BLINDSIGHT

Robin Cook

BLINDSIGHT

G. P. PUTNAM'S SONS
New York

*This is a work of fiction. The characters
and events described in this book are imaginary,
and any resemblance to actual persons, living
or dead, is purely coincidental.*

G. P. Putnam's Sons
Publishers Since 1838
200 Madison Avenue
New York, NY 10016

Library of Congress Cataloging-in-Publication Data

Cook, Robin, date
Blindsight / Robin Cook.
p. cm.
ISBN 0-399-13645-2
I. Title.
PS3553.O5545B57   1992   91-30355 CIP
813'.54—dc20

Printed in the United States of America
1   2   3   4   5   6   7   8   9   10

This book is printed on acid-free paper.

∞

TO DAVID AND LAUREL
AND THEIR NEW LIFE
TOGETHER

ACKNOWLEDGMENTS

I would like to thank the Dade County Medical Examiner's Office for putting up with me for a week, and particularly Dr. Charles Wetlie, whose patience talking with someone trained in Ophthalmology and Surgery instead of Forensic Pathology was extraordinary. I would also like to thank Dr. Charles Hirsh, Chief Medical Examiner for the City of New York, for his hospitality, and Dr. Jackie Lee for her willingness to share a glimpse into the more personal side of Forensic Pathology.

Last, but not least, I would like to thank Jean Reeds, whose intuitive sense of psychology makes her support, advice, and criticism inordinately valuable.

BLINDSIGHT

The cocaine shot into Duncan Andrews' antecubital vein in a concentrated bolus after having been propelled by the plunger of a syringe. Chemical alarms sounded immediately. A number of the blood cells and plasma enzymes recognized the cocaine molecules as being part of a family of compounds called alkaloids, which are manufactured by plants and include such physiologically active substances as caffeine, morphine, strychnine, and nicotine.

In a desperate but vain attempt to protect the body from this sudden invasion, plasma enzymes called cholesterases attacked the cocaine, splitting some of the foreign molecules into physiologically inert fragments. But the cocaine dose was overwhelming. Within seconds the cocaine was streaking through the right side of the heart, spreading through the lungs, and then heading out into Duncan's body.

The pharmacologic effects of the drug began almost instantly. Some of the cocaine molecules tumbled into the coronary arteries and began constricting them and reducing blood flow to the heart. At the same time the cocaine began to diffuse out of the coronary vessels into the extracellular fluid, bathing the hardworking heart muscle fibers. There the foreign compound began to interrupt the movement of sodium ions through the heart cells' membranes, a critical part of the heart muscle contractile function. The result was that cardiac conductivity and contractility began to fall.

Simultaneously the cocaine molecules fanned out throughout the brain, having coursed up into the skull through the carotid arteries. Like knives through butter, the cocaine penetrated the blood brain barrier. Once inside the brain, the cocaine bathed the defenseless brain cells, pooling in spaces called synapses across which the nerve cells communicated.

Within the synapses the cocaine began to exert its most perverse effects. It became an impersonator. By an ironic twist of chemical fate, an outer portion of the cocaine molecule was erroneously recognized by the nerve cells as a neurotransmitter, either epinephrine, norepinephrine, or dopamine. Like skeleton keys, the cocaine molecules insinuated themselves into the molecular pumps responsible for absorbing these neurotransmitters, locking them, and bringing the pumps to a sudden halt.

The result was predictable. Since the reabsorption of the neurotransmitters was blocked, the neurotransmitters' stimulative effect was preserved. And the stimulation caused the release of more neurotransmitters in an upward spiral of self-fulfilling excitation. Nerve cells that would have normally reverted to quiescence and serenity began to fire frantically.

The brain progressively brimmed with activity, particularly the pleasure centers deeply embedded below the cerebral cortex. Here dopamine was the principal neurotransmitter. With a perverse predilection the cocaine blocked the dopamine pumps, and the dopamine concentration soared. Circuits of nerve cells divinely wired to ensure the survival of the species rang with excitement and filled afferent pathways running up to the cortex with ecstatic messages.

But the pleasure centers were not the only areas of Duncan's brain to be affected, just some of the first. Soon the darker side of the cocaine invasion began to exert its effect. Phylogenetically older, more caudal centers of the brain involving functions like muscle coordination and the regulation of breathing began to be affected. Even the thermoregulatory area began to be stimulated, as well as the part of the brain responsible for vomiting.

Thus all was not well. In the middle of the rush of pleasurable impulses, an ominous condition was in the making. A dark cloud was forming on the horizon, auguring a horrible neurological storm. The cocaine was about to reveal its true deceitful self: a minion of death disguised in an aura of beguiling pleasure.

Prologue

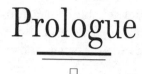

Duncan Andrews' mind was racing like a runaway train. Only a moment ago he'd been in a groggy, drugged stupor. Within seconds his dizziness and lethargy had evaporated like a drip of water falling onto a sizzling skillet. A rush of exhilaration and energy consumed him, making him feel suddenly powerful. It was as if he could do anything. In a glow of new clarity, he understood he was infinitely stronger and smarter than he'd ever realized. But just as he was beginning to savor this cascade of euphoric thoughts and this enlightened view of his abilities, he began to feel overwhelmed by intense waves of pleasure he could define only as pure ecstasy. He would have shouted for joy if only his mouth could form the proper words. But he couldn't speak. Thoughts and feelings were reverberating in his mind too rapidly to vocalize. Any fear or misgivings he had been feeling only minutes ago melted in this newfound rapture and delight.

But like his torpor, the pleasure was short-lived. The

blissful smile that had formed on Duncan's face twisted into a grimace of terror and panic. A voice called out that the people he feared were returning. His eyes darted around the room. He saw no one, yet the voice continued its message. Quickly he looked over his shoulder into the kitchen. It was empty. Turning his head, he looked down the hallway toward the bedroom. No one was there, but the voice remained. Now it was whispering a more dire prediction: he was going to die.

"Who are you?" Duncan screamed. He put his hands over his ears as if to block the sound out. "Where are you? How did you get in here?" His eyes again raced searchingly about the room.

The voice didn't answer. Duncan didn't know it was coming from inside his head.

Duncan struggled to his feet. He was surprised to realize he'd been on his living room floor. As he rose, his shoulder bumped against the coffee table. The syringe that had so recently been in his arm clattered to the floor. Duncan stared at it with hatred and regret, then reached for it to crush it between his fingers.

Duncan's hand stopped just short of the syringe. His eyes opened wide with confusion mixed with a new fear. All at once he could feel the unmistakable itch of hundreds of insects crawling on the skin of his arms. Forgetting the syringe, Duncan held out his hands with his palms up. He could feel the bugs squirming all over his forearms, but no matter how hard he searched he couldn't see them. His skin appeared perfectly clear. Then the itch spread to his legs.

"Ahhhhhh!" Duncan screamed. He tried to wipe his arms, guessing the insects were too small to be seen, but the itching only got worse. With a shiver of profound fear it dawned on him that the organisms had to be under his skin. Somehow they had invaded his body. Perhaps they had been in the syringe.

18

Using his fingernails, Duncan began to scratch his arms in a frantic attempt to allow the insects to escape. They were eating him from within. Desperately he scratched harder, digging his nails into his skin until he drew blood. The pain was intense, but the itching of the insects was worse.

Despite the terror of the insects, Duncan stopped his scratching as he became aware of a new symptom. Holding up his bloodied hand, he noticed that he was shaking. Looking down at himself he saw that his whole body was shaking, and the tremors were getting worse. For a brief instant he thought about calling 911 for help. But as the thought crossed his mind, he noticed something else. He was warm. No, he was hot!

"My God!" Duncan managed when he realized that sweat was pouring from his face. With a trembling hand he felt his forehead: he was burning up! He tried to unbutton his shirt but his tremulous hands were incapable. Impatient and desperate, he ripped the shirt open and off. Buttons flew in all directions. He did the same with his pants, throwing them to the floor. But it was to no avail; clad only in his undershorts, he still felt suffocatingly hot. Then, without a moment's warning, he coughed, choked, and vomited in a forceful stream, spattering the wall below his signed Dali lithograph.

Duncan staggered into his bathroom. Through sheer force of will he got his shaking body into the shower and turned on the cold tap full force. Gasping for breath, he stood beneath the cascade of frigid water.

Duncan's relief was brief. Involuntarily a pitiful cry escaped from his lips, and his breathing became labored as a white-hot pain stabbed into his left chest and ripped down the inside of his left arm. Intuitively Duncan knew he was having a heart attack.

Duncan clutched his chest with his right hand. Blood from his abraded arms mixed with water from the shower and swirled down the drain. Half falling and half staggering, Duncan stumbled from the bathroom and headed for the door of his apartment. Never mind that he was near naked, he needed air. His broiling brain was about to explode. Using his final reserve of strength, he gripped the knob to his front door and yanked it open.

"Duncan!" Sara Wetherbee cried. She couldn't have been more startled. Her hand was poised inches from Duncan's door. She had been about to knock when Duncan yanked it open and confronted her. He was clad in nothing but soggy Jockey shorts. "My God!" cried Sara. "What's happened to you?"

Duncan did not recognize his lover of two and a half years. What he needed was air. The crushing pain in his chest had spread throughout his lungs. It felt as if he were being stabbed over and over again. Blindly he lurched forward, reaching out to sweep Sara from his path.

"Duncan!" Sara cried again as she took in his near nakedness, the bleeding scratches on his arms, his wild, dilated eyes, and the grimace of pain on his face. Refusing to be thrust aside, she grabbed his shoulders and restrained him. "What's the matter? Where are you going?"

Duncan hesitated. For a brief moment Sara's voice penetrated his dementia. His mouth opened as if he were about to speak. But no words came. Instead he uttered a pitiful whine that ended in a gasp as his tremors coalesced into spasmodic jerks and his eyes disappeared up inside his head. Mercifully unconscious, Duncan collapsed into Sara's arms.

At first Sara struggled vainly to hold Duncan upright. But she was unable to support him, especially since Duncan's jerks became progressively more violent. As gently as possible Sara let Duncan's writhing body fall across the threshold, half into the hall. Almost the moment he touched the floor, Duncan's back arched up and his jerks rapidly coalesced into the rhythmical throes of a grand mal seizure.

"Help!" Sara screamed as she glanced up and down the hall. As she might have expected, no one appeared. Aside from the noise Duncan was making, all she could hear was the percussive thump of a nearby stereo.

Desperate for help, Sara managed to step over Duncan's convulsing and incontinent body. A glimpse of his bloody and foaming mouth appalled and frightened her. She desperately wanted to help, but she didn't know what to do save for calling an ambulance. With a trembling finger she punched 911 on Duncan's living room phone. As she impatiently waited for the connection to go through, she could hear Duncan's head repeatedly thump against the hardwood floor. All she could do was wince with each sickening sound and pray that help would be there soon.

Pulling her hands away from her face, Sara checked her watch. It was almost three o'clock in the morning. She'd been sitting on the same vinyl seat in the waiting room of the Manhattan General Hospital for over three hours.

For the umpteenth time she scanned the crowded room that smelled of cigarette smoke, sweat, alcohol, and wet wool. There was a large sign directly opposite her that read: NO SMOKING, but the notice was roundly ignored.

The injured mixed with those who'd accompanied them. There were wailing infants and toddlers, battered drunks, others clutching a towel to a cut finger or slashed chin. Most stared blankly ahead, inured to the endless wait. Some were obviously sick, others even in pain. One rather well-dressed man had his arm around his equally well-dressed female companion. Only minutes before he'd been arguing heatedly with a rather intimidatingly large triage nurse who hadn't been ruffled by his threats to call his lawyer if his companion were not seen immediately. Resigned at last, he too stared vacantly into the middle distance.

Closing her eyes again, Sara could still feel her pulse hammering at her temples. The vivid image of Duncan convulsing on the threshold of his apartment haunted her. Whatever happened tonight, she knew she would never banish the vision from her mind.

After having called the ambulance and given Duncan's address, Sara had returned to Duncan's side. Somewhere in the back of her mind she'd remembered that something should be put in a convulsing person's mouth to keep him from biting his tongue. But try as she might, she'd not been able to pry apart Duncan's clenched teeth.

Just before the EMTs arrived, Duncan finally stopped convulsing. At first Sara had been relieved, but then she noticed with renewed alarm that he was not breathing. Wiping the foam and a bit of blood from his mouth, she tried to give him mouth-to-mouth resuscitation, but she found herself fighting nausea. By then some of Duncan's hallway neighbors had appeared. To Sara's relief, one man said he'd been a corpsman in the navy, and he and a companion graciously took over the CPR until the EMTs arrived.

Sara could not imagine what had happened to Duncan. Only an hour earlier he'd called her and had asked her to come over. She thought he'd sounded a little tense and strange, but even so she'd been totally unprepared for his state once she got there. She shuddered again as she saw him standing before her in the doorway with his bloodied hands and arms and his dilated, wild eyes. It was as if he'd gone insane.

Sara's last glimpse of Duncan came after they'd arrived at the Manhattan General. The EMTs had allowed her to ride in the ambulance. Throughout the whole hair-raising trip, they'd maintained the CPR. The last she'd seen of Duncan was when he'd been rolled through a pair of white swinging doors, disappearing into the inner recesses of the emergency unit. Sara could still see the EMT kneeling on top of the gurney and continuing the chest compressions as the doors swung closed.

"Sara Wetherbee?" a voice asked, rousing Sara from her reverie.

"Yes?" Sara said as she looked up.

A young doctor sporting a heavy five o'clock shadow and a white coat slightly splattered with blood had materialized in front of her.

"I'm Dr. Murray," he said. "Would you mind coming with me. I'd like to talk with you for a moment."

"Of course," Sara said nervously. She got to her feet and pulled her purse high on her shoulder. She hurried after Dr. Murray, who'd turned on his heels almost before she'd had a chance to respond. The same white doors that had swallowed Duncan three hours before closed behind her. Dr. Murray had stopped just inside and turned to face her. She anxiously looked into the man's eyes. He was exhausted. She wanted to see some glimmer of hope, but there wasn't any.

"I understand you arc Mr. Andrews' girlfriend," Dr. Murray said. Even his voice sounded tired.

Sara nodded.

"Normally we talk to the family first," Dr. Murray said. "But I know you came in with thc patient and have been waiting. I'm sorry it has taken so long to get back to you, but several gunshot victims came in right after Mr. Andrews."

"I understand," Sara said. "How is Duncan?" She had to ask, even though she wasn't sure she wanted to know.

"Not so good," Dr. Murray said. "You can be sure our EMTs tried everything. But I'm afraid Duncan passed away anyway. Unfortunately, he was DOA. Dead on arrival. I'm sorry."

Sara stared into Dr. Murray's eyes. She wanted to see a

23

glint of the same sorrow that was welling up inside of her. But all she saw was fatigue. His apparent lack of feeling helped her maintain her own composure.

"What happened?" she asked almost in a whisper.

"We're ninety percent sure that the immediate cause was a massive myocardial infarction, or heart attack," Dr. Murray said, obviously more comfortable with his medical jargon. "But the proximate cause appears to be drug toxicity or overdose. We don't know yet what his blood level was. That takes a bit more time."

"Drugs?" Sara said with disbelief. "What kind of drug?"

"Cocaine," said Dr. Murray. "The EMTs even brought in the needle he'd used."

"I never knew Duncan used cocaine," Sara said. "He said he didn't use drugs."

"People always lie about sex and drugs," Dr. Murray said. "And with cocaine sometimes it only takes once. People don't realize how deadly the stuff can be. Its popularity has lulled people into a false sense of security. Be that as it may, we do have to get in touch with the family. Would you know the telephone number?"

Stunned by Duncan's death and the revelation about his apparent cocaine use, Sara recited the Andrews' phone number in a dazed monotone. Thinking about drugs allowed her to avoid thinking about death. She wondered how long Duncan had been on cocaine. It was all so hard to understand. She'd thought she'd known him so well.

1

The alarm of the old Westclox windup never failed to yank Laurie Montgomery from the depths of blessed sleep. Even though she'd had the clock since the first year of college, she'd never become accustomed to its fearful clatter. It always woke her up with a start, and she'd invariably lunge for the cursed contraption as if her life depended on her getting the alarm shut off as soon as humanly possible.

This rainy November morning proved no exception. As she replaced the clock on the windowsill, she could feel her heart thumping. It was the squirt of adrenaline which made the daily episode so effective. Even if she could have gone back to bed, she'd never have gotten back to sleep. And it was the same for Tom, her one-and-a-half-year-old half-wild tawny tabby who, at the sound of the alarm, had fled into the depths of her closet.

Resigned to the start of another day, Laurie stood up, wiggled her toes into her sheepskin slippers, and turned on the TV to the local morning news.

Her apartment was a small, one-bedroom affair on Nineteenth Street between First and Second avenues in a sixstory tenement. Her rooms were on the fifth floor in the rear. Her two windows faced out onto a warren of overgrown backyards.

In her tiny kitchen she turned on her coffee machine. The night before, she'd prepared it with a packet of coffee and the right amount of water. With the coffee started she padded into the bathroom and looked at herself in the mirror.

"Ugh!" she said as she turned her face from side to side, viewing the damage of another night with not enough sleep. Her eyes were puffy and red. Laurie was not a morning person. She was a confirmed night owl and frequently read until all hours. She loved to read, whether the book was a ponderous pathology text or a popular bestseller. When it came to fiction, her interests were catholic. Her shelves were crammed with everything from thrillers to romantic sagas, to history, general science, and even psychology. The night before it had been a murder mystery, and she'd read until she'd finished the book. When she'd turned out the light, she'd not had the courage to look at the time. As usual, in the morning she vowed never to stay up so late again.

In the shower Laurie's mind began to clear enough to start going over the problems that she would have to address that day. She was currently in her fifth month as an associate medical examiner at the Office of the Chief Medical Examiner for the City of New York. The preceding weekend, Laurie had been on call, which meant that she worked both Saturday and Sunday. She'd performed six autopsies: three one day and three the next. A number of these cases required additional follow-up before they could be signed out, and she began making a mental list of what she had to do.

Stepping out of the shower, Laurie dried herself briskly. One thing she was thankful about was that today would be a "paper day" for her, meaning that she would not be assigned any additional autopsies. Instead she would have the time to do the necessary paperwork on the autopsies that she'd already done. She was currently waiting for material on about twenty cases from either the lab, the medical examiner investigators, local hospitals or local doctors, or the police. It was this avalanche of paperwork that constantly threatened to overwhelm her.

Back in the kitchen Laurie prepared her coffee. Then, carrying her mug, she retreated to the bathroom to put on makeup and blow-dry her hair. Her hair always took the longest. It was thick and long and of an auburn color with red highlights she liked to burnish with henna once a month. Laurie was proud of her hair. She thought it was her best feature. Her mother was always encouraging her to cut it, but Laurie liked to keep it beyond shoulder length and wear it in a braid or piled on top of her head. As for makeup, Laurie always subscribed to the theory that "less is more." A bit of eyeliner to line her blue-green eyes, a few strokes with an eyebrow pencil to define her light, reddish blond eyebrows, and a brief application of mascara and she was nearly done. A dab of coral blush and lipstick completed the routine. Satisfied, she took her mug and retreated to the bedroom.

By then, *Good Morning America* was on. She listened with half an ear as she put on the clothes she had laid out the night before. Forensic Pathology was still largely a man's world, but that only made Laurie want to emphasize her femininity with her dress. She slipped into a green skirt and matching turtleneck. Eyeing herself in the mirror, she was pleased. She'd not worn this particular outfit before. Somehow it made her look taller than her actual height of five foot five, and even slimmer than her hundred and fifteen pounds.

With her coffee drunk, a yogurt eaten, and dried cat food poured into Tom's bowl, Laurie struggled into her trench coat. She then grabbed her purse, her lunch, which she had also prepared the night before, and her briefcase, and stepped out of her apartment. It took her a moment to secure the collection of locks on her door, a legacy of the apartment's previous tenant. Turning to the elevator, Laurie pushed the down button.

As if on cue, the moment the aged elevator began its whining ascent, Laurie heard the click of Debra Engler's locks. Turning her head, Laurie watched as the door to the front apartment opened a crack and its safety chain was pulled taut. Debra's bloodshot eye peered out at her. Above the eye was a tousle of gray frizzy hair.

Laurie aggressively stared back at the intruding eye. It was as if Debra hovered behind her door for any sound in the hallway. The repetitive intrusion grated on Laurie's nerves. It seemed like a violation of her privacy despite the fact that the hallway was a common area.

"Better take an umbrella," Debra said in her throaty, smoker's voice.

The fact that Debra was right only fanned Laurie's irritation. She had indeed forgotten her umbrella. Without giving Debra any sense of acknowledgment lest her irritating watchfulness be encouraged, Laurie turned back to her door and went through the complicated sequence of undoing the locks. Five minutes later as she stepped into the elevator, she saw that Debra's bloodshot eye was still watching intently.

As the elevator slowly descended, Laurie's irritation faded. Her thoughts turned to the case that had bothered her the most over the weekend: the twelve-year-old boy hit in the chest with a softball.

"Life's not fair," Laurie muttered under her breath as she thought about the boy's untimely death. Children's deaths were so hard to comprehend. Somehow she'd thought medical school would inure her to such senselessness, but it hadn't. Neither had a pathology residency. And now that she was in forensics, these deaths were even harder to take. And there were so many of them! Up until the accident, the softball victim had been a healthy child, brimming with health and vitality. She could still see his little body on the autopsy table; a picture of health, ostensibly asleep. Yet Laurie had had to pick up the scalpel and gut him like a fish.

Laurie swallowed hard as the elevator came to a bumping stop. Cases like this little boy made her question her career choice. She wondered if she shouldn't have gone into pediatrics, where she could have dealt with living children. The field of medicine she'd chosen could be grim.

In spite of herself, Laurie was grateful for Debra's admonition once she saw what kind of day it was. The wind was blowing in strong gusts and the promised rain had already started. The view of her street that particular day made her question her choice of location as well as her career. The garbage-strewn street was not a pretty sight. Maybe she should have gone to a newer, cleaner city like Atlanta, or a city of perpetual summer like Miami. Laurie opened her umbrella and leaned into the wind as she trudged toward First Avenue.

As she walked she thought of one of the ironies of her career choice. She'd chosen pathology for a number of reasons. For one thing she thought that predictable hours would make it easier to combine medicine with having a family. But the problem was, she didn't have a family, unless she considered her parents, but they didn't really count. In fact she didn't even have a meaningful relationship. Laurie had never thought that by age thirty-two she wouldn't have children of her own, much less that she'd still be single.

A short cab ride with a driver whose nationality she could

not even guess brought her to the corner of First and Thirtieth. She'd been shocked to get the cab. Under normal circumstances a combination of rain and rush hour meant no taxis. This morning, however, someone had been getting out of a cab just as she reached First Avenue. Yet even if she'd not been able to get one, it wouldn't have been a disaster. That was one of the benefits of living just eleven blocks away from work. Many a day she walked in both directions.

After paying her fare, Laurie started up the front steps of the Office of the Chief Medical Examiner for the City of New York. The six-story building was overshadowed by the rest of the New York University Medical Center and the Bellevue Hospital complex. Its façade was constructed of blue-glazed brick with aluminum windows and door casements of an unattractive modern design.

Normally Laurie paid no attention to the building, but on this particular rainy November Monday it wasn't spared her critical review any more than her career or her street. The place was depressing. She had to admit that. She was shaking her head, wondering if an architect could have been genuinely pleased by his handiwork, when she noticed that the foyer was packed. The front door was propped open despite the morning chill, and cigarette smoke could be seen languidly issuing forth.

Curious, Laurie pushed into the crowd, making her way with some difficulty toward the ID room. Marlene Wilson, the usual receptionist, was obviously overwhelmed as at least a dozen people pressed against her desk as they plied her with questions. The media had invaded, complete with cameras, tape recorders, TV camcorders, and flashing lights. Clearly something out of the ordinary had happened.

After a brief pantomime to get Marlene's attention, Laurie managed to get herself buzzed into the inner area. She experienced a mild sense of relief when the closing door extinguished the babble of voices and the acrid cigarette smoke.

Pausing to glance into the drab room where family members were taken to identify the deceased, Laurie was mildly surprised to find it empty. With all the commotion in the outer area, she thought she'd see people in the ID room. Shrugging her shoulders, she proceeded into the ID office.

The first person Laurie confronted was Vinnie Amendola, one of the mortuary techs. Oblivious to the pandemonium in the reception area, Vinnie was drinking coffee from a Styrofoam cup and studying the sports pages of the *New York Post*. His feet were propped up on the edge of one of the gray metal desks. As usual before eight in the morning, Vinnie was the only person in the room. It was his job to make the coffee for the coffee pool. A large, commercial-style coffeemaker was in the ID office, a room which served a number of functions, including an informal morning congregation area.

"What on earth is going on?" Laurie asked as she picked up the day's autopsy schedule. Even though she wasn't scheduled for any autopsies, she was always curious to see what cases had come in.

Vinnie lowered his paper. "Trouble," he said.

"What kind of trouble?" Laurie asked. Through the doorway leading to the communications room, she could see that the two day-shift secretaries were busy on their phones. The panels in front of them were blinking with waiting calls. Laurie poured herself a cup of coffee.

"Another 'preppy murder' case," Vinnie said. "A teenage girl apparently strangled by her boyfriend. Sex and drugs. You know, rich kids. Happened over near the Tavern On The Green. With all the excitement that first case caused a couple of years ago, the media has been here from the moment the body was brought in."

Laurie clucked her tongue. "How awful for everyone. A

life lost and a life ruined." She added sugar and a touch of
cream to her coffee. "Who's handling it?"

"Dr. Plodgett," Vinnie said. "He was called by the tour
doctor and he had to go out to the scene. It was around
three in the morning."

Laurie sighed. "Oh boy," she muttered. She felt sorry for
Paul. Handling such a case would most likely be stressful
for him because he was relatively inexperienced like herself.
He'd been an associate medical examiner for just over a
year. Laurie had been there for only four and a half months.
"Where's Paul now? Up in his office?"

"Nope," Vinnie said. "He's in doing the autopsy."

"Already?" Laurie questioned. "Why the rush?"

"Beats me," Vinnie said. "But the guys going off the
graveyard shift told me that Bingham came in around six.
Paul must have called him."

"This case gets more intriguing by the minute," Laurie
said. Dr. Harold Bingham, age fifty-eight, was the Chief
Medical Examiner of New York City, a position that made
him a powerful figure in the forensic world. "I think I'll
duck into the pit and see what's happening."

"I'd be careful if I were you," Vinnie said, struggling to
fold his paper. "I was thinking of going in there myself, but
the word is that Bingham is in a foul mood. Not that that's
so out of the ordinary."

Laurie nodded to Vinnie as she left the room. To avoid
the mass of reporters in the reception area, she took the
long route to the elevators, walking through Communications. The secretaries were too busy to say hello. Laurie
waved to one of the two police detectives assigned to the
medical examiner's office who was sitting in his cubbyhole
office off the communications room. He, too, was on the
phone.

After going through another doorway, Laurie glanced
into each of the forensic medical investigators' offices to say

good morning, but no one was in yet. Reaching the main elevators, she pushed the up button and as usual had to wait while the aged machine slowly responded. Looking down the hall to her right, she could see the mass of reporters seething in the reception area. Laurie felt sorry for poor Marlene Wilson.

As she rode up to her office on the fifth floor, Laurie thought about the meaning of Bingham's early presence not only at the office but also in the autopsy room. Both occurrences were rare and they fanned her curiosity.

Since her office-mate, Dr. Riva Mehta, was not yet in, Laurie spent only minutes in her office. She locked her briefcase, purse, and lunch in her file cabinet, then changed into green scrub clothes. Since she wasn't going to do an autopsy herself, she didn't bother putting on her usual second layer of protective, impervious clothing.

Back in the elevator Laurie descended to the basement level, where the morgue was located. This was not a basement in the true sense because it was actually the street level from the building's Thirtieth Street side. A loading dock from Thirtieth Street was the route bodies arrived and left the morgue.

In the locker room, which she rarely used as such, preferring to change in her office, Laurie got shoe covers, apron, mask, and hood. Thus dressed as if she were about to perform surgery, she pushed through the door into the autopsy room.

The "pit," as it was lovingly called, was a medium-sized room about fifty feet long and thirty feet wide. At one time it had been considered state of the art, but no longer. Like so many other city agencies, its much-needed upkeep and modernization had suffered from lack of funds. The eight stainless steel tables were old and stained from countless postmortems. Old-fashioned spring-loaded scales hung over each table. A series of sinks, countertops, X-ray view boxes, ancient glass-fronted cabinets, and exposed piping lined the walls. There were no windows.

Only one table was in use: the second from the end, to Laurie's right. As the door closed behind Laurie all three gowned, masked, and hooded doctors grouped around the table raised their heads to stare at her for a moment before returning to their grisly task. Stretched out on the table was the ivory-colored, nude body of a teenage girl. She was illuminated by a single bank of blue-white fluorescent bulbs directly overhead. The lurid scene was made worse by the sucking noise of water swirling down a drain at the foot of the table.

Laurie felt a strong intuition she should turn around and leave, but she fought the feeling. Instead she advanced on the group. Knowing the people as well as she did, she recognized each despite their coverings, which included goggles as well as masks. Bingham was on the opposite side of the table, facing Laurie. He was a stocky man of short stature with thick features and a bulbous nose.

"Goddamn it, Paul!" Bingham snapped. "Is this the first time you've done a neck dissection? I've got a news conference scheduled and you're mucking around like a first-year medical student. Give me that scalpel!" Bingham snatched the instrument from Paul's hand, then bent over the body. A ray of light glinted off the stainless steel cutting edge.

Laurie stepped up to the table. She was to Paul's right. Sensing her presence, he turned his head, and for an instant their eyes met. Laurie could tell he was already distraught. She tried to project some support with her gaze, but Paul averted his head. Laurie glanced at the morgue tech who avoided looking her way. The atmosphere was explosive.

Lowering her eyes, Laurie watched what Bingham was doing. The patient's neck had been opened with a somewhat outdated incision that ran from the point of the chin to the top of the breastbone. The skin had been flayed and

34

spread to the side like opening a high-necked blouse. Bingham was in the process of freeing the muscles from around the thyroid cartilage and the hyoid bone. Laurie could see evidence of premortal trauma with hemorrhage into the tissues.

"What I still don't understand," Bingham snapped without looking up from his labors, "is why you didn't bag the hands at the scene? Could you please tell me that?"

Laurie's eyes again met Paul's. She knew instantly that he had no excuse. She wished she could have helped him, but she didn't see how she could. Sharing her colleague's discomfort, Laurie stepped away from the table. Despite having made the effort to get dressed to observe, Laurie left the autopsy room. There was just too much tension to make it worth staying. She didn't want to make the situation any worse for Paul by giving Bingham more of an audience.

Returning back upstairs after peeling off her outer layer of protective clothing, Laurie sat down at her desk and got to work. The first order of business was to complete what she could on the three autopsies that she'd done on Sunday. The first of the cases had been the twelve-year-old boy. The second case was clearly a heroin overdose, but she reviewed the facts. Drug paraphernalia had been found with the victim. The victim had been a known heroin addict. At autopsy his arms had showed multiple sites of intravenous injection, old and new. On his right upper arm he'd had a tattoo: "Born to Lose." Internally he'd shown the usual signs of asphyxial death with a frothy pulmonary edema. Despite the fact that laboratory and microscopic studies were still pending, Laurie felt comfortable with her conclusion that the cause of death was drug overdose and the manner of death was accidental.

The third case was far from clear. A twenty-four-year-old woman flight attendant had been discovered at home in a bathrobe, having apparently collapsed in the hallway outside her bathroom. She'd been found by her roommate. She'd been healthy and had returned home from a trip to Los Angeles the previous day. She was not known to be a drug user.

Laurie had done the autopsy but had found nothing. All her findings were completely normal. Concerned about the case, Laurie had one of the medical investigators locate the woman's gynecologist. Laurie had spoken with the man and had been assured the woman had been entirely healthy. He'd seen her last only months before.

Having had a similar case recently, Laurie had instructed the medical investigator to go to the woman's apartment and bring back any personal electrical appliances found in the woman's bathroom. Sitting on Laurie's desk was a cardboard box with a note from the medical investigator, saying that the enclosed was all she could find.

Using her thumbnail, Laurie broke through the tape sealing the box, lifted the flaps, and peered inside. The box contained a blow dryer and an old metal curling iron. Laurie lifted both devices from the box and laid them on her desk. From the lower right-hand drawer of the desk, Laurie lifted out an electrical testing device called a voltohmmeter.

Examining the blow dryer first, Laurie tested the electrical resistance between the prongs of the plug and the dryer itself. In both instances, the reading was infinite ohms or no current flow. Thinking that perhaps she was again on the wrong track, she tested the hair curler. To her surprise, the result was positive. Between one of the prongs and the casing of the curler, the voltohmmeter registered zero ohms, meaning free current flow.

Taking some basic tools from her desk, including a screwdriver and a pair of pliers, Laurie opened the hair curler and immediately found the frayed wire that was making contact with the device's metal casing. It was now clear to Laurie that the poor flight attendant was the victim of low voltage electrocution. As was often the case, the victim had been shocked but had had time to put the offending device away and walk from the room before succumbing to a fatal cardiac arrhythmia. The cause of death was electrocution and the manner of death accidental.

With the hair curler "autopsied" on her desk, Laurie got out her camera and arranged the pieces to show the aberrant connection. Then she stood up to shoot directly down. As she peered through the viewfinder, Laurie felt pleased about the case. She couldn't suppress a modest smile, knowing how different her work was from what people surmised. She'd not only solved the mystery of the poor woman's untimely death, but had potentially saved someone else from the same fate as well.

Before Laurie could take the photo of the curler, her phone rang. Because of the degree of her concentration, the ringing startled her. With thinly veiled irritation, she answered. It was the operator asking Laurie if she would mind taking a call from a doctor phoning from the Manhattan General Hospital. She added that he'd requested to talk with the chief.

"Then why put him through to me?" Laurie demanded.

"The chief is tied up in the autopsy room, and I can't find Dr. Washington. Someone said he's out talking with the reporters. So I just started ringing the other doctors' numbers. You were the first to answer."

"Put him on," Laurie said with resignation. She sank back into her desk chair. She was quite confident it would be a short conversation. If someone wanted to talk with the chief, they certainly would not be satisfied talking to the lowest person in the hierarchy.

After the call had been put through, Laurie introduced herself. She emphasized that she was one of the associate medical examiners and not the chief.

"I'm Dr. Murray," the caller said. "I'm a senior medical

resident. I need to talk to someone about a drug overdose/toxicity DOA that came in this morning."

"What is it that you'd like to know?" Laurie asked. Drug deaths were a daily phenomenon at the M.E. office. Her attention partially switched back to the hair curler. She had a better idea for the photograph.

"The patient's name was Duncan Andrews," Dr. Murray said. "He was a thirty-five-year-old Caucasian male. He arrived with no cardiac activity, no spontaneous respiration, and with a core body temperature that we recorded at one hundred eight degrees."

"Uh huh," Laurie said equably. Holding the phone in the crook of her neck, she rearranged the pieces of the hair curler.

"There was massive evidence of seizure activity," Dr. Murray said. "So we ran an EEG. It was flat. The lab reported a serum cocaine level of 20 micrograms per milliliter."

"Wow!" Laurie said with a short laugh of amazement. Dr. Murray had caught her attention. "That's one hell of a high level. What was the route of administration, oral? Was he one of those 'mules' who try to smuggle the stuff by swallowing condoms filled with cocaine?"

"Hardly," Dr. Murray said with a short laugh of his own. "This guy was some kind of Wall Street whiz kid. No, it wasn't oral. It was IV."

Laurie swallowed as she struggled to keep old, unwanted memories submerged. Her throat had suddenly gone dry. "Was heroin involved as well?" she asked. In the sixties a mixture of heroin and cocaine called "speedball" had been popular.

"No heroin," Dr. Murray said. "Only cocaine, but obviously a walloping dose. If his temperature was one hundred eight when we took it, God only knows how high it had been."

"Well, it sounds pretty straightforward," Laurie said. "What's the question? If you're wondering if it's a medical examiner case, I can tell you that it is."

"No, we know it is an M.E. case," Dr. Murray said. "That's not the problem. It's more complicated than that. The fellow was found by his girlfriend who came in with him. But then his family came in as well. And I have to tell you, his family is connected, if you know what I mean. Anyway, the nurses found that Mr. Duncan Andrews had an organ-donor card in his wallet, and they called the organ-donor coordinator. Without knowing that the case was an M.E. case, the organ-donor coordinator asked the family if they would permit harvesting the eyes since that was the only tissue besides bone that might still be usable. You understand that we don't pay much attention to organ-donor cards unless the family agrees. But this family agreed. They told us that they definitely wanted to respect the decedent's wishes. Personally, I think it has something to do with their wanting to believe their son died of natural causes. But, be that as it may, we wanted to check with you people as a matter of policy before we did anything."

"The family truly agreed?" Laurie asked.

"I'm telling you, they were emphatic," Dr. Murray said. "According to the girlfriend, she and the decedent had talked about the problem of the lack of transplant organs on several occasions and had gone together to the Manhattan Organ Repository to sign up in response to the Repository's TV appeal last year."

"Mr. Duncan Andrews must have given himself some dose of cocaine," Laurie said. "Was there any suicide note?"

"No suicide note," Dr. Murray said. "Nor was the man depressed, at least according to the girlfriend."

"This sounds like a rather unique circumstance," Laurie said. "I personally don't think honoring the family's request would affect the autopsy. But I'm not authorized to make such a policy decision. What I can do is find out for you from the powers-that-be and call you back immediately."

"I'd appreciate it," Dr. Murray said. "If we're going to do something, we have to do it sooner rather than later."

Laurie hung up the phone, and with a degree of reluctance, left her disassembled hair curler, and returned to the morgue. Without donning the usual layers, she stuck her head through the door. Immediately she could see that Bingham had departed.

"The chief left you to carry on by yourself?" Laurie called out to Paul.

Paul turned to face her. "Thank God for small favors," Paul said, his voice slightly muffled by his mask. "Luckily he had to get upstairs to the news conference he's scheduled. I suppose he thinks I'm capable of sewing up the body."

"Come on, Paul," Laurie said by way of encouragement. "Remember Bingham treats everyone like an incompetent at the autopsy table."

"I'll try to keep that in mind," Paul said without conviction.

Laurie let the door close. She used the stairs at the far end of the morgue to go up to the first floor. There was no sense waiting for the elevator for a single flight.

The first-floor corridor was crowded with media people, and it was all Laurie could do to get to the double doors leading into the conference room. Over the heads of the reporters she could see Bingham's shiny bald pate reflecting the harsh lighting set up for the TV cameras. He was taking questions from the floor and perspiring copiously. Laurie knew instantly that there was no way she'd be able to discuss Manhattan General's problem with him.

Standing on her toes, Laurie scanned the crowded room for Dr. Calvin Washington, the Deputy Chief Medical Examiner. As a six-foot-seven, two-hundred-and-fifty-pound black man, he was usually easy to pick out of a crowd. Laurie finally spotted him standing near the door that led from the conference room into the chief's office.

By going out into the main reception area, then cutting through the chief's office, Laurie was able to approach Calvin from behind. When she reached him, she hesitated. Dr. Washington had a stormy temperament. Between his physique and his moods, he intimidated most people, including Laurie.

Marshaling her courage, Laurie tapped him on the arm. Immediately he spun around. His dark eyes swept over Laurie. He was not happy, that much was apparent.

"What is it?" he asked in a forced whisper.

"Could I speak to you for a moment?" Laurie asked. "There's a question of policy regarding a case over at Manhattan General."

After a glance back at his perspiring boss, Calvin nodded. He stepped beyond Laurie and closed the door to the conference room. He shook his head. "This 'preppy murder II' is going sour already. God, I hate the media. They're not after the 'truth,' whatever that is. They're nothing but a bunch of gossip hounds, and poor Harold is trying to justify why the hands weren't bagged at the murder site. What a circus!"

"Why weren't the hands bagged?" Laurie asked.

"Because the tour doctor didn't think about it," Calvin said disgusted. "And by the time Plodgett got there the body was already in the van."

"How come the tour doctor allowed the body to be moved before Paul got there?" Laurie asked.

"How should I know!" Calvin exploded. "The whole case is a mess. One screw-up after another."

Laurie cringed. "I hate to bring this up, but I noticed another potential problem downstairs."

"Oh, and what was that?" Calvin demanded.

"What I imagine were the victim's clothes were in a plastic bag on one of the countertops."

"Damn!" Calvin snapped. He stepped over to Bingham's phone and punched the extension in the "pit." As soon as the phone was answered he shouted that someone would be on the autopsy table himself if the preppy murder II victim's clothes were in a plastic bag.

Without waiting for an answer, Calvin slammed the receiver down onto the cradle. Then he glared at Laurie as if the messenger were responsible for the bad news.

"I can't imagine a fungus would have destroyed any evidence so quickly," Laurie offered.

"That's not entirely the point," Calvin snapped. "We're not out in the boondocks someplace. Screw-ups like this are not to be tolerated, especially not under this glare of publicity. It seems as if this whole case is jinxed. Anyway, what's the problem at Manhattan General?"

Laurie told Calvin about Duncan Andrews as succinctly as possible and about the attending physician's request. She emphasized that it was the family's wishes to respect the deceased's desire to be a donor.

"If we had a decent medical examiner law in this state this wouldn't even come up," Calvin growled. "I think we should honor the family's request. Tell the doctor that in this kind of circumstances he should take the eyes but photograph them prior to doing so. Also he should take vitreous samples from inside the eyes for Toxicology."

"I'll let him know immediately," Laurie said. "Thanks."

Calvin waved absently. He was already reopening the door to the conference room.

Laurie cut back through the chief's secretarial area and got Marlene to buzz her through the door into the main hall. She had to weave her way among the media people, stepping over cables powering the TV lights. Bingham's news conference was still in progress. Lauric pressed the up button on the elevator.

"Ahhhh!" Laurie squealed in response to a deliberate jab in the ribs. Laurie swung around to chastise whoever had poked her. She expected to see a colleague, but it wasn't. Before her stood a stranger in his early thirties. He had on a trench coat that was open down the front; his tie was loosened at his collar. On his face was a childlike grin.

"Laurie?" he said.

Laurie suddenly recognized him. It was Bob Talbot, a reporter for the *Daily News* whom Laurie had known since college. She'd not seen him for some time, and out of context it had taken a moment to recognize him. Despite her irritation, she smiled.

"Where have you been?" Bob demanded. "I haven't seen you for ages."

"I guess I've been a bit asocial of late," Laurie admitted. "Lots of work, plus I've started studying for my forensic boards."

"You know the expression about all work and no play," Bob said.

Laurie nodded and tried to smile. The elevator arrived. Laurie stepped in and held the door open with her hand.

"What do you think of this new 'preppy murder'?" Bob asked. "It sure is causing a fuss."

"It's bound to," Laurie said. "It's made-to-order tabloid material. Besides, it seems that we've already messed up. I suppose it's reminiscent of what happened with the first case. A little too reminiscent for my colleagues."

"What are you talking about?" Bob asked.

"For one thing, the victim's hands weren't bagged," Laurie said. "Didn't you hear what Dr. Bingham was saying?"

"Yeah, but he said it didn't matter."

"It matters," Laurie said. "Besides that, the victim's clothes ended up in a plastic bag. That's a no-no. Moisture encourages the growth of microorganisms that can affect evidence. That's another screw-up. Unfortunately the medical examiner on the case is one of us junior people. By rights it should be someone with more experience."

"Apparently the boyfriend already confessed," Bob said. "Isn't this all academic?"

Laurie shrugged. "By the time the trial rolls around, he might have a change of heart. Certainly his lawyer will. Then it's up to the evidence unless there was a witness, and in this type of case, there's seldom a witness."

"Maybe you're right," Bob said with a nod. "We'll have to see. Meanwhile, I'd better get back to the news conference. How about dinner sometime this week?"

"Maybe," Laurie said. "I don't mean to be coy, but I do have to study if I want to pass those boards. Why don't you call and we'll talk about it?"

Bob nodded as Laurie let the elevator door close. She pressed five. Back in her office, she called Dr. Murray at Manhattan General and told him what Dr. Washington had said.

"Thank you for your trouble," Dr. Murray said when Laurie was finished. "It's good to have some guidelines to follow in this kind of circumstance."

"Be sure to get good photos," Laurie advised. "If you don't, the policy could change."

"No need to worry," Dr. Murray said. "We have our own photography department. It will be done professionally."

Hanging up the phone, Laurie went back to the hair curler. She took a half dozen photos from varying angles and with varying lighting conditions. With the curler out of the way, she turned her attention to the only Sunday case remaining, and the most disturbing for her: the twelve-year-old boy.

Getting up from her desk, Laurie returned to the first

floor and visited Cheryl Myers, one of the medical investigators. She explained that she needed more eyewitnesses of the episode when the boy was hit with the softball. Without any positive finding on the autopsy, she would need personal accounts to substantiate her diagnosis of commotio cordis, or death from a blow to the chest. Cheryl promised to get right on it.

Returning to the fifth floor, Laurie went to Histology to see if the boy's slides could be speeded up. Knowing how distraught the family was, she was eager to put her end of the tragedy to rest. She found that families seemed to come to some sort of acceptance once they knew the truth. The aura of uncertainty about a death of unknown cause made grieving more difficult.

While she was in Histology, Laurie picked up slides that were ready from cases she'd autopsied the previous week. With those in hand she went down several flights of stairs and picked up reports from Toxicology and Serology. Carrying everything back to her office, she dumped all the material on her desk. Then she went to work. Except for a short break for lunch, Laurie spent the rest of the day going over the slides from Histology, collating the laboratory reports, making calls, and completing as many files as possible.

What fueled Laurie's anxiety was the knowledge that the following day she'd be assigned at least two and maybe as many as four new cases to autopsy. If she didn't stay abreast of the paperwork, she'd be swamped. There was never a dull moment at the Office of the Chief Medical Examiner for the City of New York, since it handled between fifteen and twenty thousand assigned cases each year. That translated to approximately eight thousand autopsies. Each day the office averaged two homicides and two drug overdoses.

By four o'clock in the afternoon, Laurie was beginning to

slow down. The volume of her work and its intensity had taken its toll. When her phone rang for the hundredth time, she answered with a tired voice. When she realized it was Mrs. Sanford, Dr. Bingham's secretary, she straightened up in her chair by reflex. It wasn't every day that she got a call from the chief.

"Dr. Bingham would like to see you in his office if it is convenient," Mrs. Sanford said.

"I'll be right down," Laurie answered. She smiled at Mrs. Sanford's phrase, "If it is convenient." Knowing Dr. Bingham, it was probably Mrs. Sanford's translation of: Get Dr. Montgomery down here ASAP. En route she vainly tried to imagine what Dr. Bingham wanted to see her about, but she had no idea.

"Go right in," Mrs. Sanford said. She looked at Laurie over the tops of her reading glasses and smiled.

"Close the door!" Bingham commanded as soon as Laurie was in his office. He was sitting behind his massive desk. "Sit down!"

Laurie did as she was told. Bingham's angry tone was the first warning of what was to come. Laurie immediately knew that she wasn't there for a commendation. She watched as Bingham removed his wire-rimmed spectacles and placed them on his blotter. His thick fingers handled the glasses with surprising agility.

Laurie studied Bingham's face. His steel blue eyes appeared cold. She could just make out the web of fine capillaries spread across the tip of his nose.

"You do know that we have a public relations office?" Dr. Bingham began. His tone was sarcastic, angry.

"Yes, of course," Laurie replied when Bingham paused.

"Then you must also know that Mrs. Donnatello is responsible for any information being given to the media and the public."

Laurie nodded.

"And you must also be aware that except for myself, all personnel of this office should keep their personal opinions concerning medical examiner business to themselves."

Laurie didn't respond. She still didn't know where this conversation was headed.

Suddenly, Bingham bounded out of his chair and began pacing the area behind his desk. "What I'm not sure you appreciate," he continued, "is the fact that being a medical examiner carries significant social and political responsibilities." He stopped pacing and looked across at Laurie. "Do you understand what I'm saying?"

"I believe so," Laurie said, but there was still some significant part of the conversation that eluded her. She had no idea what had precipitated this diatribe.

" 'Believing so' is not adequate," Bingham snorted. He stopped his pacing and leaned over his desk, glaring at Laurie.

More than anything, Laurie wanted to remain composed. She didn't want to appear emotional. She despised situations like this. Confrontation was not one of her strong points.

"Furthermore," Bingham snapped, "breaches in the rules pertaining to privileged information will not be tolerated. Is that clear!"

"Yes," Laurie said, fighting back unwanted tears. She wasn't sad or mad, just upset. With the amount of work that she'd been doing of late, she hardly thought she deserved such a tirade. "Can I ask what this is all about?"

"Most certainly," Bingham said. "Toward the end of my news conference about the Central Park murder, one of the reporters got up and began asking a question with the comment that you had specifically stated that the case was being mishandled by this department. Did you or did you not say that to a reporter?"

Laurie cowered in her seat. She tried to return Bingham's

glare, but she had to look away. She felt a rush of embarrassment, guilt, anger, and resentment. She was shocked that Bob would have had such little sense much less respect for her confidentiality. Finding her voice she said: "I mentioned something to that effect."

"I thought so," Bingham said smugly. "I knew the reporter wouldn't have had the nerve to make something like that up. Well, consider yourself warned, Dr. Montgomery. That will be all."

Laurie stumbled out of the chief's office. Humiliated, she didn't even dare exchange glances with Mrs. Sanford lest she lose control of the tears she'd been suppressing. Hoping she wouldn't run into anyone, Laurie sprinted up the stairs, not bothering to wait for the elevator.

She was particularly thankful that her office-mate was still apparently in the autopsy room. Locking her door behind her, Laurie sat down at her desk. She felt crushed, as if all her months of hard work had been for naught because of one foolish indiscretion.

With sudden resolve, Laurie picked up the phone. She wanted to call Bob Talbot and tell him what she thought of him. But she hesitated, then let go of the receiver. At the moment she didn't have the strength for another confrontation. Instead she took a deep breath and let it out slowly.

She tried to go back to work, but she couldn't concentrate. Instead she opened her briefcase and threw in some of the uncompleted files. After collecting her other belongings, Laurie took the elevator to the basement level and exited through the morgue loading dock onto Thirtieth Street. She didn't want to take the risk of running into anyone in the reception area.

Befitting her mood, it was still raining as she walked south on First Avenue. If anything, the city looked worse than it had that morning, with a pall of acrid exhaust fumes suspended between the buildings lining the street. Laurie kept her head down to avoid the oily puddles, the litter, and the stares of the homeless.

Even her apartment building seemed dirtier than usual, and as she waited for the elevator, she was aware of the smell of a century of fried onions and fatty meat. Getting off on the fifth floor, she glared at Debra Engler's bloodshot eye, daring her to say anything. Once inside her apartment, she slammed the door with enough force to tilt a framed Klimt print she'd gotten from the Metropolitan.

Even feisty Tom couldn't elevate her spirits as he rubbed back and forth across her shins as she hung up her coat and stashed her umbrella in her narrow hall closet. Going into her living room, she collapsed into her armchair.

Refusing to be ignored, Tom leaped to the back of the chair and purred directly into Laurie's right ear. When that didn't work, he began to paw Laurie's shoulder repeatedly. Finally Laurie responded by reaching up and lifting the cat into her lap where she began absently to stroke him.

As the rain tapped against her window like grains of sand, Laurie lamented her life. For the second time that day she thought about not being married. Her mother's criticism seemed more deserved than usual. She wondered anew if she'd made the right career choices. What about ten years from now? Could she see herself caught in the same quagmire of lonely daily life, struggling to stay ahead of the paperwork associated with the autopsies, or would she assume more administrative duties like Bingham?

With a sense of shock, Laurie realized for the first time that she had no desire to be chief. Up until that moment, she'd always tried to excel whether it was college or medical school, and aspiring to be the chief would have fit into that mold. Excelling for Laurie had been a kind of rebellion, an attempt to make her father, the great cardiac surgeon, finally acknowledge her. But it had never worked. She knew that as far as her father was concerned she'd never be able to replace her older brother who'd died at the tender age of nineteen.

Laurie sighed. It wasn't like her to be depressed, and the fact that she was depressed depressed her. She never would have guessed that she'd be quite so sensitive to criticism. Maybe she'd been unhappy and hadn't even realized it with her workload.

Laurie noticed that the red light on her answering machine was blinking. At first she ignored it, but the darker the room got, the more insistent the blinking became. After watching the light for another ten minutes, curiosity got the best of her, and she listened to the tape. The call was from her mother, Dorothy Montgomery, asking her to call the moment she got home.

"Oh, great!" Laurie said out loud. She debated about calling, knowing her mother's capacity to grate on her nerves in the best of circumstances. She wasn't feeling up to another dose of her mother's negativity and unsolicited advice just then.

Laurie listened to the message a second time and, after convincing herself that her mother sounded genuinely concerned, she made the call. Dorothy answered on the first ring.

"Thank God you called," she said breathlessly. "I don't know what I would have done if you hadn't. I was thinking of sending a telegram. We're having a dinner party tomorrow night, and I want you to come. We're having someone here I want you to meet."

"Mother!" Laurie said with exasperation. "I'm not sure I'm up for a dinner party. I've had a bad day."

"Nonsense," Dorothy exclaimed. "All the more reason to get out of that dreadful apartment of yours. You'll have a wonderful time. It will be good for you. The person I want you to meet is Dr. Jordan Scheffield. He's a marvelous ophthalmologist, known all over the world. Your father's told me. And best of all he was recently divorced from a dreadful woman."

"I'm not interested in a blind date," Laurie said with irritation. She couldn't believe that not only was her mother oblivious to her mental state, but she wanted to fix her up with some divorced eyeball doctor.

"It's about time you met someone appropriate," Dorothy said. "I never understood what you saw in that Sean Mackenzie. That boy is a shiftless hoodlum and a bad influence on you. I'm glad you finally broke up with him for good."

Laurie rolled her eyes. Her mother was in rare form today. Even if there was a certain truth in what she was saying, she didn't feel like hearing it just then. Laurie had been dating Sean on and off since college. From the start, their relationship was a rocky one. And though he wasn't exactly a hoodlum, he did hold a sort of outlaw's appeal for her between his motorcycle and bad attitude. There was a time when his "artistic" personality excited Laurie. Back then she'd even been rebellious enough to try drugs with him on several occasions. But she hoped this last breakup would be their last.

"Be here at seven-thirty," Dorothy said. "And I want you to wear something attractive, like that wool suit I gave you for your birthday in October. And your hair: wear it up. I'd love to talk longer, but I've got so much to do. See you tomorrow, dear. 'Bye."

Laurie took the phone from her ear and looked at it in the darkened room with disbelief. Her mother had hung up on her. She didn't know whether to swear, laugh, or cry. She replaced the receiver on its cradle. Finally she laughed. Her mother was certainly a character. As she played the conversation back in her mind, she couldn't believe it had taken place. It was as if she and her mother talked on different wavelengths.

51

Walking around her apartment, Laurie turned on the lights, then closed the curtains. Shielded from the world, she took her hair down and stepped out of her clothes. For some reason, she felt better. The crazy conversation with her mother had shocked her out of her depressive thoughts.

Climbing into the shower, Laurie admitted to herself that she tended to be more emotional in business situations than she would like. The realization irritated her. She didn't mind dressing femininely, but she didn't want to lend credence to the stereotype of a fragile, fickle female. In the future, she would try to be more professional. She also realized what a mistake she had made in confiding in Bob. She would have to be sure to keep her opinions to herself, particularly where the press was concerned. She was lucky Bingham hadn't fired her.

Standing under the jet of water, Laurie thought about making herself a salad and then doing some studying for her forensic boards. Then she thought about dinner the following night at her parents'. Although her initial reaction had been overwhelmingly negative, she began to have second thoughts. Maybe it would be an interesting break in her routine. Then she wondered how insufferable the newly divorced ophthalmologist would be. She also wondered how old he'd be.

2

□

"I gotta do something," Tony Ruggerio said. He was antsy and he shifted in the passenger side of the front seat of Angelo Facciolo's black Lincoln Town Car. "We've been sitting here in front of D'Agostino's grocery store for four nights. I can't stand this doing nothing, you know what I mean? I've got to have action, something, anything." His eyes nervously darted around the rain-glossed street scene in front of him. The car was parked next to a hydrant on Roosevelt Avenue.

Angelo's head swung slowly around. His lidded eyes regarded this youthful-appearing twenty-four-year-old "kid" who'd been foisted on him. Tony's nervousness and impulsiveness were enough to try the patience of Angelo. He thought the "kid," whose nickname was "the animal," was a liability in Angelo's line of work, and he'd said as much

53

to Cerino. But it didn't matter. Angelo might as well have
been talking to the wall. Cerino said that the kid's asset was
that he had no fear; he was wild and ambitious and had no
qualms and little conscience. Cerino said that he needed
more people like Tony. Angelo wasn't so sure.

Tony was short at five-foot-seven and wiry. What he
lacked in intimidation through stature, he tried to make up
for in muscle. He worked out regularly at the American
Gym in Jackson Heights. He told Angelo he took protein
supplements and occasionally steroids.

Tony's features were rounded, ethnic, southern Italian,
and his hair was shiny, black, and thick. His nose was
slightly flattened and angled to the right thanks to some
amateur boxing. He'd grown up in Woodside and never
finished high school, where he'd had frequent fights over his
stature as well as his sister, Mary, who was, in his vernacu-
lar, a "looker." He'd always been protective of his sister,
thinking that all males had the same goals as himself when
it came to females.

"I can't sit here any longer," Tony said. "I've got to get
out of the car." He reached for the door latch.

Angelo put his hand on Tony's arm. "Relax!" Angelo
said with enough threat in his voice to restrain Tony.
Cerino had been right to pair them up, in a way. Angelo, the
"dude," made an excellent foil for brash Tony. He looked
older than his thirty-four years. Where Tony was short,
Angelo was tall and gaunt, his features sharp and hatchet-
like. If Tony was sensitive about his height, Angelo was
sensitive about his skin. His face bore the scars of a near-
lethal case of chicken pox at age six and severe acne from
thirteen to twenty-one. Where Tony was wild and impul-
sive, Angelo was cautious and calculating: a seemingly calm
sociopath whose character had been molded by an endless
series of foster homes and a final stint of hard time in a
maximum security prison.

Both men were rather vain when it came to their wardrobes. Yet Tony never quite cut the figure for which he aimed; his suits, no matter how expensive, were always ill-fitting on his disproportionately muscled body. On the other hand Angelo gave even Dapper John Gotti a run for his money where sartorial elegance was concerned. He wasn't flashy, just meticulous. He wore exclusively Brioni suits, shirts, ties, and shoes. As Tony's muscle building was in response to his short stature, Angelo's fastidious attire was in response to his complexion, a subject about which he did not brook any reference.

Tony leaned back in his seat. He glanced in Angelo's direction. Angelo was one of the few people Tony feared and respected, even envied. Angelo was connected, a made man whose reputation was legendary.

"Paulie told me that Frankie DePasquale would show up at this grocery store," Angelo said. "So we're going to spend the next month waiting here if need be."

"Christ!" Tony muttered. Instead of getting out of the car, he reached into his baggy jacket and extracted his .25 caliber Beretta Bantam. Releasing the spring-loaded catch in the butt, he slid out the magazine and counted the bullets as if one of the eight shells could have disappeared since he last counted them half an hour ago.

When Tony pulled the empty gun's trigger, Angelo rolled his eyes. "Put the gun away," he said. "What's the matter with you?"

"All right, all right!" Tony said, pushing the magazine home and returning the pistol to its shoulder holster. "Take it easy, will you." He glanced at Angelo, who stared back at him for a moment. Tony held up his hands. He knew Angelo well enough to know he was irritated. "The gun's away. Relax already."

Angelo didn't say anything. He resumed looking toward the entrance of D'Agostino's, watching the people coming and going.

Tony sighed heavily. "It's been a freaking month since

the mothers threw the acid in Paulie's face. Maybe the bums have split, skipped town. That's what I would have done. The next day I would have been outta here. Gone down to Florida or out to the coast. We might be sitting here for nothing. Have you thought of that?"

"Frankie has been seen," Angelo said. "He's been seen here at D'Agostino's."

"So how did it happen?" Tony asked. "How'd they get close to Cerino in the first place?"

"It wasn't complicated," Angelo said. "Vinnie Dominick called the meeting with Cerino. There were to be no weapons. Everybody had to leave his piece in his car. We even used a metal detector that Cerino had taken from Kennedy Airport. When Terry Manso started to serve coffee, he threw a cup of acid in Paul's face. The reason we know Frankie was involved was because he came with Manso."

"How'd Frankie get away?" Tony asked.

"The moment Paulie got the acid the lights went out," Angelo said. "Then the place went crazy with Paulie screaming and everybody diving for cover in the dark. I was by the front window. I threw a chair through it and dove outside. That was when I saw Manso come out the front door. Frankie was already climbing into a car. It all happened so fast, few people could react."

"How did you manage to get Manso?" Tony asked.

"It was a race," Angelo said. "Manso lost. My car was directly in front of the restaurant with my piece on the front seat where I could get to it fast if something went wrong. I got off two shots as Manso tried to get into his car. He never made it. Both slugs went into his back."

"How many people were involved?" Tony asked. He'd been curious about the acid episode since he'd heard about it, but he'd been afraid to bring it up.

"The way I figure it, at least two more besides Manso and DePasquale," Angelo said. "Knowing for sure is one of the reasons we want to talk with Frankie."

"God, it blows my mind," Tony said with a shake of his head. "I can't imagine how much the Lucia people promised to pay for this kind of hit."

"Nobody knows for sure," Angelo said. "In fact, word has it that the punks did it on their own, thinking they'd be rewarded by the Lucia people for their balls. But as far as we can tell the Lucia people haven't even acknowledged it."

"So disrespectful," Tony muttered. "Acid in the face. Christ!"

"That reminds me," Angelo said. "Did you get that battery acid?"

"Yeah, sure," Tony said. "It's in Doc Travino's old doctor's bag on the backseat."

"Good," Angelo said. "Paulie is going to like that. It's a nice touch."

Tony stretched. He was quiet for a minute. Then he cleared his throat. "What do you say to my getting out of the car for just a second? I'd like to do a set of push-ups. My shoulders are tight."

Angelo swore under his breath and told Tony that being in the car with him was like being locked up with a two-year-old kid.

"I'm sorry," Tony said with arched eyebrows. "I'm used to more activity than this." Locking his hands together, he did a series of isometric exercises. In the middle of one of these maneuvers he stopped and stared out the side window.

"Holy crap, isn't that Frankie DePasquale coming along beside us?" Tony said excitedly.

Angelo leaned forward to see around Tony. "It sure looks like him."

"Finally!" Tony exclaimed as he fumbled to withdraw his gun and reach for the door latch. He felt Angelo's hand on his arm. He looked at his mentor in surprise.

"Not yet," Angelo said. "We have to make sure the kid's

alone. We can't screw this up. It might be our only chance and Paulie doesn't want more trouble."

Like an eager hunting dog restraining himself with difficulty from some flushed prey, Tony watched as Frankie DePasquale disappeared into the crowded grocery store. To his surprise, Angelo started the car. "Where are you going?" he demanded.

"I'm just backing up a bit," Angelo explained. "It appears that Frankie is alone. We'll take him when he comes out again."

Angelo angled back to the curb at a bus stop. He left the engine running. They waited.

Twenty minutes later, Frankie came out of the store with bundles in both arms. Angelo and Tony watched as he walked directly toward them.

"He looks like a teenager," Angelo said.

"He is," Tony said. "He's eighteen. He was in my sister's class before he started hanging around with the wrong people and dropped out of school."

"Now!" Angelo said.

In a flash both Angelo and Tony got out of the car and confronted the surprised Frankie DePasquale. Frankie's eyes opened wide and his jaw dropped.

"Hello, Frankie," Angelo said calmly. "We need to talk."

Frankie responded by dropping his groceries. The bags split when they hit the wet sidewalk and a number of cans of tomato paste rolled into the gutter. Frankie turned and fled.

Tony was on him in a flash. He grabbed him roughly from behind, knocking him to the pavement. Holding him down, he frisked him quickly, coming up with a small Saturday night special. Tony pocketed the gun, then turned the terrified boy over. Up close, Frankie looked even younger than eighteen. In fact, it didn't look as if he shaved yet.

"Don't hurt me!" Frankie pleaded.

"Shut up!" Tony snapped. The kid was such a drip. It was disgusting.

Angelo pulled the car up alongside them. With the engine running he jumped from the car. A few pedestrians had stopped beneath their umbrellas to gawk at the spectacle. Angelo pushed through them.

"All right, move on," Angelo commanded. "We're police." Angelo flashed an old police department badge that he kept in his pocket for just this sort of occasion. The fact that it said Ozone Park when they were currently in Woodside made no difference. It was the shape and the glint of metal that caused the desired effect. The small crowd started to disperse.

"They're not police!" Frankie yelled.

Tony responded to Frankie's outburst by putting his Beretta Bantam to the side of Frankie's head. "One more word and you're history, kid."

"In the car," Angelo commanded.

With Angelo on one side and Tony on the other, they stood Frankie up and dragged him to the car. Opening the rear door and pushing his head down, they shoved him inside. Tony climbed in after him. Angelo ran around and jumped into the driver's seat. With a screech of rubber they headed west on Roosevelt Avenue.

"What are you doing this for?" Frankie asked. "I haven't done anything to you guys."

"Shut up!" Angelo said from the front seat. He was keeping his eye on the rearview mirror. If there had been any sign of trouble, he would have turned on Queens Boulevard. But everything was quiet so he kept going straight. Roosevelt became Greenpoint, and Angelo began to relax.

"All right, punk," Angelo said, glancing in the rearview mirror. "Time to talk." He could just see Frankie cowering in the corner, keeping as far from Tony as possible. Tony was holding his gun in his left hand with his arm draped over the back of the seat. Tony's eyes never left Frankie.

"What do you want to talk about?" Frankie asked.

"The job you and Manso did on Paulie Cerino," Angelo said. "I'm sure you guessed that we work for Mr. Cerino."

Frankie's eyes darted from Tony's face to Tony's gun, then up to the image of Angelo in the rearview mirror. He was terrified. "I didn't do it," he said. "I was just there. It was Manso's idea. They forced me to go. I didn't want to do it, but they threatened my mother."

"Who's 'they'?" Angelo asked.

"I mean Terry Manso," Frankie said. "He was the one."

With a sudden wicked slap, Tony cracked Frankie across the face with the barrel of his gun.

Frankie screamed and pressed the palms of his hands against his face. A trickle of blood oozed between his fingers.

"What do you think we are? Stupid?" Tony sneered.

"Don't hurt him yet," Angelo said. "Maybe he'll be cooperative."

"Please don't hurt me anymore," Frankie pleaded between sobs.

Tony swore contemptuously and forced the barrel of his pistol between Frankie's fingers and into his mouth. "Your brains are going to be all over the inside of this car if you don't smarten up and stop screwing around with us."

"Who else was involved?" Angelo asked again.

Tony withdrew the barrel of his gun so Frankie could talk.

"It was just Manso," Frankie sobbed. "And he made me go along."

Angelo shook his head in disgust. "Obviously you are not cooperating, Frankie. Remember about the lights. At the same time Manso threw the acid, the lights went out. That wasn't a coincidence. Who was screwing around with the lights? And the car. Who was driving the car?"

"I don't know anything about the lights," Frankie sobbed. "I don't remember who was driving. Somebody I didn't know. Somebody that Manso got."

Angelo shook his head in disgust. Nothing was easy anymore. He hated this kind of dirty stuff. He had entertained vague hopes that Frankie would have spilled his guts the moment they got him into the car. Obviously that was not to be the case.

Glancing up into the rearview mirror, Angelo caught a glimpse of Tony's face in the flickering light of the passing streetlamps. Tony was sporting one of his contented smiles that told Angelo Tony was enjoying himself. Even Angelo thought Tony could be scary on occasion.

Once they got to the Greenpoint pier area in Brooklyn, Angelo turned right on Franklin, then left on Java. The area was run-down, especially the closer they got to the water. Abandoned warehouses lined the street. Seventy-five to a hundred years ago, the area had been a thriving waterfront, but that had long since changed save for a few isolated enterprises, like the Pepsi-Cola plant up toward Newtown Creek.

In the cul de sac where Java Street dead-ended at the East River, Angelo drove through a chain-link gate. A sign over the gate said: AMERICAN FRESH FRUIT COMPANY. The car began to vibrate on the rough cobblestone surface, but Angelo didn't slow down. When he could drive no farther, he parked.

"Everybody out," Angelo said. They were parked in the shadow of a huge warehouse built out over the pier that stuck out almost a hundred yards into the East River. Just across the river was the monumental mass of Manhattan's glittering skyline. Tony got out holding Doc Travino's little black bag and motioned for Frankie to get out too.

Angelo unlocked an overhead door to the warehouse, pulled it up, and motioned for Frankie to enter. Frankie hesitated on the dark threshold. "I've told you everything I know. What do you want from me?"

Tony gave Frankie a shove that sent the boy stumbling forward. The click of the lightswitch echoed in the cavernous warehouse as Angelo threw the switch activating the mercury vapor lights. At first the lights merely glowed, but as they walked out the pier dragging a reluctant Frankie, they became progressively brighter. Soon it was enough to illuminate the huge stacks of green bananas that filled the warehouse.

"Please!" Frankie moaned, but Angelo and Tony ignored him. They walked to the very end, unlocking a paneled door. Angelo found the lightswitch that activated a single bulb suspended by a bare wire. The room contained an old metal desk missing its drawers, a few chairs, and a large hole in the floor. Below the hole the water of the East River looked more like oil than water as it swirled around the pier's piling, flowing with the tide.

"I'm telling you the truth," Frankie wailed. "It was all Manso. I was forced to go along. I don't know anything else."

"Sure, Frankie," Angelo said. Turning to Tony he added, "Tie him to one of the chairs."

Tony put Doc Travino's bag on the desk and unsnapped it open. From within he pulled out a length of clothesline. Then, with a depraved smile, he told Frankie to sit in one of the wooden side chairs. Frankie did as he was told. While Tony tied him up, Angelo lit himself a cigarette.

Tony gave the rope a couple of yanks to test his knots. Satisfied, he stood up and nodded to Angelo.

"Once more, Frankie," Angelo said. "Who else was involved with the acid trick? Who besides you and Manso?"

"Nobody," Frankie sobbed. "I'm telling the truth."

Angelo derisively blew smoke in Frankie's face. Glancing at Tony, he said, "Time for the truth serum."

Tony pulled a small glass bottle and an eye dropper from Doc Travino's bag. He handed both to Angelo. Angelo unscrewed the cap and gingerly sniffed the contents. When he got a whiff, he pulled his head back quickly. "Geez, powerful stuff." He blinked a few times and wiped tears from the corners of his eyes.

"Any chance you want to change your story?" Angelo asked calmly after walking over to Frankie.

"I'm telling you the truth," Frankie persisted.

Angelo looked at Tony. "Hold his head back."

Tony grabbed a handful of the boy's hair just above the forehead and yanked Frankie's head back.

"Tell me, Frankie," Angelo said as he bent over the boy's upturned face. "Have you ever heard the expression 'an eye for an eye, and a tooth for a tooth'?"

Only then did Frankie realize what was happening. But despite his attempts at clamping his eyes shut, Angelo managed to empty the eye dropper into Frankie's lower right lid.

A slight spattering noise like water hitting a hot skillet preceded an ear-piercing shriek as the sulfuric acid ate into his delicate eye tissues. Angelo glanced at Tony and noticed that Tony's smile had swelled to a grin. Angelo wondered what the world was coming to with this new generation. This kid Tony was having a ball. For Angelo, this was not entertainment, it was business. Nothing more, nothing less.

Angelo set the sulfuric acid bottle on the desk and took a couple more puffs on his cigarette. When Frankie's screams had abated to choking sobs, Angelo leaned toward him and calmly asked if Frankie wanted to change his story.

"Talk to me!" Angelo commanded when it seemed that Frankie was ignoring him.

"I'm telling the truth," Frankie managed.

"Chrissake!" Angelo muttered as he went back for the acid. Over his shoulder, he called to Tony, "Hold his head back again."

"Wait!" Frankie croaked. "Don't hurt me anymore. I'll tell you what you want to know."

Angelo put the acid back on the desk and returned to Frankie. He looked at the tears streaming out of the kid's shut eyes, especially the one where he'd put the acid. "OK, Frankie," Angelo began. "Who was involved?"

"You have to get me something for my eye," Frankie whined. "It's killing me."

"We'll take care of it as soon as you tell us what we want to know," Angelo said. "Come on, Frankie. I'm losing my patience."

"Bruno Marchese and Jimmy Lanso," Frankie muttered.

Angelo looked at Tony.

Tony nodded. "I've heard of Bruno," he said. "He's a local kid."

"Where can we find these guys if we want to talk to them?" Angelo asked.

"Thirty-eight twenty-two Fifty-fifth Street, apartment one," Frankie said. "Just off Northern Boulevard."

Angelo took out a piece of paper and wrote the address down. "Whose idea was it?" he asked.

"It was Manso's," Frankie sobbed. "I was telling the truth about that. It was his idea that if we did it, we'd all become Lucia soldiers, part of the inner circle. But I didn't want to do it. They made me go along."

"Why couldn't you have told us this in the car, Frankie?" Angelo asked. "You would have saved us a lot of trouble and yourself some grief."

"I was afraid the others would kill me if they found out I'd talked," Frankie said.

"So you were more worried about your friends than us?" Angelo questioned as he stepped behind Frankie. It was enough to hurt Angelo's feelings. "That's curious. But no matter. Now you don't have to worry about your friends because we'll take care of you."

"You got to get me something for my eye," Frankie said.

"Sure," Angelo said. In a smooth motion and without a second's hesitation, Angelo pulled out his Walther TPH Auto pistol and shot Frankie in the back of the head just above the neck. Frankie's head snapped forward, then slumped down on his chest.

The suddenness of the final act surprised Tony, who winced and stepped back, anticipating a gory mess. But there wasn't any. "Why didn't you let me do that?" he whined.

"Shut up and untie him," Angelo said. "We're not here for your entertainment. We're working, remember?"

Once Tony had Frankie untied, Angelo helped carry the limp body over to the hole in the floor. On the count of three they heaved him into the river. Angelo watched just long enough to make sure that the running tide took the body out into the river proper.

"Let's head back to Woodside to pay the others a social call," Angelo said.

The address that Frankie had given was a small two-story row house with an apartment on each floor. The outer door was locked but it had a mechanism amenable to a credit card. They were inside in minutes.

Positioning themselves on either side of the door to apartment one, Angelo knocked. There was no answer. From the street they'd seen that the lights were on.

"Bust it," Angelo said, nodding toward the door.

Tony took several steps back, then kicked the door. The jamb splintered on the first kick and the door swung in. In the blink of an eye both Angelo and Tony were in the small apartment with their guns gripped in both hands. The apartment was empty save for several half-filled bottles of beer on the coffee table. The TV was on.

"What do you figure?" Tony asked.

"They must have got spooked when Frankie didn't come back," Angelo said. He lit a cigarette and thought for a moment.

"What next?" Tony questioned.

"You know where this Bruno's family lives?" Angelo asked.

"No, but I can find out," Tony said.

"Do it," Angelo said.

3

□

It was a glorious morning as Laurie Montgomery walked
north on First Avenue, nearing Thirtieth Street. Even New
York City looked good in the cool crisp air scrubbed clean
from a day of rain. It was definitely colder than the previous
days and in that sense a disturbing reminder of the coming
winter. But the sun was out and there was enough breeze to
disperse the exhaust of the vehicles jostling their way in
Laurie's direction.

Laurie's step had a definite spring to it as she approached
the medical examiner's office. She smiled to herself as she
thought how differently she felt this morning as compared
to how she'd felt when she'd left for home the night before.
Bingham's reprimand had been unpleasant but deserved.
She'd been in the wrong. If she'd been chief she would have
been equally as angry.

67

As she approached the front steps, she wondered what the day would bring. One aspect of her work she particularly enjoyed was its unpredictability. All she knew was that she was scheduled to be "on autopsy." She had no idea what kinds of cases and what kinds of intellectual puzzles she'd encounter that day. Just about every time she was on autopsy, she dealt with something she'd never seen, sometimes something she'd never even read about. It was a job that meant continual discovery.

This morning the reception area was relatively quiet. There were still a few media people hanging around for more word on the "preppy murder II" case. Yesterday's Central Park murder had made the front page of the tabloids and the local morning news.

Just shy of the inner door, Laurie stopped. Over on one of the vinyl couches she spotted Bob Talbot deep in conversation with another reporter. After a moment's hesitation Laurie strode over to the couch.

"Bob, I'd like to talk to you a moment," she said. Then to his companion, she added, "Pardon me for interrupting."

Bob eagerly got to his feet and stepped aside with Laurie. His attitude surprised her. She would have expected him to be more sheepish and contrite.

"Seeing you two days in a row must be some sort of record," Bob said. "It's a pleasure I could get used to."

Laurie started right in. "I can't believe you didn't have more respect for my confidence. What I told you yesterday was meant for your ears only."

Bob was clearly taken aback by Laurie's rebuke. "I'm terribly sorry. I didn't think what you were saying was a secret. You didn't say so."

"You could have thought about it," Laurie fumed. "It doesn't take a rocket scientist to guess what such a statement would do to my standing around here."

"I'm sorry," Bob repeated. "It won't happen again."

"You're right, it won't happen again," Laurie said. She turned and headed for the inner door, ignoring Bob as he called out to her. But although she ignored him, her anger had lessened. After all, she had been speaking the truth the day before. She wondered vaguely if she shouldn't be more uncomfortable with the social and political aspects of her job that Bingham had referred to than with Bob. One of the attractions for Laurie of pathology in general and forensics in particular was that they tried to deal with the truth. The idea of compromise for whatever reason disturbed her. She hoped she would never have to choose between her scruples and the politicking.

After Marlene Wilson buzzed her through, Laurie went directly to the ID office. As per usual Vinnie Amendola was drinking coffee and perusing the sports pages. If the date on the paper hadn't been that day's, she might have sworn he'd never left. If he noticed Laurie, he didn't give any indication. Riva Mehta, Laurie's office-mate, was in the ID office. She was a slight Indian woman with a dark complexion and a soft, silky voice. On Monday they'd not crossed paths.

"Looks like today's your lucky day," Riva teased. She was getting herself some coffee before heading up to the office. Tuesday was to be a paper day for her.

"How so?" Laurie questioned.

Vinnie gave a short laugh without looking up from his paper.

"You got a homicide floater," Riva said. A floater was a body that had been in water for a period of time. They generally were not desirable cases since they frequently were in advanced stages of decomposition.

Laurie looked at the schedule Calvin had made up that morning. Listed were that day's autopsies and the people to whom they'd been assigned. After her name were two drug overdoses and a GSW homicide. The GSW stood for Gun Shot Wound.

"The body was hauled out of the East River this morning," Riva said. "An attentive security man had apparently seen it bobbing past the South Street Sea Port."

"Lovely," Laurie said.

"It's not so bad," said Vinnie. "It hadn't been in the water long. Only a matter of hours."

Laurie nodded in relief. That meant she probably wouldn't have to do the case in the decomposing room. It wasn't the smell that bothered her on such cases as much as the isolation. The decomposing room was all by itself on the other side of the morgue. Laurie much preferred to be in the thick of things and relating to the other staff. There was a lot of give and take in the main autopsy room. Often she learned as much from other people's cases as she did from her own.

Laurie looked at the name of the victim and his age: Frank DePasquale. "Poor fellow was only eighteen," she said. "Such a waste. And like most of these homicides, the case will probably never be solved."

"Probably not," Vinnie agreed as he struggled to fold his newspaper to the next page.

Laurie said good morning to Paul Plodgett when he appeared at the door. He had dark circles under his eyes. She asked him how his famous case was progressing.

"Don't ask," Paul said. "It's a nightmare."

Laurie got herself a cup of coffee and picked up the three folders for her day's cases. Each folder contained a case worksheet, a partially filled-out death certificate, an inventory of medico-legal case records, two sheets for autopsy notes, a telephone notice of death as received by communications, a completed identification sheet, an investigative report, a sheet for the autopsy report, and a lab slip for HIV antibody analysis.

As she was shuffling through all the material, Laurie noticed the names of the other two cases: Louis Herrera and Duncan Andrews. She remembered the name Duncan Andrews from the day before.

"That was the case you asked me about yesterday," a voice said from over Laurie's shoulder. She turned and looked up into Calvin Washington's coal black eyes. He'd come up behind her and put a finger by Andrews' name. "When I saw the name, I thought you'd want the case."

"Fine by me," Laurie said.

Each one of the medical examiners had his own way of approaching his autopsy day. Some grabbed the material and went directly downstairs. Laurie had a different modus operandi. She liked to take all the paperwork up to her office to plan her day as rationally as possible. With her coffee in one hand, her briefcase in the other, and the three new files under her arm, Laurie set out for the elevator. She got as far as communications when Sergeant Murphy, one of the policemen currently assigned to the medical examiner's office, called her name. He bounded out of the police cubicle, dragging a second man behind him. Sergeant Murphy was an ebullient, red-faced Irishman.

"Dr. Montgomery, I'd like you to meet Detective Lieutenant Lou Soldano," Murphy said proudly. "He's one of the brass in the homicide department at headquarters downtown."

"Happy to meet you, Doctor," Lou said. He stuck out his hand. He was an attractive, dark-complected man of medium height, with well-defined features and bright eyes that just then were riveted to her face. His hair was cropped short in a style that seemed appropriate for his stocky, muscular body.

"Happy to meet you as well," Laurie said. "We don't see too many police lieutenants here at the medical examiner's office." Laurie felt a bit nervous under the man's unblinking stare.

"They don't let us out of our cages too often," Lou said. "I'm pretty much glued to my desk. But I still like to sneak out once in a while, especially on certain cases."

"Hope you enjoy your visit here," Laurie said. She smiled and started to leave.

"Just a moment, Doctor!" Lou said. "I was told that you were assigned to autopsy Frank DePasquale. I wonder if you would mind if I observed the post. I've already cleared it with Dr. Washington."

"Not at all," Laurie said. "If you can tolerate it, be my guest."

"I've seen a few autopsies," Lou said. "I don't think there will be any problem."

"Fine," Laurie said.

There was an awkward pause. For a moment no one spoke. Finally Laurie realized the man was waiting for some directions.

"I'm on my way to my office," Laurie said. "I usually go over the paperwork first. Would you care to come along?"

"I'd be delighted," he said.

In the elevator Laurie looked at Soldano more closely. He was a square, athletic-appearing man of obvious intelligence whose rumpled appearance vaguely reminded her of Colombo, the TV detective made famous by Peter Falk. The crease in his suit pants had long since disappeared. Despite the fact that it was only a little after eight in the morning, he had a heavy five o'clock shadow.

As if reading Laurie's mind, Lou self-consciously ran a hand up and down the sides of his face.

"I guess I look a wreck," Lou said. "I've been up since four-thirty when the DePasquale body floated to shore. Didn't have a chance to shave. Hope it doesn't offend you. I'm not trying for the Don Johnson *Miami Vice* look."

"I didn't notice," Laurie lied. "But why is a detective lieutenant so interested in an eighteen-year-old homicide victim? Is there something special about this case that I should know?"

"Not really," Lou said. "It's more personal. Before I got

promoted to lieutenant and switched to Homicide, I'd been with the organized crime unit for six years. With DePasquale the two areas overlap. DePasquale was a young hoodlum on the fringes of the Lucia crime family organization. He might have been only eighteen, but he already had a long sheet."

The elevator stopped on the fifth floor, and Laurie motioned for them to get off.

"As you've probably already guessed," Lou continued, following Laurie down the corridor, "DePasquale's death was an obvious execution."

"It was?" Laurie questioned. As of yet, nothing was obvious to her.

"Absolutely," Lou said. "You're going to find that he was shot from close range with a small caliber bullet into the base of the brain. It's the usual, proven method. No mess, no fuss."

They went into Laurie's office. Laurie introduced Lou to Riva, who was already hard at work. Laurie got a chair for Lou and put it next to her desk. They both sat down.

"You've seen these gangland-style execution cases before, haven't you?" Lou questioned.

"I'm not sure," Laurie said evasively. From medical school training, she knew how to be vague when asked a pointed question. She didn't want to give the impression she was inexperienced.

"They usually mean friction between rival organizations," Lou said. "And in this case it would mean friction between the Lucia and the Vaccarro crime families. They are the major players in the Queens area and their respective interests are controlled by midlevel bosses, Vinnie Dominick and Paul Cerino. My guess would be that Paul Cerino had a hand in poor Frank DePasquale's murder, and if he did, I'd like nothing better than to nail him with an indictment. I was after the guy for the entire six years I was

assigned to Organized Crime. I could never get an indictment to stick. But if I could link him to a capital offense like
whacking DePasquale, I'd be in fat city."

"That puts the burden on us," Laurie said as she opened
DePasquale's folder.

"If you or your lab could come up with something, I'd be
eternally grateful," Lou said. "We need some kind of break.
The problem with guys like Cerino is that they keep so
many layers between themselves and all the crime committed in their name, we seldom get any charges to stick."

"Oh, damn!" Laurie said suddenly. She'd been listening
to Lou as well as going through the DePasquale file.

"What's the matter?" Lou asked.

"They didn't take an X-ray on DePasquale," Laurie said.
She reached for her phone and dialed the morgue. "We
have to have an X-ray before the autopsy. Unfortunately
that's going to hold things up. I'll have to post one of the
other cases first. I'm sorry."

Lou shrugged.

Laurie told the mortuary tech who answered the phone to
X-ray Frank DePasquale as soon as possible. The tech said
he'd do his best. As she was hanging up, the doorway to her
office was filled by Calvin Washington.

"Laurie," Calvin said, "we've got a problem that you
should know about."

Laurie stood up when Calvin entered. "What is it?" she
asked. She noticed that Calvin was eyeing Lou question-
ingly. "Dr. Washington, I believe you met Lieutenant Soldano."

"Ah, yes," Calvin said. "Don't mind me. It's just Alz-
heimer's setting in. We met just this morning." He shook
hands with Lou, who'd stood when Laurie introduced him.

"Sit down, both of you," Calvin boomed. "Laurie, I have
to warn you that we've already been getting some heat from
the Mayor's office about this Duncan Andrews case. It

seems that the deceased has some powerful political connections. So we're going to have to cooperate. I want you to
look hard for some natural cause of death so that you can
downplay the drugs. The family would prefer it that way."

Laurie looked up at Calvin's face, half expecting it to
break out in a broad smile, saying that he was only joking.
But Calvin's expression didn't change.

"I'm not sure I understand," Laurie said.

"I can't be much clearer," Calvin said. His infamous
impatience began to show.

"What do you want me to do, lie?" Laurie asked.

"Hell, no, Dr. Montgomery!" Calvin snapped. "What do
I have to do, draw you a map? I'm just asking you to lean
as far as you can, okay? Find something like a coronary
plaque, an aneurysm, anything, and then write it up. And
don't act so surprised or self-righteous. Politics play a role
here and the sooner you learn that the better off we'll all be.
Just do it."

Calvin turned and left as quickly as he'd come.

Lou whistled and sat down. "Tough guy," he said.

Laurie shook her head in disbelief. She turned to Riva,
who hadn't paused in her work. "Did you hear that?" Laurie asked her.

"It happened to me once, too," Riva said without looking up. "Only my case was a suicide."

With a sigh, Laurie sat down in her desk chair and looked
across at Lou. "I don't know if I'm prepared to sacrifice
integrity and ethics for the sake of politics."

"I don't think that was what Dr. Washington was asking
you to do," Lou said.

Laurie felt her face flush. "It wasn't? I'm sorry, but I
think it was."

"I don't mean to tell you your business," Lou said, "but
my take was that Dr. Washington wants you to emphasize
any potential natural cause of death you find. The rest can

be left to interpretation. For some reason it makes a difference in this case. It's the real world versus the world of make-believe."

"Well, you seem pretty blasé about fudging the details," Laurie said. "In Pathology we're supposed to be dealing with the truth."

"Come on," Lou said. "What is the truth? There are shades of gray in most everything in life, so why not in death? My line of work happens to be justice. It's an ideal. I pursue it. But if you don't think politics sometimes plays a lead role in how justice is applied, you're kidding yourself. There's always a gap between law and justice. Welcome to the real world."

"Well, I don't like it one bit," Laurie said. All this was reminding her of the concerns about compromise she'd had when she'd arrived a half hour earlier.

"You don't have to like it," Lou said. "Not many do."

Laurie flipped open the file on Duncan Andrews. She leafed through the papers until she came to the investigator's report. After reading for a few moments, she looked up at Lou. "I'm beginning to get the big picture," she said. "The deceased was some kind of financial whiz kid, a senior vice president of an investment banking firm at only thirty-five. And on top of that there is a note here that says his father is running for the U.S. Senate."

"Can't get much more political than that," Lou said.

Laurie nodded, then read more of the investigator's report. When she got to the section noting who had identified the deceased at the scene, she found a name, Sara Wetherbee. In the space left to describe the witness's relationship to the deceased, the investigator had scrawled: "girlfriend."

Laurie shook her head. Discovering a loved one dead from drugs carried an ugly resonance for her. In a flash her thoughts drifted back seventeen years to when she was fifteen, a freshman at Langley School. She could remember the bright sunny day as if it had been yesterday. It was midfall, crisp and clear, and the trees in Central Park had been a blaze of color. She'd walked past the Metropolitan with its banners snapping in the gusty wind. She'd turned left on Eighty-fourth Street and entered her parents' massive apartment building on the west side of Park Avenue.

"I'm home!" Laurie called as she tossed her bookbag onto the foyer table. There was no answer. All she could hear was the traffic on Park peppered by the inevitable bleat of taxi horns.

"Anybody home?" Laurie called and heard her voice echo through the halls. Surprised to find the apartment empty, Laurie pushed through the door from the butler's pantry into the kitchen. Even Holly, their maid, was nowhere to be seen. But then Laurie remembered that it was Friday, Holly's day off.

"Shelly!" Laurie yelled. Her older brother was home from his freshman year at college for the long Columbus Day weekend. Laurie expected to find him either in the kitchen or the den. She looked in the den; no one was there, but the TV was on with the sound turned off.

For a moment Laurie looked at the silent antics of a daytime game show. She thought it odd that the TV had been left on. Thinking that someone might still be home, she resumed her tour of the apartment. For some reason the silent rooms filled her with apprehension. She began to move faster, sensing a secret urgency.

Pausing in front of Shelly's bedroom door, Laurie hesitated. Then she knocked. When there was no answer, she knocked again. When there was still no answer, she tried the door. It was unlocked. She pushed open the door and stepped into the room.

In front of her on the floor was her brother, Shelly. His face was as white as the ivory-colored china in the dining room breakfront. Bloody froth oozed from his nose.

Around his upper arm was a rubber tourniquet. On the floor, six inches from his half-opened hand, was a syringe Laurie had seen the night before. On the edge of his desk was a glassine envelope. Laurie guessed what was inside because of what Shelly had told her the night before. It had to be the "speedball" he'd boasted of, a mixture of cocaine and heroin.

Hours later the same day, Laurie endured the worst confrontation of her life. Inches from her nose was her father's angry face with his bulging eyes and purpled skin. He was beside himself with rage. His thumbs were digging into her skin where he held her upper arms. A few feet away her mother was sobbing into a tissue.

"Did you know your brother was using drugs?" her father demanded. "Did you? Answer me." His grip tightened.

"Yes," Laurie blurted. "Yes, yes!"

"Why didn't you tell us?" her father shouted. "If you'd told us, he'd be alive."

"I couldn't," Laurie sobbed.

"Why?" her father shouted. "Tell me why!"

"Because . . ." Laurie cried. She paused, then said: "Because he told me not to. He made me promise."

"Well, that promise killed him," her father hissed. "It killed him just as much as the damn drug."

Laurie felt a hand grip her arm and she jumped. The shock brought her back to the present. She blinked a few times as if waking from a trance.

"Are you all right?" Lou asked. He'd gotten up and was holding Laurie's arm.

"I'm fine," Laurie said, slightly embarrassed. She extracted herself from Lou's grip. "Let's see, where were we?" Her breathing had quickened. Perspiration dotted her forehead. She looked over the paperwork in front of her, trying to remember what had dredged up such old, painful memories. As if it had been yesterday, she could recall the anguish of the conflict of responsibility, sibling or filial, and the terrible guilt and burden of having chosen the former.

"What were you thinking about?" Lou asked. "You seemed a long way off."

"The fact that the victim had been discovered by his girlfriend," Laurie said as her eyes stumbled again onto Sara Wetherbee's name. She wasn't about to share her past with this lieutenant. To this day she had trouble talking about that tragic episode with friends, much less a stranger. "It must have been very hard for the poor woman."

"Unfortunately, homicide victims are often found by those closest to them," Lou said.

"Must have been a terrible shock," Laurie said. Her heart went out to Sara Wetherbee. "I must say, this Duncan Andrews case is certainly not the usual overdose."

Lou shrugged. "With cocaine, I'm not sure there is a usual case. When the drug went upscale in the seventies, deaths have been seen in all levels of society, from athletes and entertainers to executives to college kids to inner city hoodlums. It's a pretty democratic blight. A great leveler, if you will."

"Here at the medical examiner's office, we mostly see the lower end of the abuser spectrum," Laurie said. "But you're right in general." Laurie smiled. She was impressed by Lou. "What was your background before joining the police?"

"What do you mean?" Lou asked.

"Did you go to college?" Laurie asked.

"Of course I went to college!" Lou snapped. "What kind of question is that?"

"Sorry," Laurie said. "I didn't mean to upset you."

"And I don't mean to be testy," Lou said. "Sometimes I'm a bit self-conscious about where I went to school. I only got to go to a community college on the Island, not some Ivy League ivory tower. Where'd you go?"

"Wesleyan University, up in Connecticut," Laurie said. "Ever heard of it?"

"Of course I've heard of it," Lou said. "What do you think, all police officers are ignoramuses? Wesleyan University. I might have known. As Billy Joel says, you uptown girls live in an uptown world."

"How did you know I was from New York?"

"Your accent, Doctor," Lou said. "It's as indelible as my Long Island Rego Park accent."

"I see," Laurie said. She didn't like to think she was such an open book. She wondered what else this man could tell about her from his years as an investigator.

Laurie changed the subject. "Where you go to school matters less than what you do while you're there," she said. "You shouldn't be sensitive about your college. Obviously you got a good education."

"Easy for you to say," said Lou. "But thanks for the compliment."

Laurie looked down at the papers on her desk. Suddenly she felt a little guilty about her privileged background of a private secondary school, Wesleyan University, Columbia Medical School. She hoped she hadn't sounded patronizing.

"Let me take a quick look at the third case," Laurie said. She opened the third folder. "Louis Herrera, age twenty-eight, unemployed, found in a dumpster behind a grocery store." Laurie looked up at Lou. "Probably died in a crack house and was literally dumped. That's the usual overdose we see. Another sad, wasted life."

"In some respects maybe more tragic than the rich guy," Lou said. "I'd guess he had a lot fewer choices in life."

Laurie nodded. Lou's perspective was refreshing. She reached for the phone and dialed Cheryl Myers down in the medical investigator's department. She asked Cheryl to get all the medical records she could on Duncan Andrews. She told her that she hoped to find some medical problem that she might be able to relate to his pathology.

Hanging up the phone, Laurie glanced over at Lou. "I can't help it, but I feel like I'm cheating." She stood up and gathered all the paperwork.

"You're not cheating," Lou assured her. "Besides, why not wait until you have all the information, including the autopsy? Then you can worry about it. Who knows, maybe everything will work out."

"Good advice," Laurie said. "Let's get downstairs and get to work."

Normally Laurie changed into her scrub clothes in her office, but with Lou there, she opted to use the locker room. When they got off the elevator on the basement level, Laurie directed Lou into the men's side while she went into the women's. Five minutes later they met up in the hall. Laurie had on a layer of normal scrub clothes, then another impermeable layer, then a large apron. On her head she wore a hood. A face mask dangled from around her neck. Lou had on a single layer of scrubs, a hood, and he carried his face mask.

"You look like one of the doctors," Laurie said, eyeing Lou to make sure he'd put on the right clothing.

"I feel like I'm going into surgery instead of to see an autopsy," Lou said. "I didn't wear all this the last time. You sure I have to wear this mask?"

"Everyone in the autopsy room wears a mask," Laurie said. "Because of AIDS and other infectious problems, rules have become much stricter. If you don't wear it, Calvin will bodily throw you out."

They walked down the main corridor of the morgue, passing the stainless steel door to the walk-in cooler and past the long bank of individual refrigerated compartments. The refrigerator compartments formed a large U in the middle of the morgue.

"This place is certainly grisly," Lou commented.

"I suppose," Laurie said. "It's less so when you're used to it."

"It looks like a Hollywood set for a horror movie," Lou said. "Whoever picked out these blue tiles for the walls? And what about the cement floor? Why isn't there any covering? Look at all the stains."

Laurie stopped and gazed at the floor. Although the surface was swept clean, the stains were unspeakable. "It was supposed to be tiled long ago," she said. "Somehow it got fouled up in New York City bureaucratic red tape. At least that's what I've been told."

"And what are all those coffins doing here?" Lou asked. "That's a nice touch." He pointed to a stack of simple pine boxes piled almost to the ceiling. Others were standing on end.

"Those are Potter's Field coffins," Laurie said. "There are a lot of unidentified bodies in New York City. After their autopsies we keep them in the cooler for a number of weeks. If they go unclaimed, they are eventually buried at city's expense."

"Isn't there someplace else they could store the coffins?" Lou asked. "It looks like a garage sale."

"Not that I know of," Laurie said. "I guess I've never thought about it. I'm so used to seeing them there."

Laurie pushed into the autopsy room first, then held the door for Lou. In contrast to the previous morning, all eight tables were now occupied by corpses, each with a tag tied around its big toe. At five of the tables the posts were already under way.

"Well, well, Dr. Montgomery is starting before noon," one of the gowned and hooded doctors quipped.

"Some of us are smart enough to test the water before we jump in the pool," Laurie shot back.

"You're on table six," one of the mortuary techs called

out from a sink where he was washing out a length of intestine.

Laurie looked back at Lou, who had paused just inside the door. She saw him swallow hard. Although he'd said he'd seen autopsies before, she had the feeling that he found this "assembly line" operation a bit overwhelming. With the gut being washed out, the smell wasn't too good either.

"You can go outside anytime," Laurie said to him.

Lou held up a hand. "I'm all right," he said. "If you can take this, I can too."

Laurie walked down to table six. Lou followed her. A gowned and hooded Vinnie Amendola appeared.

"It's you and me today, Dr. Montgomery," Vinnie said.

"Fine," Laurie said. "Why don't you get everything we'll need and we'll get started."

Vinnie nodded, then went over to the supply cabinets.

Laurie put out her note papers where she could get to them, then looked at Duncan Andrews. "Handsome-looking man," she said.

"I didn't think doctors thought that way," Lou said. "I thought you guys all switched into neutral or something."

"Hardly," Laurie said. Duncan's pale body lay in apparent repose on the steel table. His eyelids were closed. The only thing that marred his appearance aside from his pasty white color were the excoriations on his forearms. Laurie pointed to them. "Those deep scratches are probably the result of what's called formication. That's a tactile hallucination of bugs under or on the skin. It's seen in both cocaine and amphetamine intoxication."

Lou shook his head. "I can't understand why people take drugs," he said. "It's beyond me."

"They do it for pleasure," Laurie said. "Unfortunately, drugs like cocaine tap into parts of the brain that developed during evolution as the reward center. It was to encourage behavior likely to perpetuate the species. If the war against drugs is to succeed, the fact that drugs can be pleasurable has to be admitted and not ignored."

"Why do I have the feeling you don't think much of the Just Say No campaign?" Lou asked.

"Because I don't. It's stupid," Laurie said. "Or at least shortsighted. I don't think the politicians who dreamed that scheme up have a clue to what growing up in today's society is like, especially for poor urban kids. Drugs are around, and when kids try them and find out that drugs are pleasurable, they think the powers-that-be are lying about the negative or dangerous side as well."

"You ever try any of that stuff?"

"I've tried pot and cocaine."

"Really?"

"Are you surprised?" Laurie asked.

"I suppose I am, to an extent."

"Why?"

Lou shrugged. "I don't know. I suppose you don't look the type."

Laurie laughed. "I guess he looks more the type than I do right now," she said, pointing to Andrews. "But when he was alive I bet he didn't look the type either. Yeah, I tried some drugs in college. Despite what happened to my brother, or maybe because of it."

"What happened to your brother?" Lou asked.

Laurie looked down at the body of Duncan Andrews. She'd not meant to bring her brother into the conversation. The comment had slipped out as if she were talking with someone with whom she was close.

"Did your brother overdose?" Lou asked.

Laurie's eyes went from Duncan's corpse to Lou. She couldn't lie. "Yes," she said. "But I don't want to talk about it."

"Fine," Lou said. "I don't mean to pry."

Laurie turned back to Duncan's body. For a second she

was immobilized by the thought it was her brother's body before her on that cold table. She was relieved to be interrupted by Vinnie returning with gloves, specimen bottles, preservatives, labels, and a series of instruments. She was eager to get started and put these reveries behind her.

"Let's do it," Vinnie said. He began applying the labels to the specimen jars.

Laurie opened the gloves and put them on. She put on her goggles and began a careful exterior examination of Duncan Andrews. After looking at Duncan's head, she motioned for Lou to step around to the other side of the table. Parting Duncan's hair with her gloved hand, she showed Lou multiple bruises.

"I'll bet he had at least one convulsion," Laurie said. "Let's look at the tongue."

Laurie opened Duncan's mouth. The tongue was lacerated in several locations. "Just what I expected," she said. "Now let's see how much cocaine this fellow has been using." With a small flashlight and a nasal speculum, she looked up Duncan's nose. "No perforations. Looks normal. Guess he hadn't been sniffing much."

Laurie straightened up. She noticed Lou's attention had been directed at a neighboring table where they were busy sawing off the top of a skull. Their eyes met.

"You okay?" Laurie questioned.

"I'm not sure," Lou said. "You actually do this every day?"

"On average, three or four days a week," Laurie said. "You want to go outside for a while? I can let you know when we do DePasquale."

"No, I'll be all right. Let's get on with it. What's next?"

"I usually check the eyes," Laurie said. She studied Lou. The last thing she wanted was for him to pass out and hit his head on the concrete floor. That had happened to a visitor once before.

"Continue," Lou urged. "I'm fine."

Laurie shrugged. Then she put her thumb and index finger on Duncan's eyelids and drew them up.

Lou gasped and turned away.

For a moment even Laurie was taken aback. The eyes were gone! The pulpy red sockets were filled with pink-stained wads of gauze. It gave the corpse a ghastly appearance.

"Okay!" Lou said. "You got me. You set me up and you got me. I'll have to give you that." He turned back to Laurie. The bit of facial skin visible between his mask and his hood was blanched. "Let me guess: this was some sort of initiation ordeal for the rookie."

Laurie let out a short, nervous laugh. "I'm sorry, Lou," she said. "I'd forgotten the eyes had been taken. Truly. This was the case where the family was insistent that the deceased's wishes to be an organ donor be honored. If the eyes can be harvested within twelve hours, they often can be used if there are no other contraindications. Occasionally it can even be longer than twelve hours if the body is chilled."

"I don't mind being the butt of a joke," Lou said.

"But it wasn't a joke," Laurie insisted. "I'm sorry. Honest. I'd been called on this case yesterday. With everything else that's happened, I'd forgotten. I just remembered this was a case where the victim took the cocaine IV. Let's see if we can find the injection site."

Laurie rotated Duncan's right arm palm up so she could examine its volar surface. Vinnie did the same with the left arm.

"Here it is," Laurie exclaimed, pointing to a minute puncture wound over one of the veins in front of the elbow area.

"I didn't know cocaine could be mainlined," Lou said.

"It's taken into the body just about every way you can imagine and some you can't," Laurie said. "IV is not common, but it's done." As she spoke, her mind took her back to the night before she found Shelly dead in his bedroom. He'd just come home from Yale, and Laurie was in his room, eager to hear about college. His open Dopp kit was on his bed.

"What's this?" Laurie questioned. She held up a pack of condoms.

"Give me that," Shelly shouted, clearly peeved to have his baby sister find such a thing in his shaving kit.

Laurie giggled as Shelly snatched the contraceptives from her hand. While Shelly was busy burying them in his top bureau drawer, Laurie looked into the Dopp kit to see what else she could find. But what she saw was more disturbing than interesting. Touching it ever so gingerly, Laurie lifted a 10 cc syringe from the bag. It was the needle she was to see the following day.

"What is this?" she demanded.

Shelly came over and tried to grab the needle, but Laurie evaded him.

"You got this from Daddy's office, didn't you?" Laurie demanded.

"Give me that or you are in serious trouble," Shelly snapped. He trapped her against the wall.

Laurie gripped the needle in both hands behind her back. Having grown up in New York City, she knew what it meant when a fellow teenager had a needle.

"Are you shooting up?" Laurie asked.

Shelly overpowered her and got the needle. He took it over to his bureau and hid it with his condoms. Then he turned back to his sister, who hadn't moved.

"I've tried it a couple of times," Shelly said. "It's called speedball. A lot of the guys at school do it. It's no big deal. But I don't want you to say anything to Mom or Dad. If you do, I'll never talk to you again. You understand? Never."

Laurie's momentary reverie was cut short by the booming voice of Calvin Washington. "What the hell is going on here?" he yelled. "Why haven't you even started this case? I came in here to see if you found anything we can hang our hats on and you haven't even started. Get busy."

Laurie sprang into action. She completed her external examination, noting only a few ecchymotic bruises on Duncan's upper arms in addition to her other findings. Then she took a scalpel and expertly made the traditional Y-shaped incision from the points of the shoulders down to the pubis. With Vinnie helping, she worked silently and quickly removing the breastbone and exposing the internal organs.

Lou tried to stay out of the way. "I'm sorry if I've slowed you down," he said when Laurie paused, allowing Vinnie to organize the specimen bottles.

"No problem," Laurie said. "When we do DePasquale I'll explain a bit more. I just want to get Andrews finished. If Calvin really gets mad there could be trouble."

"I understand," Lou said. "Would you rather I leave?"

"No, not at all," Laurie said. "Just don't get your feelings hurt when I ignore you for a while."

After Laurie inspected all the internal organs in situ, she used several syringes to take various fluids for toxicologic testing. She and Vinnie went through a precise procedure to make sure the right specimen got in the correctly labeled bottle. Then she began to remove the organs, one by one. She spent the most time on the heart, until eventually it, too, was removed.

While Vinnie took the stomach and the intestines to the sink to wash them out, Laurie carefully went through the heart, taking multiple samples for later microscopic examination. She then took similar samples from some of the other organs. By then Vinnie was back. Without any encouragement, he began on the head, reflecting the scalp. After Laurie inspected the skull, she nodded to him to use the power vibrating saw to cut through the skull in a circular fashion just above the ears.

Lou kept his distance when Laurie lifted the brain out of its skull and plopped it into a pan held by Vinnie. Wielding a long-bladed knife similar to a butcher's, she began making serial cuts as if she were dealing with a slab of processed meat. It was all an efficient, well-practiced duet requiring little conversation.

Half an hour later, Laurie led Lou out of the autopsy room. Leaving the aprons and gowns behind, they went up to the lunchroom on the second floor for coffee. They had about fifteen minutes while Vinnie took Duncan's remains away and "put up" the next case, Frank DePasquale.

"Thanks, but I don't think I'll be eating anything for a few days," Lou said when offered something from one of the several vending machines in the lunchroom. Laurie poured herself another cup of coffee. They sat at a Formica table near the microwave oven. There were about fifteen other people in the room, all engaged in animated conversation.

Seeing other people smoking, Lou took out a box of Marlboros, a pack of matches, and lit up. When he noticed Laurie's expression, he took the cigarette out of his mouth. "Okay if I smoke?" he asked.

"If you must," Laurie said.

"Just one," Lou assured her.

"Well, Duncan Andrews didn't have any pathology on gross," she said. "And I don't think I'm going to find anything on histology either."

"You can only do your best," Lou said. "If worse comes to worst, dump it in Calvin's lap. Let him decide what to do. As part of the brass, it's his job."

"Whoever does the autopsy has to sign out on the death certificate," Laurie said. "But maybe I can give it a try."

89

"I was impressed with the way you handled that knife in the autopsy room . . ." Lou said.

"Thanks for your compliment," Laurie said. "But why do I feel like I hear a 'but' coming?"

"It's just I'm surprised an attractive woman like yourself would choose this kind of work," Lou said.

Laurie closed her eyes and let out a sigh of exasperation. "That's a rather chauvinistic comment." She stared at Lou. "Unfortunately, it undermines your compliment. Did you mean to say, 'What is a pretty girl like you doing in a place like this?'"

"Hey, I'm sorry," Lou said. "I didn't mean it that way at all."

"Talking about my appearance and my abilities and re-lating the two makes a negative comment about both," Laurie said. She took a sip of her coffee. She could tell that Lou was bewildered and uncomfortable. "I don't mean to jump on you," she added. "But I'm sick of defending my career choice. And I'm also sick of hearing my looks and my gender have anything to do with my position."

"Maybe I'd better just keep my trap shut," said Lou.

Laurie glanced up at the clock on the wall. "I think we should get downstairs. I'm sure Vinnie has DePasquale on the table." She gulped down the rest of her coffee and stood up.

Lou stubbed out his cigarette and hurried after her. Five minutes later they were back in their gowns, standing in front of the X-ray view box in the autopsy room, looking at the X-rays of Frank DePasquale. The AP and the lateral of the head showed the bright silhouette of the bullet resting in the posterior fossa.

"You were right about the location of the bullet," Laurie said. "There it is in the base of the brain."

"Gangland execution is very efficient," Lou said.

"I can believe it," Laurie added. "The reason is that a

bullet into the base of the brain hits the brainstem. That's where the vital centers are for things like breathing and heartbeat."

"I suppose if I have to go, that's one way I'd like it to be," Lou said.

Laurie looked at the detective. "That's a pleasant thought."

Lou shrugged. "In my line of work you think about it."

Laurie glanced back at the X-ray. "You were also right about its being small caliber. I'd guess a twenty-two or a twenty-five at most."

"That's what they usually use," Lou said. "The more powerful stuff is just too messy."

Laurie led the way to table six, where Frankie's mortal remains were laid out. The corpse was slightly bloated. The right eye was more swollen than the left.

"He looks younger than eighteen," Laurie said.

"More like fifteen," Lou agreed.

Laurie asked Vinnie to roll the body over so they could look at the back of the head. With a gloved hand she parted his wet, matted hair and exposed a round entrance wound surrounded by a larger round area of abrasion. After taking some measurements and photographs, Laurie carefully shaved the surrounding hair to expose the wound completely.

"It was obviously a close-range shot," Laurie said. She pointed to the tight ring of gunpowder stippling around the punched-out center.

"How close?" Lou asked.

Laurie pondered for a moment. "I'd say three or four inches. Something like that."

"Typical," Lou said.

Laurie took another series of measurements and photographs. Then, with a clean scalpel, she carefully teased bits of the gunpowder residue from the depths of some of the small stippled puncture wounds. By tapping the scalpel blade against the inside of a glass collection tube, Laurie preserved this material for laboratory analysis.

"Never know what the chemists can tell us," she said. She gave the tubes to Vinnie to label.

"We need a break," Lou said. "I don't care where it comes from."

When Vinnie was finished labeling the collection tubes, Laurie had him help her turn Frank back into a supine position.

"What's wrong with the right eye?" Lou asked.

"I don't know," Laurie said. "From the X-ray it didn't look like the bullet went into the orbit, but you never know." The lid was a purplish color. Swollen conjunctiva protruded through the palpebral fissure. Gently, Laurie pulled up the eyelid.

"Ugh," Lou said. "That looks bad. The first case had no eyes; this one looks like the eye's been run over with a Mack truck. Could that have happened when he was floating around in the East River?"

Laurie shook her head. "Happened before death. See the hemorrhages under the mucous membrane? That means the heart was pumping. He was alive when this occurred."

Bending closer, Laurie studied the cornea. By looking at the reflection of the overhead lights off its surface, she could tell that the cornea was irregular. Plus, it was a milky white. Reaching over to the left eye, she lifted its lid. In contrast to the right, the left cornea was clear; the eye stared blankly at the ceiling.

"Could the bullet have done that?" Lou asked.

"I don't think so," Laurie said. "It looks more like a chemical burn the way it's affected the cornea. We'll get a sample for Toxicology. I'll look at it closely in sections under the microscope. I have to admit, I haven't seen anything quite like it."

Laurie continued her external exam. When she looked at the wrists, she pointed to them. "See these abrasions and indentations?"

"Yeah," Lou said. "What's that mean?"

"I'd say this poor guy had been tied up. Maybe the eye lesion was some kind of torture."

"These are nasty people," Lou said. "What irks me is that they hide behind this supposed code of ethics when in reality it's just a dog-eat-dog world. And what really irks me is that their screwing around tends to give all Italian-Americans a bad name."

As Laurie examined Frank's hands and legs, she asked Lou why the Vaccarro and Lucia crime families were feuding.

"For territory," Lou said. "They all have to sleep in the same bed, Queens and parts of Nassau County. They are forever at each other's throats for territory. They are in direct competition for their drugs, loan-sharking, gambling clubs, fencing, extortion rings, hot car rings, hijacking . . . You name it and they're into it. They're forever fighting and killing each other, but it's a Mexican standoff so in a way they also have to get along. It's a weird world."

"All this illegal activity goes on even today?" Laurie questioned.

"Absolutely," Lou said. "And what we know about is just the tip of the iceberg."

"Why don't the police do something?"

Lou sighed. "We're trying, but it ain't easy. We need evidence. As I explained before, that's hard to get. The bosses are insulated and the killers are pros. Even when we've got the goods on them they still have to go through the courts, and nothing is guaranteed. We Americans have always been so worried about tyranny from the authorities, that we legally give the bad guys the edge."

"It's difficult to believe so little can be done," Laurie said.

"Something can only be done if we get hard evidence. Take Frank DePasquale here. I'm ninety-nine percent sure Cerino and his crew are responsible for whacking him. But I can't do anything without some proof, some break."

"I thought the police had informers," Laurie said.

"We have informers," Lou agreed. "But nobody who really knows anything. The people that could really point a finger are more scared of each other than they are of us."

"Well, maybe I'll come up with something with this post," Laurie said, redirecting her gaze to Frank DePasquale's corpse. "The trouble is that bodies in water tend to be washed of evidence. Of course, there is the bullet. At the very least I can give you the bullet."

"I'll take whatever I can get," Lou said.

Laurie and Vinnie tackled the autopsy. At each step she explained to Lou what they were doing. The only difference between Frank's autopsy and Duncan's was the way Laurie did the brain. With Frank she was meticulously careful to follow the bullet's path. She noted that it never came near to the swollen eye. She was also careful not to touch the bullet with a metal instrument. Once she'd retrieved it, she put it into a plastic container to avoid scratching it. Later, after it was dry, she marked it on its base, then photographed it before sealing it in a small envelope. The envelope was then attached to a property receipt, ready to be turned over to the police, meaning Sergeant Murphy or his partner upstairs.

"It's been quite a morning," Lou said as they exited the autopsy room. "It's been very instructive, but I think I'll pass on your third case."

"I was surprised you tolerated two," Laurie said.

They paused outside the locker room. "I'll go through the microscopic material on Frank DePasquale, and I'll let you know if anything interesting turns up. The only thing that I think might be interesting is the eye. But who knows?"

94

"Well, it's been fun . . ." Lou said. He shifted his weight from one foot to the other.

Laurie looked into the lieutenant's dark eyes. She had a feeling he wanted to ask her something else, but couldn't seem to get it out. "I'm heading upstairs for another shot of coffee," she said. "Would you care for another before you run off?"

"Sounds good," Lou said without hesitation.

Up in the lunchroom they found themselves at the same table they'd occupied earlier. Laurie couldn't understand why the confident Lou had become so fidgety and awkward. She watched while he took out his cigarettes and matches and fumbled to light up.

"You've been smoking for a long time?" Laurie asked, just to make conversation.

"Since I was twelve," Lou said. "In my neighborhood it was the thing to do." He shook out his match and took a long drag.

"Have you ever considered stopping?" Laurie asked.

"Absolutely," Lou said. He blew smoke over his shoulder. "It's easy to stop. I've been doing it weekly for a year. Seriously though, I do want to quit. But it's hard at headquarters. Most everybody smokes."

"I'm sorry that we didn't come up with a breakthrough with DePasquale," Laurie said.

"Maybe the bullet will help somehow," Lou said. He dropped his cigarette into the ashtray while trying to balance it on the edge. "The ballistics people are pretty resourceful. Ouch!" Lou pulled his hand away from the ashtray. He'd burned his finger on his cigarette.

"Lou, are you all right?" Laurie asked.

"I'm fine," Lou said too quickly. He tried again and this time succeeded in retrieving his cigarette.

"You seem upset about something," Laurie said.

"Just have a lot on my mind," Lou said. "But there is something I'd like to ask. Are you married?"

In spite of herself, Laurie smiled and shook her head. "Now there's a question out of the blue."

"I agree," Lou said.

"Also, under the circumstances, it's not very professional," Laurie said.

"I can't argue with that either," Lou admitted.

Laurie paused as she had a mini-argument with herself. "No," she said finally. "I'm not married."

"Well, in that case . . ." Lou said, struggling for words, ". . . maybe we could have lunch someday."

"I'm flattered, Lieutenant Soldano," Laurie said uneasily. "But I usually don't mix my private life with work."

"Nor do I," Lou said.

"What if I say maybe, and I'll think about it?"

"Fine," Lou said. Laurie could tell he regretted having put the question to her. He stood up abruptly. Laurie got up, too, but Lou motioned for her to stay where she was. "Finish your coffee. I can testify that you need a break, believe me. I'll just run downstairs, change, and be on my way. Let me hear from you." With a wave, Lou left. At the door, he turned and waved again.

Laurie waved back as Lou's figure disappeared from view. He really was a bit like Colombo: intelligent yet lumbering and mildly disorganized. At the same time, he had a basic blue-collar charm and a refreshing, down-to-earth lack of pretense that appealed to her. He also seemed lonely.

Finishing her coffee, Laurie got up and stretched. As she walked out of the lunchroom, she realized that Lou also reminded her a bit of her on-again, off-again boyfriend, Sean Mackenzie. No doubt her mother would find Lou equally as inappropriate. Laurie wondered if part of the reason she found herself attracted to such a type was because she knew her parents would disapprove. If that was true, she wondered when she'd get this rebelliousness out of her system for good.

Pressing the down button on the elevator, it dawned on Laurie that after Lou had surprised her with his question, she'd failed to ask him if he were married. She decided that if he called, she'd ask. She checked her watch. She was doing fine: only one more autopsy to go and it was still before noon.

Laurie checked the address she'd jotted on a piece of paper, then looked up at the impressive Fifth Avenue apartment building. It was in the mid-Seventies, bordering on Central Park. The entrance had a blue canvas, scalloped awning that extended to the curb. A liveried doorman stood expectantly just behind the glazed, wrought-iron door.

As Laurie approached the door, the doorman pushed it open for her then politely asked if he could help her.

"I'd like to speak to the superintendent," Laurie said. She unbuttoned her coat. While the doorman struggled with an old-fashioned intercom system, Laurie sat on a leather couch and glanced around the foyer. It was tastefully decorated in restrained, muted tones. An arrangement of fresh fall flowers stood on a credenza.

It was not difficult for Laurie to imagine Duncan Andrews striding confidently into the foyer of his apartment building, picking up his mail, and waiting for the elevator. Laurie glanced over at the bank of mailboxes discreetly shielded by a Chinese wooden screen. She wondered which one was Duncan's and if letters awaited his arrival.

"Can I help you?"

Laurie stood and looked eye-to-eye at a mustachioed Hispanic. Stitched into his shirt above his breast pocket was the name "Juan."

"I'm Dr. Montgomery," Laurie said. "I'm from the medical examiner's office." Laurie flipped open the leather cover of her wallet to reveal her shiny medical examiner's badge. It looked like a police badge.

"How can I help you?" Juan asked.

"I would like to visit Duncan Andrews' apartment," Laurie said. "I'm involved with his postmortem examination and I'd like to view the scene."

Laurie purposefully kept her language official. In truth, she felt uncomfortable about what she was doing. Although some jurisdictions required medical examiners to visit death scenes, the New York office didn't. Policy had evolved to delegate such duties to the forensic medical investigators. But when Laurie was training in Miami, she had had a lot of experience visiting scenes. In New York, she missed the added information such visits afforded. Yet she wasn't visiting Duncan's apartment for such a reason. She didn't expect to find anything that would add to the case. She felt compelled more for personal reasons. The idea of a privileged, accomplished young man ending his life for a few moments of drug-induced pleasure made her think of her brother. This death had stirred up feelings of guilt she'd suppressed for seventeen years.

"Mr. Andrews' girlfriend is up there," Juan said. "At least I saw her go up half an hour ago." Directing his attention to the doorman, he asked if Ms. Wetherbee had left. The doorman said she hadn't.

Turning back to Laurie, Juan added, "It's apartment 7C. I'll take you up there."

Laurie hesitated. She'd not expected anyone to be in the apartment. She really didn't want to talk with any of the family members, much less Andrews' girlfriend. But Juan was already in the elevator pressing the floor button and holding the door for her. Having presented herself in her official capacity, she felt she couldn't leave.

Juan pounded on the door to 7C. When it didn't open immediately, he pulled out a ring of keys the size of a baseball and began flipping through them. The door opened just as he was about to insert a key.

Standing in the doorway was a woman about Laurie's

98

height with blond, curly hair. She was wearing a sweatshirt over acid-washed jeans. Fresh tears stained her cheeks.

Juan introduced Laurie as being from the hospital, then excused himself.

"I don't remember seeing you at the hospital," Sara said.

"I'm not from the hospital," Laurie said. "I'm from the medical examiner's office."

"Are you going to do an autopsy on Duncan's body?" Sara asked.

"I already have," Laurie said. "I just wanted to see the scene where he died."

"Of course," Sara said. She stepped back from the door. "Come in."

Laurie stepped into the apartment. She felt extremely uncomfortable knowing she was intruding on this poor woman's grief. She waited while Sara locked the door. The apartment was spacious. Even from the foyer Laurie could see out over the leafless expanse of Central Park. Unconsciously she shook her head at the senselessness of Duncan Andrews' taking drugs. At least on the surface his life seemed perfect.

"Duncan actually collapsed right here in the doorway," Sara said. She pointed at the floor by the door. Fresh tears spilled down her cheeks. "Just before I knocked he pulled it open. It was as if he'd gone crazy. He was heading outside practically naked."

"I'm terribly sorry," Laurie said. "Drugs can do that to people. Cocaine can make them feel like they're burning up."

"I didn't even know he took drugs," Sara sobbed. "Maybe if I'd gotten over here faster after he called, it wouldn't have happened. Maybe if I'd stayed Sunday evening . . ."

"Drugs are such a curse," Laurie said. "No one is going to know the reason Duncan took them. But it was his choice. You can't blame yourself." Laurie paused. "I know how you feel," she said at last. "I found my big brother after he'd overdosed."

"Really?" Sara said through her tears.

Laurie nodded. For the second time that day Laurie had admitted a secret that she'd not shared with anyone for seventeen years. This job was getting to her, all right, but in a way she had never expected. The case of Duncan Andrews had touched her in a fashion no other case had ever done.

4

□

"Christ!" Tony exclaimed. "Here we are waiting again. Every night we wait. I thought last night when we finally caught that prick DePasquale, things would move along. But oh no, we're back here waiting like nothing happened."

Angelo leaned forward and tapped the ash from his cigarette into the ashtray, then leaned back. He didn't say anything. He'd promised himself earlier that afternoon to ignore Tony. Angelo regarded the busy street scene. People were heading home after work, walking their dogs, or coming back from the grocery store. He and Tony were parked in a loading zone on Park Avenue between Eighty-first and Eighty-second, headed north. Both sides of the street were filled with high-rise apartment buildings whose first floors were filled with professional office suites.

"I'm going to get out and do some push-ups," Tony said.

101

"Shut the hell up!" Angelo snapped, despite his vow to disregard his partner. "We went over this last night. You don't get out and do push-ups when we're waiting for action. What's the matter with you? You want a neon sign or something to let the cops know we're sitting here? We're not supposed to call attention to ourselves. Can't you understand that?"

"All right," Tony said. "Don't get pissed. I won't get out!"

In utter frustration, Angelo blew through pursed lips and beat a nervous rhythm on the steering wheel with the first two fingers of his right hand. Tony was wearing even for Angelo's practiced calm.

"If we want to hit the doctor's office, why don't we just go in there and do it?" Tony said after a pause. "It don't make sense wasting all this time."

"We're waiting for the secretary," Angelo said. "We want to be sure the place is empty. Plus, she can let us in. We don't want to break down any doors."

"If she lets us in, then she's there and it's not empty anymore," Tony said. "It doesn't make sense."

"Trust me," Angelo said. "This is the best way to do what we have to do."

"Nobody ever tells me anything," Tony brooded. "This whole operation is weird. Breaking into a doctor's office is crazy. It's even crazier than when we broke into the Manhattan Organ Repository. At least there we got a few hundred in cash. What the hell are we going to find in a doctor's office?"

"If it doesn't take too long we can see if there's any cash in here, too," Angelo said. "Maybe we can also look for Percodan and stuff like that if it will make you happy."

"Hard way to get a few pills," Tony muttered.

Angelo laughed in spite of his aggravation.

"What do you think about old Doc Travino?" Tony

asked. "Do you think he knows what the hell he's talking about?"

"Personally, I have my doubts," Angelo said. "But Cerino trusts him and that's what's important."

"Come on, Angelo," Tony whined. "Tell me why we're going in there. Isn't Cerino happy with this doc?"

"Cerino loves the guy," Angelo said. "He thinks he's the best in the world. In fact, that's why we're going in."

"But why?" Tony asked. "Tell me that and I'll shut up."

"For some of the guy's records," Angelo said.

"I knew it was crazy," Tony said, "but not that crazy. What are we going to do with the guy's records?"

"You told me you would shut up if I told you what we were after. So shut up! Besides, you're not supposed to ask so many questions."

"There, that's just what I was complaining about," Tony said. "Nobody tells me what's going on. If I knew more about what was happening, I could do more; I could be more help."

Angelo laughed sarcastically.

"I can tell you don't believe me," Tony complained. "But it's true. Try me! I'm sure I'd have some suggestions, even for this job."

"Everything is going fine," Angelo assured him. "Planning is not your strong suit. Whacking people is."

"That's true," Tony agreed. "That's what I like best. Bam! It's over. None of this complicated stuff."

"There'll be enough whacking over the next couple of weeks to satisfy even you," Angelo promised.

"I can't wait," Tony said. "Maybe it will make up for all this waiting around."

"There she is," Angelo said. He pointed ahead to a heavyset woman emerging from one of the apartment buildings. She was busy buttoning a red coat with one hand and holding a hat to her head with the other.

103

"Okay, let's go," Angelo said. "But keep your piece out of sight and let me do all the talking."

Angelo and Tony got out of the car. They walked over to the woman just as she joined a cab line.

"Mrs. Schulman!" Angelo called.

The woman turned toward Angelo. Her distrustful hauteur evaporated as soon as she recognized the man. "Hello, Mr. . . ." she said, trying to remember Angelo's name.

"Facciolo," Angelo offered.

"Of course," she said. "And how is Mr. Cerino getting along?"

"Just great, Mrs. Schulman," Angelo said. "He's getting pretty good with his cane. But he asked me to come over here to talk to you. Do you have a minute?"

"I suppose," Mrs. Schulman said. "What is it you'd like to talk about?"

"It's confidential," Angelo said. "I'd prefer if you came over to the car for a moment." Angelo gestured toward the black Town Car.

Obviously discomfited by this request, Mrs. Schulman muttered something about having to be somewhere shortly.

Angelo slipped a hand into his jacket pocket and lifted his Walther automatic pistol just enough so Mrs. Schulman could see its butt.

"I'm afraid I have to insist," Angelo said. "We won't take much of your time and afterwards we'll be sure to drop you off someplace convenient."

Mrs. Schulman glanced at Tony, who smiled back. "All right," she said nervously. "As long as it doesn't take too long."

"That will be up to you," Angelo said, motioning toward the car again.

Tony led the way. Mrs. Schulman slid into the front seat when Tony opened the door for her with a courteous bow. Tony got in the back while Angelo climbed into the driver's seat.

"Does this have something to do with my husband, Danny Schulman?" Mrs. Schulman asked.

"Danny Schulman from Bayside?" Angelo said. "Is he your old man?"

"Yes, he is," Mrs. Schulman said.

"Who's Danny Schulman?" Tony asked from the back-seat.

"He owns a joint in Bayside called Crystal Palace," Angelo said. "A lot of the Lucia people go there."

"He's very well connected," Mrs. Schulman said. "Maybe you men would like to talk with him."

"No, this has nothing to do with Danny," Angelo said. "All we want to know is if the good doctor's office is empty."

"Yes, everyone has gone for the day," Mrs. Schulman said. "I locked up as I usually do."

"That's good," Angelo said, "because we want you to go back inside. We're interested in some of the doctor's records."

"What records?" Mrs. Schulman asked.

"I'll tell you when we get inside," Angelo said. "But before we go I want you to know that if you decide to do anything foolish, it'd be the last foolish thing you do. Do I make myself clear?"

"Quite clear," Mrs. Schulman said, regaining some of her composure.

"This isn't a big deal," Angelo added. "I mean, we're civilized people."

"I understand," Mrs. Schulman said.

"Okay! Let's go," Angelo said, and he opened his door.

"Hello, Miss Montgomery," George said. George was one of the doormen at Laurie's parents' apartment house. He'd been there for decades. He looked sixty but he was actually seventy-two. He liked to tell Laurie that he'd been the one to open the cab door the day her mother had brought Laurie home from the hospital just days after her birth.

After a brief chat with George, Laurie went on up to her parents'. So many memories! Even the smell of the place was familiar. But more than anything, the apartment reminded her of that awful day she'd found her brother. She'd almost wished her parents had moved after the tragedy, just so she wouldn't have to be constantly reminded of her brother's overdose.

"Hello, dear!" her mother crooned as she let Laurie into the foyer. Dorothy Montgomery bent forward and offered her daughter a cheek. She smelled of expensive perfume. Her silver-gray hair was cut short in a style that was making the covers of women's fashion magazines lately. Dorothy was a petite, vibrant woman in her mid-sixties who looked younger than her years, thanks to a second face-lift.

As Dorothy took Laurie's coat, she cast a critical eye over her daughter's attire. "I see you didn't wear the wool suit I bought for you."

"No, Mother, I did not," Laurie said. She closed her eyes, hoping her mother wouldn't start in on her this early.

"At least you could have worn a dress."

Laurie refrained from responding. She'd chosen a jacquard blouse embellished with mock jewels and a pair of wool pants that she'd gotten from a mail order catalogue. An hour earlier she'd thought it was one of her best outfits. Now she wasn't so sure.

"No matter," Dorothy said after hanging up Laurie's coat. "Come on, I want you to meet everyone, especially Dr. Scheffield, our guest of honor."

Dorothy led Laurie into the formal living room, a room reserved exclusively for entertaining. There were eight people in the room, each balancing a drink in one hand and a canapé in the other. Laurie recognized most of these guests, four married couples who'd been friends of her parents for years. Three of the men were physicians, the other a banker. Like her own mother, the wives weren't career women. They devoted their time to charities just as her mother did.

After some small talk, Dorothy dragged Laurie down the hall to the library where Sheldon Montgomery was showing Jordan Scheffield some rare medical textbooks.

"Sheldon, introduce your daughter to Dr. Scheffield," Dorothy commanded, interrupting her husband in midsentence.

Both men looked up from a book in Sheldon's hands. Laurie's gaze went from her father's dour aristocratic face to Jordan Scheffield's, and she was pleasantly surprised. She had expected Jordan to look more like her image of an ophthalmologist; that he'd be older, heavier, stodgy, and far less attractive. But the man who stood before her was dramatically handsome with sandy blond hair, tanned skin, bright blue eyes, and rugged, angular features. Not only didn't he look like an ophthalmologist, he didn't even look like a doctor. He looked more like a professional athlete. He was even taller than her father, who was six-two. And instead of a glenn plaid suit like her father was wearing, he had on tan slacks, a blue blazer, and a white shirt open at the collar. He wasn't even wearing a tie.

Laurie shook hands with Jordan as Sheldon made the introductions. His grip was forceful and sure. He looked directly into her eyes and smiled pleasantly.

The fact that Sheldon liked Jordan was immediately apparent to Laurie as he pounded him on the back, insisting he get him some more of the special Scotch he usually hid when company came. Sheldon went to get the prized liquor, leaving Laurie alone with Jordan.

"Your parents are extremely hospitable," Jordan said.

"They can be," Laurie said. "They enjoy entertaining. They certainly were looking forward to your coming tonight."

"I'm glad to be here," Jordan said. "Your father had nothing but nice things to say about you. I've been looking forward to meeting you."

"Thank you," Laurie said. She was mildly surprised to hear that her father had spoken of her at all, let alone spoken well. "Likewise," said Laurie. "Frankly, you're not what I'd expected."

"What did you expect?" Jordan asked.

"Well," said Laurie, suddenly slightly embarrassed, "I thought you'd look like an ophthalmologist."

Throwing his head back, Jordan laughed heartily. "And just what does an ophthalmologist look like?"

Laurie was relieved when her father came back with Jordan's refill, thus sparing her an explanation. Her father told Jordan that he wanted to show him some ancient surgical instruments in the den. As Jordan obediently followed his host, he sent a conspiratorial smile Laurie's way.

At dinner, Jordan was responsible for lightening the atmosphere. He managed to force even the most reserved of Laurie's parents' friends to open up. Hearty laughter filled the room for the first time in recent memory.

Sheldon encouraged Jordan to tell certain stories he'd told Sheldon about his famous patients. Jordan was only too happy to oblige, and he recounted the stories in an exuberant, almost boastful manner that had everyone laughing. Even Laurie's emotional day receded into the background as she heard Jordan's amusing tales of the rich and famous who passed through his office each day.

Jordan's specialty was the anterior part of the eye, particularly the cornea. But he also did some plastic surgery, even cosmetic plastic surgery. He'd treated celebrities ranging from movie stars to royalty. He had everyone in stitches about a prince from Saudi Arabia who'd come to his office along with dozens of servants. Then he went on to name drop a few sports figures he was treating. Finally, he mentioned he'd even treated the occasional Mafioso.

"As in Mafia?" Dorothy asked with horrified disbelief.

"Absolutely," Jordan said. "God is my witness. Honest-to-goodness mobsters. In fact just this month I've been seeing a Paul Cerino, who is obviously connected to the underworld over in Queens."

Laurie choked on her white wine at Jordan's mention of Paul Cerino's name. Hearing it for the second time that day startled her. The conversation stopped as everyone looked at her with concern. She waved off their attention and managed to say she was all right. Once she could speak again, she asked Jordan what he was treating Paul Cerino for.

"Acid burns in his eyes," Jordan said. "Someone had thrown acid into his face. Luckily he had been smart enough to rinse his eyes with water almost immediately."

"Acid! How dreadful," Dorothy said.

"It's not as bad as alkali. Alkali can eat right through the cornea."

"Sounds ghastly," Dorothy said.

"How are Cerino's eyes doing?" Laurie asked. She was thinking of Frank DePasquale's right eye, wondering if that could be the beginning of the break that Lou had been hoping for.

"The acid opacified both corneas," Jordan said. "But the fact that he washed his eyes out saved the conjunctiva from extensive damage. So he should do well with corneal transplants which we'll be doing soon."

"Does it frighten you to be involved with these people?" one guest asked.

"Not at all," Jordan said. "They need me. I'm of use to them. They wouldn't harm me. In fact I find it all rather comical and entertaining."

"How do you know this Cerino is a mobster?" one of the other guests asked.

Jordan gave a short laugh. "It's pretty apparent. He comes in with several bodyguards who have obvious telltale bulges in their suits."

"Paul Cerino is a known mobster," Laurie said. "He's one of the midlevel bosses of the Vaccarro crime family, which is currently warring with the Lucia organization."

"How do you know that?" Dorothy asked.

"This morning I autopsied a gangland-style execution victim. The authorities believe the murder was a direct result of the feud, and they would like nothing better than to associate the killing with Paul Cerino."

"How hideous!" Dorothy said with disdain. "Laurie, that's enough! Let's talk about something else."

"This isn't appropriate dinner conversation," Sheldon agreed. Then, turning to Jordan, he added: "You'll have to excuse my daughter. Since she abandoned her medical education and went into pathology, she's somewhat lost her sense of etiquette."

"Pathology?" Jordan questioned. He looked over at Laurie. "You didn't tell me you are a pathologist."

"You didn't ask me," Laurie said. She smiled to herself, knowing that Jordan had been too busy talking about his own affairs to have asked about hers. "Actually I'm a forensic pathologist currently working for the Office of the Chief Medical Examiner here in New York."

"Maybe we should talk about this season at Lincoln Center," Dorothy suggested.

"I don't know much about forensics," Jordan said. "We only had two lectures on it in medical school and before them we were told that the material would not be on the exam. So guess what I did?" Jordan pretended to fall asleep by snoring and allowing his head to drop onto his chest.

Sheldon laughed at Jordan's antics. "We only had one lecture and I cut it," he confessed.

"I think we should change the subject," Dorothy said.

"The problem with Laurie," Sheldon said to Jordan, "was that she didn't go into surgery, where she could have been dealing with the living. We have a gal in the thoracic program who's unbelievable, as good as a man. Laurie could have done equally as well."

It took every ounce of self-restraint Laurie possessed not to lash out at her father's inane, sexist remark. Instead, she calmly defended her specialty. "Forensics very much deals with the living, and it does it by speaking for the dead." She told the story of the curling iron and how knowledge of the cause of that fatality could potentially save someone else's life.

When Laurie finished, there was an uncomfortable pause. Everyone looked down at their place settings and toyed with their flatware. Even Jordan seemed strangely subdued. Finally Dorothy broke the silence by announcing that dessert and cognac would be served in the living room.

By the time the group had reassembled in the living room, Laurie was uncomfortable enough to consider leaving. As she watched the others fall effortlessly into conversations, she debated taking her mother aside and making the excuse that it was a "school night." But before she could decide, a discreet maid hired for the evening appeared at Laurie's side with her serving tray filled with brandy snifters. Accepting a cognac, Laurie turned her back on the group. With drink in hand, she slipped down the hall and into the den.

"Mind if I join you?" Jordan had followed her from the living room.

"Not at all," Laurie said, mildly startled. She thought her exit had not been noticed. She tried to smile. She sat in a leather club chair while Jordan leaned comfortably against a massive rear-projection TV. Sounds of laughter drifted in from the living room.

"I didn't mean to make fun of your specialty," he said. "I actually find pathology fascinating."

"Oh?" Laurie said.

"I enjoyed the story about the curling iron," he added. "I had no idea you could get electrocuted with such an appliance unless you dropped it in the tub while you were taking a bath."

"You might have said so at the time." She knew she wasn't being polite, but she wasn't feeling particularly hospitable just then.

Jordan nodded. "Sorry," he said. "I guess I felt a little inhibited by your parents. It's pretty obvious they are not wild about your specialty choice."

"Is it that obvious?" Laurie asked.

"Indeed," Jordan said. "I couldn't believe your father's remark about that woman in their thoracic program. And your mother kept trying to change the subject of the conversation."

"You should have heard my mother's comment the day I told her I was going into forensics. She said: 'What will I tell people at the club who ask me what you do?' That gives you a pretty good idea of her feelings. And my father, the quintessential cardiac surgeon! He thinks that anything other than surgery, specifically thoracic surgery, is for the weak, the timid, and the retarded."

"Not an easy pair to please. It must be hard on you."

"Frankly, I've caused them some heartache through the years. I was a pretty rebellious kid: dating rough types, riding motorcycles, staying out late, the usual. Maybe I trained my parents to be wary of everything I do. They've never been particularly supportive. In fact they've kind of ignored me, especially my father."

"Your father certainly speaks highly of you now," Jordan said. "Practically every time I run into him in the surgical lounge."

"Well, it's news to me," Laurie said.

"Anybody want more cognac?" Sheldon called. He'd stuck his head into the den, waving the bottle of cognac.

Jordan said no. Laurie merely shook her head. Sheldon told them to give a yell if they changed their minds. Then he left them.

"Enough," said Laurie. "This is much too serious a conversation. I didn't mean to put a damper on the evening." She actually was sorry she'd revealed so much to Jordan. It wasn't like her to confide in a relative stranger this way, similar to what she'd done with Lou Soldano. But she'd been feeling vulnerable all day, ever since she'd been assigned Duncan Andrews.

"You didn't put a damper on anything," Jordan assured her. Then he looked at his watch. "Say," he said. "It's getting late, and I have surgery in the morning. My first case, at seven-thirty, is an English baron who sits in the House of Lords."

"Really," Laurie said without much interest.

"I think I'll be calling it a night," Jordan added. "I'd be delighted to give you a lift home. That is, of course, if you are intending to leave."

"I'd love a ride home," Laurie said. "I've been thinking about leaving since we got up from the table."

After the appropriate goodbyes during which Dorothy let Laurie know her coat was far too thin for late fall, Jordan and Laurie left the party and waited at the elevator.

"Mothers!" Laurie said once the doors had closed behind them.

As they rode down, Jordan started talking about the parade of celebrities due in his office the next day. Laurie wasn't sure if he was trying to impress her or merely cheer her up.

Emerging from the building into the cold November air, Jordan switched the conversation to the surgical aspect of his practice. Laurie was nodding as if listening. In reality she was waiting for some signal from Jordan whether he'd parked his car to the north or to the south. For a moment

113

they stopped directly in front of the building while Jordan told Laurie how many surgical cases he did in a year.

"Sounds like you're busy," Laurie said.

"Could be busier," Jordan admitted. "If I had my way, I'd be doing twice the amount of surgery I'm doing now. Surgery is what I enjoy; it's what I'm best at."

"Which way is your car?" Laurie finally asked. She was shivering.

"Oh, I'm sorry," he said. "It's right here." He pointed to a long black limousine sitting directly in front of her parents' building. As if on cue, a liveried driver leaped out and held the rear door open for Laurie.

"This is Thomas," Jordan said.

Laurie said hello and slipped in the sleek automobile. Thomas looked as though he could have moonlighted as a bouncer; he was powerfully built. The limo's interior was elegantly luxurious, complete with a cellular phone, dictaphone, and fax.

"Well," Laurie said, noticing all the equipment. "You look ready for business or pleasure."

Jordan smiled. He was clearly pleased with his style of living. "Where to?" he asked.

Laurie gave her address on Nineteenth Street and they pulled out into traffic.

"I never imagined you had a limo," Laurie said. "Isn't it a bit extravagant?"

"Perhaps a bit," Jordan agreed. His white teeth shone in the half-light of the car's interior. "But there is a practical side to this ostentation. I do all my dictation work to and from work and even between work and the hospital. So in a sense, the car pays for itself."

"That's an interesting way of looking at it."

"It's not merely a rationalization," Jordan said. He went on to describe other ways he'd organized his practice to boost his productivity.

114

As Laurie listened she couldn't help compare Jordan Scheffield with Lou Soldano. They couldn't have been more opposite. One was self-effacing, the other arrogantly narcissistic; one was provincial, the other sophisticated; and where one could be awkward, the other was smoothly adroit. Yet despite their differences, Laurie found each attractive in his own way.

As they turned onto Nineteenth Street, Jordan's monologue stopped abruptly. "I'm boring you with all this shop talk," he said.

"I can see you are committed," Laurie said. "I like that."

Jordan stared at her. His eyes sparkled.

"I've truly enjoyed meeting you tonight," he said. "I wish we'd had more time to talk. How about having dinner with me tomorrow night?"

Laurie smiled. It had been a day of surprises. She'd not been dating much since her ninetieth breakup with Sean Mackenzie. Yet she found Jordan interesting despite his seemingly overbearing nature. Impulsively she decided it might be fun to see a little more of the man, even if her parents did approve of him.

"I'd love to have dinner," Laurie said.

"Wonderful," Jordan said. "How about Le Cirque? I know the maître d' there and he'll give us a great table. Is eight o'clock okay?"

"Eight is fine," Laurie said, although she began to have second thoughts as soon as Jordan suggested Le Cirque. For a first date she would have preferred a less formal environment.

"What the hell time is it?" Tony asked. "My battery must have died in my watch." He shook his wrist, then tapped the crystal.

Angelo extended his arm and glanced at his Piaget. "It's eleven eleven."

"I don't think Bruno's coming out," Tony said. "Why don't we go in and see if he's there?"

"Because we don't want Mrs. Marchese to see us," Angelo said. "If she sees us then we got to do her too, and that's not right. The Lucia people might do that kind of stuff, but we don't. Besides, look. Here comes the punk now." Angelo pointed to the front entrance of the tiny two-story row house.

Bruno Marchese emerged into the night dressed in a black leather jacket, freshly pressed Guess jeans, and sunglasses. He paused for a moment on the front steps of the house to light a cigarette. Tossing the match into the shrubbery, he started toward the sidewalk.

"Get a load of those shades," Angelo said. "Must think he's Jack Nicholson. My guess is that he's going socializing. He should have stayed home. The trouble with you young guys is that your brains are in your balls."

"Let's get him," Tony urged.

"Hold on," Angelo said. "Let him round the corner. We'll nab him when he walks under the railroad tracks."

Five minutes later they had Bruno cowering in the backseat, staring into Tony's smiling face. The pickup had gone even more smoothly than it had with Frankie. The only casualty had been Bruno's sunglasses, which ended up in the gutter.

"Surprised to see us?" Angelo asked after they had driven a short while. Angelo looked at Bruno in the rearview mirror.

"What's this about?" Bruno demanded.

Tony laughed. "Oh, a tough guy. Tough and dumb. How about I give him a few whacks with my gun?"

"It's about the Cerino incident," Angelo said. "We want to hear about it from you."

"I don't know anything about it," Bruno said. "I never even heard of it."

116

"That's funny," Angelo said. "We've had it from a friend of yours that you were involved."

"Who?" Bruno asked.

"Frankie DePasquale," Angelo said. He watched Bruno's expression change. The kid was terrified, and for good reason.

"Frankie didn't know crap," Bruno said. "I don't know anything about any Cerino incident."

"If you don't know anything about it, how come you're hiding out at your mother's house?" Angelo asked.

"I'm not hiding out," Bruno said. "I got kicked out of my apartment so I'm just staying there a few days."

Angelo shook his head. They drove to the American Fresh Fruit Company in silence. Once they were there, Angelo and Tony brought Bruno to the same spot they'd brought Frankie.

As soon as Bruno saw the hole in the floor, his tough-guy stance melted. "All right, you guys," he said. "What do you want to know?"

"That's better," Angelo said. "First sit down."

Once Bruno had complied, Angelo leaned toward him and said, "Tell us about it." He took out a cigarette and lit up, blowing smoke up toward the ceiling.

"I don't know much," Bruno said. "I only drove the car. I wasn't inside. Besides, they made me do it."

"Who made you do it?" Angelo asked. "And remember, if you give me any bull now, you'll be in deep trouble."

"Terry Manso," Bruno said. "It was all his idea. I didn't even know what was going on until after it was all over."

"Who else beside you, Manso, and DePasquale were involved in all this?" Angelo said.

"Jimmy Lanso," Bruno said.

"Who else?" Angelo demanded.

"That's all," Bruno insisted.

"What did Jimmy do?" Angelo asked.

"He went into the place early to locate the electrical panel," Bruno said. "He made the lights go out."

"Who ordered this hit?" Angelo asked.

"I told you," Bruno said. "It was all Manso's idea."

Angelo took another long pull on his cigarette, then tilted his head back as he blew out the smoke. He tried to think if there was anything else that he needed to ask this punk. When he decided there wasn't, he glanced at Tony and nodded.

"Bruno, I'd like to ask a favor," Angelo said. "I'd like you to take a message back to Vinnie Dominick. Do you think you could do that for me?"

"No problem," Bruno said. A bit of his earlier toughness returned to the timbre of his voice.

"The message is—" Angelo began. But he didn't finish. The sound of Tony's Bantam made Angelo flinch. When it wasn't your own gun, it always sounded louder.

Since they hadn't tied Bruno to the chair, his whole body sagged forward and crumpled to the floor. Angelo stood over him and shook his head. "I think Vinnie will get the message," he said.

Tony looked at his gun with a mixture of admiration and pleasure, then took out a handkerchief and wiped the soot from the muzzle. "It gets easier every time I do it," he said to Angelo.

Angelo didn't respond. Instead, he squatted down next to Bruno's body and pulled out his wallet. There were several hundred-dollar bills and a few smaller denominations. He handed one of the hundreds to Tony. The rest he pocketed. Then he put the wallet back.

"Give me a hand," he told Tony. Together they carried Bruno over to the hole and tossed him into the river. Like Frankie, Bruno obligingly floated quickly away, pausing only momentarily against one of the pier's piles. Angelo brushed off his trousers. Bruno's body had kicked up some dust from the floor.

"You hungry?" Angelo asked.

"I'm starved," Tony said.

"Let's go over to Valentino's on Steinway Street," Angelo said. "I'm in the mood for a pizza."

A few minutes later Angelo backed up the Town Car, then made a three-point turn to exit through the chain-link gate. At the junction of Java and Manhattan Avenue, he made a left, then gunned the car.

"It's amazing how easy it is to whack somebody," Tony said. "I remember when I was a kid, I used to think it was a big deal. There was a guy who lived on the next block. We kids had heard that he'd bumped somebody off. We used to sit outside his house just to see him come out. He was our hero."

"What kind of pizza you want?" Angelo asked.

"Pepperoni," Tony said. "I remember the first time I whacked somebody I was so excited I got the trots. It even gave me bad dreams. But now it's just fun."

"It's work," Angelo said. "I wish you'd understand that."

"Which list we going to work off of after we eat?" Tony asked. "The old one or the new one."

"The old one," Angelo said. "I want to show the new one to Cerino just to be sure. No sense making work for ourselves."

5

□

From where Laurie was standing she could see her brother heading for the lake. He was walking quickly; Laurie was afraid he might break into a run. She thought he knew about the mud and how dangerously deep it was. Yet he kept going as if he didn't care.

"Shelly!" Laurie cried. Either he was ignoring her or he couldn't hear. Laurie yelled again as loud as she could but still he didn't respond. She started running after him. He was only a step away from the horrid ooze. "Stop!" Laurie yelled. "Don't go near the water! Stay away!"

But Shelly kept walking. By the time Laurie reached the lakeside, he was already in black mud up to his waist. He had turned back toward shore. "Help me!" he cried.

Laurie came to a stop just at the edge. She reached out for him, but their hands could not touch. Laurie turned and

121

screamed for help, but no one was in sight. Turning back to Shelly, she saw that he had sunk up to his neck. There was pure terror in his eyes. As he sank further, his mouth opened and he screamed.

Shelly's scream merged into a mechanical ringing that pulled Laurie from her sleep. Still desperate to help Shelly, Laurie's hand shot out and swept the Westclox from the windowsill. The same movement toppled a half-full glass of water and collided with the book she'd been reading the night before. The clock, the glass of water, and the book all fell to the floor.

Laurie's sudden movement and the crash of the things on the floor so surprised Tom that he leaped first to the top of the bureau, where he knocked off most of Laurie's cosmetics, then to the valance over the window. Unable to make the top of the valance, Tom's claws sank into the upholstered front, and the sudden weight brought the valance down.

With the commotion and the noise Laurie was out of bed before she knew what she was doing. It was a few seconds before the sound of the alarm clock shocked her into full awake. Reaching down for it, she managed to shut it off.

For a moment Laurie stood in the ruins of her room to catch her breath. She'd not had that particular nightmare for years, probably not since college, and its effect was more upsetting than the disarray of her room. Perspiration dotted her forehead, and she could feel her heart beating in her chest.

After she'd sufficiently recovered, she went into the kitchen for the dustpan to clean up the broken glass. Next she picked up the cosmetics from the floor and stacked them on her bureau. The valance was too big a task. She decided to leave that for later in the day.

She found Tom hiding under the sofa in the living room. After coaxing him out, she held him in her lap and stroked him for a few minutes until he started purring.

About ten minutes later, she was about to step into the shower when the doorbell rang. "Now what?" she thought. Clutching a towel, she went to her intercom and asked who was there.

"It's Thomas," a voice said.

"Thomas who?" Laurie yelled back.

"Dr. Scheffield's driver," the voice said. "I'm here to deliver something at the request of the doctor. He couldn't come himself because he's already in surgery."

"I'll be right down," Laurie said.

Laurie quickly threw on a pair of jeans and a sweatshirt. "You're early this morning." Debra Engler was poised, as usual, at her door.

Laurie was grateful when the elevator arrived.

Thomas tipped his hat when he saw her. He said he hoped he hadn't woken her. What he had for her was a long white box tied with a thick red ribbon. Laurie thanked him for the package and went back upstairs.

Putting the box on the kitchen table, she untied the red bow, opened the box, and spread the inside tissue paper. Nestled within the paper were several dozen long-stemmed red roses. On top of the flowers was a card that said: *Until tonight, Jordan.*

Laurie caught her breath. Never having been the recipient of such a flamboyant gesture, she didn't know quite how to react. She wasn't even sure if accepting them was appropriate or not. But what could she do? She couldn't send them back.

Reaching into the box, Laurie lifted one of the blossoms and smelled its springlike sweetness and looked at its deep ruby color. Even though the arrival of the roses confused her and made her feel uncomfortable, she also had to admit that it was romantic and flattering.

Getting the largest vase she had, Laurie put half of the roses into water, then carried them into the living room. She put the vase on her coffee table. She thought she could get used to having cut flowers in her apartment. The effect was amazing.

Returning to the kitchen, Laurie put the cover on the box and retied the ribbon. If a dozen roses could do so much for her apartment, she could only guess what they would do for her office.

"Oh, my God!" Laurie said when she saw the time. In a panic, she tore off her clothes and jumped into the shower.

It was almost eight-thirty before Laurie arrived at the medical examiner's office, a good half hour later than usual. Feeling guilty, she went directly to the ID office even though, given the box of roses, she would have preferred to go to her office first.

"Dr. Bingham wants to see you," Calvin said as soon as he saw Laurie. "But get your butt back here on the double. We got a lot of cases to do."

Laurie put her briefcase and box of roses down on an empty desk. She was self-conscious about the roses, but if Calvin noticed, he didn't give any indication. Hurrying back through the reception area, Laurie presented herself to Mrs. Sanford. Given her last time in the chief's office, Laurie was apprehensive to say the least. She tried to imagine what he wanted this time, but she couldn't.

"He's on the phone right this minute," Mrs. Sanford said. "Would you care to sit down? It should only be a moment."

Laurie went over to a couch, but before she could sit down, Mrs. Sanford was speaking into her intercom: Dr. Bingham was ready to see her.

Taking a deep breath, Laurie walked into the chief's office. As she approached his desk, his head was down. He was writing. He made Laurie stand while he finished his note. Then he looked up.

For a moment he studied her with his cold blue eyes. He shook his head and sighed. "After months of flawless work, you seem to have developed a penchant for trouble. Don't you like your work, Doctor?"

"Of course I like my work, Dr. Bingham," Laurie said, alarmed.

"Sit down," Bingham said. He folded his hands and placed them resolutely on his blotter.

Laurie sat down on the very edge of the chair facing Dr. Bingham.

"Then perhaps you do not like working at this particular office," he said. It was half question, half statement.

"Quite the contrary," Laurie said. "I love being here. What makes you think I don't?"

"Only because it is the only way I can explain your behavior."

Laurie returned his gaze evenly. "I have no idea what behavior you are referring to," she said.

"I'm referring to your visit yesterday afternoon to the apartment of the deceased, Duncan Andrews, where you apparently gained access by flashing your official credentials. Did you go there or have I been misinformed?"

"I was there," Laurie said.

"Didn't Calvin tell you that we have been getting some pressure from the mayor's office about this case?"

"He said something to that effect," Laurie said. "But the only aspect of the case he discussed with me with regard to that pressure concerned the official cause of death."

"Wouldn't that make you think that this was somehow a sensitive case and that maybe you should be as circumspect as possible in all respects?"

Laurie tried to imagine who would have complained about her visit. And why? Certainly not Sara Wetherbee. While she was thinking she realized Dr. Bingham was waiting for a response. "I didn't think that visiting the scene would upset anyone," she said at last.

"It is true you didn't think," Dr. Bingham said. "That is

painfully obvious. Can you tell me why you went to visit this scene? After all, the body was gone. Hell, you'd already finished the autopsy. And on top of that we have medical investigators to do that type of thing; medical investigators whom we had warned not to meddle in this particular case. So that brings me back to the question: Why did you go?"

Laurie tried to think of an explanation without becoming personal. She did not want to discuss her brother's overdose with Dr. Bingham, particularly not now.

"I asked you a question, Dr. Montgomery," Bingham said when Laurie failed to respond.

"I hadn't found anything on autopsy," Laurie said finally. "There was no pathology. I suppose I went in desperation to see if the scene might reveal a plausible alternative to the drugs the man had obviously taken."

"This is in addition to asking Cheryl Myers to look into the man's medical history."

"That's right," Laurie said.

"Under normal circumstances," Bingham said, "such initiative might be commendable. But under the present circumstances it has added to the problems of this office. The father, who happens to be very politically connected, found out you were there and screamed bloody murder, as if we're out to ruin his senatorial campaign. And all this is on top of the Central Park Preppy II case, which has already caused enough trouble with the mayor's office. We don't need any more. Do you understand?"

"Yes, sir," Laurie said.

"I hope so," Bingham said. He looked down at the work on his desk. "That will be all, Dr. Montgomery."

Laurie walked out of the chief's office and took a deep breath. This was the closest she had ever come to being fired. Two unpleasant summonses to the chief's office in three days. Laurie couldn't help but think that one more time in front of Bingham and she would be out.

"You and the chief square things away?" Calvin asked when Laurie reappeared.

"I hope so," Laurie said.

"Me too," Calvin said. "Because I need you in top form." He handed her a pack of folders. "You've got four cases today. Two more overdoses like the Duncan Andrews case and two more floaters. Fresh floaters, I might add. I figured since you did the same kind of cases yesterday, you'd be the fastest today. There's a lot of work for everyone. I had to give several people five cases, so consider yourself lucky."

Laurie flipped through the folders to make sure that they were complete. Then she took them, her briefcase, and her box of roses up to her office. Before she did anything else, she went to the lab and borrowed the largest flask she could find. Taking the roses from the box, she arranged them and filled the flask with water. After putting the flowers on the lab bench, she stepped back. She had to smile; they were so glaringly out of place.

Sitting down at her desk, Laurie started with the first folder. She didn't get far. The moment she opened it there was a knock on her door. "Come in," she said.

The door opened slowly and Lou Soldano poked his face in. "Hope I'm not bothering you too much," he said. "I'm sure you didn't expect to see me."

He looked as though he'd never gone to bed the previous night. He was wearing the same baggy, unpressed suit and he still hadn't managed to shave.

"You're not bothering me," Laurie said. "Come in!"

"So how are you today?" he asked once he'd come in and sat down. He put his hat in his lap.

"Except for a little run-in with the boss, I guess I'm fine."

"Wasn't about my being here yesterday, was it?" Lou asked.

"No," Laurie said. "Something I did yesterday afternoon

which I suppose I shouldn't have. But it's always easy to say that after the fact."

"I hope you don't mind my coming back today, but I understand you have a couple more cases like poor Frankie's. They were found almost in the same spot by the same night security guard. So I was back out at the South Street Sea Port at five in the morning. Wow!" he said, suddenly spotting Laurie's flask. "Fancy flowers. They weren't here yesterday."

"You like them?" she asked.

"Pretty impressive," Lou said. "They from an admirer?"

Laurie wasn't sure how to answer. "I guess you'd call him that."

"Well, that's nice," Lou said. He looked down at his hat and straightened the brim. "Anyway, Dr. Washington said he assigned the cases to you, so here I am. Do you mind if I tag along again?"

"Not at all," Laurie said. "If you think you can take several more autopsies, I'm glad to have you."

"I'm pretty sure at least one of the deaths is related to Frankie's," Lou said, moving forward in his chair. "The name is Bruno Marchese. Same age as Frankie and about the same position in the organization. The reason we know so much so quickly is that his wallet was found on his body, just as Frankie's was. Obviously whoever killed him wanted the fact of his death to be immediately known, like an advertisement. When it happened with Frankie we thought it had been a lucky accident. When it happens twice, we know it's deliberate. And it has us worried: something big might be about to happen, like an all-out war between the two organizations. If that's the case, we've got to stop it. A lot of innocent people get killed in any war."

"Was he killed the same way?" Laurie asked as she went through the folders until she came across Bruno's.

"Same way," Lou said. "Gangland-style execution. Shot in the back of the head from close range."

"And with a small-caliber bullet," Laurie added as she finished with Bruno's folder and picked up the phone. She dialed the morgue. When someone answered, she asked for Vinnie.

"Are we together again today?" Laurie asked.

"You're stuck with me all week," Vinnie said.

"We got two floaters," Laurie said. "Bruno Marchese and . . ." Laurie looked over at Lou. "What's the name of the other one."

"We don't know," Lou said. "There's been no ID."

"No wallet?" Laurie asked.

"Worse than that," Lou said. "Both the head and the hands are missing. This one they didn't want us to identify at all."

"Lovely!" Laurie said sarcastically. "The post will be of limited value without the head." To Vinnie she said, "I want to be sure Bruno Marchese and the headless man get X-rayed."

"We're already working on it," Vinnie said. "But it's going to be a while. They're in line. Busy down here today. There was some kind of gang war up in Harlem last night, so we're knee deep in gunshot wounds. And by the way, the headless corpse is a woman, not a man. When will you be down here?"

"Shortly," Laurie said. "Make sure we have a rape-kit for the female." She hung up and looked over at Lou. "You didn't tell me one of the floaters was a woman."

"I didn't have a chance," Lou said.

"Well, no matter," Laurie said. "Unfortunately, the cases you are interested in won't be first. I'm sorry."

"No problem," Lou said. "I like to watch you work."

Laurie scanned the material in the folder on the headless woman. Then she perused one of the overdose folders. She'd only got as far as the investigator's report before she reached for the last folder and scanned its investigator's report. "This is amazing," she said. She looked up at Lou.

"Dr. Washington said these cases were the same as Duncan Andrews. I had no idea he was speaking so literally. What a coincidence."

"Are they cocaine overdoses?" Lou asked.

"Yes," Laurie said. "But that's not what makes them such a coincidence. One's a banker, the other an editor."

"What's so amazing about that?" Lou asked.

"It's the demographics," Laurie said. "All three were successful professionals, actively employed, young single people. Hardly the usual overdose we're accustomed to seeing around here."

"Like I said: what's so amazing about that? Aren't these people the kind of yuppies who made coke popular? What's the big surprise?"

"The fact that they took cocaine is not the surprising aspect," Laurie began slowly. "I'm not naive. Behind the veneer of material success can lie some pretty serious addictions. But as I told you the overdose cases we get in here are usually the truly down and out. With crack you see a lot of very impoverished, lower-class people. We do see more prosperous people from time to time, but usually by the time the drugs kill them, they've already lost everything else: job, family, money. These recent cases just don't strike me as typical overdoses. It makes me wonder if there wasn't some kind of poison in the drug. Now where did I put that article from the *American Journal of Medicine?*" she said, talking more to herself. "Ah, here it is."

Laurie pulled out a reprint of an article and handed it to Lou. "Street cocaine is always cut with something, usually sugars or common stimulants, but sometimes with weird stuff. That article is about a series of poisonings resulting from a kilo of cocaine cut with strychnine."

"Wow," Lou said as he scanned the article. "That would be quite a trip."

"It'd be a quick trip in here to the morgue," Laurie agreed. "Seeing three rather atypical OD cases with such strikingly similar demographics in two days makes me wonder if they each got the cocaine from the same contaminated source."

"I think it's a long shot," Lou said. "Especially with only three cases. And quite frankly, even if your hunch is right, I'm not that interested."

"Not interested?" Laurie couldn't believe what she was hearing.

"With all the problems this city has, with all the violence and street crime going down, it's hard for me to muster much sympathy for a trio of fancy pants who have nothing better to do with their leisure time than do illegal drugs. Frankly I'm much more concerned about poor slobs like that headless female floater we got downstairs."

Laurie was stunned, but before she could launch into a rebuttal, her phone rang. She was surprised to hear Jordan Scheffield on the other end when she picked up.

"I finished my first case," he said. "Went perfectly. I'm sure the Baron will be pleased."

"Glad to hear it," Laurie said, glancing self-consciously at Lou.

"Did you get the flowers?" Jordan asked.

"Yes," Laurie said. "I'm looking at them this very minute. Thank you. They were just what the doctor ordered."

"Very clever," Jordan laughed. "I thought it would be an appropriate way to let you know that I'm looking forward to seeing you tonight."

"The gesture might fall into the same category as your limo," Laurie said. "A bit on the extravagant side. But I appreciate your thinking of me."

"Well, I just wanted to check in. I've got to get back to surgery," Jordan said. "See you at eight."

"I'm sorry," Lou said once Laurie had hung up. "You

could have told me it was a personal call. I would have stepped out into the hall."

"I usually don't get personal calls here," Laurie said. "It took me by surprise."

"A dozen roses. A limo. Must be an interesting guy."

"He is interesting," Laurie said. "In fact, he said something last night that I think you'll find interesting."

"That's hard to believe," Lou said. "But I'm all ears."

"The man on the phone is a doctor," Laurie said. "His name is Jordan Scheffield. You may have heard of him. Supposedly he's quite well known. At any rate, he told me last night that he has been taking care of the man you are so interested in: Mr. Paul Cerino."

"No fooling!" Lou said. He was surprised. He was also interested.

"Jordan Scheffield is an ophthalmologist," Laurie said.

"Wait a sec," Lou said. He held up a hand while he reached into his jacket and pulled out a tattered pad of paper and a ballpoint pen. "Let me write this down." While he bit on his tongue, he wrote out Jordan's name. Then he asked Laurie to spell ophthalmologist.

"Is that the same as optometrist?" Lou asked.

"No," Laurie said. "An ophthalmologist is a medical doctor trained to do surgery as well as manage medical eye care. An optometrist is trained more to correct visual problems with eyeglasses and contact lenses."

"What about opticians?" Lou asked. "I've always mixed these guys up. No one ever explained it to me."

"Opticians fill the eyeglass prescriptions," Laurie said. "Either from an ophthalmologist or an optometrist."

"Now that I have that straight," Lou said. "Tell me about Dr. Scheffield and Paul Cerino."

"That's the most interesting part," Laurie said. "Jordan said that he was treating Mr. Cerino for acid burns of the eyes. Someone had thrown acid in Paul Cerino's eyes to blind him."

"You don't say," Lou said. "That could explain a lot. Like maybe these two gangland-style executions of Lucia people. And what about Frankie's eye? Could that have been acid?"

"Yes," Laurie said. "It could have been acid. It will be tough to determine since Frankie was in the East River, but on the whole, the damage to his eye was definitely consistent with an acid burn."

"Can you try to have your lab document that it was acid? This could be the start of the lucky breakthrough I've been praying for."

"Of course we'll try," Laurie said. "But like I said, his having been in the river might make it tough. We'll also examine the bullet in the present case. Maybe it will match the one from Frankie."

"I haven't been this excited for months," Lou said.

"Come on," Laurie said. "Let's see what we can do."

Together they went down to the lab. Laurie found the director, a toxicologist, Dr. John DeVries. He was a tall, thin man with gaunt cheeks and an academic's pallor. He was dressed in a soiled lab coat several sizes too small.

Laurie made introductions, then asked if any of the results on the previous day's cases were available.

"Some might be," John told her. "You have the accession numbers?"

"Absolutely," Laurie said.

"Come in my office," John said. He led them to his office, a narrow cubbyhole filled with books and stacks of scientific journals.

John leaned across his desk and punched a few keys on his computer. "What are the accession numbers?" he asked.

Laurie gave Duncan Andrews' number and John entered it.

"There was cocaine in the blood and urine," John said, reading off the screen. "And apparently in high concentration. But this was only by thin-layer chromatography."

"Any contaminants or other drugs?" Laurie asked.

"Not so far," John said, straightening up. "But we'll be using gas chromatography and mass spectrometry as soon as we have time. We got a lot of work around here."

"This was a cocaine overdose case but it's a little atypical in that the deceased did not appear to be a habitual user. And if he did use drugs—which his family swears he didn't—it wasn't interfering with his life. The man was very successful, a solid citizen: the kind of person you do not expect to overdose. So his death was unusual perhaps, but not extraordinary. Cocaine can be an upscale drug. But now I've got two more OD's with similar profiles the very next day. I'm concerned that a batch of cocaine may be poisoned with some kind of contaminant. That's what may be killing these seemingly casual users. I'd really appreciate it if you ran the samples sooner rather than later. We might be able to save some lives."

"I'll do what I can," John said. "But as I told you, we're busy. Was there another case you wanted to know about now?"

Laurie gave Frank DePasquale's accession number and John consulted the screen. "Only a trace of cannabinoid in the urine. Otherwise, nothing on screening."

"There was a sample of eye tissue," Laurie said. "Find anything there?"

"Hasn't been processed yet," John said.

"The eye appeared burned," Laurie added. "We now suspect acid. Could you look for acid? It might be important if we can document it."

"I'll do what I can."

Laurie thanked John, then motioned for Lou to follow her to the elevator. As they walked, Laurie shook her head. "It's like squeezing water out of a stone to get information out of him," she complained.

"He seems exhausted," Lou said. "Or he hates his job. One of the two."

"In his defense, he is busy," Laurie said. "Like everything else here, his funding is limited and getting progressively worse, so he's stretched thin when it comes to staff. But I hope he can find the time to search for a contaminant in the drug cases. The more I think about it the more sure I am."

When they got to the elevators, Laurie glanced at her watch. "I have to get a move on!" She lifted her eyes to Lou. "I can't afford to have Dr. Washington mad at me as well as Dr. Bingham. I'll be out pounding the pavement, looking for a new job."

Lou gazed into her eyes. "You really are upset about these overdose cases, aren't you?"

"Yes, I am," Laurie admitted. She averted her eyes and glanced up at the floor indicator. Lou's comment brought up the memory of the nightmare she'd had that morning. She hoped that he wouldn't mention her brother. Thankfully the elevator door opened, and they boarded.

They changed into scrub clothes and entered the main autopsy room. It was a beehive of activity; every table was occupied. Laurie saw that even Calvin was working at table one. Things were definitely hopping for him to be there; it was not customary for Calvin to do routine cases.

Laurie's first case was on the table. Vinnie had taken the liberty of getting all the paraphernalia he anticipated she'd need. The deceased's name was Robert Evans, aged twenty-nine.

Laurie set out her papers and switched into her professional persona, beginning her meticulous external exam. She was halfway through when she realized that Lou was not across from her. Raising her head, she saw him standing to the side.

"I'm sorry I haven't been including you," she said.

"I understand," Lou said. "You do your thing. I'm fine. I can tell that you are all very busy. I don't want to be in the way."

"You won't be in the way," Laurie said. "You wanted to watch, so come over and watch."

Lou stepped around the table being careful where his feet touched the floor. His hands were clasped behind his back. He looked down at Robert Evans. "Find anything interesting?" he asked.

"This poor fellow convulsed just like Duncan Andrews," Laurie said. "He has all the consequent bruises and badly bitten tongue to prove it. He also has something else. Look here in the antecubital fossa. See that blanched puncture mark? Remember seeing that on Duncan Andrews?"

"Sure," Lou said. "That was the intravenous site where he mainlined the cocaine."

"Exactly," Laurie said. "In other words, Mr. Evans took his cocaine the same way Mr. Andrews did."

"So?" Lou questioned.

"I told you yesterday that cocaine can be taken lots of ways," Laurie said. "But sniffing, or the medical term, insufflation, is the usual recreational route."

"What about smoking?" Lou asked.

"You're thinking of crack. Cocaine hydrochloride, the salt, is poorly volatile and can't be smoked. For smoking it has to be converted to its free base: crack. The point is that although the usual form of cocaine can be injected, it usually isn't. The fact that it had been used that way on both these cases is curious, not that I know what to make of it."

"Wasn't it common in the sixties to shoot cocaine?" Lou asked.

"Only when it was combined with heroin in what they call speedball." Laurie closed her eyes for a moment, took a deep breath, and let it out with a sigh.

"Are you all right?" Lou asked.

"I'm fine," Laurie said.

"Maybe what we're seeing is the beginning of a new fad," Lou suggested.

"I hope not," Laurie said. "But if it is, it's much too deadly to be a fad for long."

Fifteen minutes later, when Laurie plunged the scalpel into Robert's chest, Lou winced. Despite the fact that Robert was dead and that there was no blood, Lou could not dismiss the idea that the razor-sharp knife was cutting into human tissue just like his own skin.

With no pathology apparent, Laurie finished the internal aspect of Robert Evans' autopsy in short order. While Vinnie took the body away and brought in Bruno Marchese, Laurie and Lou went to the X-ray view box to look at Bruno's X-rays and the one of the headless woman.

"The bullet is in just about the same location," Laurie said, pointing to the bright dot inside the outline of Bruno's skull.

"Looks like slightly larger caliber," Lou said. "I could be wrong, but I don't think it's from the same gun."

"I'll be impressed if you're right," Laurie said.

Laurie put up Bruno's full-body X-ray. She scanned the film with a practiced eye. When she saw no abnormalities she replaced it with the X-ray of the unfortunate woman.

"It's a good thing we took this X-ray," Laurie said.

"Oh?" Lou said, staring at the foggy-appearing shadows.

"You mean you don't see the abnormality?" Laurie asked.

"No," Lou said. "At the same time I don't know how you doctors can see much in these things. I mean a bullet jumps out at you, but the rest just looks like a bunch of smudges."

"I can't believe you can't see it," Laurie said.

"All right, I'm blind," Lou said. "So tell me!"

"The head and the hands!" Laurie said. "They're gone."

"You miserable slut!" Lou laughed in a forced whisper to keep those at a nearby table from hearing.

"Well, it's an abnormality," Laurie teased.

Finished with the X-rays, Laurie and Lou returned to the table just in time to help Vinnie move Bruno from the gurney onto the table. Lou started to help, but Laurie shooed him away since he was not gloved. To save time, Laurie started out with the body prone.

The entrance wound looked much like Frankie's although the diameter of the stippling was slightly larger, suggesting the gun had been a bit farther away. After taking all the appropriate photographs and samples, she and Vinnie turned the body supine.

The first thing Laurie did then was check the eyes. They were normal.

"After what you said upstairs I was hoping the eyes might tell us something," Lou said.

"I was hoping as well," Laurie admitted. "I'd love to give you that break you need."

"It still might be important," Lou said. "If Paul Cerino had acid thrown in his eyes, and if Frank DePasquale did too, it's certainly a link. I think it's worth my while to take a trip out to Queens and have a chat with Paul."

After finishing the rest of the external exam, Laurie accepted a knife from Vinnie and began the internal. Again, with no pathology, it went very quickly.

As soon as Bruno's autopsy was completed, Vinnie rolled him away and brought in the second floater. As Laurie helped Vinnie transfer the body to the table, someone from a nearby table called out: "Where'd that body come from, Laurie? Sleepy Hollow?"

After the laughter died down, Lou leaned over to Laurie's ear. "That was crude," he whispered teasingly. "Want me to go over and slug the guy?"

Laurie laughed. "Black humor," she said. "It has always played a role in pathology."

Laurie inspected the woman's severed limbs and neck. "The mutilation was done after death," she said.

"That's comforting," Lou said. He felt his tolerance was getting lower with every case. He was having more trouble dealing with this dismembered body than with the others.

"The decapitation and the removal of the hands was done crudely," Laurie said. "Look at the rough saw marks on the exposed bones. Of course some of this tissue appears to have been eaten by fish or crabs."

Lou forced himself to look even though he would have preferred not to. He was feeling slightly nauseated.

"The rest of the torso looks okay," Laurie said. "No human bite marks."

Lou swallowed again. "Would you have expected bite marks?" he asked weakly.

"If rape was involved," Laurie said, "then bite marks are occasionally seen. You have to think about them, otherwise you can miss them."

"I'll try to remember that," Lou said.

Laurie carefully inspected the chest and abdomen. The only finding of note was a right upper quadrant scar following the line of the ribs.

"This could turn out to be important for ID purposes," Laurie said, pointing at the scar. "I'd guess it was a gall-bladder operation."

"What if the body is never identified?" Lou asked.

"It will stay in the walk-in cooler for a number of weeks," Laurie said. "If by then we still don't know who she is, she'll end up in one of those pine coffins in the hall."

Laurie opened up the rape-kit and spread out the contents. "Most of this is probably academic after the body has been in the river, but it's still worth a try." As she took the appropriate samples, she asked Lou if he thought the case was related to Frank's or Bruno's.

"I can't be sure, but I have my suspicions. I have a number of people including police divers out looking for the heads and hands. I'll tell you one thing: whoever dumped this woman didn't want her to be identified. Given the East River's tidal and current patterns, the fact that she was found in the same general vicinity as Frankie and Bruno suggests she was dumped from the same place. So, yeah, I think there could be a connection."

"What do you think the chances are of finding the head or the hands?" Laurie asked.

"Not great," Lou said. "They could have sunk where the body was dumped or they might not have been dumped in the river."

Laurie had moved on to the internal portion of the autopsy. She noted that the victim had had two surgeries in the past: a gallbladder removal, as Laurie had surmised, and a hysterectomy.

With three of her four cases out of the way before noon, Laurie felt comfortable enough with her progress to suggest that she and Lou have a quick cup of coffee. Lou happily agreed, saying he could use the fortification after the morning's ordeal. Besides, he would have to leave to get back to his office. Having seen the autopsies of the two "floaters," he couldn't rationalize any more time. He jokingly told Laurie that she'd have to do the second overdose without his assistance.

After taking off her goggles, apron, and gown, Laurie took Lou up to the coffeemaker in the ID room. It was just one floor up, so they used the stairs. Laurie sat in a desk chair while Lou sat on the corner of a desk. Just as happened the previous day, Lou's demeanor suddenly changed when he was about to leave. He became clumsy and self-conscious. He even managed to spill some of his coffee down the front of his scrub shirt.

"I'm sorry," he said, dabbing at the coffee spots with a napkin. "I hope it doesn't stain."

"Don't be silly, Lou," Laurie said. "These scrub clothes have had lot worse stains than coffee."

"I guess you're right," he said.

"Is something on your mind?" Laurie asked.

"Yeah," Lou said. He stared into his coffee. "I wanted to know if you'd like to grab a bite to eat tonight. I know a great place down in Little Italy on Mulberry Street."

"I'd like to ask you a question," Laurie said. "Yesterday you asked if I was married. You never said whether you're married."

"I'm not married," he said.

"Have you ever been married?" Laurie asked.

"Yeah, I was married," Lou said. "I've been divorced for a couple of years. I have two kids: a girl seven and a boy five."

"Do you ever see them?"

"Of course I see them," Lou said. "What do you think? I wouldn't see my own kids? I get 'em every weekend."

"You don't have to be defensive," Laurie said. "I was just curious. Yesterday I realized after you'd left that you'd asked me about my marital status without telling me yours."

"It was an oversight," Lou said. "Anyway, how about dinner?"

"I'm afraid I have plans tonight," Laurie said.

"Oh, fine," said Lou. "Give me the third degree about my marital and parental status, then turn me down. I suppose you're seeing the fancy doctor with the roses and the limo. Guess I'm not quite in his league." He stood up abruptly. "Well, I better be going."

"I think you're being overly sensitive and silly," Laurie said. "I only said I was busy tonight."

"Overly sensitive and silly, huh? I'll keep that in mind. It's been another illuminating morning. Thank you so very much. If you come up with anything interesting on any of the floaters, please give me a call." With that, Lou tossed his Styrofoam cup into a nearby wastebasket and walked out of the room.

Laurie remained in her seat for a moment, sipping her

coffee. She knew that she'd hurt Lou's feelings, and that made her feel uncomfortable. At the same time she thought he was being immature. Some of that "blue collar" charm she'd noted the day before was wearing thin.

After finishing her coffee, Laurie returned to the autopsy room and her fourth case of the day: Marion Overstreet, aged twenty-eight, editor for a major New York publishing house.

"You want anything special for this case?" Vinnie asked. He was eager to get under way.

Laurie shook her head no. She looked at the young woman on the table. Such a waste. She wondered if this woman would have gambled with drugs if she could have anticipated such a terrible price.

The autopsy went quickly. Laurie and Vinnie worked well together as a team. Conversation was kept to a minimum. The case was remarkably similar to both Duncan Andrews' and Robert Evans', down to the fact that Overstreet had injected the cocaine, not snorted it. There were only a few minor surprises that Laurie would have Cheryl Myers or one of the other forensic investigators check out. By twelve forty-five Laurie walked out of the main autopsy room.

After changing to her street clothes, Laurie took it upon herself to carry the specimens from each of the day's cases to Toxicology. She hoped to have another chat with the resident toxicologist. She found John DeVries in his office eating his lunch. An old-fashioned lunch box with a Thermos built into its vaulted cover was open on his desk.

"I finished the two overdoses," Laurie said. "I've brought up their toxicology samples."

"Leave the samples on the receiving desk in the lab," he told her. He held an uncut sandwich in both hands.

"Any luck finding a contaminant in the Andrews case?" she asked hopefully.

"It's only been a few hours since you were here last. I'll call you if I find anything."

"As soon as possible," Laurie encouraged. "I don't mean to be a bother. It's just that I'm more convinced than ever that a contaminant of some sort is involved. If there is, I want to find it."

"If it's there, we'll find it. Just give us a chance, for Chrissake."

"Thanks," Laurie said. "I'll try to be patient. It's just that—"

"I know, I know," John interrupted. "I get the picture already. Please!"

"I'm out of here," Laurie said. She put her hands in the air to signify her surrender.

Back in her office, Laurie ate some of the lunch, dictated the morning's autopsies, and tried to tackle some of her paperwork. She found she couldn't take her mind off the drug overdose cases.

What worried her was the specter of more cases. If there was some source of contaminated cocaine in the city, it meant there would be more deaths. At this point the ball was in John's court. There was nothing more she could do.

Or was there? How could she prevent more deaths? The key lay in warning the public. Hadn't Bingham just lectured her on the fact that they had social and political responsibilities?

With that thought in mind, Laurie picked up the phone and called the chief's office. She asked Mrs. Sanford if Dr. Bingham might have a moment to see her.

"I believe I could squeeze you in," Mrs. Sanford said, "but you have to come immediately. Dr. Bingham is due at a luncheon at City Hall."

When she entered Bingham's office, she could tell the chief medical examiner was not prepared to give her more than a minute of his time. When he asked her what it was she wanted, Laurie outlined the facts surrounding the three cocaine overdose cases as succinctly as possible. She emphasized the upscale demographics, the fact that none of the victims appeared to have been in the depths of addiction, and that all three had mainlined the drug.

"I get the picture," Bingham said. "What's your point?"

"I'm afraid that we are seeing the beginning of a series," Laurie said. "I'm concerned about a toxic contaminant in some cocaine supply."

"With only three cases, don't you think that's a rather fanciful leap?"

"The point is," Laurie said, "I'd like to keep it at three cases."

"An admirable goal," Bingham said. "But are you certain about this alleged contaminant? What does John have to say?"

"He's looking," Laurie said.

"He hasn't found anything?"

"Not yet," Laurie admitted. "But he's only used thin-layer chromatography so far."

"So I guess we have to wait for John," Bingham said. He stood up.

Laurie held her seat. Having come this far, she wasn't about to give up yet. "I was thinking that maybe we should make a statement to the press," Laurie said. "We could put out a warning."

"Out of the question," Bingham said. "I'm not about to gamble the integrity of this office on a supposition based on three cases. Aren't you coming to me a little prematurely? Why don't you wait and see what John comes up with? Besides, making that kind of statement would require names, and the Andrews organization would have the mayor at my throat in an instant."

"Well, it was just a suggestion," Laurie said.

"Thank you, Doctor," Bingham said. "Now if you'll excuse me, I'm late as it is."

Laurie was chagrined Bingham didn't give her suggestion more credence, but without more conclusive proof she could hardly force the issue. She only wished there was something she could do before more of the same kind of overdoses showed up on her schedule.

It was then she had a thought. Her training in forensics in Miami had involved direct on-the-scene investigation. Maybe if she toured any future scenes, some critical clue might present itself.

Laurie went to the forensic medical investigative department, where she found Bart Arnold, chief of the investigators, sitting at his desk. Between two of his innumerable telephone conversations, she told him that she wanted to be notified if any more overdoses were called in that were similar to the three that she had had. She was very explicit. Bart assured her that he'd let the others know, including the tour doctors who took calls at night.

Laurie was about to return to her office when she remembered that she should also request that the autopsies of any similar overdoses be assigned to her. That meant seeing Calvin.

"It always worries me when one of the troops wants to see me," Calvin said when Laurie poked her head in his office. "What is it, Dr. Montgomery? It better not be about scheduling your vacation. With the current case load, we've decided to cancel all this year's vacations."

"Vacation! I wish!" Laurie said with a smile. Despite his gruff manner, she had a genuine fondness and respect for Calvin. "I wanted to thank you for assigning me those two overdose cases this morning."

Calvin raised an eyebrow. "Well, this is a first. No one ever thanked me for assigning him a case. Why do I have the feeling there's more to this visit?"

"Because you are naturally suspicious," Laurie teased. "I truly have found the cases interesting. More than interesting. In fact I'd like to request that any other similar case that comes in be assigned to me."

"A grunt looking for work!" Calvin said. "It's enough to make a poor administrator's heart glow. Sure. You can have all you want. Just so I don't make any mistakes, what do you mean by similar? If you took all our overdoses you'd be here 'round the clock."

"Upscale overdose or toxicity cases," Laurie said. "Just like the two you gave me this morning. People in their twenties or thirties, well educated, and in good physical condition."

"I'll personally see that you get them all," Calvin said cheerfully. "But I have to warn you now. If you put in for overtime, I'm not paying."

"I'm hoping there will be no overtime," Laurie said.

After saying goodbye to Calvin, Laurie returned to her office and sat down to work. The positive meeting with Calvin had compensated for the meeting with Bingham, and with a modicum of peace of mind, Laurie was able to concentrate. She was able to accomplish more work than she'd expected and signed out a number of cases including most of the weekend's autopsies. She even had time to counsel a devastated family about the "crib death" of their infant. Laurie was able to assure them they were not at fault.

The only problem that intruded during the early afternoon was a call from Cheryl Myers. She told Laurie that she'd been unable to find any medical conditions in Duncan Andrews' past. His only brush with a hospital had occurred nearly fifteen years ago when he broke his arm during a high school football game. "You want me to keep looking?" Cheryl asked after a pause.

"Yes," Laurie said. "It can't hurt. Try to go back to his

childhood." Laurie knew that she was hoping for nothing less than a miracle, yet she wanted to be complete. Then she could turn the whole problem over to Calvin Washington. She decided Lou had been right: if the powers-that-be wanted to distort the record for political expediency, they should do it themselves.

By late afternoon Laurie's thoughts drifted back to the drug cases. On a whim she decided to check out where Evans and Overstreet lived. She caught a cab on First Avenue and asked to go to Central Park South. Evans' address was near Columbus Circle.

When the cab arrived at the destination, Laurie asked him to wait. She hopped out of the cab to get a good look at the building. She tried to remember who else lived around there. It was some movie star, she was sure. Probably dozens of stars lived nearby. With a view of the park and its proximity to Fifth Avenue, Central Park South was prime real estate. In Manhattan it didn't get much better than that.

Standing there, Laurie tried to picture Robert Evans striding confidently down the street and turning into his building, briefcase in hand, excited about the prospects of a social evening in New York. It was hard to jibe such an image with so untimely and profligate a demise.

Getting back in the cab, Laurie directed the driver to Marion Overstreet's: a cozy brownstone on West Sixty-seventh Street a block from Central Park. This time she didn't even get out of the car. She merely gazed at the handsome residence and again tried to imagine the young editor in life. Satisfied, she asked the confused driver to take her back to the medical examiner's office.

After the confrontation with Bingham that morning over her visit to Duncan Andrews' apartment, Laurie had not intended going inside either victim's building. She'd merely wanted to see them from the outside. She didn't know why she'd had the compulsion to do so, and when she got back to the medical examiner's, she wondered if it had been a bad idea. The excursion had saddened her since it made the victims and their tragedies more real.

Back in her office, Laurie ran into her office-mate, Riva. Riva complimented Laurie on the beauty of her roses. Laurie thanked her and stared at the flowers. In her current state of mind, they had changed their ambience. Although they had suggested celebration that morning, now they seemed more the symbol of grief, almost funereal in their appearance.

Lou Soldano was still irritated as he drove over the Queensboro Bridge from Manhattan to Queens. He felt like such a fool having set himself up so conveniently for rejection. What had he been thinking, anyway? She was a doctor, for Chrissake, who'd grown up on the East Side of Manhattan. What would they have talked about? The Mets? The Giants? Hardly. Lou was the first to admit that he wasn't the most educated guy in the city, and except for law enforcement and sports, he didn't know much about most other things.

"Do you ever see your kids?" Lou said out loud, doing a mockingly crude imitation of Laurie's much higher voice. With a short little yell, Lou pounded the steering wheel and mistakenly honked the horn of his Chevrolet Caprice. The driver in front of him turned around and threw him a finger.

"Yeah, to you too," Lou said. He felt like reaching down and putting his emergency light on the dashboard and pulling the guy over. But he didn't. Lou didn't do things like that. He didn't abuse his authority, although he did it in his fantasy on a regular basis.

"I should have taken the Triborough Bridge," he mumbled as the traffic bogged down on the Queensboro. From the last third of the bridge all the way to the juncture with

Northern Boulevard it was stop and go, and mostly stop. It gave Lou time to think about the last time he had seen Paul Cerino.

It had been about three years previously when Lou had just made detective sergeant. He was still assigned to Organized Crime at the time and had been pursuing Cerino for a good four years. So it was a surprise when the operator at the station had said that a Mr. Paul Cerino was on the line. Confused as to why the man he was after was calling him, Lou had picked up the phone with great curiosity.

"Hey, how you doing?" Paul had said as if they were the best of friends. "I have a favor to ask of you. Would you mind stopping at the house this afternoon when you leave work?"

Having been invited to a gangster's house had been such a weird occurrence that Lou had been reluctant to tell anybody about it. But finally he'd told his partner, Brian O'Shea, who'd thought he'd gone crazy for accepting.

"What if he's planning on doing you in?" Brian asked.

"Please!" Lou had said. "He wouldn't call me up here at the station if he was going to bump me off. Besides, even if he decided to do it, he wouldn't get anywhere near it himself. It's something else. Maybe he wants to deal. Maybe he wants to finger somebody else. Whatever it is, I'm going. This could be something big."

So Lou went with great expectations of some major breakthrough that he thought might even have resulted in a commendation by the chief. Of course the visit was against Brian's better judgment, and Brian insisted on going with him but waiting in the car. The deal had been that if Lou didn't come out in a half hour, Brian was going to call in a SWAT team.

It was with a lot of anxiety that Lou had mounted the front steps of Cerino's modest house on Clintonville Street in Whitestone. Even the house's appearance added to Lou's unease. There was something wrong about it. With the huge amount of money the man had to be making from all his illegal activities plus his only legal endeavor, the American Fresh Fruit Company, it was a mystery to Lou why he lived in such a small, unpretentious house.

With a final glance back at Brian, whose concerns had only served to fan Lou's anxiety to a fevered pitch and with a final check to make sure his Smith and Wesson Detective Special was in its holster, Lou rang the front bell. Mrs. Cerino had opened the door. Taking a deep breath, Lou had entered.

Lou laughed heartily, bringing tears to his eyes. The experience was still capable of doing that after three years. While still laughing, Lou glanced into the car immediately to his left. The driver was looking at him as if he were crazy, laughing as he was in such abominable traffic.

But the traffic notwithstanding, Lou could still laugh at the shock he had had when he'd stepped into Cerino's house that day expecting the worst. What he had unexpectedly walked into was a surprise party for himself in celebration of his having been promoted to detective sergeant!

At the time Lou had been recently separated from his wife, so the promotion had gone unnoticed except at the station. Somehow Cerino had heard about this and had decided to give him a party. It had been Mr. and Mrs. Cerino and their two sons, Gregory and Steven. There'd been cake and soda. Lou had even gone out to get Brian.

The irony of the whole thing had been that Lou and Paul had been enemies for so long they had almost become friends. After all, they knew so much about each other.

It took Lou almost an hour to get out to Paul's, and by the time he mounted the front steps, it was just about the same time of day as when Paul had thrown the surprise party. Lou could remember it as if it had been yesterday.

Looking through the front windows, Lou could see that

the living room lights were on. Outside it was getting dark even though it was only five-thirty. Winter was on its way.

Lou pressed the front doorbell and heard the muted chimes. The door was opened by Gregory, the older boy. He was about ten. He recognized Lou, greeted him in a friendly fashion, and invited him inside. Gregory was a well-mannered boy.

"Is your dad home?" Lou asked.

No sooner had he asked than Paul appeared from the living room in his stocking feet clutching a red-tipped cane. A radio was on in the background.

"Who is it?" he asked Gregory.

"It's Detective Soldano," Gregory said.

"Lou!" Paul said, coming directly toward Lou and extending a hand.

Lou shook hands with Paul and tried to see his eyes behind a pair of reflective sunglasses. Paul was a big man, moderately overweight, so that his small facial features were sunk into his fleshy face. He had dark hair cut short, and large, heavily lobed ears. On both cheeks were red patches of recently healed skin. Lou guessed it had been from the acid.

"How about some coffee?" Paul said. "Or a little wine?" Without waiting for a response, Paul yelled for Gloria. Gregory reappeared with Steven, the younger Cerino. He was eight.

"Come in," Paul said. "Sit down. Tell me what's been happening. You married yet?"

Lou followed Paul back into the living room. He could tell that Paul had adapted well to his reduced visual acuity, at least in his own home. He didn't use the cane to navigate to the radio to turn it off. Nor did he use it to find his favorite chair, into which he sank with a sigh.

"Sorry to hear about your eye problem," Lou said, sitting opposite Paul.

151

"These things happen," Paul said philosophically.

Gloria appeared and greeted Lou. Like Paul, she was overweight—a buxom woman with a kind, gentle face. If she knew what her husband did for a living, she never let on. She acted like the typical, lower-middle-class suburban housewife who had to scrimp to get along on a budget. Lou wondered what Paul did with all the money he had to be accumulating.

Responding to Lou's positive reply regarding coffee, Gloria disappeared into the kitchen.

"I heard about your accident just today," Lou said.

"I haven't told all my friends," Paul said with a smile.

"Did this involve the Lucia people?" Lou asked. "Was it Vinnie Dominick?"

"Oh no!" Paul said. "This was an accident. I was trying to jump-start the car and the battery blew up. Got a bunch of acid in my face."

"Come on, Paul," Lou said. "I came all the way out here to commiserate with you. The least you can do is tell me the truth. I already know that the acid was thrown into your face. It's just a matter of who was responsible."

"How do you know this?" Cerino asked.

"I was specifically told by someone who knows," Lou said. "In fact it ultimately came from a totally reliable source. You!"

"Me?" Paul questioned with genuine surprise.

Gloria returned with an espresso for Lou. He helped himself to sugar. Gloria then retreated from the room. So did the boys.

"You have awakened my curiosity," Paul said. "Explain to me how I was the source of this rumor about my eyes."

"You told your doctor, Jordan Scheffield," Lou said. "He told one of the medical examiners by the name of Laurie Montgomery, and the medical examiner told me. And the reason I happened to be talking to the medical examiner was because I went over there to watch a couple of autopsies on homicide victims. The names might be familiar to you: Frankie DePasquale and Bruno Marchese."

"Never heard of them," Paul said.

"They are Lucia people," Lou said. "And one of them, curiously enough, had acid burns in one of his eyes."

"Terrible," Cerino said. "They certainly don't make batteries the way they used to."

"So you're still telling me that you got battery acid in your eyes?" Lou asked.

"Of course," Paul said. "Because that's what happened."

"How are the eyes doing?" Lou asked.

"Pretty good, considering what could have happened," Paul said. "But the doctor says I'll do fine as soon as I have my operations. First I have to wait a while, but I'm sure you know about that."

"What are you talking about?" Lou said. "I don't know anything about eyes except how many you got."

"I didn't know much either," Paul said. "At least not before this happened. But I've been learning ever since. I used to think they transplanted the whole eye. You know, like changing an old-fashioned-type radio tube. Just plug the thing in with all the prongs in the right place. But that's not how it works. They only transplant the cornea."

"That's all news to me," Lou said.

"Want to see what my eyes look like?" Paul asked.

"I'm not sure," Lou said.

Paul took off his reflective sunglasses.

"Ugh," Lou said. "Put your glasses back on. I'm sorry for you, Paul. It looks terrible. It looks like you have a couple of white marbles in your eyes."

Paul chuckled as he put his glasses back on. "I would have thought a hardened cop like you would have felt satisfaction that his old enemy took a fall."

"Hell no!" Lou said. "I don't want you handicapped. I want you in jail."

Paul laughed. "Still at it, huh?"

"Putting you away is still one of my ultimate goals in life," Lou said agreeably. "And finding that acid burn in Frankie DePasquale's eye gives me some hope. At this point it looks mighty suspicious that you were behind the kid's murder."

"Aw, Lou," Paul said. "It hurts my feelings that you'd think something nasty about me after all these years."

6

□

At first Laurie thought the experience was unique enough to
be tolerable, but as the time approached eight forty-five she
began to get irritated. Thomas, Jordan's driver, had shown
up exactly at the agreed-upon time, eight o'clock, and had
rung Laurie's bell. But when Laurie got down to the car, she
learned that Jordan was not there. He was still in surgery
doing an emergency operation.

"I'm supposed to take you to the restaurant," Thomas
had said. "Dr. Scheffield will be meeting you there."

Taken by surprise with this situation, Laurie had agreed.
She'd felt strange entering the fancy restaurant by herself,
but she was quickly put at ease by the maître d', who had
been expecting her. She'd been discreetly ushered to a waiting table wedged among others near to the window. Next to
the table stood a wine stand icing down a bottle of Meur-
sault.

155

The sommelier had appeared instantly and had shown Laurie the label of the wine. After she'd nodded, he'd opened it, poured her a dollop, waited for her OK, then filled her glass. All this had been accomplished without words.

Finally at five minutes before nine, Jordan arrived.

He came into the room with a flourish, and although he waved a greeting at Laurie, he didn't join her immediately. Instead he weaved his way through the crowded room, stopping at several tables to say hello. Each group of diners greeted him with gusto; animated conversation and smiles followed in his wake.

"Sorry," he said, finally sitting down. "I was in surgery, but I guess Thomas told you as much."

"He did," Laurie said. "What kind of emergency surgery was it?"

"Well, it wasn't exactly an emergency," Jordan said, nervously rearranging his place setting. "My surgery has picked up recently, so I have to squeeze standby cases in whenever the operating room can give me a slot. How's the wine?"

The wine steward had reappeared and gave Jordan a taste of the wine.

"The wine is fine," Laurie said. "Seems that you know a lot of people here."

Jordan took a sip of his wine and for a moment he looked pensive while he swished it around inside his mouth. He nodded with satisfaction after he swallowed, motioned for his glass to be filled, then looked at Laurie. "I usually run into a few of my patients here," he said. "How was your day? I hope it was better than mine."

"Some sort of trouble?" Laurie asked.

"Plenty of trouble," Jordan said. "First, my secretary, who's been with me for almost ten years, didn't show up in the morning. She's never not shown up without calling. We tried calling her but there was no answer. So scheduling got all fouled up by the time I came in from the hospital. Then, to make matters worse, we discovered that someone had broken into the office the night before and had stolen our petty cash as well as all the Percodans we kept on hand."

"How awful," Laurie said. She remembered how it had felt to be robbed. Her room at college had been ransacked one day. "Any vandalism?" she asked. Whoever had broken into her room had smashed what they couldn't carry away.

"No," Jordan said. "But strangely enough the burglar rifled through my records and used the copy machine."

"That sounds like more than a simple robbery," Laurie said.

"That's what makes me uneasy," Jordan said. "The petty cash and the few Percodans I could care less about. But I don't like the thought of someone in my records, not with the high accounts receivable I have. I've already called my accountant to run a tape; I want to make sure there isn't some big change. Have you looked at the menu?"

"Not yet," Laurie said. Her irritation was fading now that Jordan had arrived.

Responding to Jordan's gesture, the maître d' appeared with two menus. Jordan, who ate there frequently, was full of suggestions. Laurie ordered from the daily specials menu attached to the main menu.

She thought the food was wonderful although the frenetic atmosphere made it difficult for her to relax. But Jordan seemed in his element.

While they were waiting for dessert and coffee, Laurie asked Jordan about the effects of acid in the eye. He warmed to the request immediately, going on at length about the cornea's and the conjunctiva's responses to both acid and alkali. Laurie lost interest halfway through his discourse, but her gaze remained steady. She had to admit:

he was an attractive man. She wondered how he maintained such a fabulous tan.

To Laurie's relief, the arrival of dessert and coffee interrupted Jordan's impromptu lecture. As he began his flourless chocolate cake, he changed the subject. "I probably should be thankful those crooks didn't take any of the valuables last night, like the Picassos in the waiting room."

Laurie set her coffee cup down. "You have Picassos in your waiting room?"

"Signed drawings," Jordan said casually. "About twenty of them. It's truly a state-of-the-art office, and I didn't want to scrimp on the waiting area. After all, that's the place the patients spend the most time." Jordan laughed for the first time since he'd sat down.

"That's even more extravagant than the limo," Laurie said. Actually, she felt more strongly than she let on. The idea of such ostentation in a medical setting seemed obscene, especially given the runaway cost of medical care.

"It's quite an office," Jordan said proudly. "My favorite feature of it is that the patients move. I don't go to them, they come to me."

"I'm not sure I understand," Laurie said.

"Each one of my five examining rooms is built on a circular mechanism. You've seen these revolving restaurants at the tops of certain buildings. It's kind of like that. When I push a button in my office, the whole thing turns and the examining room I want lines up with my office. Another button lifts the wall. It's as good as a ride in Disneyland."

"Sounds very impressive," Laurie said. "Expensive but impressive. I suppose your overhead is pretty high."

"Astronomical," Jordan said. He sounded proud of it. "So high that I hate to take a vacation. It's too expensive! Not the vacation itself, but letting the office sit idle. I also have two operating rooms for outpatient procedures."

"I'd like to see this office sometime," Laurie said.

"I'd love to show it to you," Jordan said. "In fact, why not now? It's just around the corner on Park Avenue."

Laurie said she thought that was a great idea, so as soon as Jordan took care of the bill, they were off.

The first room they entered was Jordan's private office. The walls and furniture were entirely of teak, waxed to a high gloss. The upholstery was black leather. There was enough sophisticated ophthalmological equipment to outfit a small hospital.

Next they entered the waiting room, which was paneled in mahogany. Just as Jordan had said, the walls were lined with Picasso drawings. Down a short hall from the waiting room was a circular room with five doors on its perimeter. Opening one, Jordan asked Laurie to sit in the examining chair.

"Now stay right there," he said before leaving the room.

Laurie did as she was told. Next thing she knew, she felt like the room was moving. Then the movement—real or imagined—stopped abruptly and the lights in the room began to dim. Simultaneously, the far wall rose. Its disappearance effectively joined Laurie's examination room to Jordan's private office. Jordan was sitting at his desk, backlit, and leaning back in his chair.

"What's that line about not having Mohammed go to the mountain, but the mountain going to him? Same principle applies here. I like my patients to feel they are in powerful hands. I actually believe it makes them heal more quickly. I know that sounds a bit hocus-pocus, but it works for me."

"I'm impressed," Laurie said. "Obviously I've never seen anything quite like this. Where do you keep your records?"

Jordan took Laurie through another door that led from his office into a long hall. At the end of the hall was a windowless room with a bank of file cabinets, a copy machine, and a computer terminal.

"All the records are in the file cabinets," he said. "But most of the material is duplicated on the computer on hard disk."

"Are these the records that the burglars went through?" Laurie asked.

"They are," Jordan said. "And that's the copy machine. I'm very meticulous about my records. I could tell someone had been in them because the contents in some had been put out of order. I know the copy machine was used after we closed because I have my secretary record the number from the machine at the end of each day."

"What about Paul Cerino's record?" Laurie asked. "Was that disturbed?"

"I don't know," Jordan said. "But it's a good question."

Jordan flipped through his "C" drawer and pulled out a manila folder.

"You were right," he said after paging through. "This one was disturbed as well. See this information sheet? It's supposed to be in the front. Instead it's in the back."

"Is there any way to tell if it had been copied?"

Jordan thought for a moment but shook his head. "Not that I can think of. What's going through your mind?"

"I'm not sure," Laurie said. "But maybe this supposed burglary should convince you to be a bit more careful. I know you think taking care of this Cerino character is mildly entertaining, but you have to understand that he is apparently one nasty man. And maybe even more important, he has some very nasty enemies."

"You think Cerino could have been responsible for my break-in?" Jordan asked.

"I truly don't know," Laurie said. "But it's possible, one way or the other. Maybe his enemies don't want you to fix him up. There are all sorts of possibilities. The only thing I do know is that these guys play for keeps. Over the last two days I've done autopsies on two young men who'd been

160

murdered gangland style, and one of them had what looked like acid burns in his eye."

"Don't tell me that," Jordan said.

"I'm not trying to scare you just to scare you," Laurie said. "I'm only saying this so that you will think about what you are getting yourself involved with by taking care of these people. I've been told that the two major crime families, the Vaccarros and the Lucias, are currently at each other's throats. That's why Cerino got the acid slung in his face. He's one of the Vaccarro bosses."

"Wow," Jordan said. "This does put a different complexion on things. Now you got me worried. Luckily I'll be operating on Cerino soon, so this will all be behind me."

"Is Cerino scheduled?" Laurie asked.

Jordan shook his head. "Not exactly," he said. "I'm waiting on material, as usual."

"Well, I think you should do it as soon as possible. And I wouldn't advertise the date and the time."

Jordan put the contents of Cerino's file back into its proper order and replaced it in the file drawer. "Want to see the rest of the office?" he asked.

"Sure," Laurie said.

Jordan took Laurie deeper into the office complex, showing her several rooms devoted to special ophthalmologic testing. What impressed her most were the two state-of-the-art operating rooms complete with all the requisite ancillary equipment.

"You have a fortune invested here," Laurie said once they'd reached the final room, a photography lab.

"No doubt about it," Jordan agreed. "But it pays off handsomely. Currently I'm grossing between one point five and two million dollars a year."

Laurie swallowed. The figure was staggering. Although she knew her father, the cardiac surgeon, had to have a huge income to cover his life-style, she'd never before been slapped with such an astronomical figure. Knowing what she did about the plight of American medicine and even the shoestring budget the medical examiner's office ran under, it seemed like an obscene waste of resources.

"How about coming by and seeing my apartment?" Jordan said. "If you like the office, you'll love the apartment. It was designed by the same people."

"Sure," Laurie said, mainly as a reflex. She was still trying to absorb Jordan's comment about his income.

As they retraced their route through the office, Laurie asked after Jordan's secretary. "Did you ever hear from her?"

"No," Jordan said, obviously still angry about the no-show. "She never called and there was never any answer at her home. I can only imagine it has something to do with her no-good husband. If she'd not been such a good secretary, I would have gotten rid of her just because of him. He has a restaurant in Bayside, but he's also involved with a number of shady deals. She confided in me in order to borrow bail on several occasions. He's never been convicted, but he's spent plenty of time on Rikers Island."

"Sounds like a mobster himself," Laurie said.

Once they got into the back of the car, Laurie asked Jordan his missing secretary's name.

"Marsha Schulman," Jordan said. "Why do you ask?"

"Just curious," Laurie said.

It didn't take long for Thomas to pull up to the private entrance of Trump Tower. The doorman opened the door for Laurie to get out, but she held back.

"Jordan," she said, looking at him in the dim light of the interior of the limo, "would you be angry if I asked for a raincheck on seeing your apartment? I just noticed the time, and I have to get up for work in the morning."

"Not at all," Jordan said. "I understand perfectly. I've got surgery again myself at the crack of dawn. But there is a condition."

"Which is?"

"That we have dinner again tomorrow night."

"You can put up with me two evenings in a row?" Laurie asked. She'd not been "rushed" like this since high school. She was flattered but wary.

"With pleasure," Jordan said, humorously affecting an English accent.

"All right," Laurie said. "But let's pick a place not quite so formal."

"Done," Jordan said. "You like Italian?"

"I love Italian."

"Then it will be Palio," Jordan said. "At eight."

Vinnie Dominick paused outside of the Vesuvio Restaurant on Corona Avenue in Elmhurst and took advantage of his reflection in the window to smooth his hair and adjust his Gucci tie. Satisfied, he motioned to Freddie Capuso to open the door.

Vinnie's nickname since junior high school was "the Prince." He'd been considered a handsome fellow whom the neighborhood girls had found quite attractive. His features were full but well sculpted. Favoring a tailored look, he heavily moussed his dark hair and brushed it straight back from his forehead. He looked considerably younger than his forty years and, unlike most of his contemporaries, he prided himself on his physical prowess. A high school basketball star, he'd kept his game over the years, playing three nights a week at St. Mary's gym.

Entering the restaurant, Vinnie scanned the room. Freddie and Richie crowded in behind him. Vinnie quickly spotted whom he was looking for: Paul Cerino. The restaurant still had a few diners since its kitchen stayed open until eleven, but most of its clientele had already departed. It was a good location and time for a meeting.

Vinnie walked to Paul's table with the confidence of one meeting an old, good friend. Freddie and Richie followed several steps behind. When Vinnie reached the table, the two men sitting with Paul stood. Vinnie recognized them as Angelo Facciolo and Tony Ruggerio.

"How are you, Paul?" Vinnie asked.

"Can't complain," Paul said. He stuck out a hand for Vinnie to shake.

"Sit down, Vinnie," Paul said. "Have some wine. Angelo, pour the man some wine."

As Vinnie sat down, Angelo picked up an open bottle of Brunello from the table and filled the glass in front of Vinnie.

"I want to thank you for agreeing to see me," Vinnie said. "After what happened last time, I consider it a special favor."

"When you said it was important and involved family, how could I turn you down?"

"First I want to tell you how much I sympathize with your eye problem," Vinnie said. "It was a terrible tragedy and it never should have happened. And right now in front of these other people I want to swear on my mother's grave I knew nothing about it. The punks did it on their own."

There was a pause. For a moment no one said anything. Finally Cerino spoke. "What else is on your mind?"

"I know that your people whacked Frankie and Bruno," Vinnie said. "And even though we know this we have not retaliated. And we're not going to retaliate. Why? Because Frankie and Bruno got what they deserved. They were acting on their own. They were out of step. And we're also not going to retaliate because it is important for you and me to get along. I don't want a war. It gets the authorities up in arms. It makes for bad business for us both."

"And how do I know I can trust this gesture of peace?" Cerino asked.

"By my good faith," Vinnie answered. "Would I ask for a meeting like this at a place of your choosing if I wasn't serious? Furthermore, as another token of my desire to settle the matter, I'm willing to tell you where Jimmy Lanso, the fourth and final guy, is hiding out."

"Really?" Cerino asked. For the first time in the conversation he was genuinely surprised. "And where might that be?"

"His cousin's funeral parlor. Spoletto Funeral Home in Ozone Park."

"I appreciate your openness in all of this," Paul said. "But I have the feeling that there is more."

"I have a favor to ask of you," Vinnie said. "I want to ask you as a colleague to show some good faith to me. I want to ask you to spare Jimmy Lanso. He's family. He's a nephew of my wife's sister's husband. I'll see to it that the punk is punished, but I'd like to ask you as a friend not to whack him."

"I'll certainly give it serious thought," Paul said.

"Thank you," Vinnie said. "After all, we are civilized people. Kids can make mistakes. You and I have had our differences, but we respect each other and understand our common interests. I'm sure that you will take all this into account." Vinnie stood up.

"I'll take everything into consideration," Paul said.

Vinnie turned around and walked out of the restaurant.

Paul lifted his wineglass and took a sip. "Angelo," he called over his shoulder. "Did Vinnie touch his wine?"

"No," Angelo said.

"I didn't think so," Paul said. "And he calls himself civilized?"

"What about Jimmy Lanso?" Angelo asked.

"Kill him," Cerino said. "Take me home, then do it."

"What if it is a setup?" Angelo asked.

Paul took another sip of his wine. "I seriously doubt it," he said. "Vinnie wouldn't lie about family."

* * *

165

Angelo did not like the situation at all. The idea of a funeral home gave him the creeps. Besides, he didn't trust Vinnie Dominick to tell the truth whether it was about family or business. In Angelo's opinion there was a good chance this was a setup, despite Cerino's thoughts to the contrary. And if it was a setup, it was going to be very dangerous to go breaking into the Spoletto Funeral Home. Angelo decided this was a good occasion to let Tony take the lead. And Tony was so eager, he'd no doubt be pleased. He'd been crying for a year that he was never able to do something on his own.

"So what's your take?" Angelo asked once he and Tony were parked across the street from the funeral parlor. It was a rather large, white clapboard building with Greek columns supporting a small front porch.

"I think it's perfect," Tony said. His eyes sparkled with excitement.

"Don't you feel it's a little creepy?" Angelo asked.

"Nah," Tony said. "My uncle's cousin had a home. I even worked there for a summer when I needed a job for the parole board. The work is definitely not your usual nine to five, but for what we have in mind, I think it's convenient. We whack him, they embalm him. It's all done in-house." Tony laughed.

"You get it?"

"Of course I get it," Angelo snapped.

"Well, let's do it," Tony said. "I can see a light on in the back. Must be the embalming room. That must be where Lanso's hiding out."

"You say you worked in a funeral home?" Angelo asked as he scanned the neighborhood for signs of trouble.

"For about two months," Tony said.

"Since you're familiar with this kind of place maybe you should go in first." He hoped it would sound as if the idea had just occurred to him. "Once you get Lanso cornered, you can flip the light on and off. Meanwhile I'll hang out here and make sure it isn't a setup."

"Sounds great," Tony said. With that, he was off.

Getting up from the cot, Jimmy Lanso stepped over to the tiny TV and turned down the sound. He thought he'd heard a noise again, just like he had the last couple of nights. He listened intently but he didn't hear anything except his own heart thumping in his chest and a slight ringing in his ears from all the aspirin he'd been taking. Not having slept for sixty or so hours except short snatches, he was a nervous, exhausted wreck. He'd been hiding out in the funeral home ever since he and Bruno abandoned their pad in Woodside after Frankie didn't return or call.

The last month had been a nightmare for Jimmy. Ever since the stupid acid episode, he'd been living in constant fear. Up until the dirty deed actually went down, he'd been convinced that his part in it would "make" his career. Instead, he seemed to have guaranteed his own death. The first terrible shock was Terry Manso's getting killed trying to get into the car. And now he'd heard that both Frankie and Bruno had ended up floating in the East River. It couldn't be long before they got him, too.

Jimmy's only hope was that his uncle had talked to Vinnie Dominick, his brother-in-law by marriage, and Vinnie had promised to take care of things. But until Jimmy heard that everything was copacetic, he couldn't relax, not for a second.

Jimmy heard a slight thump in the embalming room. It was not his imagination. With the TV turned down it had been as clear as day. He froze, wondering if he'd hear the sound again. Beads of perspiration dotted his forehead. When all remained quiet, he mustered the courage to check it out by stepping over to the door of the utility room he was using to hide out.

ROBIN COOK

Opening the door as soundlessly as possible, Jimmy let his eyes slowly roam around the unilluminated embalming room. There was a series of high windows along one wall that allowed some light in from a streetlamp, but most of the room was lost in shadow. Jimmy could see the two shrouded corpses that his cousin had embalmed that evening since they were on gurneys pushed against the wall opposite the windows. Their white sheets seemed to glow in the half-light. In the center of the room was the embalming table, but Jimmy could just make out its outline. Against the far wall was a large, glass-fronted cabinet that loomed out of the shadows. On the wall below the windows were several porcelain sinks.

With trembling fingers, Jimmy reached into the room and switched on the light. Immediately he saw the source of the noise. A large rat was on the embalming table. Disturbed in its foraging, it stared at Jimmy with angry, gleaming eyes. Then it leaped from the table and scampered to a grate in the floor and disappeared down a drain.

Jimmy felt disgusted and relieved at the same time. He hated rats, but he also hated hiding in a funeral home. The place gave him the willies and reminded him of all the horror comic books he'd read as a child. His imagination had conjured up all sorts of explanations for the noises he'd been hearing. So seeing a rat was far better than seeing one of the embalmed corpses stalking around the room like *Tales From the Crypt.*

Stepping out into the embalming room, Jimmy hurried over to a large metal box the size of a small trunk. Pushing it along the floor, he used it to cover the grate where the rat had disappeared. With that accomplished, he headed back toward his room. But he didn't get far. He heard another slight thump through the door to the supply room.

Thinking the rat had surfaced in the supply room, Jimmy grabbed the broom that he'd been using on his clean-up chores. Planning on beating the crap out of the rat, he threw open the supply room door. He even took a step forward before he froze. Blood drained from his face. In front of him was an upright figure whose features were lost in shadow.

A muffled scream issued from between Jimmy's lips as he staggered back. The broom slipped from his hands and fell to the tiled floor with a clatter. Jimmy's wildest fears had become a reality. One of the corpses had come alive.

"Hi, Jimmy," said the figure.

Panic could not overcome paralysis in Jimmy's brain. He stood rooted to the floor as the figure in front of him stepped from the shadows of the supply room along with a cold breeze from an open window.

"You look a little pale," Tony commented. He was holding his gun, but it was pointed toward the floor. "Maybe you'd better climb up on that old porcelain table and lie down." Tony pointed with his free hand toward the embalming table.

"They made me do it," Jimmy slobbered when he comprehended he was not dealing with a supernatural creature but rather a live human being obviously associated with Cerino's organization.

"Yeah, sure," Tony said in a falsely consoling tone of voice. "But get on the table just the same."

As Jimmy stepped over to the embalming table with shaky legs, Tony walked over to the wall switch and turned the light on and off several times.

"On the table!" Tony commanded when he noticed that Jimmy was hesitating.

With some effort Jimmy got himself up on the table, sitting on the edge.

"Lie down!" Tony snapped. When Jimmy did so, Tony walked over and looked down on him. "Great place to hide out," he said.

"It was all Manso's idea," Jimmy blurted out. His head

was propped up on a black rubber block. "All I did was turn the lights off. I didn't even know what was going down."

"Everybody says it was Manso's idea," Tony complained. "Of course he's the only one who didn't make it from the scene. Too bad he's not around to defend himself."

A thump in the supply room heralded Angelo's entrance. He came into the room warily, looking like a caged animal. He did not like the funeral home. "This place stinks," he said.

"That's formaldehyde," Tony said. "You get used to it. You don't even smell it after a while. Come over and meet Jimmy Lanso."

Angelo walked over to the embalming table, eyeing Jimmy with contempt. "Such a little prick," he said.

"It was Manso's idea," Jimmy insisted. "I didn't do anything."

"Who else was involved?" Angelo demanded. He wanted to be sure.

"Manso, DePasquale, and Marchese," Jimmy said. "They made me go."

"Nobody wants to take any responsibility," Angelo said with disgust. "Jimmy, I'm afraid you've got to go for a little ride."

"No, please," Jimmy begged.

Tony leaned over and whispered into Angelo's ear. Angelo glanced over at the embalming equipment, then back down at Jimmy cowering on the embalming table.

"Sounds appropriate," Angelo said with a nod. "Especially for such a gutless piece of dog turd."

"Hold him down," Tony said with glee. He darted over to the embalming equipment and turned on a pump. He watched the dials until sufficient suction was produced. Then he wheeled the aspirator over to the table.

Jimmy observed these preparations with growing alarm.

Having avoided watching any of the embalming procedures his cousin had performed, he had no idea what Tony was up to. Whatever it was, he was sure he wasn't going to like it.

Angelo leaned across his chest and held his hands down. Without giving Jimmy a chance to guess what was happening, Tony plunged the knife-sharp embalming trocar into Jimmy's abdomen and roughly rooted the tip around.

With a stifled scream Jimmy's face seemed to pull inward as his cheeks went hollow and pale. The canister on the aspirator filled with blood, bits of tissue, and partially digested food.

Feeling queasy, Angelo let go of the boy and turned away. For a second Jimmy's hands tried to grab the trocar from Tony, but they quickly went limp as the boy lapsed into unconsciousness.

"What do you think?" Tony asked as he stepped away to view his handiwork. "Pretty neat, huh? All I'd have to do is pump him full of embalming fluid with the embalming machine and he'd practically be ready for the grave."

"Let's get out of here," Angelo said. He felt a little green. "Wipe off any prints from that machine."

Five minutes later they retraced their steps and climbed back out the window. They'd considered using the door but decided against it in case it was wired.

Once in the car, Angelo began to relax. Cerino had been right. Dominick hadn't been lying. It hadn't been a setup. As he pulled away from the curb, Angelo felt a sense of accomplishment. "Well, that's the end of the acid boys," he said. "Now we have to get back to real work."

"Did you show the second list to Cerino?" Tony asked.

"Yeah, but we'll still start from the first list," Angelo said. "The second list will be easier."

"Makes no difference to me," Tony said. "But what do you say we eat first? Sitting around the Vesuvio made me hungry. How about another pizza?"

"I think we'd better get one job done first," Angelo said.

He wanted to put a little distance between the grisly scene at the Spoletto Funeral Home and his next meal.

Embroiled again in the recurrent nightmare about her brother sinking into the bottomless black mud, Laurie was thankful for her alarm's jangle that pulled her from her deep sleep. Barely awake she reached over to the alarm and turned it off. Before she could retract her arm back into the warm covers, the alarm went off again. That was when Laurie realized it wasn't the alarm. It was the telephone.

"Dr. Montgomery, this is Dr. Ted Ackerman," the caller said. "I'm sorry to bother you at this hour, but I'm the tour doctor on call and I got a message that I should call you if a certain kind of case came in."

Laurie was too bewildered to respond. Glancing down at the clock she saw it was only two-thirty in the morning. No wonder she was having a tough time getting her bearings.

"I just got a call," Ted continued. "It sounds like the demographics you had mentioned. It also sounds like cocaine. The deceased is a banker, aged thirty-one. The name is Stuart Morgan."

"Where?" Laurie asked.

"Nine-seventy Fifth Avenue," Ted said. "Do you want to take the call or shall I just go? I don't mind either way."

"I'll go," Laurie said. "Thanks." She hung up the phone and stood up. She felt miserable. Tom, on the other hand, seemed pleased to be awake. Purring contentedly, he rubbed against her legs.

Laurie threw on some clothes and grabbed a camera and several pairs of rubber gloves. She left her apartment still buttoning her coat and dreaming of returning home to climb back in bed.

Outside, Laurie found her street deserted, but First Avenue had traffic. In five minutes she was in the back of a taxi with an Afghani freedom fighter for a driver. Fifteen min-

utes later she got out of the cab at 970 Fifth. An NYPD car
and a city ambulance were pulled up on the sidewalk. Both
vehicles had their emergency lights blinking impatiently.

Inside, Laurie flashed her medical examiner's badge and
was directed to Penthouse B.

"You the medical examiner?" a uniformed policeman
asked with obvious amazement when Laurie entered the
apartment and again showed her badge. His name tag read
"Ron Moore." He was a muscular, heavyset fellow in his
late thirties.

Laurie nodded, feeling little tolerance or reserve for what
was coming.

"Hell," Ron said, "you don't look like any of the medical
examiners I've ever seen."

"Nonetheless I am," Laurie said without humor.

"Hey, Pete!" Moore yelled. "Get a load of what just
walked in. A medical examiner who looks more like a Play-
boy Bunny!"

Another uniformed but younger-appearing policeman
poked his head from around a doorway. His eyebrows went
up when he saw Laurie. "Well, I'll be damned," he said. He
had a handful of correspondence in both hands.

"Who is in charge here?" Laurie questioned.

"I am, honey," Ron said.

"My name is Dr. Montgomery," Laurie said. "Not
honey."

"Sure, Doc," Ron answered.

"Who can give me a tour of the scene?" Laurie asked.

"Might as well be me," Ron said. "This here's the living
room, obviously. Notice the drug paraphernalia on the coffee table. The victim apparently injected himself there, then
went into the kitchen. That's where the body is. You get to
the kitchen through the den."

Laurie took a quick look around the apartment. It was
tiny but beautifully decorated. From her spot in the foyer,

she could see the living room and part of the den. In the living room two large windows with a southern exposure afforded an extraordinary view. But more than the view, Laurie was interested in the clutter on the floor. It appeared that the room had been ransacked.

"Was this a robbery?" Laurie asked.

"Nah," Ron said. "We did this. Part of our usual thorough investigation, if you know what I mean."

"I'm not sure I do," Laurie said.

"We're always exhaustive in our search," Ron said.

"For what?" Laurie demanded.

"For proper identification," Ron said.

"You didn't notice all these diplomas here on the foyer walls?" Laurie questioned while making a sweeping gesture. "The name seems to be rather obvious."

"Guess we didn't see them," Ron said.

"Where's the body?" Laurie asked.

"I told you," Ron said. "It's in the kitchen." He pointed toward the den.

Laurie walked ahead, avoiding the debris on the floor, and stepped into the den. All the drawers to the desk were open. The contents looked as if they'd been roughly gone through.

"I suppose you were looking for identification in here as well?" she said.

"That's right, Doc," Ron said.

Passing through the den, Laurie walked to the threshold of the kitchen. There she stopped. The kitchen was as messy as the other rooms. The entire refrigerator was emptied, including its shelves. Laurie also noticed some clothing scattered across the floor. The refrigerator's door was slightly ajar. "Don't tell me you were looking for identification in here as well?" she asked sarcastically.

"Hell, no!" Ron said. "The victim did this himself."

"Where's the body?" Laurie asked.

"In the refrigerator," Ron said.

Laurie stepped to the refrigerator and opened the door. Ron wasn't kidding. Stuart Morgan was wedged into the refrigerator compartment. He was almost naked, clothed only in Jockey shorts, a money belt, and socks. His face was bone white. His right arm was raised, his hand balled into a tight fist.

"I can't understand why he wanted to climb into the refrigerator," Ron said. "Weirdest thing I've seen since I joined the force."

"It's called hyperpyrexia," Laurie said, staring at Stuart Morgan. "Cocaine can make people's temperature go sky high. The users get a little crazy. They'd do anything to get their temperature down. But this is the first one I've seen in a refrigerator."

"If you'll release the body we can let the ambulance boys take Stuart away," Ron said. "We're pretty much done otherwise."

"Did you touch the body?" Laurie asked suddenly.

"What are you talking about?" Ron said nervously.

"Just what I said. Did you or Pete touch the body?"

"Well . . ." Ron said. He didn't seem inclined to answer.

"It's a simple question."

"We had to find out if he were dead," Ron said. "But that was pretty easy since he was cold as one of those cucumbers on the floor."

"So you merely reached in and felt for a pulse?" Laurie suggested.

"That's right," Ron said.

"Which pulse?" Laurie asked.

"The wrist," Ron said.

"The right wrist?" Laurie asked.

"Hey, you're getting too specific," Ron said. "I can't remember which wrist."

"Let me tell you something," Laurie said as she removed

175

the lens cap from her camera and started taking pictures of the body in the refrigerator. "See that right arm in the air?"

"Yeah," Ron said.

"It's staying up in the air because of rigor mortis," Laurie said. Her camera flashed as she took a photo.

"I've heard of that," Ron said.

"But rigor mortis develops after the arm has been flaccid for a while," Laurie said. "Does that suggest something to you about this body?" Laurie took another photo from a different angle.

"I don't know what you're talking about," Ron said.

"It suggests that the body was moved after death," Laurie said. "Like perhaps out of the refrigerator and then back. And it had to be several hours after death because it takes about two hours for rigor mortis to set in."

"Well, isn't that interesting," Ron said. "Maybe Pete should hear about this." Ron went to the door to the den and yelled for Pete to come into the kitchen. When he did, Ron explained what Laurie had told him.

"Maybe this guy's girlfriend pulled him out," Pete suggested.

"This overdose was found by the deceased's girlfriend?" Laurie asked. The torture drug abusers put their loved ones through was horrible.

"That's right," Pete said. "The girlfriend called 911. So maybe she pulled him out."

"And then stuffed him back in?" Laurie questioned with skepticism. "Hardly likely."

"What do you think happened?" Ron asked.

For a moment Laurie stared at the two policemen, wondering what approach she should take.

"I don't know what to think," she said finally. She pulled on her rubber gloves. "But for now I want to examine the body, release it to the hospital people, and go home."

Laurie reached in and touched Stuart Morgan's body. It

was hard, due to the rigor mortis, and cold. As she examined him, it was obvious that his other limbs were in unnatural positions as well as the right arm. She noticed an IV site in the antecubital fossa of the left arm. Except for the refrigerator, the case certainly seemed uncannily similar to the Duncan Andrews, Robert Evans, and Marion Overstreet overdoses.

Straightening up, Laurie turned to Ron. "Would you mind helping me lift the body out of the refrigerator?" she asked.

"Pete, you help her," Ron said.

Pete made an expression of annoyance but accepted the rubber gloves from Laurie and put them on. Together they lifted Stuart Morgan from the refrigerator and laid him out on the floor.

Laurie took several more photos. To her trained mind, it was obvious from the attitude of the body that the rigor mortis had taken place while the body had been in the refrigerator. That much was clear. But it was also clear that the position the body was in when she found it was not the position it had been in originally.

As she was photographing the body, Laurie noticed that the money belt was partially open. Its zipper was caught on some paper money. She moved in for a close-up.

Putting her camera aside, Laurie bent down to examine the money belt more closely. With some difficulty, she managed to work the zipper loose and open the pouch. Inside were three single dollar bills with torn edges from having been caught in the zipper.

Standing up, Laurie handed the three dollars to Ron. "Evidence," she said.

"Evidence of what?" Ron said.

"I've heard of cases where police steal from the scenes of accidents or homicides," Laurie said. "But I'd never expected to be confronted by such an obvious case."

"What the hell are you talking about?" Ron demanded.

"The body can be moved, Sergeant Moore," Laurie said. "And I am supposed to extend an invitation to you to come and see the autopsy. Frankly, I hope I never see you again."

Laurie snapped off her rubber gloves, threw them in the trash, grabbed her camera, and left the apartment.

"I can't eat another bite," Tony said as he pushed the remains of a pizza away from him. He pulled the napkin from his collar where he'd tucked it and wiped his mouth of tomato stains. "What's the matter. You don't like pepperoni? You're eating like a bird."

Angelo sipped his San Pellegrino mineral water. Its fizz tended to settle his stomach which was still churning from the Spoletto Funeral Home visit. He'd tried several bites of the pizza, but it hadn't appealed to him. In fact it made him nauseated, so he'd been impatient for Tony to finish.

"You done?" Angelo asked Tony.

"Yeah," Tony said, sucking his teeth. "But I wouldn't mind having a coffee."

They were sitting in a small all-night Italian pizza joint in Elmhurst, not far from the Vesuvio. There was a handful of customers sitting at widely spaced Formica tables despite the fact it was three-thirty in the morning. An old-fashioned juke box was playing favorites from the fifties and sixties.

Angelo had another mineral water while Tony had a quick espresso.

"Ready?" Angelo asked when Tony's empty espresso cup clanked against the saucer. Angelo was eager to get going, but felt he owed it to Tony to relax for a while. After all, they had been busy.

"Ready," Tony said with a final wipe with his napkin. They stood up, tossed some bills on the table, and walked out into the cold November night. Tucking their heads into their coats, they dashed for the car. It had started drizzling.

With the motor running to get the heater up to temperature, Angelo took the second list from the glove compartment and scanned it. "Here's one in Kew Garden Hills," he said. "That's nice and convenient, and it should be fast and easy."

"This is going to be fun," Tony said eagerly. He burped. "Love that pepperoni."

Angelo put the sheet back into the glove compartment. As he pulled out into the deserted street, he said, "Working at night sure makes it easier to get around town."

"The only problem is getting used to sleeping all day," Tony said. He pulled out his Beretta Bantam and screwed the silencer on over the muzzle.

"Put that thing away until we get there," Angelo said. "You make me nervous."

"Just getting ready," Tony said. He tried to jam the gun back into the holster, but with its silencer it didn't quite fit. The butt stuck out of his jacket. "I've been looking forward to this part of the operation because we don't have to be so careful pussyfooting around."

"We still have to be careful," Angelo snapped. "In fact we always have to be careful."

"Calm down," Tony said. "You know what I mean. We won't have to worry about all that crazy stuff. Now it's going to be fast and we leave. I mean, boom, it's over and we're out the door." He pretended to shoot a pedestrian with his index finger extended from his hand, sighting down his knuckle.

It took them a while to find the house, a modest, two-story affair made of stone and stucco with a slate roof. It was situated on a quiet street that dead-ended into a cemetery.

"Not bad," Tony said. "These people must have a few bucks."

"And possibly an alarm system," Angelo said. He pulled

over to the side of the road and parked. "Let's hope it's nothing complicated. I don't want any complications."

"Who gets whacked?" Tony asked.

"I forgot," Angelo said. He reached over to the glove compartment and took out the second list. "The woman," he said after locating the name. He returned the list to the glove compartment. "And let's get this straight so there will be no confusion: I'll do her. They'll probably be in bed, so you cover the man. If he wakes up, whack him. You understand?"

"Of course I understand," Tony said. "What do you think I am? An imbecile? I understand perfectly. But you know how much I enjoy this stuff, so how's about I do her and you cover the man."

"Jesus H. Christ!" Angelo said. He took out his gun and attached a silencer. "This is work, not some turkey shoot. We're not here to have fun."

"What difference does it make if you whack her or I whack her?" Tony asked.

"Ultimately, no difference at all," Angelo said. "But I'm in charge, and I'm shooting the woman. I want to make sure she's dead. I'm the one who has to answer to Cerino."

"So you think you can shoot someone better than me?" Tony said. He seemed insulted.

"For Chrissake, Tony," Angelo said. "You can do the next one. How about we take turns?"

"Okay, that's fair," Tony said. "Share and share alike."

"Glad you approve," Angelo said. Then, looking briefly up at the ceiling of the car, he added: "I feel like I'm back in kindergarten. All right, let's go!"

They climbed out of the car, crossed the street, and melted into the dense, wet shrubbery surrounding the house in question. Arriving at the back door, Angelo studied it carefully, running his hand over the architrave, peering through the cracks with a small flashlight, and inspecting the hardware. He straightened up.

"No alarm," Angelo said with amazement, "unless it's something I haven't seen."

"You want to go through a window or a door?" Tony asked.

"The door should be easy enough," Angelo said.

With his pocketknife Tony made short work of the caulking around one of the glass panes bordering the door. With a pair of needle-nosed pliers, he pulled out the wire brads, then lifted the pane out. Reaching inside, he unbolted the door and turned the knob.

The door opened with only a minor squeak of protest. No alarms sounded and no vicious dogs barked. Angelo silently stepped inside, holding his gun up alongside of his head. He let his eyes roam around the room. It seemed to be a family room with gingham-covered couches and a large-screen television. He listened for a minute, then lowered his gun. After testing for alarms, he began to relax. Everything seemed to be fine; the place was there for the taking.

Motioning for Tony to follow, Angelo moved silently to the front entrance hall. Together the two men crept up a grand circular staircase. The stairs led them to an upstairs corridor with a half-dozen doors opening onto it. Each of the doors was slightly ajar save for one. Trusting his instincts, Angelo made his way straight for it. When he was sure Tony was right behind him, he tried the door. It pushed open at his touch.

Loud snores came from the bed against the far wall. Angelo wasn't sure who was snoring, but once he was convinced both were still sound asleep, he motioned for Tony to follow him. Together they advanced to the bed.

It was a king-sized bed covered with a down-filled comforter. In the bed were a man and a woman of late middle age. They were both on their backs, their arms at their sides.

Angelo veered to the right to be on the same side as the woman. Tony went to the opposite side. The victims did not stir. Angelo motioned for Tony's attention, pointing toward his Walther in the half-light of the bedroom, indicating that he was about to dispatch the woman and that Tony should keep his eye on the man.

Tony nodded. And as Angelo brought up his gun to bear on the sleeping, female head, Tony did the same across the bed. Angelo advanced the gun to the point where he'd be unable to miss, aiming at the temple, just above and in front of the ear. He wanted the bullet to penetrate into the base of the brain, approximately where it would end up if he were able to shoot her from behind.

The report was loud in relation to the silence that prevailed in the room, but when compared with normal noise, it was a soft, hissing thump, like a fist striking a pillow.

Hardly had Angelo recovered from the wince he made after pulling the trigger when there was another similar hissing thump. Out of the corner of his eye he saw the man's head rebound off the pillow, then settle back. A dark stain that looked black in the half-light began to spread.

"I couldn't help it," Tony said. "I heard you shoot and I couldn't help pulling the trigger myself. I like it. It gives me such a rush."

"You're a goddamn psychopath," Angelo said angrily. "You weren't supposed to shoot the guy unless he moved. That was the plan."

"What the hell difference does it make?" Tony said.

"The difference is that you have to learn to follow orders," Angelo snapped.

"All right already," Tony said. "I'm sorry. I couldn't help it. Next time I'll play exactly how you say."

"Let's get out of here," Angelo said. He started toward the door.

"How about looking around for some cash or valuables?" Tony asked. "After all, we're here."

"I don't want to take the time," Angelo said. At the door

to the hall he turned. "Come on, Tony! We're not here to turn a profit. Cerino's already paying us enough."

"But what Cerino doesn't know can't hurt him," Tony said. He picked up a wallet on the night-table along with a Rolex watch. "How about I take a souvenir?"

"Fine," Angelo said. "Now let's get out of here."

Three minutes later they were speeding away.

"Holy crap!" Tony exclaimed.

"What's the matter?"

"There's over five hundred big ones in here," Tony said, waving the bills in the air. He already had the gold Rolex watch on his wrist. "Add that to what Cerino is paying us and we're doing okay."

"Just be sure to get rid of that wallet," Angelo said. "It could finger us for sure."

"No problem," Tony said. "I'll drop it in the incinerator."

Angelo pulled up to the curb and put the car in park.

"Now what?" asked Tony.

Angelo leaned over and took the list out of the glove compartment. "I want to see if there's anybody else in this area," he said. "Bingo," Angelo said after a brief perusal. "Here's two in Forest Hills. That's right around the corner. We can do both before dawn no problem. I'd say that'd make it a pretty good night."

"I'd say it'd make it a fabulous night," Tony said. "I've never made this kind of money."

"All right!" Angelo said, studying a map. "I know where both of these houses are. Expensive part of town." He placed the map and the list down on the center console, put the car in gear, and drove off.

It took less than half an hour for Angelo to cruise past the first house. It was a large white mansion set far back from the street. Angelo guessed the house sat on at least two acres. Several leafless elms lined a long, curving driveway.

"Which one this time?" Tony asked as he gazed up at the big house.

"The man," Angelo said. He was trying to decide where to leave the car. In such a ritzy part of town there weren't many vehicles parked on the street. In the end, he decided to drive right up the driveway since it looped behind the house. He could park so that the car wasn't visible from the street. He turned his lights off as he came up the drive, hoping the darkened car wouldn't attract any attention.

"Now remember," Tony said as they prepared to move in. "This time it's my turn."

Angelo looked to the heavens as if to say, "Why me, God?" Then he nodded and the two went to the house.

The white mansion proved more difficult than the more modest stone house. The white mansion had several overlapping alarm systems that took Angelo some time to figure out as well as neutralize. It was a half hour before they broke out a whole sash in a window into a laundry room.

Angelo went in first to make sure there were no infrared detectors or lasers. When he determined the coast was clear, Tony climbed over the windowsill.

They stayed together and moved slowly through the kitchen, where they could hear a TV playing in a nearby room.

As carefully as possible they moved toward the sound. It was coming from a room off the front hall. Angelo went first and peered around the corner.

The room was a den with a wet bar built into one wall, a giant rear-projection TV in another. In front of the TV was a chintz-upholstered chesterfield. Asleep in the center of the couch was an enormously overweight man, dressed in a blue bathrobe. His stubby, surprisingly skinny legs stuck out from beneath the corpulent mass of his abdomen and were propped up on a hassock. On his feet were leather slippers.

Angelo pulled back to talk with Tony. "He's asleep and alone. We'll have to assume the wife, if there is one, is upstairs."

"What are we going to do?" Tony questioned.

"You wanted to whack him," Angelo said. "So go in and do it. Just do it right. Then we'll check on the woman."

Tony smiled and stepped beyond Angelo. His gun with the silencer in place was in his right hand.

Rounding the corner, Tony boldly strode into the den. He went directly up to the man on the couch. Pointing the gun at the man's temple just above the ear, he purposefully bumped the man's thigh with his leg.

The man sputtered as his heavily lidded eyes struggled up. "Gloria, dear?" he managed.

"No, honey, it's me—Tony."

The hissing thump knocked the man over onto his right side on the couch. Tony leaned over and placed the muzzle of his silencer at the base of the skull and fired again. The man didn't move.

Tony straightened up and looked back at Angelo. Angelo waved for him to follow him. Together they went up the stairs. On the second floor they had to search through several rooms before finding Gloria. She was fast asleep with the lights on but with black eyeshades over her eyes and earplugs in her ears.

"Looks like she thinks she's a movie star," Tony said. "This is going to be a snap."

"Let's go," Angelo said. He gave Tony's arm a tug.

"Aw, come on," Tony said. "She's like a sitting duck."

"I'm not going to argue," Angelo snarled. "We're getting out of here."

Back in the car, Tony pouted while Angelo checked the fastest route to the next house. Angelo didn't care how long Tony brooded. At least it kept him quiet.

The final house was a two-story row house with a metal

awning forming a carport in front of the single-car garage. A small chain-link fence demarcated a postage-stamp-sized lawn that contained two pink flamingo statues.

"The man or the woman?" Tony asked, breaking his silence for the first time.

"The woman," Angelo said. "And you can do her if you want." He was feeling magnanimous with the evening's work drawing to a close.

Breaking into the final house was a breeze. They did it from the alleyway, going through the back door. To their surprise they found the husband sleeping on the couch with an empty six-pack on the floor next to him.

Angelo told Tony to go upstairs by himself and that he'd keep his eye on the man. Angelo could see Tony's eager smile in the half-light, and he thought the kid's appetite for "whacking" was insatiable.

Several minutes later Angelo could barely hear the silenced report of Tony's gun, followed quickly by another shot. At least the kid was thorough. A few minutes after that Tony reappeared.

"The guy move?" Tony asked.

Angelo shook his head and motioned for them to leave.

"Too bad," Tony said. His eyes lingered a second on the sleeping man before he turned to follow Angelo out the door.

On the back stoop Angelo stretched and looked up at the brightening sky. "Here comes the sun," he said. "How about some breakfast?"

"Sounds great," Tony said. "What a night. It doesn't get any better than this." As he walked to the car he unscrewed his silencer from his gun.

7

□

Although she hadn't slept much thanks to her late-night call, Laurie made it a point to arrive at work a little early to compensate for having been late the day before. It was only seven forty-five as she mounted the steps to the medical examiner's office.

Going directly to the ID office, she detected a mild electricity in the air. Several of the other associate medical examiners who usually didn't come in until around eight-thirty were already on the job. Kevin Southgate and Arnold Besserman, two of the older examiners, were huddled around the coffeepot in heated debate. Kevin, a liberal, and Arnold, an arch-conservative, never agreed on anything.

"I'm telling you," Arnold was saying when Laurie squeezed through to get herself some coffee, "if we had more police on the streets, this kind of thing wouldn't happen."

"I disagree," Kevin said. "This kind of tragedy—"

"What happened now?" Laurie asked as she stirred her coffee.

"A series of homicides in Queens," Arnold said. "Gunshot wounds to the head from close range."

"Small-caliber bullets?" Laurie asked.

Arnold looked at Kevin. "I don't know about that yet."

"The posts haven't been done yet," Kevin explained.

"Were they pulled out of the river?"

"No," Arnold said. "These people were asleep in their own homes. Now, if we had more police presence—"

"Come on, Arnold!" Kevin said.

Laurie left the two to their bickering and went over to check the autopsy schedule. Sipping her coffee, she checked at who was on autopsy besides herself and what cases were assigned. After her own name were three cases, including Stuart Morgan. She was pleased. Calvin was sticking by his promise.

Noting that the other two cases were drug overdose/toxicity cases as well, Laurie flipped through the investigator's reports. She was immediately dismayed to see that profiles of the deceased resembled the previous suspicious cases. Randall Thatcher, thirty years old, was a lawyer; Valerie Abrams, thirty-three, was a stockbroker.

The day before she'd feared there'd be more cases, but she'd hoped her fears wouldn't materialize. Obviously that wasn't to be the case. Already there were three more. Overnight her modest series had jumped one hundred percent.

Laurie walked through Communications on her way to the medical forensic investigative department. Spotting the police liaison office, she wondered what she should do about the suspected thievery at the Morgan apartment. For the moment she decided to let it go. If she saw Lou she might discuss the matter with him.

Laurie found Cheryl Myers in her tiny windowless office.

"No luck so far on that Duncan Andrews case," Cheryl told her before she could say a word.

"That's not why I stopped by," Laurie said. "I left word last evening with Bart that I wanted to be called if any upscale drug overdose cases came in like Duncan Andrews or Marion Overstreet. I was called last night for one. But this morning I discovered there were two others that I wasn't called on. Have you any idea why I wasn't called?"

"No," Cheryl said. "Ted was on last night. We'll have to ask him this evening. Was there a problem?"

"Not really," Laurie admitted. "I'm just curious. Actually I probably couldn't have gone to all three scenes. And I will be handling the autopsies. By the way, did you check with the hospital about the Marion Overstreet case?"

"Sure did," Cheryl said. "I spoke with a Dr. Murray and he said that they were just following policy orders from you."

"That's what I figured," Laurie said. "But it was worth a check. Also, I have something else I'd like to ask you to do. Would you see what kind of medical records you can get, particularly surgical, on a woman by the name of Marsha Schulman. I'd love to get some X-rays. I believe she lived in Bayside, Queens. I'm not sure of her age. Let's say around forty." Ever since Jordan had told Laurie about his secretary's husband's shady dealings and arrest record, she'd had a bad feeling about the woman's disappearance, particularly in view of the odd break-in at Jordan's office.

Cheryl wrote the information down on a pad on her desk. "I'll get right on it."

Next Laurie sought out John DeVries. As she'd feared, he was less than cordial.

"I told you I'd call you," John snapped when Laurie asked about a contaminant. "I've got hundreds of cases besides yours."

"I know you're busy," Laurie said, "but this morning I

have three more overdoses like the three I had before. That brings the body count to a total of six young, affluent, well-educated career people. Something has to be in that cocaine, and we have to find it."

"You're welcome to come up here and run the tests yourself," John said. "But I want you to leave me alone. If you don't, I'll have to speak to Dr. Bingham."

"Why are you acting this way?" Laurie asked. "I've tried to be nice about this."

"You're being a pain in the neck," John said.

"Fine," Laurie said. "It's wonderful to know we have a nice cooperative atmosphere around here."

Exasperated, Laurie stalked out of the lab, grumbling under her breath. She felt a hand grip her arm and she spun around, ready to slap John DeVries for having the nerve to touch her. But it wasn't John. It was one of his young assistants, Peter Letterman.

"Could I talk to you a moment?" Peter said. He glanced warily over his shoulder.

"Of course," Laurie said.

"Come into my cubbyhole," Peter said. He motioned for Laurie to follow him. They entered what had originally been designed as a broom closet. There was barely enough room there for a desk, a computer terminal, a file cabinet, and two chairs. Peter closed the door behind them.

Peter was a thin, blond fellow with delicate features. To Laurie he appeared as the quintessential graduate student, with a marked intensity to his eyes and demeanor. Under his white lab coat was an open-necked flannel shirt.

"John is a little hard to get along with," he said.

"That's an understatement," Laurie answered.

"Lots of artists are like that," Peter continued. "And John is an artist of sorts. When it comes to chemistry and toxicology in particular, he's amazing. But I couldn't help overhearing your conversations with him. I think one of the reasons he's giving you a hard time is to make a point with the administration that he needs more funding. He's slowing up a lot of reports, and for the most part it makes little difference. I mean the people are dead. But if your suspicions are right it sounds like we could be in the lifesaving business for a change. So I'd like to help. I'll see what I can do for you even if I have to put in some overtime."

"I'd be grateful, Peter," Laurie said. "And you're right."

Peter smiled self-consciously. "We went to the same school," he said.

"Really?" Laurie said. "Where?"

"Wesleyan," Peter said. "I was two years behind you, but we shared a class. Physical chemistry."

"I'm sorry but I don't remember you," Laurie said.

"Well, I was kinda a nerd then. Anyway, I'll let you know what I come up with."

Laurie returned to her office feeling considerably more optimistic about mankind with Peter's generous offer to help. Going through the day's autopsy folders, she came up with only a few questions on two of the cases similar to her question about Marion Overstreet. Just to be thorough she called Cheryl to ask her to check them out.

After changing in her office, Laurie went down to the autopsy room. Vinnie had Stuart Morgan "up" and was well prepared for her arrival. They started work immediately.

The autopsy went smoothly. As they were finishing the internal portion, Cheryl Myers came in holding a mask to her face. Laurie glanced around to make sure Calvin wasn't in sight to complain that Cheryl had not put on scrubs. Happily he wasn't in the room.

"I had some luck with Marsha Schulman," she said, waving a set of X-rays. "She'd been treated at Manhattan General because she worked for a doctor on the staff. They had recent chest film which they sent right over. Want me to put it up?"

"Please," Laurie said. She wiped her hands on her apron

and followed Cheryl over to the X-ray view box. Cheryl stuck the X-rays into the holder and stepped to the side.

"They want them back right away," Cheryl explained. "The tech in X-ray was doing me a favor by letting them out without authorization."

Laurie scanned the X-rays. They were an AP and lateral of the chest taken two years before. The lung fields were clear and normal. The heart silhouette looked normal as well. Disappointed, Laurie was about to tell Cheryl to remove the films when she looked at the clavicles, or collarbones. The one on the right had a slight angle to it two-thirds along its length, associated with a slight increase in radiopacity. Marsha Schulman had broken her collarbone sometime in the past. Though well healed, there had definitely been a fracture.

"Vinnie," Laurie called out. "Get someone to bring the X-ray we took on the headless floater."

"See something?" Cheryl asked.

Laurie pointed out the fracture, explaining to Cheryl why it appeared as it did. Vinnie brought the requested X-ray over to the view box. He snapped the new film up next to Marsha Schulman's.

"Well, look at that!" Laurie cried. She pointed to the fractured clavicle. They were identical on both films. "I think we're looking at the same person," she said.

"Who is it?" Vinnie asked.

"The name is Marsha Schulman," Laurie said, pulling down the X-rays from the Manhattan General and handing them to Cheryl. Then she asked Cheryl to check if Marsha Schulman had had a cholecystectomy and a hysterectomy. She told her it was important and asked her to do it immediately.

Pleased with this discovery, Laurie started her second case, Randall Thatcher. As with her first case of the day, there was essentially no pathology. The autopsy went quickly and smoothly. Again Laurie was able to document with reasonable certainty that the cocaine had been taken IV. By the time they were sewing up the body, Cheryl was back in with the news that Marsha Schulman had indeed had both operations in question. In fact, both had been performed at Manhattan General.

Thrilled by this additional confirmation, Laurie finished up and went to her office to dictate the first two cases and to make several calls. First she tried Jordan's office, only to learn that Dr. Scheffield was in surgery.

"Again?" Laurie sighed. She was disappointed not to get him right away.

"He's been doing a lot of transplants lately," Jordan's nurse explained. "He always does quite a bit of surgery, but lately he's been doing even more."

Laurie left word for Jordan to call back when he could. Then she called police headquarters and asked for Lou.

To Laurie's chagrin, Lou was unavailable. Laurie left her number and asked that he return her call when he could.

Somewhat frustrated, Laurie did her dictation, then headed back to the autopsy room for her third and final case of the day. As she waited for the elevator she wondered if Bingham might be willing to change his mind about making some kind of public statement now that there were six cases.

When the elevator doors opened, Laurie literally bumped into Lou. For a moment they looked at each other with embarrassment.

"I'm sorry," she said.

"It was my fault," Lou told her. "I wasn't looking where I was going."

"I was the one who wasn't looking," Laurie said.

Then they both laughed at their self-conscious behavior.

"Were you coming to see me?" Laurie asked.

"No," Lou said. "I was looking for the Pope. Someone said he was up here on the fifth floor."

"Very funny," Laurie said, leading him back to her office. "Actually I just this minute tried to call you."

"Oh, sure!" Lou teased.

"Honest," Laurie said. She sat down at her desk. Lou took the chair he'd been in the day before. "I made an ID on the headless floater that was found with Marchese. The name is Marsha Schulman. She is Jordan Scheffield's secretary."

"You mean Dr. Roses? She was his secretary?" Lou pointed at the flowers, which had not lost any of their freshness.

"One and the same," Laurie said. "Just last night he told me that she'd not shown up for work. But he also told me that her husband, who's no Boy Scout, has ties to organized crime."

"What's the husband's name?" Lou asked.

"Danny Schulman," Laurie said.

"Could that be the Danny Schulman who owns a restaurant in Bayside?" he asked.

"That's the one," Laurie said. "Apparently he's had several brushes with the law."

"Damn right he has. He's associated with the Lucia crime family. At least they used his place to run some of their operations like fencing stolen goods, gambling, that sort of thing. We picked up old Danny-boy hoping he'd finger some of the higher-ups, but the guy took the fall without talking."

"You think his wife might have gotten killed because of his business?" Laurie asked.

"Who knows?" Lou admitted. "Threats could have been made, warnings not heeded. I'll certainly look into that angle."

"What a nasty business," Laurie said.

"That's an understatement," Lou said. "And speaking of nasty business, have you gotten any results on Frankie DePasquale's eyes? Could they document acid?"

"I'm afraid I haven't heard back yet. Dr. DeVries has not been terribly accommodating. I don't think he's looked at the specimen yet. But there is some good news: a young assistant of his is going to help me on the q.t. I think I'll finally start getting some results."

"I hope so," Lou said. "Something big is about to happen in the Queens crime world. There were four gangland-style slayings there last night. People shot in their own homes. And on top of that a friend of Frankie's and Bruno's was killed in a funeral home in Ozone Park. Whatever tensions were brewing are bubbling big time."

"I'd heard there were a number of homicides in Queens," Laurie said.

"One couple was shot right in their bed while they were sleeping. The other two, one man and one woman, were sleeping as well. As far as we can tell, none of these people had any previous association with organized crime."

"Sounds like you're not convinced."

"I'm not. The manner in which they were killed is almost an indictment. Anyway, I've got three separate detective teams working on the three cases, and this is in addition to the organized crime unit who is doing the same. We have so many people out there they are running into each other."

"Sounds like the Vaccarro and Lucia families are moving toward a showdown," Laurie said. "But you know something? Somehow mobsters offing mobsters doesn't bother me so much. At least not as much as the deaths of the accomplished people I'm seeing with this rash of cocaine overdoses. I've got three more today. That makes six."

"I guess we view things from a different perspective," Lou said. "I feel just the opposite. As far as I'm concerned, I can't get too overly sympathetic about rich, privileged people doing themselves in trying to get high. In fact I couldn't care less about druggies of any sort ODing, because they are the ones that create the demand for drugs. If it weren't for the demand there wouldn't be a drug problem. They're more to blame for this current national disaster than the starving peasant down in Peru or Colombia growing coca leaves. If the druggies knock themselves off, all the better. With each death there is that much less demand."

"I can't believe I'm hearing you correctly," Laurie snapped. "These are productive members of society that we are losing. People on whom society has spent time and money educating. And why are they dying? Because some bastard put a contaminant in the drug or cut it with something lethal. Stopping these unnecessary deaths is a lot more important than stopping a bunch of gangsters from killing each other. Hell, they're the ones who are doing a service to society."

"But not only gangsters get hurt when crime wars break out," Lou yelled. "Besides, organized crime reaches way down into our lives. In a city like New York it is all around us. Take trash collection—"

"I don't care about trash collection!" Laurie yelled. "That's the most stupid comment that I—"

All of a sudden Laurie stopped in midsentence. She realized she'd become angry, and that getting angry at Lou was ridiculous.

"I'm sorry for raising my voice," Laurie said. "I sound like I'm mad at you, but I'm not. I'm just frustrated. I can't get anyone else to share my concern about these particular overdose deaths—not even you—and I think future deaths are preventable. But at the rate I'm going we're like to have forty more ODs before anybody blinks about them."

"And I'm sorry for raising my voice," Lou said. "I suppose I'm frustrated too. I need some kind of break. Plus I have the police commissioner breathing down my back. I've only been a lieutenant on homicide for a year. I want to save lives, but I also want to save my job. I like being a policeman. I can't imagine doing anything else."

"Speaking of police," Laurie said, changing the subject, "I had a little shock last night I wanted to share with you. I'd like your advice."

Laurie described the experience she'd had the night before at Stuart Morgan's apartment. She tried to be as objective as possible since there had been no hard evidence. Yet as she told the story, especially with the three dollars remaining in the money belt, she became even more convinced that the uniformed patrolmen had stolen things from the Stuart Morgan apartment.

"That's too bad," Lou said dejectedly.

There was a pause. Laurie looked at Lou expectantly.

"Is that all you can say?" Laurie questioned finally.

"What else can I say? I hate to hear stories like that, but it happens. What can you do?"

"I thought you'd demand to know the names of the officers involved so that you could reprimand them and—"

"And what?" Lou asked. "Get them fired? I'm not going to do that. You have to expect a little thievery once in a while with the kind of money the typical uniformed patrolman pulls down. A few bucks here and there. It's like incentive pay. Remember, police work is Godawful frustrating as well as dangerous. So it's not so surprising. Not that I personally condone it, but you have to expect some."

"That sounds like convenient morality," Laurie said. "When you start allowing the 'good guys' to break the law, where do you stop? And not only is this kind of thievery morally objectionable, it's also a disaster from a medical-legal point of view. These guys mucked around with a scene, distorting and destroying evidence."

"It's bad and it's wrong, but I'm not about to make an issue about this kind of illicit behavior at a drug overdose

197

scene. I'd feel differently if it had been a homicide. I'm sure the officers would too."

"I can't believe what a double standard you have! Any drug user can drop dead as far as you're concerned, and if cops steal from a victim before the M.E. arrives, so much the better."

"I'm sorry to disappoint you," Lou said, "but this is just the way I feel. You asked me how I felt, I've told you. If you want to pursue the matter, I suggest you call Internal Affairs at police headquarters and tell the story to them. Me, I'd rather concentrate on serious bad guys."

"Once again I can't believe I'm hearing you correctly," Laurie said. "I'm floored. What am I, too naive?"

"I take the fifth amendment," Lou said, trying to lighten the atmosphere. "But I tell you what. Why don't we discuss it further this evening. How about dinner tonight?"

"I have plans," Laurie said.

"Of course," Lou said. "How silly of me to think you might be available. I suppose it is Dr. Roses again. But don't tell me. What's left of my ego couldn't take it. With his limo and all, he's probably taking you to those places where I couldn't afford to check my coat. Like I said yesterday, let me know if your lab decides to do any of the tests that might show anything. Ciao!"

With that, Lou got up and left the room. Laurie was happy to see him go. He could be so irritating. If he wanted to take personally her turning him down for that evening, he was welcome to. What did he expect her to do? Drop everything?

She was about to call Internal Affairs as Lou had facetiously suggested, but before she could pick up the receiver, the phone rang. It was Jordan returning her call.

"I hope you didn't call to cancel for tonight," he said.

"Nothing like that," Laurie said. "It's about your secretary, Marsha Schulman."

"You mean my former secretary," Jordan said. "She didn't show up or call this morning either, so I'm in the process of replacing her. I already have a temp."

"I'm afraid she's dead," Laurie said.

"Oh, no!" Jordan said. "Are you serious?"

Laurie explained how she had made the identification of the headless corpse with the chest X-ray, and the fact of the two surgeries.

"The forensic medical investigators are following up to make the identification even more certain," Laurie said, "but with what we have already, I think we can be quite confident."

"I wonder if that bastard husband was involved," Jordan wondered aloud.

"I'm sure the police will be looking into the possibility," Laurie said. "Anyway, I thought you should know."

"I'm not sure I want to know," Jordan said. "What horrible news."

"Sorry to be the bearer of sad tidings," Laurie said.

"It's not your fault," Jordan said. "And I had to be told. Anyway, I'll still see you at eight."

"Eight it is."

Laurie hung up and dialed Internal Affairs. She spoke to a disinterested secretary who took down the details of her story, promising to pass them along to her boss.

Laurie sat at her desk to compose her thoughts before returning to the autopsy room for her last case. She was beginning to feel overwhelmed. It felt as if every aspect of her life—personal, professional, ethical—was spinning out of control.

"I'm Lieutenant Lou Soldano," Lou said politely. He passed his credentials to the bright-eyed secretary at the reception desk.

"Homicide?" she asked.

"That's right," Lou said. "I'd like to speak with the doctor. I only need a few minutes of his time."

"If you'll have a seat in the waiting room, I'll let him know you're here."

Lou sat down and idly flipped through a recent edition of *The New Yorker*. He noticed the drawings on the walls, especially one that was blatantly pornographic. He wondered if someone had actually chosen them or if they had come with the office. Either way, thought Lou, there was no accounting for some people's taste.

Other than the drawings, Lou was impressed with the waiting room. The walls were paneled with mahogany. A tasteful, inch-thick oriental carpet covered the floor. But then Lou already knew the good doctor did quite well for himself.

Lou looked at the faces of the patients who paid for this opulence, plus the limo and the roses. There were about ten in the waiting room, some with eyepatches, some who looked totally healthy, including one middle-aged woman draped in jewels. Lou would have loved to ask her what she was there for, just to get an idea, but he didn't dare.

Time passed slowly as one by one the patients disappeared into the depths of the office. Lou tried to contain his impatience, but after three-quarters of an hour, he began to get irritated. He began to think it was a deliberate snub on Jordan Scheffield's part. Although Lou didn't have an appointment, he'd expected to be seen relatively quickly, perhaps to schedule a future visit if it were needed. It wasn't every day a detective lieutenant from Homicide dropped by someone's office. Besides, Lou hadn't planned on taking much of the doctor's time.

Lou's reason for the visit was twofold. He wanted to find out more about Marsha Schulman, but he also wanted to talk about Paul Cerino. It was a kind of fishing trip; the doctor might be able to fill him in on some details he didn't yet know. He resisted the nagging thought at the back of his mind: he was really there to check out the guy who was seeing Doctor Laurie Montgomery every night for dinner.

"Mr. Soldano," the secretary said at last, "Dr. Scheffield will see you now."

"It's about time," Lou mumbled as he got to his feet and tossed his magazine aside. He walked toward the door being held open by the secretary. It wasn't the same door that all the patients had disappeared into.

After a short hall, Lou was shown into Jordan's private office. He strode into the center of the room. Behind him he heard the door close.

Lou looked at the top of Jordan's blond head. The doctor was writing in a record.

"Sit down," Jordan said without looking up.

Lou debated what he wanted to do. The idea of disregarding what sounded more like a command than an offer appealed to him, so he stayed where he was. His eyes roamed the office. He was impressed and couldn't help compare the environment with his own utilitarian, metal-desked, peeling-walled rathole. Who said life was fair? Lou mused.

Redirecting his attention to the doctor, Lou couldn't tell much other than that the man was well groomed. He was dressed in a typical doctor white coat that appeared to be whiter than white and starched to boardlike stiffness. On his ring finger he wore a large gold signet ring, probably from some fancy school.

Jordan finished his writing and meticulously organized the pages of the record before folding over its cover. Then he looked up. He appeared genuinely surprised that Lou was still standing in the middle of his office, hat in hand.

"Please," Jordan said. He got to his feet and gestured toward one of the two chairs facing his desk. "Sit down. Sorry to have made you wait, but I'm tremendously busy these days. Lots of surgery. What can I do for you? I suppose you are here about my secretary, Marsha Schulman. Tragic situation. I hope you people are planning on looking into her husband's probable involvement."

Lou's eyes traveled up to Jordan's face. He was dismayed the man was so tall. It made him feel short by comparison, although he was almost six feet himself.

"What do you know about Mr. Schulman?" Lou asked. With Jordan's more cordial offer, Lou sat down. Jordan did the same. Lou listened while Jordan told all he knew about Marsha's husband. Since Lou already knew considerably more than Jordan, he took the time to observe the "good" doctor, noticing things like a mild yet probably fake English accent. Before Jordan had even finished talking about Danny Schulman, Lou had decided that Jordan was a pompous, affected, arrogant creep. Lou couldn't understand what a down-to-earth girl like Laurie could see in him.

Lou decided it was time to change the subject. "What about Paul Cerino?" he asked.

Jordan hesitated for a moment. He was surprised at the mention of Paul's name. "Pardon me for asking," he said, "but what does Mr. Cerino have to do with anything?"

Lou was glad to see Jordan squirm. "I'd appreciate your telling me all you know about Mr. Cerino."

"Mr. Cerino is a patient," Jordan said stiffly.

"I already know that," Lou said. "I'd like to hear how his treatment is coming along."

"I don't talk about my patients," Jordan said coldly.

"Really?" Lou asked, raising his eyebrows. "That's not what I've heard. In fact, I have it from a reliable source that you've been discussing Mr. Cerino's case in detail."

Jordan's lips narrowed some.

"But we can leave that subject for the moment," Lou said. "I also wanted to ask if you or any of your staff had been the subject of any extortion attempt."

"Absolutely not," Jordan said. He laughed nervously. "Why would anyone threaten me?"

"When you start involving yourself with people like Cerino, things like extortion have a way of happening. Could your secretary have been threatened in some way?"

"For what?"

"I don't know," Lou said. "You tell me."

"Cerino wouldn't want to extort me or any of my employees. I'm taking care of the man. I'm helping him."

"These organized-crime people think differently than normal people," Lou said. "They consider themselves special and above the law: in fact above everything. If they don't get exactly what they want, they kill you. If they do get what they want but decide they don't like you or they owe you too much money, they kill you."

"Well, I'm certainly giving them what they want."

"Whatever you say, Doc. I'm just trying to explore all the angles. You've got one dead secretary and somebody whacked her rather brutally. And whoever did it didn't want anyone finding out who she was anytime soon. I want to know why."

"Well, all I can tell you is I'm quite certain Marsha's disappearance, or death, hasn't anything to do with Mr. Cerino. Now if you'll kindly excuse me, I have patients to attend to. If you have any additional questions, perhaps you should contact me through my attorney."

"Sure, Doc, sure," Lou said. "I'll be on my way. But a word to the wise: I'd be very careful where Paul Cerino is concerned. The Mafia may seem glamorous when you read about them or see them in the movies, but I think you'd develop a different point of view if you got a glimpse of what Mrs. Schulman looks like now. And one last piece of advice. I'd be careful about sending him a bill. Thank you for your time, Doctor."

Lou walked out of the building, embarrassed to an extent that he had come. It had been a worthless encounter that had only annoyed him. He couldn't stand pompous silver-spoon-fed fools like Jordan Scheffield. If he got into trouble with Paul Cerino, it was his own fault. He was so full of his own self-importance that he couldn't see the danger.

Half an hour later Lou arrived at his office at police headquarters. For a moment he stood on the threshold, surveying the mess within. His digs were a far cry from Jordan Scheffield's posh surroundings. The furniture was the usual gray metal, city issue with the burns from innumerable cigarettes left on the edges and with stains from spilled coffee. The floor was dried and cracked linoleum. The walls had been painted years previously in a pale green that had blistered from a water leak from the floor above. Papers and reports were stacked on every horizontal surface, since the file cabinets were full.

Lou had never thought much about his office, but today it seemed oppressively dingy. It was irrational, he knew, but he got mad at the smug doctor all over again.

Just then Harvey Lawson, another detective lieutenant on the force, interrupted Lou's thoughts. "Hey, Lou," Harvey called, "you know that broad you were talking about yesterday? The one from the medical examiner's office?"

"Yeah?"

"I just heard she called Internal Affairs. Made some beef about two uniformed guys stealing from an overdose scene. What do you think of that?"

Tony and Angelo were back in Angelo's Town Car. They were parked across the street from the Greenblatt Pavilion of Manhattan General Hospital. The Greenblatt Pavilion was the fancy part of the hospital where pampered, wealthy patients could order from special menus that included amenities such as wine, provided their doctors permitted such treats as part of their diet.

It was 2:48 in the afternoon and Tony and Angelo were

exhausted. They'd hoped to sleep after their busy night, but Paul Cerino had other plans for them.

"What time did Doc Travino say we should pull this off?" Tony asked.

"Three o'clock," Angelo said. "Supposedly that's the time there's most confusion in the hospital. That's when the day shift of nurses are getting ready to leave and the evening shift is just coming on."

"If that's what the doc says, it's good enough for me."

"I don't like it," Angelo said. "I still think it's too risky." He surveyed the vicinity with wary eyes. There was a lot of activity and plenty of cops. In the ten minutes they'd been parked there, Angelo had spotted three squad cars cruising by.

"Think of it as a challenge," Tony suggested. "And think about all the money we're getting."

"I like working at night better," Angelo said. "And I don't need any challenges at this point of my life. Besides, I should be sleeping right this minute. I shouldn't be working when I'm so tired. I might make a mistake."

"Lighten up," Tony said. "This should be fun."

But Angelo wouldn't let it go. "I got a bad feeling about this job," he said. "Maybe we should just go home and sleep. We got another big night ahead of us tonight."

"Why don't you wait here and I'll go in by myself. I'll still split the money with you."

Angelo bit his lip. It was tempting to send the kid into the hospital alone, but if anything went wrong he knew Cerino would be furious. And even under the best circumstances, if Tony went in by himself, there was a good chance things would go awry. Reluctantly, Angelo came to the conclusion that he really didn't have a choice.

"Thanks for the offer," Angelo said, scanning the neighborhood once more, "but I think we should do this together." It was then that Angelo turned to Tony and saw, to his horror, that Tony had his gun out. He was checking the magazine.

"For Chrissake!" Angelo shouted. "Put your goddamn gun away. What if someone was to walk by the car and see you monkeying around with that thing? There's cops all over this place."

"All right already," Tony exclaimed. He clicked the magazine back into his gun and slipped the gun into its holster. "You are in one hell of a bad mood. I looked around before I took my piece out. What do you think I am, a moron? There's nobody anywhere near this car."

Angelo closed his eyes and tried to calm himself. His headache was getting worse. His nerves were frayed. He hated being so tired.

"It's getting close to three," Tony said.

"All right," Angelo said. "You remember the plan of what we're going to do when we get inside the hospital?"

"I remember what we're supposed to do," Tony repeated. "No problem."

"All right," Angelo said again. "Let's do it."

They got out of the car. Angelo gave one more glance around the immediate area. Satisfied, he led Tony across the street and into the lobby of bustling Manhattan General Hospital.

Their first stop was the hospitality shop, where Angelo purchased two bunches of cut flowers. Handing one to Tony, Angelo carried the other. Taking the flowers back to the entrance area, they waited in line for information.

"Mary O'Connor," Angelo said politely once it was his turn.

"Five zero seven," the desk attendant told him after consulting her computer screen.

Joining the crowd at the elevators, Tony leaned toward Angelo and whispered: "So far so good."

Angelo glowered at Tony again, but said nothing. Nurses

just coming on duty had them surrounded. It was no time
for a reprimand. At the fifth floor Angelo and Tony got off
the elevator along with three nurses.

Angelo waited to see which way the nurses went, then
chose the opposite direction. He immediately saw that
room 507 was the other way, but he walked until the nurses
had reached the busy nurses' station before retracing his
steps.

Angelo behaved as if he knew exactly where he was
going. He sauntered past the nurses' station without so
much as a glance in its direction.

Once beyond the nurses' station, it was easy to find 507.
Slowing down, Angelo glanced inside. Satisfied that no staff
was in the room, he stepped over the threshold and looked
at the woman in the bed. She was watching a TV mounted
on a mechanical arm attached to the bed frame.

The woman had an eyepatch over one eye. Her un-
protected eye switched its attention from the TV to Angelo.
She gave him a questioning look.

"Good afternoon, Mrs. O'Connor," Angelo said affably.
"You have a visitor."

Angelo waved for Tony to come into the room.

"Who are you?" Mrs. O'Connor asked.

Tony came smiling into the room with his bouquet of
flowers out in front of him. Mrs. O'Connor's eyes went
from Angelo to Tony. She smiled.

"I think you must have the wrong room," she said.
"Maybe the wrong O'Connor."

"Oh?" Angelo questioned. "Aren't you the O'Connor
who's scheduled for surgery later today?"

"Yes," Mrs. O'Connor said, "but I don't know either of
you. Do I?"

"I can't imagine you do," Angelo said. He stepped back
to the door and looked up and down the hall. The nurses'
station was still a flurry of activity. No one was coming the

other way. "I think it's time for Mrs. O'Connor's treatment."

Tony's smile broadened. He laid his flowers on the night table.

"What treatment?" Mrs. O'Connor asked.

"Relaxation therapy," Tony said. "Let me take your pillow."

"Did Dr. Scheffield order this?" Although she was suspicious, Mrs. O'Connor did not resist as Tony pulled the pillow from beneath her head. She wasn't accustomed to second-guessing her physicians.

"Not exactly," Tony said.

The confession emboldened Mrs. O'Connor. "I'd like to speak with Nurse Lang," she began to say. But she didn't get a chance to finish. Tony crammed the pillow down over her face, then sat on her chest.

A few muffled sounds followed, but Mrs. O'Connor didn't struggle for long. She kicked several times, but the move seemed less defensive than an uncontrollable reaction to being deprived of air.

Angelo acted as lookout throughout. He kept his eyes on the nurses' station. No problem there. The nurses were engrossed in conversation. Angelo looked down the hall in the other direction. His heart missed a beat when he spotted a middle-aged woman approaching 507 pushing a cartful of water pitchers. She was only fifteen feet away.

Stepping back into the room, Angelo closed the door. Tony hadn't quite finished dispensing his "treatment." He was still sitting on top of Mrs. O'Connor.

"Someone's coming!" Angelo warned him. He pulled his gun from his pocket and fumbled with the silencer.

Tony kept pressure on the pillow. There was a knock at the door.

Angelo motioned toward the bathroom. "Come on," he urged in a whisper when Tony failed to follow him in. After another ten seconds there was a second knock. Tony reluctantly lifted the pillow. Mary O'Connor was blue and motionless. Her unpatched eye stared blankly at the ceiling.

Frantically Angelo motioned for Tony to join him in the bathroom as a third knock sounded. Then, as the door to the hall opened, Tony pushed off the bed and crowded into the bathroom, forcing Angelo to straddle the toilet. Tony pulled the bathroom door partially closed as the woman with the cart of water pitchers entered the room.

Angelo had his gun ready. The silencer was in place. He did not like the idea of using it, but he was afraid he didn't have any choice. With the bathroom door open a fraction of an inch, he was able to watch as the woman switched O'Connor's water pitcher for a fresh one. He held his breath. The woman was only a few feet away. His plan was to wait for her to spot Mrs. O'Connor before he made his move. To his surprise, the woman disappeared from view without so much as a glance in Mrs. O'Connor's direction.

After waiting for a full minute, Angelo told Tony to take a careful peek.

Slowly Tony opened the bathroom door enough so that he could get his head around the door.

"She's gone," Tony said.

"Let's get out of here," Angelo said.

Exiting the bathroom, Tony paused at the bedside. "You think she's dead?" he questioned.

"You can't be that blue and still be alive," Angelo said. "Come on. Grab your flowers. I want to be long gone before they find her."

They made it to the car without incident. Angelo was thinking it was a good thing he'd gone in. Trigger-happy Tony would have left a trail of bodies in his wake.

Angelo was just pulling away from the curb when Tony confided in him. "Smothering wasn't bad. But I still like shooting them better. It's surer, quicker, and definitely more satisfying."

* * *

Lou took out a cigarette and lit up. He didn't even feel like smoking particularly. He was just interested in killing time. The meeting was to have started half an hour earlier but officers were still drifting in. The subject was the three gangland-style executions that had occurred in Queens overnight. Lou had thought the cases would have inspired a sense of urgency in the department, but three detectives were missing.

"Screw them," Lou said finally, referring to the missing officers. He motioned to Norman Carver, a detective sergeant, to start. Norman was nominally in charge of the investigation, although in point of fact the three units covering the cases were acting independently.

"I'm afraid we don't have much," Norman said. "The only link we've established between the three cases, other than the manner of murder, is that each of the men was involved in the restaurant business in one way or another, either as an owner, partner, or supplier."

"That's not much of an association," Lou commented. "Let's review each case."

"The first one was the Goldburgs in Kew Gardens," Norman said. "Both Harry and Martha Goldburg were shot dead in their sleep. The preliminary report suggests two guns were involved."

"And Harry's occupation?" Lou asked.

"Owned a successful restaurant here in Manhattan," Norman said. "Place is called La Dolce Vita. East side. Fifty-fourth. He was partners with an Anthony DeBartollo. So far we've come up with no problems, financial or personal, involving the partnership or the restaurant."

"Next," Lou said.

"Steven Vivonetto of Forest Hills," Norman said. "Owned a chain of fast-food joints all over Nassau County called Pasta Pronto. Again no financial problems that we've come across, but these are all just preliminaries."

"And finally."

"Janice Singleton, also of Forest Hills," Norman said. "Married to Chester Singleton. He has a restaurant-purveyor business and was recently picked up by the Vivonetto chain as a supplier. Again, no financial problems. In fact things had been looking up with the Pasta Pronto account."

"Who'd been supplying the Pasta Pronto before Singleton?" Lou asked.

"Don't know that yet," Norman said.

"I think we should find that out," Lou said. "Did the Singletons and the Vivonettos know each other personally?"

"We haven't established that yet," Norman said. "But we will."

"What about any organized-crime associations?" Lou asked. "The way these people were killed certainly suggests as much."

"That's what we thought when we started," Norman said. He glanced around at the five other men in the room. They all nodded. "But we've found almost nothing. A couple of the restaurants that Singleton supplied have some loose association, but nothing major."

Lou sighed. "There's got to be some connection linking the three."

"I agree," Norman said. "The slugs we got from the medical examiners suggest that Harry Goldburg, Steven Vivonetto, and Janice Singleton were shot with the same gun, Martha Goldburg from another. But that's not the ballistics report. It's just from preliminary examination. But they were all the same caliber. So we have a strong suspicion the same people were behind all three murders."

"What about burglary?" Lou asked.

"Relatives of the Goldburgs say that Harry had a big gold Rolex. We haven't found it. Also his wallet could not be located. But at the other scenes, nothing seems to have been taken."

"Seems that the answer has to be in the restaurant connection," Lou said. "Get detailed financial statements on all the operations. Also try to find out if these guys had been subjected to extortion or other threats. And do it sooner rather than later. The commissioner is on my back."

"We've got people working around the clock," Norman said.

Lou nodded.

Norman handed a typewritten sheet to Lou. "Here's a summary of what I just told you. Sorry for the typos."

Lou read it over quickly. He took a thoughtful drag on his cigarette. Something big and bad was going on in Queens. There was no doubt about it. He wondered if these murders could have had anything to do with Paul Cerino. It seemed unlikely. But then Lou thought of Marsha Schulman. He wondered if any of the deceased were acquainted with her husband, Danny. It was a long shot, but there was a chance he was the connecting thread.

8

□

3:00 P.M., THURSDAY
MANHATTAN

After getting a cup of coffee from the ID office that looked
more like sludge than coffee by that time of the day, Laurie
pushed her way into the Thursday afternoon conference
which was held in the conference room connected to Bingham's office. This was the one opportunity for all the city's
medical examiners to get together and share cases and discuss diagnostic problems. Although the office of the chief
medical examiner handled deaths in the Bronx as well as
Manhattan, the boroughs of Queens, Brooklyn, and Staten
Island had their own offices. Thursday was the day they all
got together. Coming to the conference was not an option.
As far as Bingham was concerned, it was a command per-
formance.

As usual, Laurie took a seat near to the door. When the
discussions became too administrative or political for her
taste, she liked to slip away.

213

The most interesting part of these weekly conferences usually occurred before the meeting was called to order. It was in these casual conversations beforehand that Laurie was able to pick up interesting tidbits and details of particularly baffling or gruesome cases. In that respect, this Thursday's meeting proved no different.

"I'd thought I'd seen it all," Dick Katzenburg told Paul Plodgett and Kevin Southgate. Dick was a senior medical examiner assigned to the Queens office. Laurie's ears perked up.

"It was the weirdest homicide I'd seen," Dick continued. "And God knows I've seen some strange ones."

"Are you going to tell us or do we have to beg?" Kevin asked, obviously as eager for the story. Medical examiners loved to swap "war stories" that were either intellectually stimulating or grotesquely bizarre.

"It was a young guy," Dick said. "Done in a funeral home with the aspirator that they use for embalming."

"He was bludgeoned to death?" Kevin asked. So far he was unimpressed.

"No!" Dick said. "With the trocar. The aspirator was running. It was as if the kid was embalmed alive."

"Ugh," Paul said, obviously impressed. "That *is* weird. It reminds me of the case—"

"Dr. Montgomery," a voice called.

Laurie turned. Dr. Bingham stood before her. "I'm afraid there is something else I have to discuss with you," he said.

Laurie felt queasy. She wondered what she'd done now.

"Dr. DeVries came to see me," Bingham said. "He complained that you have been coming in his lab bothering him about some test results. Now I know that you are eager for those results, but you're not the only one waiting. Dr. DeVries is swamped right now. I don't think I have to tell you. But don't expect special treatment.

You're going to have to wait like everyone else. I'll thank you not to harass Dr. DeVries any further. Do I make myself clear?"

Laurie was tempted to say something like DeVries had a hell of a way of going after more funding, but Bingham turned away. Before Laurie had a chance to dwell on this, her third reprimand in four days, Bingham called the meeting to order.

Bingham began the conference, as usual, by summarizing the statistics for the previous week. Then he gave a short report on the status of the Central Park murder case since it had been so much in the news. He again rebutted the media's charges of mismanagement of the case on the part of the medical examiner's office. He concluded by advising everyone not to offer any personal opinions.

Laurie was certain that last remark was directed at her. Who else had been offering opinions from within the medical examiner's ranks?

Following Bingham's talk, Calvin spoke about administrative issues, particularly concerning how reduced city funding was affecting operations. Every other week one service or supply was being curtailed or eliminated.

Following Calvin's talk, each of the deputy medical examiners from the other borough offices gave summaries. Some of the people present yawned, others nodded off.

When the borough chiefs were finished, the floor was opened up for general discussion. Dick Katzenburg described a few cases, including the rather grisly one at the Queens funeral home.

Once he was through, Laurie cleared her throat and began to address the group. She presented her six overdose cases as succinctly as possible, careful to delineate the demographic differences that set them apart from usual overdoses. Laurie described the deceased as single yuppies whose drug use came as a surprise to friends and family. She explained the cocaine was mainlined although not mixed with heroin.

"My concern," Laurie said, avoiding looking at Bingham, "is that we are seeing the beginning of a series of unusual overdose deaths. I suspect a contaminant in the drug is to blame, but so far none has been found. What I'd like to request is that if anybody sees any cases similar to the ones I've described, please send them to me."

"I've seen four myself over the last several weeks," Dick said once Laurie was through. "Since we see so many overdose/toxicity cases I didn't give the demographics much thought. But now that you mention it, all four seemed like overachievers. In fact, two were professionals. And three of the four took the cocaine intravenously, the fourth orally."

"Orally?" someone echoed with surprise. "An oral cocaine overdose? That's pretty uncommon. You usually only see that in drug-smuggling 'mules' coming from South America whose condoms break."

"I'm never surprised what druggies do," Dick said. "One of the cases that I had was found wedged in the refrigerator. Apparently he got so hot, he had to crawl into the ice box for relief."

"One of mine climbed into a refrigerator, too," Laurie said.

"I had one also," Jim Bennett said. He was the chief at the Brooklyn office. "And now that I think about it, I had another who ran out into the street stark naked before he had a terminal seizure. He'd taken the drug orally but only after attempting to take it IV."

"Did these two cases have the same unlikely demographics for a drug overdose?" Laurie asked Jim.

"Sure did," Jim said. "The man who ran out in the street was a successful lawyer. And the families in both cases swore up and down that the deceased didn't do drugs."

Laurie looked to Margaret Hauptman, who headed the

Staten Island office. "Have you seen any similar cases?" she asked.

Margaret shook her head.

Laurie asked Dick and Jim if they would mind faxing over the records on the cases they'd described. They immediately said that they would.

"One thing I have to mention," Dick said. "In three out of four I've had a lot of pressure from the involved families to sign the case out as natural."

"That's a point I want to underline," Bingham said, speaking for the first time since the beginning of the discussion. "With upscale overdose deaths like these the families will certainly want to keep the whole episode low profile. I think we should cooperate in this regard. Politically we cannot afford to alienate this constituency."

"I don't know what to make of this refrigerator aspect," Laurie said. "Although it brings me back to the contaminant idea. Perhaps there is some chemical that has a synergistic effect with cocaine vis-à-vis causing hyperpyrexia. At any rate I'm concerned that all these deaths are coming from the same source of the drug. Now that we have this many cases we ought to be able to prove it by comparing the percentages of its natural hydrolysates. Of course we will need the lab to cooperate."

Laurie looked nervously at Bingham to see if his expression changed with her reference to the lab. It didn't.

"I don't think a contaminant is a given," Dick said. "Cocaine is fully capable of causing these deaths all by itself. On the four cases I've seen, the serum level was high. Very high. These people took big doses. Maybe the cocaine wasn't cut with anything; maybe it was one-hundred-percent pure. We've all seen that kind of death with heroin."

"I still think a contaminant is involved," Laurie said. "With the general intelligence of this group of victims, it's hard for me to believe that so many would mess up if it were purely dose related."

Dick shrugged. "You may be right," he admitted. "All I'm saying is let's not jump to hasty conclusions."

Leaving the conference, Laurie felt a strange and disturbing mixture of excitement, yet a renewed frustration and anxiety. Within a couple of hours her "series" had doubled from six cases to twelve. That was ominous. Her intuition about the number of cases increasing was already coming to pass, and at an alarming rate.

Now, even more than before, Laurie felt that the public had to be warned, especially this group of yuppie types. The problem was how to do it. Certainly she dared not go back to Bingham. But she had to do something.

Suddenly she thought of Lou. The police had a whole division devoted to drugs and vice. Perhaps that division had a way of putting out the word that a certain drug was particularly dangerous. With growing resolve, she went to her office and dialed Lou immediately. When he answered, she felt relieved.

"I'm so glad you're still there," she said with a sigh.

"You are?" Lou asked.

"I want to come right down and talk to you," Laurie said.

"You do?"

"Will you wait for me?" Laurie demanded.

"Sure," Lou said. He was puzzled and elated at the same time. "Come on down."

Laurie hung up the phone, grabbed her briefcase, opened it, threw in some half-finished records, snapped it shut, snatched her coat, and literally ran down to the elevator.

A slight rain was falling as she stepped out onto First Avenue. She despaired of catching a cab, but as luck would have it, one pulled up to the curb and let off a passenger right in front of her. Laurie got in before the passenger had a chance to close the door.

Never having been to New York City police headquarters, Laurie was surprised to find it a relatively modern brick structure. Entering the front entrance, she had to sign in while a security person called up to Lou to make sure she was expected. Then they went through her briefcase. Armed with a visitor's pass and directions, she found his office. Like the entire building, it reeked of cigarette smoke.

"Can I take your coat?" Lou asked as she stepped inside. Lou took the coat and hung it on a coatrack. While he was doing so he caught Harvey Lawson giving him a dirty look from across the hall. Lou closed his office door.

"You sounded excited on the phone," Lou commented as he went around behind his desk. Laurie had taken one of the two straight-backed chairs. Her briefcase was on the floor next to her.

"I need your help," Laurie said. She was intense and obviously nervous, clutching her hands in her lap.

"Oh, really?" Lou commented. "I was hoping this excitement had something to do with dinner tonight, like you had changed your mind." He couldn't keep the sarcasm from his voice. He was obviously disappointed.

"My 'series' has doubled," Laurie said. "There are now twelve cases, not six."

"That's interesting," Lou said flatly.

"I was hoping that you might know some way we can warn the public," Laurie said. "I think we're about to see a flood of these cases unless something is done, and done soon."

"What would you have me do?" Lou asked. "Have an ad posted in *The Wall Street Journal:* 'Yuppies, Just Say No'?"

"Lou, I'm serious," Laurie said. "I'm truly worried about this."

Lou sighed. He took out a cigarette and lit up.

"Must you smoke?" Laurie asked him. "I'll only be here a few moments."

"Jesus Christ," Lou snapped. "It's my office."

"Then try to blow the smoke away, please," Laurie said.

"I'll ask you again," Lou said. "What do you want me to do? You must have had something in mind if you bothered coming all the way down here."

"No, nothing specific," Laurie admitted. "I just thought the police narcotics squad might have some way of warning the public. Couldn't they make some kind of announcement to the press?"

"Why doesn't the medical examiner's office do it?" Lou asked. "The police are around to arrest people with drugs, not help them."

"The chief refuses to take a public stand so far. I'm sure he'll come around, but in the meantime lives are being lost."

Lou took a drag on his cigarette and blew the smoke over his shoulder. "What about the other medical examiners? Are they as convinced as you about this thing exploding into a glut of dead yuppies?"

"I haven't polled them," Laurie said.

"Don't you think you might be a little overly sensitive about these deaths because of your brother?" Lou offered.

Laurie became enraged. "I didn't come down here for you to play amateur psychologist. But while we're on the subject, sure, I'm sensitive. I know how it feels to lose a loved one to drugs. But I would say that kind of empathy is a boon to my work. Maybe if a few more jaded policemen like yourself had a little more empathy, we civil servants would be in the business of saving lives instead of picking corpses' pockets."

Lou held his temper. "Frankly, Dr. Montgomery, I'd love to be in the lifesaving business. In fact, I already consider myself to be in the lifesaving business. But unless you furnish me with more proof as to this grand contaminant theory of yours, I'm afraid Narcotics won't do anything more than laugh me back to Homicide."

"Isn't there anything you can do?"

"Me? A detective lieutenant in Homicide?" Lou was exasperated but he knew Laurie was genuinely concerned. "Can't you go to the media?"

"I can't," Laurie said. "If I go to the media behind Dr. Bingham's back, I'll be looking for work. That much I know. We already had a run-in about that. How about you?"

"Me?" Lou questioned with surprise. "A homicide lieutenant suddenly involved with drug overdoses! They'd want names and where I got them, and I'd have to say I got them from you. Besides my bosses would wonder why I was worried about druggies and not solving the problem with the gangland slayings. No, I can't go either. If I went to the media I'd probably be out looking for work as well."

"Won't you try talking with the narcotics division?" Laurie asked.

"I got an idea," Lou said. "What about your boyfriend, the doctor. It's sorta natural that a doctor would be interested in this kind of problem. Besides he seems to be pretty high profile with a limo and that posh office."

"Jordan is not my boyfriend," Laurie said. "He's a male acquaintance. And how do you know about his office?"

"I went to see him this afternoon," Lou said.

"Why?" Laurie asked.

"You want the truth or what I told myself?" Lou said.

"How about both," Laurie said.

"I wanted to ask him about his patient Paul Cerino," Lou said. "And also about his secretary now that she is a homicide victim. But I was also curious to meet the guy. And if you want my opinion, he's a creep."

"I don't want your opinion," Laurie snapped.

"What I don't understand," Lou persisted, "is why you'd be interested in such a fake, pompous, ostentatious bum. I've never seen such an office for a doctor. And a limo . . . please! The guy must be robbing his patients blind. Excuse the pun! What is it that attracts you? His money?"

"No!" Laurie said indignantly. "And as long as you are bringing up money, I called your Internal Affairs department—"

"So I heard," Lou interrupted. "Well, I hope you sleep better now that you've probably gotten some poor patrolman in hot water while he's trying to send his kids to college. Bravo for your strict morality. Now if you'll excuse me, I've got to go out to Forest Hills and try to solve some real crime." Lou stubbed out his cigarette and got to his feet.

"So you won't talk to your drug division?" Laurie asked, trying one more time.

Lou leaned over his desk. "No, I don't think so," he said. "I believe I'll just let you rich people look after yourselves."

Having reined in her anger over the last few minutes, Laurie now gave in to it. "Thanks for nothing, Lieutenant," she said superciliously. Getting up, she got her coat, picked up her briefcase, and stalked out of Lou's office. Downstairs she threw her visitors pass on the Security table and walked out.

Catching a cab was easy as they came in from the Brooklyn Bridge. With just about a straight shot up First Avenue, she was home in no time. Getting off the elevator on her floor, she glared at Debra Engler, then slammed her door.

"And at one point you thought he was charming," she said out loud, ridiculing herself as she stripped down and got into the shower. She couldn't believe that she had allowed herself to sit for as long as she had in Lou Soldano's office absorbing all that abuse in the futile hopes that he might deign to help her. It had been a degrading experience.

Ensconced in a white terry robe, Laurie went to her answering machine and listened to her messages while a hun-

222

gry Tom rubbed across her legs and purred. One was from her mother and the other was from Jordan. Both asked her to call when she got home. Jordan had left a number different from his home number with an extension.

When she called Jordan at the number he'd left, she was told that he was in surgery but that she should hold on.

"Sorry," said Jordan once he picked up a few minutes later. "I'm still in surgery. But I insisted on being told when you called."

"You're in the middle of an operation right now?" Laurie couldn't believe it.

"It doesn't matter," Jordan said. "I can break scrub for a few minutes. I wanted to ask if we could make dinner tonight a bit later. I don't want to keep you waiting again, but I have another case to go."

"Maybe it would be just as well if we took a raincheck."

"No, please!" Jordan said. "It's been a hell of a day and I've been looking forward to seeing you. Remember, you took a raincheck last night."

"Won't you be tired? Especially if you have another case."

Laurie herself felt exhausted. The idea of going straight to bed sounded wonderful to her.

"I'll get a second wind," Jordan said. "We can make it an early evening."

"What time can you meet for dinner?"

"Nine o'clock," Jordan said. "I'll send Thomas around then."

Reluctantly, Laurie agreed. After she hung up, she called Calvin Washington at home.

"What is it, Montgomery?" Calvin demanded once his wife called him to the phone. He sounded grumpy.

"Sorry to bother you at home," Laurie said. "But now that I have twelve cases in my series, I'd like to ask that I be assigned any more that might come in tomorrow."

"You're not on autopsy tomorrow. It's a paper day for you."

"I know. That's why I'm calling. I'm not on call this weekend so I can catch up with my paperwork then."

"Montgomery, I think you ought to cool it. You're getting much too carried away with all this. You're too emotionally involved; you're losing your objectivity. I'm sorry, but tomorrow is a paper day for you no matter what comes through the door feetfirst."

Laurie hung up the phone. She felt depressed. At the same time she knew there was a certain amount of truth in what Calvin had said. She was emotionally involved in the issue.

Sitting by the phone, Laurie thought about returning her mother's call. The last thing she wanted to go through was the third degree about her budding relationship with Jordan Scheffield. Besides, she hadn't quite decided what she thought of him herself. She decided to wait on calling back her mother.

As Lou drove through the Midtown Tunnel and out the Long Island Expressway, he wondered why he insisted on continually bashing his head up against a brick wall. There was no way a woman like Laurie Montgomery would look at someone like himself other than as a city servant. Why did he keep entertaining delusions of grandeur in which Laurie would suddenly say: "Oh, Lou, I've always wanted to meet a police detective who's gone to a community college"?

Lou slapped the steering wheel in embarrassed anger. When Laurie had suddenly called and insisted on coming down to his office, he'd believed she'd wanted to see him for personal reasons, not some harebrained idea of using him to publicize a yuppie cocaine epidemic.

Lou exited the Long Island Expressway and got onto Woodhaven Boulevard, heading to Forest Hills. Feeling the need to do something rather than play with paper clips at his desk, he'd decided to go out and do a little gumshoeing on his own by visiting the surviving spouses. It was also better than going back to his miserable apartment on Prince Street in SoHo and watching TV.

Pulling up the Vivonettos' long, curved driveway, Lou couldn't help but be awed. The house was a mansion with white columns. Right away, lights went off in Lou's head. This kind of opulence suggested serious money. And Lou had a hard time believing a simple restaurateur could make that kind of dough unless he had organized-crime connections.

Lou parked the car by the front door. He'd called ahead so Mrs. Vivonetto was expecting him. When he rang the bell, a woman wearing a ton of makeup came to the door. She was wearing a white, off-the-shoulder wool dress. There was not much suggestion of aggrieved mourning.

"You must be Lieutenant Soldano," she said. "Do come in. My name is Gloria Vivonetto. Can I offer you a drink?"

Lou said that just water would be fine for him. "You know, on duty," he muttered by way of explanation. Gloria poured him a glass at the bar in the living room. She fixed herself a vodka gimlet.

"I'm sorry about your husband," Lou said. It was his standard intro for occasions like this.

"It was just like him," Gloria said. "I'd told him time and time again he shouldn't stay up and watch television. And now he goes and gets himself shot. I don't know anything about running a business. I'm sure people are going to rob me blind."

"Was there anyone that you know of who would have wanted your husband dead?" Lou asked. It was the first question in the standard protocol.

"I've been all over this with the other detectives. Do we have to go through it again?"

"Perhaps not," Lou said. "Let me be frank with you,

Mrs. Vivonetto. The way your husband was killed suggests an organized-crime involvement. Do you know what I'm saying?"

"You mean Mafia?"

"Well, there's more to organized crime than the Mafia," Lou said. "But that's the general idea. Is there any reason that you can think of why people like the Mafia would want your husband killed?"

"Ha!" Gloria laughed. "My husband was never involved with anything as colorful as the Mafia."

"What about his business?" Lou persisted. "Did Pasta Pronto have any connection whatsoever with organized crime?"

"No," Gloria said.

"Are you sure?" Lou questioned.

"Well, no, I guess I'm not sure," Gloria answered. "I wasn't involved with the business. But I can't imagine he ever had anything to do with the Mafia. And anyway, my husband was not a well man. He wasn't going to be around much longer anyway. If someone wanted him out of the way they could have waited for him to keel over naturally."

"How was your husband sick?" Lou asked.

"In what ways wasn't he sick?" Gloria shot back. "Everything was falling apart. He had bad heart problems and had had two bypass operations. His kidneys weren't great. He was supposed to have his gallbladder removed but they kept putting it off, saying his heart wouldn't take it. He was going to have an eye operation. And his prostate was messed up. I'm not sure what was wrong with that, but his whole lower half didn't work anymore. Hadn't for years."

"I'm sorry," Lou said, unsure of what else to say. "I suppose he suffered a lot."

Gloria shrugged her shoulders. "He never took care of himself. He was overweight, drank a ton, and he smoked like a chimney. The doctors told me he might not last a year unless he changed his ways, which wasn't something he was about to do."

Lou decided there wasn't much more he'd learn from the not-so-aggrieved widow. "Well," he said, standing up, "thank you for your time, Mrs. Vivonetto. If you think of anything else that might seem important, please give me a call." He handed her one of his business cards.

Next Lou headed for the Singleton residence. The place was a simple, two-story, brick row house with two pink flamingos stuck in the front lawn. The street reminded him of his old neighborhood only a half dozen blocks away in Rego Park. He felt a stab of nostalgia for the evenings in the alleyway, playing stickball.

Mr. Chester Singleton opened the door. He was a big man, middle-aged and quite balding. He had a hounddog look thanks to his beefy jowls. His eyes were red and streaked. The instant Lou saw him he knew he was in the presence of true grief.

"Detective Soldano?"

Lou nodded and was immediately invited inside.

Inside, the furniture was plain but solid. A crocheted comforter was folded over the back of a plaid, well-worn couch. Dozens of framed photos lined the walls, most of them black and white.

"I'm very sorry about your wife," Lou said.

Chester nodded, took a deep breath, and bit his lower lip.

"I know that other people have been by," Lou continued. He decided to go right to the heart of the matter. "I wanted to ask you flat-out why a professional gunman would come into your home to shoot your wife."

"I don't know," Chester said. His voice quavered with emotion.

"Your restaurant-supply business supplied some restaurants with organized-crime connections. Do any of the restaurants you supply have any complaints with your service?"

"Never," Chester said. "And I don't know anything about any organized crime. Sure, I heard rumors. But I never met anyone or saw anyone I would call a mobster type."

"What about Pasta Pronto?" Lou asked. "I understand you had new business there."

"I recently got some of their business, that's true. But only a piece of it. I think they were just trying me out. I hoped to get more of their business eventually."

"Did you know Steven Vivonetto?" Lou asked.

"Yes, but not well. He was a wealthy man."

"You know he got shot last night as well?" Lou said.

"I know. I read about it in the paper."

"Had you received any threats lately?" Lou asked. "Any attempts at extortion? Any kind of protection racket knocking on your door?"

Chester shook his head.

"Can you think of any reason your wife and Steven Vivonetto should have been killed during the same night, possibly by the same person?"

"No," Chester said. "I can't think of any reason why anyone would have wanted to kill Janice. Everyone loved Janice. She was the warmest, nicest person in the world. And on top of that, she was ill."

"What was wrong with her?" Lou asked.

"Cancer. Unfortunately it had spread before they found it. She never liked to go to the doctor. If only she'd gone sooner, they might have been able to do more. As it was, she only had chemotherapy. She seemed okay for a while, but then she got this awful rash on her face. Herpes zoster they call it. It even got into one of her eyes and blinded it so that she needed to have an operation."

"Did the doctors hold out much hope for her?" Lou asked.

"I'm afraid not," Chester said. "They told me that they couldn't say for sure, but they thought that it might be only a year or so, and shorter if the cancer came back quicker."

"I'm so sorry to hear all this," Lou said.

"Well, maybe what happened was just as well. Maybe it saved her a lot of suffering. But I miss her so. We were married for thirty-one years."

After offering additional condolences and his business card, Lou bade farewell to Mr. Singleton. Driving back to Manhattan, he reviewed what little he'd learned. The organized-crime connection to either case was at best tenuous. He'd been surprised to learn that both victims were terminally ill. He wondered if their killers had known.

By reflex he reached into his jacket pocket and took out a cigarette. He pushed in the lighter. Then he thought about Laurie. Rolling down the window, he tossed the unlit cigarette into the street just as the lighter popped out. He sighed, wondering where that pompous Jordan Scheffield was taking her for dinner.

Vinnie Dominick came into the locker room at St. Mary's and sat wearily on the bench. He was perspiring heavily. He was bleeding slightly from a small scratch on his cheek.

"You're bleeding, boss," Freddie Capuso said.

"Get out of my face," Vinnie snapped. "I know I'm bleeding. But you know what bugs me? That bum Jeff Young said he never touched me and whined for ten minutes when I called a foul."

Vinnie had just finished an hour's worth of pickup three-on-three basketball. His team had lost and he was in a foul mood. His mood got even worse when his most trusted lieutenant, Franco Ponti, came in with a long face.

"Don't tell me it's true?" Vinnie asked.

Franco came over to the bench. He put one foot on it and leaned on his knee. His nickname since high school had been "falcon," mostly because of his face. With a narrow hooked nose, thin lips, and beady eyes he resembled a bird of prey.

"It's true," Franco said. He spoke in a monotone. "Jimmy Lanso got whacked last night in his cousin's funeral home."

Vinnie bolted off the bench and hammered one of the metal lockers. The crashing noise reverberated around the small locker room like a clap of thunder. Everyone winced except Franco.

"Christ!" Vinnie cried. He began pacing. Freddie Capuso got out of his way.

"What am I going to tell my wife?" Vinnie cried. "What am I going to tell my wife?" he repeated, raising his voice. "I promised her I'd take care of it." He pounded one of the lockers again. Perspiration flew off his face.

"Tell her that you made a mistake trusting Cerino," Franco suggested.

Vinnie stopped in his tracks. "It's true," he snarled. "I thought Cerino was a civilized man. But now I know otherwise."

"And there's more," Franco said. "Cerino's men have been busy whacking all sorts of people besides Jimmy Lanso. Last night they hit two in Kew Gardens and two in Forest Hills."

"I saw that on the news." Vinnie was astounded. "That was Cerino's people?"

"Yup," Franco said.

"Why?" Vinnie asked. "I didn't recognize any of the names."

"Nobody knows." Franco shrugged his shoulders.

"There must be some reason."

"For sure," Franco said. "I just don't know what it is."

"Well, find out!" Vinnie ordered. "It's one thing putting up with Cerino and his bums as business rivals, but it's quite another to sit around watching them ruin things for everyone."

"There arc cops crawling all over Queens," Franco agreed.

"That's just what we don't need," Vinnie said. "With the authorities up in arms, we'll have to suspend a significant part of our operations. You have to find out what Cerino is up to. Franco, I'm depending on you."

Franco nodded. "I'll see what I can do."

"You're not eating much," Jordan said.

Laurie looked up from her plate. They were dining at a restaurant called Palio. Although the food was Italian, the décor was a relaxing meld of oriental and modern. Before her was a delicious seafood risotto. Her wineglass was filled with a crisp Pinot Grigio. But Jordan was right; she wasn't eating much. Although she hadn't eaten much that day, she just wasn't hungry.

"You don't like the food?" Jordan asked. "I thought you said you liked Italian." His dress was as casually elegant as ever; he had on a black velvet blazer with a silk shirt open at the neck. He was not wearing a tie.

The logistics had worked much better this evening. As Jordan had promised, he'd called just before nine when he was leaving surgery, saying that Thomas was on his way to pick her up while he went back to his apartment to change. By the time Thomas and Laurie got back to the Trump Tower, Jordan was waiting curbside. From there it had been a short ride over to West Fifty-first Street.

"I love the food," Laurie said. "I guess I'm just not that hungry. It's been a long day."

"I've been avoiding talking about the day," Jordan admitted. "I thought it better to get a bit of wine under our belts. As I mentioned on the phone, my day was atrocious. That's the only word for it, starting from your phone call about poor Marsha Schulman. Every time I think about her, I get this sick feeling. I even feel guilty about being so angry with her for not showing up to work, and here she

231

was a headless corpse floating in the East River. Oh, God!"
Jordan couldn't continue. He buried his face in his hands
and shook his head slowly. Laurie reached across the table
and put a hand on Jordan's arm. She felt for him but was
also relieved to see this display of emotion. Up until this
moment she'd felt he'd been incapable of such demonstra-
tiveness and rather dispassionate about his secretary's murder. He suddenly seemed a lot more human.

Jordan pulled himself together. "And there's more," he
said sadly. "I lost a patient today. Part of the reason I went
into ophthalmology was because I knew I'd have a hard
time dealing with death, yet I still wanted to do surgery.
Ophthalmology seemed an ideal compromise, until today. I
lost a preop by the name of Mary O'Connor."

"I'm sorry," Laurie said. "I understand how you feel.
Dealing with dying patients was hard for me too. I suppose
it's one of the reasons I went into pathology, especially
forensics. My patients are already dead."

Jordan smiled weakly. "Mary was a wonderful woman
and such an appreciative patient," he said. "I'd already
operated on one eye and was about to do the other this
afternoon. She was a healthy lady with no known heart
trouble, yet she was found dead in her bed. She'd died
watching television."

"What a terrible experience for you," Laurie sympa-
thized. "But you have to remember that occult medical
problems are always found in such cases. I imagine we'll be
seeing Mrs. O'Connor tomorrow, and I'll be sure to let you
know what it was. Sometimes knowing the pathology
makes it easier to deal with the death."

"I'd appreciate that," Jordan said.

"I suppose my day wasn't as bad as yours," Laurie said.
"But I'm beginning to understand how Cassandra felt when
Apollo made sure that she was not to be heeded."

Laurie told Jordan all about her overdose series and that

she was sure there would be more cases if no appropriate warnings were issued. She told him how upsetting it had been that she'd been unable to convince the chief medical examiner to go public with the story. Then she told him she'd gone to the police, and even they refused to help.

"Sounds frustrating," Jordan said. "There was one good thing about my day," he said, changing the subject. "I did a lot of surgery, and that makes me and my accountant very happy. Over the last couple of weeks I've been doing double my normal number of cases."

"I'm glad," Laurie said. She couldn't help but notice Jordan's propensity for turning the conversation to himself.

"I just hope it keeps up," he said. "There are always fluctuations. I can accept that. But I'm getting spoiled at the current rate."

Once they had finished their meal and their places were cleared, the waiter rolled a tempting dessert trolley to their table. Jordan selected a chocolate cake. Laurie chose berries. Jordan had an espresso, Laurie a decaf. As she stirred her coffee, she discreetly glanced at her watch.

"I saw that," Jordan said. "I know it's getting late. I also know it's a 'school night.' I'll get you home in a half hour if we can make the same deal we made last night. Let's have dinner again tomorrow night."

"Again?" Laurie asked. "Jordan, you're sure to get sick of me."

"Nonsense," Jordan said. "I'm enjoying every minute. I just wish it weren't so rushed, and tomorrow is Friday. It's the weekend. Maybe you'll even have some news about Mary O'Connor. Please, Laurie."

Laurie couldn't believe she was being asked to dinner for a third night in a row. It was certainly flattering. "All right," she said at last. "You have yourself a date."

"Wonderful," Jordan said. "Have any suggestions for a restaurant?"

"I think you have a lot more experience," Laurie said. "You pick."

"Okay, I will. Shall we say nine o'clock again?"

Laurie nodded as she sipped her decaf. Looking into Jordan's clear eyes, she thought of Lou's negative description of the man. For a second Laurie was tempted to ask how the meeting with the detective lieutenant had gone, but decided against it. Some things were better left unsaid.

9

□

"Not bad," Tony said. He and Angelo were just leaving an all-night pizza joint on Forty-second Street near Times Square. "I was surprised. The place looked like such a dump."

Angelo didn't answer. His mind was already on the job that lay ahead.

When they arrived at the parking garage, Angelo nodded toward his Town Car. The garage owner, Lenny Helman, paid money to Cerino. Since Angelo usually collected it, he parked for free.

"Better not have scratched the car," Angelo said after the attendant drove the car up to the curb. Once he was satisfied there wasn't a mark on its highly polished surface, Angelo got in. Tony did the same. They pulled out onto Forty-second Street.

235

"What's next?" Tony asked, sitting sideways so he could look directly at Angelo. The light from the glittering neon marquees of the neighborhood movie theaters played over Angelo's gaunt face, making him look like an unraveled mummy in a museum.

"We're going to switch to the 'demand' list," Angelo told him.

"Great," Tony said with enthusiasm. "I'm getting tired of the other. Where to?"

"Eighty-sixth," Angelo said. "Near the Metropolitan Museum."

"Good neighborhood," Tony said. "I'll bet there'll be souvenirs for the taking."

"I don't feel good about it," Angelo said. "Wealthy neighborhood means fancy alarms."

"You handle all that stuff like a breeze," Tony said.

"Things have been going a little too well," Angelo said. "I'm starting to get concerned."

"You worry too much," Tony said with a laugh. "The reason things have been going so well is because we know what we're doing. And the more we do it, the better we get. It's the same thing with everything."

"Screw-ups happen," Angelo said. "No matter how much you prepare. We have to expect it. And be able to handle it when it does."

"Ah, you're just a pessimist," Tony said.

Engrossed in their banter, neither Tony nor Angelo took note of a black Cadillac cruising two cars behind them. At the wheel, a relaxed Franco Ponti was enjoying a tape of *Aida*. Thanks to a tip from a contact in the Times Square area, Franco had been tailing Angelo and Tony since their stop at the pizza place.

"Which one are we doing?" Tony asked.

"The woman," Angelo said.

"Whose turn?" Tony asked. He knew Angelo was due but hoped he might have forgotten.

"I don't give a damn," Angelo said. "You can do her. I'll watch the man."

Angelo drove by the brownstone several times before parking. It was five stories tall with a double door at the top of a short flight of granite steps. Beneath the stoop at the ground level was another door.

"The service entrance is probably the way to go," Angelo said. "We'll be a little shielded by the stoop. I can see there's an alarm, but if it's the kind I think it is, it won't be a problem."

"You're the boss," Tony said. He took his gun out and attached the silencer.

They parked almost a block away and walked back. Angelo carried a small flight bag full of tools. When they got to the house, Angelo told Tony to wait on the sidewalk and let him know if anyone was coming. Angelo descended the few steps to the service entrance door.

Tony kept an eye out, but the street was quiet. No one was in sight. What Tony didn't see was Franco Ponti parked only a few doors down, blocking a driveway.

"All right," Angelo whispered from the shadows of the service entrance. "Come on."

They entered a long hallway, moving quickly to the stairs. There was an elevator but they knew better than to use it. Taking two steps at a time, they climbed to the first floor and listened. Save for a large antique clock ticking loudly in the dark, the house was quiet.

"Can you imagine living in a place like this?" Tony whispered. "It's like a palace."

"Shut up," Angelo snapped.

They continued upstairs, climbing a curving, double staircase that circled a chandelier Tony guessed was six feet across. On the second floor they peered into a series of sitting rooms, a library, and a den. On the third floor they hit pay dirt: the master bedroom.

Angelo stood to one side of the double doors that no

doubt led to the master suite. Tony took the other side. Both men had their guns drawn. Their silencers were attached.

Angelo slowly turned the door handle and pushed the door in. The room was larger than any bedroom either of them had ever seen. On the far wall—which seemed very far to Angelo—stood a massive canopied bed.

Angelo stepped into the room, motioning for Tony to follow. He went to the right side of the bed, where the man was sleeping. Tony went to the other side. Angelo nodded. Tony extended his gun while Angelo did the same.

Tony's gun went off with its familiar hissing thump and the woman recoiled. The man must have been a light sleeper. No sooner had the shot gone off than he sat bolt upright, eyes wide. Angelo shot him before he had a chance to say a word. He toppled over toward his wife.

"Oh, no!" Angelo said out loud.

"What's the matter?" Tony questioned.

Using the tip of the silencer, Angelo reached over and separated the fingers of the dying man. Clutched in his hand was a small plastic device with a button.

"He had a goddamn alarm," Angelo said.

"What does that mean?" Tony asked.

"It means we have to get the hell out of here," Angelo said. "Come on."

Moving as quickly as they could in the semidarkness, they ran down the stairs. Rounding the bend onto the first floor, they practically ran into a housekeeper who was on her way up.

The housekeeper screamed, turned, and fled back down the way she'd come. Tony fired his Bantam, but at distances greater than six feet, his gun wasn't accurate. The slug missed the housekeeper, shattering a large gold-framed mirror instead.

"We have to get her," Angelo said, knowing that the

woman had gotten a good look at them. He threw himself down the stairs, the flight bag bouncing its shoulder straps. Reaching the bottom, he skidded on the marble strewn with shards of mirror. Regaining his footing, he hurled himself down the first-floor hallway toward the back of the house. Ahead he could see the woman struggling to open a pair of French doors leading to the backyard.

Before he could catch her, she was out the door, pulling it closed behind her. Angelo got there just seconds behind her. Tony was right behind him. They ran out after her only to trip on a pair of garden chairs they couldn't see in the dark.

Angelo peered into the darkness. The backyard could have passed for a public park. There was a rectangular reflecting pool in the center of the space. To the right was an ivy-covered gazebo that was lost in shadow. A thick oak had a swing hanging from a broad branch. Nowhere could Angelo spot the woman.

"Where did she go?" Tony whispered.

"If I knew would I be standing here?" Angelo said. "You go that way and I'll go this way." He pointed to either side of the pool.

The two men groped their way around the garden. They strained to look into the dark recesses of the ferns and shrubbery.

"There she is!" Tony said, pointing back at the house.

Angelo fired two shots at the fleeing woman. The first bullet shattered the glass of the French doors. After the second, he saw the woman stumble and fall.

"You got her!" Tony cried.

"Let's get out of here," Angelo said. He could hear sirens in the distance. It was hard to be sure, but they seemed to be approaching.

Not wanting to risk coming out of the front of the house, Angelo turned to the back wall of the garden. Spotting a door on the far side of the pond, he yelled, "Come on!" to Tony. Angelo reached the door first. He unbolted the dead bolt securing the door and rushed into a debris-strewn alleyway. They made their way down the darkened path, trying each garden door they passed. Tony finally found one with nearly rotten planking and broke through.

The garden they found themselves in seemed as neglected as the door.

"Now what?" Tony said.

"That way," Angelo said. He pointed to a dark passageway leading toward the front of the house. At the end of the passageway they came to a bolted door, but it was bolted from the inside. Passing through it, they found themselves on Eighty-fifth Street.

Angelo brushed off his clothes. Tony followed his example. "Okay," said Angelo. "Now be cool, confident, relaxed."

The pair walked slowly down the street and around the corner as if they called the neighborhood home. Slowly they made their way to Angelo's car. The sirens had indeed been heading for the brownstone they'd just left. Ahead they could see three squad cars with emergency lights flashing, blocking the street in front of the house where they'd made the hit.

Angelo unlocked his car doors with a remote control and the two men climbed in.

"That was awesome!" Tony said excitedly once they were a half dozen blocks away. "That was the coolest thing I've ever seen."

Angelo scowled at him. "It was a disaster," he said.

"What do you mean?" Tony questioned. "We got away. No problem. And you got the housekeeper. You dropped her right in her tracks."

"But we didn't check her," Angelo said. "How do I know if I really got her or just winged her? We should have checked her. She looked directly at both of us."

"She dropped quickly," Tony said. "I think you hit her real good."

"This is what I mean: screw-ups happen. How would we have guessed the guy would sleep holding a panic-button alarm?" Angelo was glad he had the wheel to grip; his hands were shaking.

"Okay, so we got the 'bad luck' hit out of the way," Tony said. "Now you can't say that things are going too well. What's next?"

"I'm not sure," Angelo said. "Maybe we should call it a night."

"What for?" Tony questioned. "The night is young. Come on! Let's at least do one more. We can't pass up this kind of money."

Angelo thought for a minute. Intuition told him to call it a night, but Tony was right. The money *was* good. Besides, hits were like riding horses: you fall off, you get back on. Otherwise you may never ride again.

"All right," he said finally. "We'll do one more."

"That's what I like to hear," Tony said. "Where to?"

"Down in the Village. Another town house."

Angelo took the Ninety-seventh Street transverse across Central Park and got on the Henry Hudson Parkway.

For a while they didn't talk. Each was recovering from the opposite ends of the emotional spectrum: Angelo from fear and anxiety and Tony from pure exhilaration. Neither noticed the black Cadillac in the distance.

"It will be up here on the left," Angelo said once they turned onto Bleecker Street. He pointed to a three-story town house with a lion's head knocker on the front door. Tony nodded as they drove past.

Angelo felt his pulse start quickening. "It's the man this time," he said. "Same plan as before. You do him, I'll cover the wife."

"Got it," Tony said, thrilled to have yet another turn.

This time Angelo parked farther away than usual. They

walked back in silence except for the occasional clank of tools in Angelo's flight bag. They passed a few pedestrians. The streets weren't empty as they had been uptown; the Village was always livelier than the Upper East Side.

The alarm at the targeted house was child's play for Angelo. Within minutes he and Tony were tiptoeing up the creaking stairs.

Conveniently, there was a small night-light plugged into a socket in the upstairs hall. The rosy glow it cast was just enough to see by.

The first door Angelo tried proved to be an empty guest room. Since there was only one other door on the floor, he assumed it was to the master suite.

Once again the two men positioned themselves on either side of the door, holding their guns alongside their heads. Angelo turned the knob and briskly pushed open the door.

Angelo managed one step into the room when a snarling dog sprang at him in the half-light. The beast's paws hit him in the chest, knocking him back through the door to the opposite wall of the hall. The dog snapped at him, biting through his jacket, shirt, and even a bit of his skin. Angelo wasn't sure, but he thought it was a Doberman. It was too long and lean for a pit bull, although it certainly had the temperament. Whatever it was, it had Angelo terrorized and effectively pinned.

Tony moved quickly. He stepped to the side and shot the dog from point-blank range in the chest. He was sure he'd hit his mark, but the dog didn't flinch. With a snarl he ripped another large patch of cloth out of Angelo's jacket and spit it out. Then he lunged for another bite.

Tony waited until he had a clear shot before pulling the trigger again. This time he hit the dog in the head, and the animal went instantly limp, hitting the floor with a solid thud.

A woman's scream sent new chills down Angelo's spine.

242

The woman of the house had awakened just in time to see her dog slaughtered. She was standing a few feet from the foot of her bed, her face contorted in horror.

Tony raised his gun, and again there was a hissing thump. The woman's scream was cut short. Her hand went to her chest. Pulling her hand away, she looked at the spot of blood. Her facial expression was one of bewilderment, as if she could not believe she'd been shot.

Tony stepped over the threshold into the bedroom. Raising his gun again, he shot her at point-blank range in the center of her forehead. Like the dog, she collapsed instantly in a heap on the floor.

Angelo started to speak, but before he could say anything, there was a frightful yell from the first floor as the husband charged up the stairs with a double-barrel twelve-gauge shotgun. He held the gun in both hands at waist height.

Sensing what was about to happen, Angelo threw himself onto the floor just as the shotgun discharged with a powerful concussion. In the confined area the sound was horrendous, making Angelo's ears ring. The concentrated buckshot blew a hole twelve inches in diameter in the wall where Angelo had been standing.

Even Tony had to react by reflex, throwing himself to the side to avoid the open bedroom doorway. The second blast of the shotgun traveled the length of the bedroom and blew out one of the rear windows.

From his position on the floor, Angelo fired his Walther twice in rapid succession, hitting the husband in the chest and the chin. The force of the bullets stopped the man's forward momentum. Then, in a kind of slow motion he tipped backward. With a terrible racket he fell down the stairs and ended up on the floor below.

Tony reappeared from the bedroom and ran down the stairs to put an additional bullet into the fallen man's head.

Angelo picked himself and his flight bag off the floor. He was shaking. He'd never come so close to death. Rushing down the stairs on shaky legs, he told Tony that they had to get the hell out of there.

When they got to the front door, Angelo stood on his tiptoes to look out. What he saw he didn't like. There was a handful of people gathered in front of the building, gazing up at its façade. No doubt they'd heard glass smash when the bedroom window was blown out. Maybe they'd heard both shotgun blasts.

"Out the back!" Angelo said. He knew they couldn't risk a confrontation with this crowd. They easily scaled the chain-link fence in the backyard. There wasn't even any barbed wire at the top to worry about. Once they made it over, they went through a neighboring backyard and through to another street. Angelo was glad he'd parked as far away as he had. They made it to his car without incident. Sirens started in the distance just as they were pulling away.

"What the hell kind of dog was that?" Tony asked as they cruised up Sixth Avenue.

"I think it was a Doberman," Angelo said. "It scared the life out of me."

"You and me both," Tony agreed. "And that shotgun. That was close."

"Too close. We should have called it quits after the first job." Angelo shook his head in disgust. "Maybe I'm getting too old for this stuff."

"No way," Tony said. "You're the best."

"I used to think so," Angelo said. He glanced down at his tattered Brioni jacket in despair. By force of habit he glanced in the rearview mirror, but nothing he saw worried him. Of course, he was looking for cop cars, not Franco Ponti's sedan, which was pursuing them at a discreet distance.

244

10

□

Ordinarily Laurie would be pleased to have slept through the night. Although no one from the medical examiner's office had called her to report any more upscale overdose cases for her series, she wondered if that meant there had been no such overdoses or, as her intuition suggested, there had been and she had simply not been called. She dressed as quickly as she could and didn't even bother with coffee, so eager was she to get to work and find out.

The moment she stepped inside the medical examiner's office, she could tell that something out of the ordinary had happened. Once again there was a group of reporters huddled in the reception area. Laurie felt the knot in her stomach tighten as she wondered what their restless presence could mean.

Going directly to the ID office, she helped herself to a cup of coffee before doing anything else. Vinnie, as usual, had his nose in the sports page. Apparently none of the other associate medical examiners had yet arrived. Laurie picked up the sheet at the scheduling desk to check the cases to be posted that day.

As her eyes ran down the list, she saw four drug overdoses. Two were scheduled for Riva and two were scheduled for George Fontworth, a fellow who'd been with the office for four years. Laurie flipped through the folders intended for Riva and glanced at the investigator's report sheet. Judging by the Harlem addresses, Laurie figured they were the common crack-house deaths. Relieved, Laurie put the folder down. Then she picked up the two for George. Reading the first investigator's report, her pulse quickened. The deceased was Wendell Morrison, aged thirty-six, a medical doctor!

With a shaky hand, Laurie opened the last folder: Julia Myerholtz, aged twenty-nine, art historian!

Laurie breathed out. She hadn't been aware that she'd been holding her breath. Her intuition had been correct: there'd been two more cocaine overdose cases with similar demographics as the others. She felt a mixture of emotions including anger about not having been called as she'd requested and confirmation that her fears had come to pass. At the same time she felt sorry there had been two more potentially preventable deaths.

Laurie went straight to the forensic investigator's office and found Bart Arnold. She knocked loudly on his door and walked in before he had a chance to invite her.

"Why wasn't I called? I spoke to you specifically about this. I told you I wanted to be called on cocaine overdoses that fall within certain demographic parameters. Last night there were two. I wasn't called. Why?"

"I was told you were not to be called," Bart said.

"Why not?" Laurie questioned.

"I wasn't given a reason," Bart said. "But I passed the word on to the tour doctors when they came on duty."

"Who told you this?" Laurie asked.

"Dr. Washington," Bart said. "I'm sorry, Laurie. I would have told you myself, but you had already gone for the day."

Laurie abruptly turned and walked out of Bart's office. She was more angry than hurt. Her worst fears had been confirmed: she hadn't been overlooked accidentally, there was a deliberate effort going on to keep her out of the way. Just outside the police liaison office she saw Lou Soldano.

"Can I talk to you for a minute?" Lou asked.

Laurie stared at him. Didn't the guy ever get any sleep? Once again he looked as if he'd been up all night. He hadn't shaved and his eyes were red-rimmed. His close-cropped hair was matted down on his forehead.

"I'm quite busy, Lieutenant," Laurie said.

"Just a moment of your time," Lou repeated. "Please."

"All right," Laurie relented. "What is it?"

"I had a little time to think last night," Lou said. "I wanted to apologize for being such a boob yesterday afternoon. I came on a little stronger than I should have. So, I'm sorry."

The last thing she'd expected from Lou was an apology. Now that it was being offered, she was gratified to hear it.

"As kind of an explanation," Lou continued, "I'm under a lot of pressure from the commissioner about these gangland-style murders. He thinks that since I'd spent time on organized crime, I should be the one to solve them. Unfortunately he's not a patient man."

"I guess we're both pretty stressed," Laurie said. "But your apology is accepted."

"Thank you," Lou said. "At least that's one hurdle out of the way."

"So what brings you here this morning?"

ROBIN COOK

"You haven't heard about the homicides?"

"What homicides?" Laurie asked. "We get homicides every day."

"Not like these," Lou said. "More gangland stuff. Professional hits. Two couples here in Manhattan."

"Floating in the river?" Laurie asked.

"Nope," Lou said. "Shot in their homes. Both of the couples were well-to-do, one in particular. And the wealthier one is also politically connected."

"Uh-oh," Laurie said. "More pressure."

"You'd better believe it," Lou said. "The mayor is livid. He's already chewed out the commissioner, and guess who the commissioner has decided to target: yours truly."

"Do you have any ideas?" Laurie asked.

"I wish I could tell you I did," Lou said. "Something big time is going on, but for the life of me I don't have a clue as to what it is. The night before last there were three similar hits in Queens. Now these two in Manhattan. And there doesn't seem to be any organized-crime connection. Certainly not with the two last night. But the m.o. of the killers is definitely gangland style."

"So you're here for the autopsies?" Laurie asked.

"Yeah," Lou said. "Maybe I can get a job here after I'm fired from the police department. I'm spending as much time here as in my office."

"Who's doing the cases?" Laurie asked.

"Dr. Southgate and Dr. Besserman," Lou said. "How are they, all right?"

"They're excellent. Both are very experienced."

"I'd kinda hoped you'd be doing them," Lou said. "I was beginning to think we worked well together."

"Well, you're in good hands with Southgate and Besserman," she assured him.

"I'll let you know what we find," Lou said. He fumbled with his hat.

"Please do," Laurie answered. All of a sudden she had that same feeling that she'd gotten on previous days. Lou seemed to become painfully self-conscious, as if he wanted to say something but couldn't.

"Well . . . I'm glad I ran into you," Lou said, avoiding Laurie's eyes. "Well . . . I'll see you. 'Bye." Lou turned and started back toward the police liaison office.

For a second Laurie watched Lou's lumbering gait and again was impressed by a sense of the man's loneliness. She wondered if he had intended asking her out once again.

For a minute after Lou disappeared from view, Laurie forgot where she'd been headed. But her anger returned the minute she remembered Calvin's attempt to get her off her overdose series. With a renewed sense of purpose, she marched to Calvin's office and knocked on the open door. She was inside facing him before he had a chance to say a word.

She found Calvin seated behind a mountain of paperwork. He looked up over the tops of his wire-rimmed reading glasses that were dwarfed by his broad face. He didn't seem happy to see her. "What is it, Montgomery?"

"There were two more overdoses last night similar to the kind that I am interested in," Laurie began.

"You're not telling me anything I don't already know," Calvin said.

"I know this is scheduled as a paper day for me, but I would appreciate it if you would let me do the autopsies. Something tells me these cases are related. By my doing them all, maybe I'll make some connections."

"We went over this on the phone," Calvin said. "I told you I think you are getting carried away. You've become less than objective."

"Please, Dr. Washington," Laurie pleaded. She hated to beg.

"No! Goddamn it!" Calvin exploded. He slammed an

249

open palm on his desk, sending some of his papers flying. He stood up. "George Fontworth is doing the overdoses, and I want you to stick to your own work. You're behind in signing out some of your cases as it is. I don't think I need to tell you. Now, I don't need this kind of aggravation. Not with the pressure this office is under."

Laurie nodded, then walked out of the office. If she weren't so enraged, she would probably have been in tears. Leaving Calvin's office, she went directly to Bingham's.

This time Laurie waited to be asked in. Bingham was on the phone, but he waved her in.

Laurie got the impression Bingham was speaking to someone at city hall, since his side of the conversation reminded her of speaking with her mother. Bingham was saying "yes," "certainly," and "of course" over and over.

When he finally hung up and peered at Laurie she could tell he was already exasperated. It was not an opportune time for her visit. But since she was already there, and there was no one else to whom she could appeal, Laurie pressed on.

"I'm being deliberately prevented from further involvement with these upscale overdose cases," she said. She tried to sound firm but her voice was filled with emotion. "Dr. Washington will not let me perform the relevant autopsies that have come in today. He made sure I wasn't called to any of the scenes last night. I don't think barring me from these cases is in the best interests of the department."

Bingham put his face in his hands and rubbed, particularly his eyes. When he looked up again at Laurie his eyes were red. "We're dealing with a lot of bad press about possibly mishandling a Central Park murder case; we've got a rash of brutal, professional homicides that are on top of the usual nighttime New York mayhem; and on top of that, you're in here causing trouble. I don't believe it, Laurie. Truly I don't."

"I want to be allowed to pursue these cases," Laurie said evenly. "Now there are at least fourteen. Someone has to be looking at the whole picture. I think I'm the person to do it. I'm convinced we're on the brink of a widespread disaster. If there is a contaminant, and I'm convinced there is, we must issue a public warning!"

Bingham was incredulous. Gazing up at the ceiling and throwing his hands up in the air, he muttered to himself: "She's been on the staff for about five months and she's telling me how to run the department." He shook his head. Then he turned his attention back to Laurie. This time he sounded a lot fiercer.

"Calvin is an able administrator. In fact, he is more than able. He's excellent. What he says goes. You hear me?! That's it; the issue is closed." With that, he turned his attention to the pile of letters stacked in his in-box.

Laurie headed straight for the lab. She decided it was better to keep moving. If she paused to think about these last two interviews, she might do something rash she'd later regret.

She was looking for Peter Letterman but ran into John DeVries instead. "Thanks for putting in a good word for me with the chief," she said sarcastically. As angry as she was, she couldn't contain herself.

"I don't like to be pestered," John said. "I warned you."

"I wasn't pestering," Laurie snapped. "I was merely asking you to do your job. Have you found a contaminant?"

"No," John said. He pushed past her without giving her the courtesy of a more detailed reply.

Laurie shook her head. She wondered if her days at the New York Medical Examiner's Office were numbered.

She found Peter over in the corner of the lab, working on the largest and newest of the gas chromatographs.

"I think you should try to avoid John," he said. "I couldn't help overhearing."

"Believe me, I wasn't looking for him," Laurie answered.

"I haven't found any contaminant, either," Peter said. "But I've been running samples on this gas chromatograph. It has what they call a 'trap.' If we're going to pick something up, this is the apparatus that will do it."

"Keep at it," Laurie said. "We're up to fourteen cases now."

"I did learn something," Peter said. "As you know, cocaine naturally hydrolyzes to benzoylecgonine, ecgonine methyl ester, and ecgonine."

"Yes," Laurie said. "Go on."

"Each batch of cocaine that is made has a unique percentage of these hydrolysates," Peter said. "So by analyzing the concentrations, you can make a pretty educated guess as to the origin of the samples."

"And?" Laurie asked.

"All the samples that I've recovered from the syringes have the same percentages," Peter said. "That means the cocaine has all come from the same batch."

"Meaning the same source," Laurie added.

"Exactly," Peter said.

"That's what I suspected," Laurie said. "It's nice to have it documented."

"I'll let you know if I find any contaminant with this machine."

"Please do," Laurie said. "If I had proof of a contaminant I think Dr. Bingham would make a statement." But as she returned to her office, Laurie wondered if she could be sure of anything.

"Don't hold my arm!" Cerino shouted. Angelo had been trying to guide him through the entrance to Jordan Scheffield's office. "I can see more than you think I can." Cerino was carrying his red-tipped cane but wasn't using it. Tony came in last and pulled the door shut.

One of Jordan's nurses guided the group down the corridor, making sure that Cerino was comfortably seated in one of the examination chairs.

When Cerino came to Jordan's office, he did not use the usual entrance, and he bypassed the waiting room altogether. That was the customary modus operandi for all of Jordan's VIP patients.

"Oh dear!" the nurse said as she eyed Tony's face. There was a deep scratch that extended down from in front of his left ear to the corner of his mouth. "That's a nasty cut on your cheek. How'd you get it?"

"A cat," Tony said, self-consciously putting a hand to his face.

"I hope you got a tetanus shot," the nurse said. "Would you like us to wash it out?"

"Nah," Tony said, embarrassed at the attention in front of Cerino.

"Let me know if you change your mind," the nurse said, heading for the door.

"Gimme a light," Paul said as soon as the nurse had left the room. Angelo hastily lit Paul's cigarette, then pulled one out for himself.

Tony found a chair off to the side and sat down. Angelo remained standing a little to Cerino's left and a little behind. Both he and Tony were exhausted, having been roused out of bed for Cerino's unexpected doctor's visit. Both were also still suffering the late effects of the experiences at the last two hits, particularly Angelo.

"Here we are in Disneyland again," Paul said.

The room stopped and the wall lifted. Jordan was poised at the edge of his office with Cerino's record in hand. As he stepped forward he immediately smelled the cigarettes.

"Excuse me," he said. "There is no smoking in here."

Angelo nervously looked around for someplace to deposit his smoldering cigarette. Cerino grabbed his arm and motioned for him not to move.

"If we want to smoke, we're going to smoke," Paul said.

"Like I told you when you called me on the phone, Doc, I'm a bit disappointed in you and I don't mind telling you again."

"But the instruments," Jordan said, pointing toward the slit lamp. "Smoke is detrimental to them."

"Screw the instruments, Doc," Paul said. "Let's talk about you blabbing all over town about my condition."

"What are you talking about?" Jordan asked. He'd known Cerino was angry about something from their phone call. He'd figured it had something to do with the wait for a suitable cornea transplant. But Cerino's true complaint came as a complete surprise to him.

"I'm talking about a detective by the name of Lou Soldano," Paul said. "And a broad by the name of Dr. Laurie Montgomery. You talked to the broad, the broad talked to the detective, and the detective came to me. And I'll tell you something, Doc. It pisses me off. I was trying to keep the details of my little accident a secret. For business purposes, you understand."

"We doctors sometimes discuss cases," Jordan said. He suddenly felt very warm.

"Give me a break, Doc," Paul said derisively. "I hear this supposed colleague is a medical examiner. And in case you haven't noticed, I'm not dead yet. And if you two had been consulting for some strange reason, she wouldn't have blabbed to a homicide detective. You'll have to give me a better explanation than that."

Jordan was at a loss. He couldn't think of any plausible excuse.

"The bottom line, Doctor, is that you haven't respected my confidentiality. Isn't that the fancy word you doctors use? The way I understand it, I could go to a lawyer and slap a malpractice suit on you, couldn't I?"

"I'm not sure . . ." Jordan couldn't even complete a phrase. He was instantly aware of his legal vulnerability.

"Now I don't want to hear any of your double-talk,"

Paul told him. "I probably won't go to a lawyer. You know why? I have lots of friends who are cheaper than lawyers and a hell of a lot more effective. You know, Doc, my friends are kind of like you: specialists for kneecaps, leg bones, and knuckles. I can just imagine what it would do to your practice if you happened to have your hand crushed by a car door."

"Mr. Cerino . . ." Jordan said in a conciliatory tone, but Paul cut him off.

"I think I've made myself clear, Doc. I'm counting on you not to go blabbing anymore. Am I right?"

Jordan nodded. His hands were trembling.

"Now, Doc, I don't mean to make you nervous. I want you in nothing but good shape. 'Cause that's what you're going to put me in: good shape. I was very pleased when your nurse called this morning to say I could come in for my operation."

"I'm glad, too," Jordan said, trying to regain some of his professionalism and composure. "You're lucky your chance came up so quickly. The waiting period has been much shorter than usual."

"Not short enough for me," Paul said. "In my line of work you have to have all your senses and then some. There are any number of sharks who'd love to put me out to pasture or worse. So let's get it over with."

"Fine by me," Jordan said nervously. He laid Cerino's record on the lens stand. Straddling a small wheeled stool, he pushed up to Cerino's ophthalmic examination chair. Swinging around the slit lamp, he motioned for Cerino to put his chin on the chin rest.

Reaching below with a trembling hand, Jordan switched on the slit lamp. As he did so he got a whiff of garlic from Cerino's breath.

"I understand you've been doing more surgery than usual lately," Paul said.

"That's true," Jordan replied.

255

"As a businessman myself I would imagine you'd like to do as much surgery as possible," Cerino said. "I imagine that's where the big bucks are."

"That's also true," Jordan said. He moved the slit lamp's beam so that it fell across Cerino's badly scarred cornea.

"I have some ideas about keeping your surgery up," Cerino said. "Would that interest you?"

"Of course," Jordan said.

"Fix me up first, Doc," Cerino said. "If you do, we'll remain friends. Then who knows? Maybe we can do some business."

Jordan wasn't certain he wanted to be friends with this guy, but he certainly didn't want to be enemies. He had a feeling Paul Cerino's enemies didn't last too long. He was determined to do his best by Cerino. And he'd already made up his mind: he wouldn't be sending the man a bill.

Laurie put down her pen and leaned back in her desk chair. She'd been struggling to keep her mind on her paperwork, but she wasn't making much headway. Her thoughts kept drifting back to those drug overdoses. She couldn't believe she wasn't down in the autopsy room working on the two cases that had come in overnight.

She'd resisted the temptation to sneak down and watch as Fontworth went about his business. Calvin would have exploded if he'd seen her.

Laurie looked at her watch. She decided it was late enough to slip downstairs to see if Fontworth had turned up anything. No sooner had she stood up than Lou walked in.

"On your way out?" he asked.

Laurie sat back down. "It's probably better if I don't."

"Yeah?" said Lou.

She could tell he wasn't sure what she was talking about.

"It's a long story," Laurie said. "How are you doing? You look exhausted."

"I am," Lou admitted. "I've been up since three. And doing autopsies with people other than you is just plain work."

"Are they finished?" Laurie asked.

"Hell, no," Lou said. "I'm the one who's finished. I couldn't stand up any longer. But it will probably take the two doctors all day to finish the four cases plus the dog."

"The dog?"

"Clipper," Lou said. "At one of the homes the killer shot the dog as well as the man and the woman. But I'm only kidding. They're not autopsying the dog."

"Find out anything useful?" Laurie asked.

"I don't know. The caliber of the bullets looks similar to the cases in Queens, but we'll have to wait to hear what Ballistics says before we're certain they're from the same guns. And of course Ballistics is weeks behind."

"No ideas yet?" Laurie asked.

Lou shook his head. "Afraid not. The Queens cases suggested a restaurant connection, but the two cases downstairs have nothing to do with the business. One guy was a big-shot banker who'd contributed heavily to the mayor's campaign. The other is an executive for one of the big auction houses."

"Still no organized-crime association?" Laurie asked.

"Nope," Lou said. "But we're still working on it. There's no question that these were professional hits. I've got two more investigative teams on these two Manhattan cases. Between the three teams in Queens and these two new ones, I'm running out of manpower. The only positive break so far is that the housekeeper at one of the homes is still alive. If she makes it, we'll have our first witness."

"I'd like to get a break with my series," Laurie said. "If only one of these overdoses wouldn't die. I wish I had some manpower to try to find the source of the coke that's killing all these people."

"You think it's from a single source?"

"I know so," Laurie said. She explained how Peter had determined it scientifically.

Just then Lou's beeper sounded. Lou checked the number. "Speaking of manpower," he said, "that's one of my boys. May I use your phone?"

Laurie nodded.

"What is it, Norman?" Lou asked once he got through. Laurie was flattered that Lou put the call on speakerphone so she could hear.

"Probably nothing," Norman said. "But I thought I'd tell you anyway. I've found one note of commonality in these three cases: a doctor."

"Really?" Lou said. He rolled his eyes at Laurie. This wasn't exactly the break he had been looking for. "That's not the sort of association that's going to be much help in this kind of murder case, Norman."

"I know," Norman said. "But it's the only thing that's turned up. Remember you told me that Steven Vivonetto and Janice Singleton were both terminal?"

"Yeah," Lou said. "Was one of the Kaufmans terminally ill too?"

"No, but Henriette Kaufman had a medical condition she was being treated for. And she was seeing the same doctor that Steven Vivonetto and Janice Singleton were seeing. Of course, Steven and Janice were seeing about a dozen doctors. But there was one doctor who was seeing all three."

"What kind of a doctor?" Lou asked.

"An eye doctor," Norman said. "His name is Jordan Scheffield."

Lou blinked. He couldn't believe what he'd heard. He glanced at Laurie. Her eyes registered equal surprise.

"How did you find this out?" Lou asked.

"Just by accident," Norman replied. "After you told me

about Steven and Janice being terminal, I looked into everybody's health. I didn't even realize the connection until I got back to my office and started going over all the material that had been coming in. Do you think it's important?"

"I don't know," Lou said. "It's certainly weird."

"You want me to follow up on it in any way?"

"I wouldn't even know how to follow up. Let me think about it and I'll get back to you. Meanwhile keep the investigation going."

Lou hung up the phone. "Well, it's a real small world. Either that or that boyfriend of yours really gets around."

"He's not my boyfriend," Laurie said irritably.

"I'm sorry," Lou said. "I forgot. Your male acquaintance who happens to be a friend."

"You know, the night that Marsha Schulman disappeared, Jordan told me that his office had been broken into. Someone had gone through his records."

"Some had been stolen?" Lou asked.

"No," Laurie said. "Apparently some had been copied. I had him check Cerino's record; it was one of the ones that had been disturbed."

"No kidding!" Lou said. He sat in bemused silence for a few minutes.

Laurie was quiet, too.

"It doesn't make a lot of sense," Lou said at last. "Could the Lucia family have gotten involved because Cerino is seeing Scheffield? I'm trying to fit Cerino's rival, Vinnie Dominick, into the picture, but I can't make any sense of it."

"One thing we could do is check the gangland-style homicides that came in today. See if any of them are Jordan's patients."

Lou's face brightened. "You know, that's a good idea. Glad I thought of it." His smile told Laurie he was kidding.

In mock anger Laurie threw a paper clip at him.

Five minutes later, dressed in scrubs, Laurie and Lou entered the autopsy room. Luckily Calvin was nowhere in sight.

Both Southgate and Besserman were on their second cases. Southgate was almost finished; the Kaufmans were fairly straightforward cases, given their simple head wounds. Besserman's cases were more difficult. First he had Dwight Sorenson, who had three bullet paths to trace. The work had been laborious and time-consuming, so Besserman was just starting on Amy Sorenson when Lou and Laurie got there.

With the permission of the respective doctors, Laurie and Lou glanced through the folders on each case. Unfortunately, the medical histories were meager.

"I've got a better idea," Laurie said. She went to the phone and called Cheryl Myers.

"Cheryl, I've got a favor to ask," Laurie said.

"What is it?" Cheryl asked cheerfully.

"You know the four Manhattan homicides we got today?" Laurie said. "The ones that everybody's up in arms about? I want to know if any of them have ever seen an ophthalmologist by the name of Jordan Scheffield."

"Will do," Cheryl said. "I'll call you back in a few minutes. Where are you?"

"I'm down in the pit," Laurie said.

Laurie told Lou they'd hear back soon. Then Laurie went over to George Fontworth. He was just finishing up the second of his two overdose cases: Julia Myerholtz.

"Calvin said I wasn't supposed to talk with you today," George told her. "I don't want to cross him."

"Just answer me this. Was the cocaine mainlined?"

"Yeah," George said. His eyes darted around the room as if he expected Calvin to come thundering by.

"Were the autopsies normal except for signs of the overdose and toxicity?" Laurie asked.

"Yes," George said. "Come on, Laurie, don't put me in this situation."

"One last question," Laurie said. "Were there any surprises?"

"Just one," George said. "But you know about that. I'd just not heard it was standard policy on this kind of case. I think it should have been brought up at Thursday conference."

"What are you talking about?" Laurie asked.

"Please," George said. "Don't act dumb. Calvin told me it was your doing."

"I don't know what you're talking about," Laurie said.

"Oh, God!" George said. "Here comes Calvin. 'Bye, Laurie."

Laurie turned in time to see Calvin's hulking figure enter through the swinging door. Even dressed in his scrubs and protective gloves, there was no mistaking that body. Laurie quickly stepped away from George's table, making a beeline for the master sheet of the day's autopsies. She wanted to have a cover in case Calvin asked why she was there. Quickly, she searched for Mary O'Connor's name. Finding it, she noted that Paul Plodgett had been scheduled for the autopsy. He was at the far table near the wall. Laurie joined him.

"I've found a lot of stuff," Paul said when Laurie asked how the autopsy was going.

Laurie glanced over her shoulder. Calvin had gone directly to Besserman's table.

"What's your feeling about the cause of death?" Laurie asked. She was relieved that Calvin hadn't seen her, or if he had, he didn't seem concerned about her presence.

"Undoubtedly cardiovascular," Paul said, gazing down at Mary O'Connor's body. The woman was considerably overweight. The face and head were a deep blue, almost purple.

"A lot of pathology?" Laurie asked.

"Enough," Paul said. "Moderate coronary disease for starters. Also the mitral valve was in pretty bad shape. The heart itself seemed awfully flabby. So there are a lot of candidates for the final culprit."

Laurie thought Jordan would appreciate the news.

"She's awfully purple," Laurie commented.

"True," Paul said. "Quite a bit of congestion in the head and the lungs. Must have been a lot of terminal, agonal effort. She didn't want to die, poor lady. She apparently even bit her lip."

"Really?" Laurie asked. "Do you think she had some kind of seizure?"

"Could have," Paul said. "But it's more like an abrasion, like she was chewing her lip."

"Let's see."

Paul reached over and drew back Mary O'Connor's upper lip.

"You're right," Laurie said. "What about the tongue?"

"Normal," Paul said. "That's why I doubt there was a seizure. Maybe she had a lot of terminal pain. Well, perhaps the microscopic of the heart will show something pathognomonic, but I bet this case will fall into that category of an unknown coup de grâce, at least specifically. In general I know it was cardiovascular."

Laurie nodded but looked at Mary O'Connor. Something bothered her about the case. It was triggering a memory she couldn't quite put a finger on.

"What about these petechiae on her face?" Laurie asked.

"It's consistent with terminal heart disease," Paul said.

"This much?"

"As I said, there must have been a lot of agonal effort."

"Would you mind letting me know what you find on microscopic?" she asked. "She was a friend's patient. I know he'll be interested in what you find."

"Will do," Paul said.

Laurie saw that Calvin had moved from Besserman to Fontworth. Lou had wandered back to Southgate's table. Laurie headed over to him.

"Sorry," she said to Lou as she came alongside.

"No problem," Lou said. "I'm starting to feel right at home here."

"Hey, Laurie, the phone's for you," a voice yelled out over the general background noise of the busy autopsy room. Laurie walked to the phone, cringing that her presence had been so blatantly broadcasted. She didn't dare look in Calvin's direction. She picked up the receiver: it was Cheryl.

"I wish all your requests were so easy," Cheryl said. "I called over to Dr. Scheffield's office and the secretary couldn't have been more helpful. Henriette Kaufman and Dwight Sorenson were both patients. Does that help you?"

"I'm not sure," Laurie said. "But it is interesting indeed. Thanks."

Laurie went back to Lou and told him what she had learned.

"Wow!" he said. "That takes it out of the realm of coincidence. At least I think it does."

"Five for five," Laurie said. "The possibility of that happening by chance is extremely small."

"But what does it mean?" Lou asked. "It seems like an awfully strange way to get at Cerino, if that's what it's about. It doesn't make any sense."

"I agree," Laurie said.

"One way or the other," Lou said, "I've got to look into it immediately. I'll be in touch." He was gone before Laurie could say so much as goodbye.

Laurie hazarded one last glance at Calvin. He was still talking with George and didn't seem the least perturbed by her presence.

Back in her office, Laurie called Jordan. As usual he was in surgery. Laurie left a message for him to please call back.

Trying to go back to work, Laurie wasn't much more successful than she'd been earlier. Her mind was in a turmoil concerning her precarious job situation from having alienated so many people, her overdose series, and the odd coincidence that Jordan was treating a string of five gangland-style murder victims.

Laurie's thoughts drifted back to Mary O'Connor. She suddenly remembered what she'd been trying to think of earlier. The abrasions on the lip, the florid petechiae, and the face's deep purple discoloration suggested "burking," the suffocation by compressing the chest while occluding the mouth.

With that thought in mind, Laurie phoned down to the autopsy room and asked for Paul.

"I've had a thought," Laurie said once he was on the line.

"Shoot," Paul said.

"What do you think about burking as a possible cause of death in the O'Connor case?"

Her suggestion was met with silence.

"Well?" Laurie questioned.

"The victim was in Manhattan General," Paul said. "She was in a private room in the Goldblatt wing."

"Try to forget where she was," Laurie said. "Just look at the facts."

"But as forensic pathologists we're supposed to take the scene into consideration. If we didn't, we'd misdiagnose tons of cases."

"I understand that," Laurie said. "But sometimes the scene can be misleading. What about homicides set up to look like suicides?"

"That's different," Paul said.

"Is it?" Laurie questioned. "Anyway I just wanted you to give burking some thought. Think about the lip abrasion, the petechiae, and the amount of congestion of the face and the head."

As soon as Laurie put down the receiver, the phone rang. It was Jordan.

"I'm glad you called," Jordan said. "I was about to call you. I'm up in surgery and I only have a second. I've got a number of cases, including, you'll be glad to hear, Mr. Paul Cerino."

"I am glad—" Laurie said.

"And I have a favor to ask," Jordan said, cutting Laurie short. "In order to get Cerino on the schedule, I've had to do some juggling. So I'm going to be stuck here until late. Could we take a raincheck on our dinner plans? How about tomorrow night?"

"I suppose," Laurie said. "But Jordan, I have some things I have to talk to you about now."

"Make it fast," Jordan said. "My next patient is already in the operating room."

"First, about Mary O'Connor," Laurie said. "She had heart disease."

"That's reassuring," Jordan said.

"Do you know anything about her personal life?"

"Not much."

"What would you say if I told you she'd been murdered?"

"Murdered!" Jordan sputtered. "Are you serious?"

"I don't know," Laurie admitted. "But if you told me she had twenty million dollars and was about to cut her wicked grandson out of her will, the possibility of murder might enter into my thinking."

"She was well-off but not wealthy," Jordan said. "And do I have to remind you that you were supposed to make me feel better about her death, not more uneasy?"

"The doctor who did her autopsy is convinced that she died from heart disease," Laurie said.

"That's better," Jordan said. "Where did this murder question originate?"

"My fertile imagination," Laurie said. "Plus some other rather startling news. Are you sitting down?"

"Please, Laurie, no games. I was due in the OR ten minutes ago."

"Do the names Henriette Kaufman and Dwight Sorenson mean anything to you?" Laurie questioned.

"They're two of my patients. Why?"

"They were your patients," Laurie said. "They were both killed last night along with their spouses. Their autopsies are going on as we speak."

"My God!" Jordan said.

"And that's not all," Laurie said. "The night before last three other patients of yours were murdered. All of them were shot in a manner that suggests an organized-crime connection. At least that's what I've been told."

"Oh, my God," Jordan said. "And Paul Cerino was in my office threatening me just this morning. This is a nightmare."

"How did he threaten you?" Laurie asked.

"I don't even want to discuss it," Jordan said. "But he's quite angry with me and I'm afraid I have you to thank."

"Me?"

"I wasn't going to bring this up until we got together," Jordan said, "but now that we're on the subject—"

"What?"

"Why did you tell a detective Soldano about my treating Cerino?"

"I didn't think it was a secret," Laurie said. "After all, you talked about it at my parents' dinner party."

"I suppose you're right," Jordan said. "But how did you happen to tell a homicide detective of all people?"

"He was here observing autopsies," Laurie said. "Cerino's name came up in relation to some homicides:

several gangland-style execution victims pulled out of the East River."

"Oh, boy," Jordan said.

"I'm sorry to be the Greek messenger with all this bad news."

"It's not your fault," Jordan said. "And I guess I'm better off knowing. Thankfully I'll be doing Cerino this evening. At this point the sooner I get rid of him the better."

"Just be careful," Laurie said. "Something strange is going on. I'm just not sure what."

Jordan didn't need Laurie to remind him to be careful, not after Cerino's threat to crush his hands. And now this news that five of his patients had been murdered and another one dead, possibly also murdered. It was too much.

Preoccupied with this bizarre yet terrifying set of circumstances, Jordan got up from the chair in the surgical lounge of the Manhattan General Hospital and traipsed into the OR. He wondered if he should go to the police and tell them about Cerino's threat. Yet if he did go to the police, what would they do? Probably nothing. What would Cerino do? Probably what he threatened. Jordan shivered with fear at the thought and wished that Cerino had never walked through his door.

As he scrubbed his hands, Jordan tried to think of why five and possibly six of his patients would be killed. And what about Marsha? But try as he might, he couldn't think of a reason. Holding his hands in the air, he pushed into the operating room.

Surgery for Jordan was a cathartic experience. He was relieved to be able to lose himself in the exacting procedure of a corneal transplant. For the next few hours he completely forgot about threats, mob hits, Marsha Schulman, and unsolved homicides.

"Wonderful job," the junior resident commented after Jordan had finished.

"Thank you," Jordan said. He beamed. Then, to the nursing staff, he added: "I'll be in the surgical lounge. Let's turn the room around as soon as possible. The next case is one of my VIPs."

"Yes, your Highness," the scrub nurse teased.

Walking back to the surgical lounge, Jordan was glad that Cerino was next. He just wished it was already over. Although complications were rare for Jordan, they did occur. He shivered to think of the consequence of a postoperative infection: not for Cerino, for himself.

Gripped by his scary thoughts, Jordan was oblivious of his surroundings. And when he sank into one of the armchairs in the lounge and closed his eyes he hadn't noticed the man sitting directly across from him.

"Good afternoon, Doctor!"

Jordan opened his eyes. It was Lou Soldano.

"Your secretary told me you were up here," Lou said. "I told her it was important that I talk with you. I hope you don't mind."

Jordan sat bolt upright and his eyes nervously darted around the room. He knew Cerino had to be close, probably in the holding area at that moment. And that meant that the tall gaunt fellow would be around someplace. Cerino had insisted on it, and the administration had agreed. Jordan did not relish the idea of Cerino's man seeing him with Lou Soldano. He didn't want to be forced to explain it to Cerino.

"Certain facts have come up," Lou continued. "I'm hoping you might have some explanations."

"I have another operation," Jordan said. He started to get up.

"Sit down, Doctor," Lou said. "I only want a minute of your time. At least at the moment. We've been puzzling over five recent homicides which we have reason to believe were done by the same person or persons, and the only way we have been able to associate them so far, other than the manner in which they were killed, is that they were your patients. Naturally we'd like to ask you if you have any idea why this has happened."

"I'd just been informed about it an hour ago," Jordan said nervously. "I haven't the slightest idea why. But I can tell you there is no way that it could involve me."

"So we can assume they have all paid their bills?" Lou asked.

"Under the circumstances, Lieutenant," Jordan snapped, "I don't think that is a very funny comment."

"Excuse my black humor," Lou said. "But guessing how much that office of yours had to cost and knowing you have a limo—"

"I don't have to talk with you if I don't want to," Jordan said, interrupting Lou and again motioning to get up.

"You don't have to talk with me now," Lou said. "That's true. But you'd have to talk with me eventually, so you might as well try to cooperate. After all, this is one hell of a serious situation."

Jordan sat back. "What do you want from me? I don't have anything to add to what you already know. I'm sure you know much more than I."

"Tell me about Martha Goldburg, Steven Vivonetto, Janice Singleton, Henriette Kaufman, and Dwight Sorenson."

"They were patients of mine," Jordan said.

"What were their diagnoses?" Lou asked. He took out his pad and pencil.

"I can't tell you that," Jordan said. "That's privileged information. And don't cite my mentioning the Cerino case to Dr. Montgomery as a precedent. I made a mistake talking about him."

269

"I'll be able to get the information from the families," Lou said. "Why don't you just make it easy for me?"

"It's up to the families to tell you if they so choose," Jordan said. "I am not at liberty to divulge that information."

"OK," Lou said. "Then let's talk generalities. Did all these people have the same diagnosis?"

"No," Jordan said.

"They didn't?" Lou questioned. He visibly sagged. "Are you sure?"

"Of course I'm sure," Jordan said.

Lou looked down at his blank pad and thought for a moment. Raising his eyes he asked: "Were these patients related in some unlikely way? For example, were they customarily seen on the same day, anything like that?"

"No," Jordan said.

"Could their records have been kept together for some reason?"

"No, my records are alphabetical."

"Could any of these patients have been seen on the same day as Cerino?"

"That I can't say," Jordan admitted. "But I can tell you this. When Mr. Cerino came to see me, he never saw any other patient nor did any other patient see him."

"Are you sure of that?" Lou asked.

"Positive," Jordan said.

The intercom connecting the surgical lounge to the OR crackled to life. One of the OR nurses told Jordan that his patient was in the room waiting for him.

Jordan got to his feet. Lou did the same.

"I've got surgery," Jordan said.

"OK," Lou said. "I'm sure we'll be in touch."

Lou put on his hat and walked out of the surgical lounge.

Jordan followed him to the door and watched as Lou continued down the long hallway to the main hospital elevators. He watched as Lou pushed the button, waited, then boarded and disappeared from view.

Jordan's eyes swept the hallway for Cerino's man. Stepping across the hall, he peered into the surgical waiting room. He was encouraged when he didn't see the gaunt man anyplace.

Turning back into the surgical lounge, Jordan sighed. He was relieved that Lou had left. The meeting with him had left Jordan feeling more rattled than ever, and it wasn't only because of the fear that Cerino's man would see them talking. Jordan sensed the detective didn't like him much, and that could mean trouble. Jordan was afraid he'd have to put up with the man's annoying presence in the future.

Stepping into the men's locker room, Jordan splashed his face with cold water. He needed to pull himself together to try to relax a moment before going into the OR and doing Cerino. But it wasn't easy. So much was happening. His mind was in a turmoil.

One of the thoughts that was particularly disturbing was that he'd realized there was one way that the five homicides were related, including Mary O'Connor. He'd realized it while Lou Soldano had been talking with him, but Jordan had chosen not to say anything about it. And the fact that he had so chosen confused him. He didn't know if the reason he'd not mentioned it was because he wasn't sure of its significance or because it scared him. Jordan certainly did not want to become a victim himself.

Walking down toward the operating room where Paul Cerino was waiting, Jordan decided that the safest course of action for him was to do nothing. After all, he was in the middle.

Suddenly Jordan stopped. He'd realized something else. Despite all these problems, he was doing more surgery than ever. There had to be another part to it all. As he started walking again, it all began to make a kind of grotesque, malicious sense. He picked up his pace. Definitely playing dumb was the way he should handle it. It was the safest by far. And he liked to do surgery.

Pushing into the operating room, he went up to Cerino, who was significantly sedated.

"We'll have you done in no time," Jordan said. "Just relax."

After giving Cerino a pat on the shoulder, Jordan turned and headed out to scrub. As he passed one of the orderlies in scrubs, he realized it wasn't one of the orderlies. Jordan had recognized the eyes. It was the gaunt one.

11

□

Laurie was hesitant to visit the lab again. She didn't want to risk another run-in with John DeVries. But attempting any more paperwork just then was ridiculous. She was far too distracted. She decided to find Peter. Surely he had to have more results by then.

"I know you promised to call if you found anything," Laurie said once she'd found him, "but I couldn't help but stop by just to check how you were doing."

"I haven't found a contaminant yet," Peter said. "But I did learn something that might be significant. Cocaine is metabolized in the body in a variety of different ways producing a variety of metabolites. One of the metabolites is called benzoylecgonine. When I calculated the ratio of cocaine and benzoylecgonine in the blood, urine, and brain of your victims, I can estimate the amount of time from injection to death."

273

"And what did you find?" Laurie asked.

"I found it was pretty consistent," Peter said. "Roughly an hour in thirteen of the fourteen. But in one of the cases it was different. For some reason Robert Evans had practically no benzoylecgonine at all."

"Meaning?" Laurie questioned.

"Meaning that Robert Evans died very quickly," Peter said. "Maybe within minutes. Maybe even less, I really can't say."

"What do you think the significance is?" Laurie questioned.

"I don't know," Peter said. "You're the medical detective, not me."

"I suppose he could have suffered an instantaneous cardiac arrhythmia."

Peter shrugged. "Whatever," he said. "And I haven't given up on a contaminant. But if I find something, it's going to be in nanomoles."

Leaving the toxicology department, Laurie felt discouraged. Despite all her efforts she didn't feel any further along in her investigation of these unlikely overdoses than she had been at the start. Intending to talk again with George Fontworth and have him explain what had surprised him on the autopsies, Laurie descended to the basement level and poked her head into the autopsy room. She didn't see George, but she saw Vinnie and asked about George.

"He left about an hour ago," Vinnie said.

Laurie went upstairs to George's office. The door was open but he wasn't there. Since his room was adjacent to one of the serology labs, Laurie went in and asked if anyone had seen George.

"He had a dentist's appointment," one of the techs said. "He mentioned he'd be back later, but he didn't know when."

Laurie nodded.

Stepping out of the lab, she paused outside George's office. From where she was standing she could see the autopsy folders from the two overdose cases he'd handled that day.

Looking over her shoulder to make sure no one was watching, Laurie stepped into the office and opened the top folder. It was Julia Myerholtz's file. That was the case George had been working on when Laurie had gone over to his table. She hastily read through George's autopsy notes. Immediately she understood what he had meant by the "surprise." Obviously he'd responded the same way Laurie had with Duncan Andrews.

Looking at the forensic investigator's report, Laurie noticed that the victim had been identified at the scene by "Robert Nussman, boyfriend."

Taking a piece of scratch paper from a pad on George's desk, Laurie jotted down Julia's address.

Laurie was just about to open the second file when she heard someone coming down the hall. Sheepishly, she closed the folder, pocketed the piece of scrap paper, and stepped back out into the hall. She nodded and smiled guiltily as one of the histology techs passed by.

Although Bingham had chastised Laurie for visiting Duncan Andrews' apartment, she decided she would go to Julia Myerholtz's place. Hailing a cab, she convinced herself that Bingham's anger had more to do with the unique fact that the case was such a political hot potato. He hadn't objected to examination of the scene per se—or so Laurie rationalized.

Julia's apartment was in a large posh building on East Seventy-fifth Street. Laurie was quite surprised when the doorman came to the curb to open her door for her as she paid the cab fare. It amazed her to experience the kind of style some people enjoyed in the city. The ambience was certainly a far cry from her own in Kips Bay.

"May I help you, madame?" the doorman asked. He had a thick Irish brogue.

Laurie showed her medical examiner's badge and asked to see the superintendent. A few minutes later the man appeared in the foyer.

"I'd like to view Julia Myerholtz's apartment," Laurie told him. "But before I go up, I want to make certain that no one is there just now."

The superintendent asked the doorman if the apartment was empty.

"It is indeed," the doorman said. "Her parents aren't due in until tomorrow. You want the key?"

The superintendent nodded. The doorman opened a small cabinet, took out a key, and handed it to Laurie.

"Just give it back to Patrick here when you leave," the superintendent said.

"I'd prefer if you came along."

"I have a hot water leak in the basement," the superintendent explained. "You'll be okay—9C. It's to the right when you get off the elevator."

The elevator stopped on 9, and Laurie got out. Just to be sure, she rang the bell of 9C several times and even pounded on the door before going in. She didn't want to run into any of the deceased's loved ones this time around.

The first thing Laurie noticed were the shards of a plaster cast statue scattered over the floor of the foyer. Judging by the larger pieces, Laurie guessed the piece had been a replica of Michelangelo's David.

The roomy apartment was decorated in a comfortable, country style. Not sure of what she was looking for, Laurie simply roamed from room to room, surveying the scene.

In the kitchen Laurie opened the refrigerator. It was well stocked with health food: yogurt, bean sprouts, fresh vegetables, and skim milk.

In the living room the coffee table was loaded with art books and magazines: *American Health, Runner's World,*

Triathlon, and *Prevention.* The room was lined with book-shelves filled with more art books. On the mantel, Laurie noticed a small plaque. She went closer to read the inscription: "Central Park Triathlon, Third Place, 30–34."

In the bedroom Laurie discovered an exercise bike and lots of framed photographs. Most of the photos featured an attractive woman and a handsome young man in various outdoor settings: on bikes in a mountain setting, camping in a forest, finishing a race.

As she wandered back into the living room, Laurie tried to imagine why an amateur athlete like Julia Myerholtz was apparently taking drugs. It just didn't make any sense. The health food, the magazines, and the accomplishments just didn't jibe with cocaine.

Laurie's musings were abruptly cut short when she heard a key in the door. For a second of absolute panic she contemplated trying to hide, as if she expected Bingham to come through the door.

When the door opened, the young man who entered seemed as surprised as Laurie to meet someone in the apartment. Laurie recognized him as the man in many of the bedroom photos.

"Dr. Laurie Montgomery," Laurie said, flipping open her badge. "I'm from the medical examiner's office, investigating Miss Myerholtz's death."

"I'm Robert Nussman. I was Julia's boyfriend."

"I don't mean to be a bother," Laurie said, moving to leave. "I can come back at another time." She did not want Bingham to get wind of this.

"No, it's all right," Robert said, holding up a hand. "Please stay. I'll only be here a moment."

"Terrible tragedy," Laurie said. She felt the need to say something.

"Tell me about it," Robert said. He suddenly looked very sad. He also acted as if he needed to talk.

"Did you know she took drugs?" Laurie asked.

"She didn't," he said. "I know that's what you people say," he added as his face flushed, "but I'm telling you, Julia never did drugs. It just wasn't in her nature. She was totally into health. She got me into running." He smiled at the memory. "Last spring she had me do my first triathlon. I just can't figure it. My God, she didn't even drink."

"I'm sorry," Laurie said.

"She was so gifted," Robert said wistfully. "So strong-willed, so committed. She cared about people. She was religious: not overly, but enough. And she was involved in everything, like pro choice, the homeless, AIDS, you name it."

"I understand you identified her here at the scene," Laurie said. "Were you the one who found her?"

"Yes," Robert managed. He looked away, struggling with tears.

"It must have been awful," Laurie said. Memories of finding her brother crowded in with graphic intensity. She did her best to dismiss them. "Where was she when you came in?"

Robert pointed toward the bedroom.

"Was she still alive at that point?" Laurie asked gently.

"Sort of," Robert said. "She was breathing off and on. I gave her CPR until the ambulance got here."

"How did you happen to come by?" Laurie asked.

"She'd called me earlier," Robert said. "She said to be sure to come over later on."

"Was that customary?" Laurie asked.

Robert looked puzzled. "I don't know," he said. "I guess."

"Did she sound normal?" Laurie asked. "Could you tell if she'd taken any drugs yet?"

"I don't think she'd taken anything," Robert said. "She didn't sound high. But I guess she didn't seem normal either. She sounded tense. In fact, I was a little afraid she was

278

planning on telling me something bad, like she wanted to break up or something."

"Was there some problem in your relationship?" Laurie asked.

"No," Robert said. "Things were great. I mean, I thought they were great. It's just that she sounded a little funny."

"What about that broken statue by the front door?"

"I saw that the second I came through the door last night," Robert said. "It was her favorite possession. It was a couple of hundred years old. When I saw it was broken, I knew something bad was going on."

Laurie glanced over at the shattered statue and wondered if Julia could have broken it while in the throes of a seizure. If so, how did she get from the foyer to the bedroom?

"Thank you for your help," Laurie said. "I hope I haven't upset you with my questions."

"No," Robert said. "But why are you going to all this trouble? I thought medical examiners just did autopsies and only got involved with murders, like Quincy."

"We try to help the living," Laurie said. "That's our job. What I'd really like to do is prevent future tragedies like Julia's. The more I learn, the more I may be able to do that."

"If you have any more questions, call me," Robert said. He handed Laurie his card. "And if it somehow turns out that it wasn't drugs, please let me know. It would be important because . . ." Suddenly overcome with emotion, he wasn't able to continue.

Laurie nodded. She gave Robert her own business card after scribbling her home phone number on the back. "If you have any questions for me or if you think of anything I should know, please give me a call. You can call anytime."

Leaving Robert to grieve in private, Laurie left the apartment and boarded the elevator. As she was riding down, she recalled that Sara Wetherbee had said that Duncan had invited her over the night he'd overdosed. Laurie thought both Duncan's and Julia's invitations to their significant others were odd. If both were doing such a good job hiding their drug abuse, why invite someone over the very night they were indulging?

Laurie returned the key to Patrick the doorman and thanked him on her way out. She was a half dozen steps from the door when she turned around and went back.

"Were you on duty last night?" Laurie asked him.

"Indeed I was," Patrick said. "Three to eleven. That's my shift."

"Did you happen to see Julia Myerholtz yesterday evening?" Laurie asked.

"I did," Patrick said. "I'd see her most every evening."

"I suppose you've heard what happened to her," Laurie said. She didn't want to offer any information the doorman might not be privy to.

"I have," Patrick said. "She took drugs like a lot of young people. It's a shame."

"Did she seem depressed when she came in last night?" Laurie asked.

"I wouldn't say depressed," Patrick said. "But she didn't act normal."

"In what way?" Laurie asked.

"She didn't say hello," Patrick said. "She always said hello except for last night. But maybe that was because she wasn't alone."

"Do you remember who was with her?" Laurie questioned with interest.

"I do," Patrick said. "Normally I can't remember things like that since we have a lot of traffic going in and out. But since Ms. Myerholtz hadn't said hello, I looked at her companions."

"Did you recognize them?" Laurie said. "Had they been here before?"

"I didn't know who they were," Patrick said. "And I don't think I'd ever seen them. One was tall, thin, and well dressed. The other was muscular and on the short side. No one said anything when they came in."

"Did you see them when they went out?" Laurie asked.

"No, I didn't," Patrick said. "They must have left during my break."

"What time did they come in?" Laurie asked.

"Early evening," Patrick said. "Something like seven o'clock."

Laurie thanked Patrick yet again and hailed a cab to return to her office. It was almost dusk. The skyscrapers were already lit and people were hurrying home from work. As the cab headed downtown in the heavy traffic, she thought about her conversations with the boyfriend and the doorman. She wondered about the two men Patrick had described. Although they were probably co-workers or friends of Julia's, the fact that they had visited the same night that Julia overdosed made them important. Laurie wished there was some way she could find out their identities so she could talk with them. The thought even went through her mind that they could have been drug dealers. Could Julia Myerholtz have had a secret life her boyfriend wasn't privy to?

Back at the medical examiner's building, Laurie went first to George's office to see if he'd returned from the dentist. Obviously he had come and gone; his office was dark. Disappointed, Laurie tried the door, but it was locked. Not being able to talk with George, she'd had the sudden idea to get the address of the other overdose, Wendell Morrison.

Leaving her coat in her room and picking up some rubber gloves, Laurie went down to the morgue. She found the evening mortuary tech, Bruce Pomowski, in the mortuary office.

"Any idea of the dispensation of the Myerholtz remains?" Laurie asked. "Have they been picked up?"

"Was she one of today's cases?" Bruce asked.

"Yes," Laurie said.

Bruce opened a thick ledger and ran a finger down the day's entries. When he got to Myerholtz, his finger ran across the page. "Hasn't been picked up yet," he said. "We're waiting on a call from an out-of-town funeral home."

"Is she in the walk-in?" Laurie asked.

"Yup," Bruce said. "Should be on a gurney near the front."

Laurie thanked him and walked down the corridor toward the walk-in refrigerator. In the evenings the environment of the morgue changed considerably. During the day it was full of frantic activity. But now as Laurie walked she could hear the heels of her shoes echo through the deserted and mostly dark, blue-tiled corridors. All at once she remembered Lou's response when they'd come down Tuesday morning. He'd called it a grisly scene.

Laurie stopped and looked down at the stained cement floor that Lou had pointed out. Then she raised her eyes to the stacks of pine coffins destined for Potter's Field with unclaimed, unidentified remains. She started walking again. It was amazing how her normal mental state shielded the ghastly side of the morgue from her consciousness. It took a stranger like Lou and a time when the morgue was empty of the living for her to appreciate it.

Reaching the large, cumbersome stainless-steel door of the walk-in, Laurie put on her gloves and pressed the thick handle to release the latch. With a hefty yank she pulled the heavy door open. A cold, clammy mist swirled out around her feet. Reaching in, she turned on the light.

Reacting to her mind-set of only moments earlier, Laurie viewed the interior of the walk-in cooler from the perspective of a nonprofessional person, not the forensic pathologist she was. It was definitely horrifying. Bare wooden shelves lined the walls. On the shelves was a ghoulish collection of cold, dead bodies and body parts that having been autopsied and examined were waiting to be claimed. Most were nude, although a few were covered with sheets stained with blood and other body fluids. It was like an earthly view of hell.

The center of the room was crowded with old gurneys, each bearing a separate body. Again, some were covered, others naked and blankly staring up at the ceiling like some sort of macabre dormitory.

Feeling uncharacteristically squeamish, Laurie stepped over the threshold, her eyes nervously darting around the gurneys to locate Julia Myerholtz. Behind her the heavy door slammed shut with a loud click.

Irrationally, Laurie spun around and rushed back to the door, fearful that she'd been locked into the cooler. But the latch responded to her push and the door swung open on its bulky hinges.

Embarrassed at her own imagination, Laurie turned back into the refrigerator and began methodically going through the bodies on the gurneys. For identification purposes each body had a manila name tag tied around the right big toe. She found Julia not far from the doorway. Her body was one of those that had been covered.

Stepping up to the head, Laurie drew down the sheet. She gazed at the woman's pallid skin and her delicate features. Judging by her appearance alone, if she hadn't been so pale, she could have been sleeping. But the rude, Y-shaped autopsy incision dispelled any hope that she might still be alive.

Looking more closely, Laurie saw multiple bruised areas on Julia's head, an indication of her probable seizure activity. In her mind's eye Laurie could see the woman bumping up against her statue of David and knocking it to the floor. Opening up Julia's mouth, Laurie looked at the tongue, which had not been removed. She could see that it had been bitten severely: more evidence of seizure activity.

Next Laurie looked for the IV site where Julia had injected herself. She found it as easily as she had the others. She also noticed that Julia had scratched her arms the way Duncan Andrews had done. She had probably experienced similar hallucinations. But Laurie noticed Julia's scratches were deeper, almost as if they had been done with knives.

Looking at Julia's carefully manicured nails, Laurie could see why the scratches were so deep. Julia's nails were long and immaculately polished. While she was admiring the woman's nails, Laurie noted a bit of tissue wedged beneath the nail of the right middle finger.

After finding no other tissue under any of the other nails, Laurie went to the autopsy room for two specimen jars and a scalpel. Returning to Julia's side, she teased a bit of tissue free and put it into one of the specimen jars. Using the scalpel, she sliced a small sliver of skin from the margin of the autopsy wound and slipped it into the other specimen jar.

After covering Julia's body with the sheet, Laurie took the two samples up to the DNA lab, where she labeled them and signed them in. On the request form she asked for a match. Even though it was fairly obvious the woman had scratched herself, Laurie thought it was worth checking. Just because the M.E.'s office was overworked was no reason not to be thorough. Still, she was relieved that it was evening and the lab was empty. She wouldn't have wanted to explain the need for this test.

Laurie walked back to her office. With everyone else gone, she thought she might take advantage of the quiet and turn her attention to some of that paperwork she'd been so studiously neglecting.

Still feeling slightly tense from her strange reaction to the cooler door closing, Laurie was ill prepared to deal with what awaited her in her office. As she rounded the corner of the doorway, preoccupied with her thoughts, a figure shouted and leaped at her.

Laurie screamed from someplace deep down in her being. It was a purely reflex response, and of a power that caused the sound to reverberate up and down the cinderblocked hallway like some charged subatomic particle in an accelerator. She'd had no control. Simultaneous with the scream her heart leaped in her chest.

But the attack that Laurie feared did not occur. Instead her brain frantically changed the message and told her that the terrifying figure had cried "Boo!"—hardly what a mad rapist or some supernatural demon would yell. At the same time her brain identified the face as belonging to Lou Soldano.

All this had happened in the blink of an eye, and by the time Laurie was capable of responding, her fear had changed to anger.

"Lou!" she cried. "Why did you do that?"

"Did I scare you?" Lou asked sheepishly. He could see that her face had turned to ivory. His ears were still ringing from her scream.

"Scare me?" she yelled. "You terrified me, and I hate to be scared like that. Don't ever do that again."

"I'm sorry," Lou said contritely. "I suppose it was juvenile. But this place has been scaring me; I thought I could get you back a little."

"I could bop you in the nose," Laurie said, shaking a clenched fist in front of his face. Her anger had already subsided, especially with his apology and apparent remorse. She walked around her desk and fell into her chair. "What on earth are you doing here at this hour anyway?" she asked.

"I was literally driving by," Lou said. "I wanted to talk with you, so I pulled into the morgue loading dock on the chance that you'd be here. I really didn't expect you to be, but the fellow downstairs said you'd just been in his office."

"What did you want to talk to me about?"

"Your boyfriend, Jordan," Lou said.

"He's not my boyfriend," Laurie snapped. "You're really going to irritate me if you persist in calling him that."

"What's the problem?" Lou asked. "It seems to me to be a relatively accurate term. After all, you go out with him every night."

"My social life is no one's business but mine," Laurie said. "But for your information, I do not 'go out' with him every night. I'm obviously not going out tonight."

"Well, three out of four ain't bad," Lou said. "But look, down to business: I wanted to let you know that I talked with Jordan about his patients being professionally bumped off."

"What did he have to say?" Laurie asked.

"Not a lot," Lou said. "He refused to talk about any of his patients specifically."

"Good for him."

"But more important than what he said was how he acted. He was really nervous the whole time I was there. I don't know what to make of that."

"You don't think he was involved with these murders in any way, do you?"

"No," Lou said. "Robbing his patients blind—no pun intended—yes, shooting them, no. He'd be killing the golden goose. But he was definitely nervous. Something's on his mind. I think he knows something."

"I think he has plenty of reason to be nervous," Laurie said. "Did he tell you that Cerino threatened him?"

"No, he didn't," Lou said. "How did he threaten him?"

"Jordan wouldn't say," Laurie said. "But if Cerino is the kind of person you say he is, then you can just imagine."

Lou nodded. "I wonder why Jordan didn't tell me."

"Probably he doesn't think you could protect him. Could you?"

"Probably not," Lou said. "Certainly not forever. Not someone as high profile as Jordan Scheffield."

"Did you learn anything helpful talking with him?" Laurie asked.

"I did learn that the murder victims did not have the same diagnosis," Lou said. "At least according to him. That was one harebrained idea I had. And I learned that they are not related in any other obvious way vis-à-vis Jordan Scheffield other than being his patients. I asked about every way I could imagine. So, unfortunately, I didn't learn much."

"What are you going to do now?" Laurie asked.

"Hope!" Lou said. "Plus I'll have my investigative teams find out the individual diagnoses. Maybe that will tell us something. There has to be some aspect I'm missing in all this."

"That's the way I feel about my overdose cases," Laurie said.

"By the way," Lou said. "What are you doing here so late?"

"I was hoping to get some work done. But with my pulse still racing thanks to you, I'll probably take the paperwork home and tackle it there."

"What about dinner?" Lou asked. "How about coming with me down to Little Italy. You like pasta?"

"I love pasta."

"How about it then?" Lou asked. "You already told me you aren't going out with the good doctor, and that's your favorite excuse."

"You are persistent."

"Hey, I'm Italian."

Fifteen minutes later Laurie found herself in Lou's Caprice heading downtown. She did not know if it was a good idea to have dinner with the man, but she really hadn't been able to think of a reason not to go. And although he'd been somewhat rude on previous occasions, now he seemed nothing but charming as he regaled her with stories of growing up in Queens.

Although Laurie had grown up in Manhattan, she'd never been to Little Italy. As they drove up Mulberry Street she was delighted by the ambience. There was a multitude of restaurants and throngs of people strolling the streets. Just like Italy itself, the place seemed to be throbbing with life.

"It's definitely Italian," Laurie said.

"It looks it, doesn't it?" Lou said. "But I'll tell you a little secret. Most of the real estate here is owned by Chinese."

"That's strange," Laurie said, a bit disappointed although she didn't know why.

"Used to be an Italian neighborhood," Lou said, "but the Italians for the most part moved out to the suburbs, like Queens. And the Chinese with a nose for business came in and bought up the properties."

They pulled into a restricted parking zone. Laurie pointed to the sign.

"Please!" Lou said. He positioned a little card on the dash by the steering wheel. "Once in a while I'm entitled to take advantage of being one of New York's finest."

Lou led her down a narrow street to one of the less obvious restaurants.

"It doesn't have a name," Laurie said as they entered.

"It doesn't need one."

The interior was a kitschy blend of red and white checked tablecloths and trellis interlaced with artificial ivy and plastic grapes. A candle stuck in a jug with wax drippings coating the sides served as each table's light fixture. A few black velvet paintings of Venice hung on the walls. There were about thirty tables packed tightly in the narrow room; all seemed to be occupied. Harried waiters dashed about attending to the customers. Everyone seemed to know each other by their first names. Over the whole scene hung a babble of voices and a rich, savory, herbed aroma of spicy food.

Laurie suddenly realized how hungry she was. "Looks like we should have made a reservation," she said.

Lou motioned for her to be patient. In a few minutes a very large and very Italian woman appeared and gave Lou an enveloping hug. She was introduced to Laurie. Her name was Marie.

As if by magic, an available table materialized and Marie seated Laurie and Lou.

"I have a feeling you're pretty well known here," Laurie said.

"With as many times as I've eaten here I'd better be. I've put one of their kids through college."

To Laurie's chagrin there were no menus. She had to listen to the choices as they were recited by a waiter with a heavy Italian accent. But no sooner had he finished his impressive litany than Lou leaned over and encouraged her to choose the ravioli or the manicotti. Laurie quickly settled on the ravioli.

With dinner ordered and a bottle of white wine on the table, Lou disappointed Laurie by lighting a cigarette.

"Maybe we could compromise," Laurie said. "How about you having only one."

"Fine by me."

After a glass of wine, Laurie began to revel in the chaotic atmosphere. When their entrées arrived, Giuseppe, the owner-chef, appeared to pay his respects.

Laurie thought the dinner was wonderful. After the last few nights in such formal settings, this lively spot was a welcome relief. Everyone seemed to know—and love—Lou. He received much good-natured kidding for having brought Laurie along. Apparently he usually dined solo.

For dessert Lou insisted they take a walk up the street to

an Italian-style coffee bar that served decaf espresso and gelato.

With their espressos and ice creams before them, Laurie looked up at Lou. "Lou," she said, "there's something I want to ask you."

"Uh-oh," Lou said. "I was hoping we could avoid any potentially troublesome subjects. Please don't ask me to go to the narc boys again."

"I only want your opinion," Laurie said.

"OK," Lou said. "That's not so scary. Shoot."

"I don't want you to laugh at me, OK," Laurie said.

"This is starting to sound interesting," Lou said.

"I have no definitive reason why I've been thinking this," Laurie said. "Just some little facts that bother me."

"It's going to take you all night to get this out at this rate," Lou said.

"It's about my overdose series," Laurie said. "I want to know what your opinion would be if I suggested that they were homicides, not accidental overdoses."

"Keep talking," Lou said. Absently he took out a cigarette and lit it.

"A case came in where a woman died suddenly in the hospital," Laurie said. "She has lots of cardiac disease. But when you looked at her and you examined her carefully, you couldn't help but think that she could have been smothered. The case is being signed out as 'natural' mainly because of the other details—where she was, the fact that she was overweight, and had a history of heart disease. But if the lady had been found someplace else, it might have been considered a homicide."

"How does this relate to your overdoses?" Lou asked. He leaned forward, the cigarette stuck in the corner of his mouth. His eyes were squinting from the smoke.

"I started thinking about my overdoses in the same light. Take away the fact that these people were found alone in their apartments with syringes by their sides. It's hard not to view murders in context. But what if the cocaine wasn't self-administered?"

"Wow—that would be a twist," Lou said. He sat back and took the cigarette from his mouth. "It's true; homicides have been committed with drugs. There's no doubt about that. But the motive is usually more apparent: robbery, sex, retribution, inheritance. A lot of small-time pushers get killed by their disgruntled clients that way. The cases in your series don't fit that mold. I thought the whole reason these cases are so striking is the fact that in each case the deceased was apparently such a solid citizen with no history of drug abuse or run-ins with the law."

"That's true," Laurie admitted.

"Do you mean to say you think these yuppies were forcibly administered the cocaine? Laurie, get real. With users willing to pay big bucks for the stuff, why would anyone go on a personal crusade to rid the city of some of its best and brightest? What would they have to gain? Isn't it likelier that these people were really into drugs on the sly, maybe even dealing?"

"I don't think so," Laurie said.

"Besides," Lou said, "didn't you say that these people were shooting the coke rather than sniffing it?"

"That's right," Laurie said.

"Well, how is someone going to stick a needle in someone who isn't cooperating? I mean, don't nurses in hospitals have a hard enough time sticking patients? Now you're telling me some struggling victim who's trying to just say no can get shot up against his will? Give me a break."

Laurie closed her eyes. Lou had stumbled upon the weakest point of her homicide theory.

"If these people were being injected against their will, there would be signs of struggle. Have there been any?"

"No," Laurie admitted. "At least I don't think so." She

suddenly recalled the shattered statue in Julia's apartment.

"The only other way I could conceive of this happening is if the victims had been drugged to beat the band with some kind of knockout cocktail beforehand. Correct me if I'm wrong, but you people at the M.E. office would have found a drug like that if there'd been one. Am I right?"

"You're right," Laurie conceded.

"Well, there you go," Lou said. "I'm not going to fault you for considering homicide, but I think it's a mighty remote possibility."

"There are a few other facts I've discovered that have made me suspicious," Laurie persisted. "I visited the apartment of one of the more recent overdose cases today, and the doorman said that on the evening the woman died, she'd come home with two men he'd never seen before."

"Laurie, you can't mean to tell me that the fact a woman comes home with two men the doorman doesn't recognize has spawned this huge conspiracy theory. Is that it?"

"OK! OK!" Laurie said. "Go easy on me. Do you mind that I bring this stuff up? The problem is that these things are bothering me. It's like a mental toothache."

"What else?" Lou said patiently. "Out with it."

"On two of the cases the respective girlfriend or boyfriend was called by the victim an hour or so before and asked to come over."

"And?" said Lou.

"And nothing," said Laurie. "That's it. I just thought it was curious that these people who were allegedly hiding their drug abuse invited their non-druggie significant others over if they were planning a night of coked-out debauchery."

"These two could have called for a million different reasons. I don't think either had any idea this trip was going to turn out the way it did. If anything, it's more support for self-administration. They probably believed in the popular myth of cocaine's aphrodisiac powers and wanted their playmates to be available at the height of their turn-on."

"You must think I'm nuts," Laurie said.

"Not at all," Lou insisted. "It's good to be suspicious, particularly in your line of work."

"Thank you for the consult. I appreciate your patience."

"My pleasure," Lou said. "Any time you want to run something by me, don't hesitate."

"I enjoyed dinner very much," Laurie said. "But I think I'd better be thinking of getting home. I still have to make good on my plans to get some work done."

"If you liked this restaurant," Lou said, "I'd love to take you to one in Queens. It's out in the middle of a real Italian neighborhood. Authentic Northern Italian cuisine. How about tomorrow night?"

"Thank you for asking," Laurie said, "but I do have plans."

"Of course," Lou said sarcastically. "How could I forget Dr. Limo."

"Lou, please!" Laurie said.

"Come on," Lou said, pushing back his chair. "I'll take you home. If you can stand my humble, stripped-down Caprice."

Laurie rolled her eyes.

Franco Ponti pulled his black Cadillac up in front of the Neapolitan Restaurant on Corona Avenue up the street from the Vesuvio and got out. The valet recognized him and rushed over to assure him that good care would be taken of his car. Franco gave the valet a ten-dollar bill and walked through the door.

At that hour on a Friday night, the restaurant was in full swing. An accordion player went from table to table serenading the customers. Between the laughter and din, an air of conviviality marked the evening. Franco paused for a moment, just inside the red velvet curtain separating the foyer from the dining area. He easily spotted Vinnie Dominick, Freddie Capuso, and Richie Herns at one of the upholstered booths along with a pair of buxom, miniskirted bimbos.

Franco walked directly to the table. When Vinnie saw him, he patted the girls and told them to go powder their noses. As soon as they left, Ponti sat down.

"You want something to drink?" Vinnie asked.

"A glass of wine would be fine," Franco said.

Vinnie snapped his fingers. A waiter instantly appeared for instructions. Just as quickly, he reappeared with the requested glass. Vinnie poured Franco some wine from the bottle standing on the table.

"You got something for me?" Vinnie asked.

Franco took a drink and twisted the bottle around to look at the label.

"Angelo Facciolo and Tony Ruggerio are with Cerino tonight. So they're idle. But last night they were out hustling. I don't know what they did early in the evening because I'd lost them. But after some midnight pizza I picked them up again, and they were busy. You read about those murders in Manhattan last night?"

"You mean that big-shot banker and the auction house guy?" Vinnie asked.

"Those are the ones," Franco said. "Angelo and Tony did both those jobs. And they were messy. They almost got nabbed both times. In fact, I had to be careful not to get picked up for questioning, especially on the banker job. I was parked out front when the cops came."

"What the hell did they whack them for?" Vinnie said. His face had gotten quite red and his eyes started to bulge.

"I still don't know," Franco said.

"Every day the cops are more agitated!" Vinnie bellowed. "And the more of an uproar they're in, the worse it gets for business. We've had to shut most of our gambling clubs down temporarily." He glared at Franco. "You got to find out what's going on."

"I've put out some feelers," Franco said. "I'll be asking around as well as tailing Angelo and Tony. Somebody's got to know."

"I have to do something," Vinnie said. "I can't sit around forever while they ruin everything."

"Give me a couple more days," Franco said. "If I can't figure it out, I can get rid of Angelo and Tony."

"But that would mean a war," Vinnie said. "I'm not sure I'm ready for that either. That's even worse for business."

"You know something, Doc?" Cerino said. "That wasn't so bad at all. I really was worried but I didn't feel a thing when you operated. How'd it go?"

"Like a dream," Jordan said. He was holding a small penlight and shining it in the eye on which he'd just performed surgery. "And it looks fine now. The cornea's as clear as a bell and the chamber's deep."

"If you're happy," Cerino said, "I'm happy."

Cerino was in one of the private rooms of the Goldblatt wing of Manhattan General Hospital. Jordan was making late postoperative rounds since he'd finished his last corneal transplant only half an hour earlier. He'd done four in that day alone. In the background Angelo was leaning against the wall. In an armchair next to the door to the bathroom, Tony was fast asleep.

"What we'll do is give this eye a few days," Jordan said, straightening up. "Then if all goes well, which I'm sure it will," he hastily added, "we'll do the other eye. Then you'll be as good as new."

"You mean I have to wait for the other operation, too?" Cerino demanded. "You didn't tell me about that. When we started you just said I had to wait for the first operation."

"Relax!" Jordan urged. "Don't get your blood pressure up. It's good to put a little time between operations so that your eye has a chance to recover before I work on the other one. And at the rate we've been going today, you shouldn't have long to wait."

"I don't like surprises from doctors," Cerino warned. "I don't understand this second waiting period. Are you sure this eye you operated on is doing OK?"

"It's doing beautifully," Jordan assured him. "No one could have done better, believe me."

"If I didn't believe you I wouldn't be laying here," Cerino said. "But if I'm doing this good and if I got to wait for a few days what am I doing in this depressing room. I want to go home."

"It's better that you stay. You need medication in your eye. And should any infection set in—"

"Anybody can put a couple of drops in my eyes," Paul said. "With all that's happened, my wife Gloria has gotten pretty good at it. I want out of here!"

"If you are determined to go, I can't keep you," Jordan said nervously. "But at least be sure to rest and stay quiet."

Three quarters of an hour later an orderly pushed Cerino to Angelo's car in a wheelchair. Tony had already moved the Town Car to the curb in front of the hospital's entrance. He had the engine idling.

Cerino had paid his hospital bill in cash, a feat that had stunned the cashier who was on duty. After a snap of his boss's fingers, Angelo had peeled hundred-dollar bills off a big roll he had in his pocket until he'd surpassed the total.

"Hands off," Cerino said when Angelo tried to help him out of the wheelchair when it reached the side of the car and the orderly had activated the wheel brakes. "I can do it myself. What do you think I am, handicapped?" Cerino pushed himself into a standing position and swayed for a moment getting his considerable bulk directly over his legs.

He was dressed in his street clothes. Over his operated eye he had a metal shield with multiple tiny holes.

Slowly he eased himself into the front passenger seat. He allowed Angelo to close the door for him. Angelo got in the backseat. Tony started driving, but as he reached the street he misjudged the curb. The car bounced.

"Jesus Christ!" Cerino yelled.

Tony cowered over the steering wheel.

They drove through the Midtown Tunnel and out the Long Island Expressway. Cerino became expansive.

"You know something, boys," Cerino beamed, "I feel great! After all that worry and planning, it finally happened. And as I told the doc, it wasn't half bad. Of course I felt that first needle stick."

Angelo cringed in the backseat. He'd been squeamish about going into the operating room from the start. When he'd seen Jordan direct that huge needle into Cerino's face, just below the eye, Angelo had almost passed out. Angelo hated needles.

"But after the needle," Cerino continued, "I didn't feel a thing. I even fell asleep. Can you believe that? Can you, Tony?"

"No, I can't," Tony said nervously.

"When I woke up it was done," Cerino said. "Jordan might be an ass, but he's one hell of a surgeon. And you know something? I think he's smart. I know he's practical. We might very well go into business, he and I. What do you say about that, Angelo?"

"An interesting idea," Angelo said without enthusiasm.

12

□

Since it was Saturday, Laurie did not set her alarm. But she woke up before eight anyway, again troubled by her nightmare about Shelly. Vaguely she wondered if it would help if she were to see someone professional.

Despite not being on call, Laurie had decided to go into the office. Her intentions notwithstanding, she'd not been productive with her work the previous evening after Lou had dropped her off. Wine and work did not mix well with Laurie.

Emerging from her building, Laurie was pleasantly surprised to find a crisp fall day. The sun had already taken on its weak winter look, but the sky was clear and the temperature moderate. Being a Saturday, the traffic and its resultant exhaust was minimal on First Avenue, and Laurie enjoyed the walk up to Thirtieth Street.

As soon as she arrived, Laurie went straight to the ID office to check on that day's cases. She was relieved to see there were no new candidates for her overdose series. The schedule was filled with the usual Friday-night homicides and accident cases reflecting a normal night of murder and mayhem in the Big Apple.

Next Laurie headed for the toxicology lab. She was relieved she wouldn't have to dodge John DeVries. He certainly wouldn't be in on a Saturday. She was pleased to find hardworking Peter at his usual spot in front of the newest gas chromatograph.

"Nothing yet along the lines of a contaminant," Peter told her, "but with that huge new sample I got yesterday, we might be in luck."

"What kind of sample?" Laurie asked. "Blood?"

"No," Peter said, "pure cocaine taken from the gut."

"Whose gut?" Laurie asked.

Peter checked the specimen tag before him. "Wendell Morrison. One of Fontworth's cases from yesterday."

"But how did he get a sample from the gut?"

"I can't help you there," Peter said. "I have no idea how he got it, but by giving me as much as he did, it makes my job considerably easier."

"I'm glad," Laurie said, puzzled by this unexpected bit of news. "Let me know what you find."

Laurie left the toxicology lab and went to her office. After finding his number in the office directory, she called George Fontworth at home. He answered on the second ring; Laurie was relieved not to have awakened him.

"Don't tell me you're in the office," he said when he heard who it was.

"What can I say?" Laurie said.

"You're not even on call," George said. "Don't work so hard. You'll make the rest of us look bad."

"Sure," Laurie laughed. "I'm not impressing anyone

around here. You know what Calvin told you: you weren't even supposed to talk with me yesterday."

"That was kinda stupid," George agreed. "What's on your mind?"

"I'm curious about the first case you did yesterday," Laurie said. "Wendell Morrison."

"What do you want to know?" George asked.

"Toxicology told me that you had given them a cocaine sample from the deceased's gut. How did you come by that?"

"Dr. Morrison took the drug orally," George said.

"I thought you told me both your cases mainlined it," Laurie said.

"Only the second case," George said. "When you asked me the route of administration, I thought you were only referring to that one."

"All of my cases took the drug IV, but one of Dick Katzenburg's took it orally only after trying to take it IV."

"Same with Dr. Morrison," George said. "His antecubital fossae looked like pincushions. The guy was overweight and his veins were deep, but you'd think a doctor would have been a bit better at venipuncture."

"There was still a lot of cocaine in the gut?" Laurie asked.

"A ton," George said. "I can't imagine how much the guy ate. Part of the gut was infarcted where the cocaine had closed down the blood supply. It was just like one of those cocaine 'mule' cases where the condoms break in transit."

"Was there anything else of note?"

"Yes," George said. "He had a CVA from a small aneurysm. It probably burst during a seizure."

Before Laurie hung up she told George about the little bit of tissue she'd taken from beneath Julia Myerholtz's fingernail and sent up to the lab.

"I hope you don't mind my butting in on your case," Laurie said.

301

"Hell no," George said. "I'm just embarrassed I missed it. With the way she had excoriated herself, I should have looked under her nails."

After wishing George a good weekend, Laurie finally settled down to her paperwork. But as she experienced lately, she couldn't take her mind off the troubling aspects of her overdose series. Despite her conversation with Lou, some of the details of the Myerholtz case continued to bother her.

Laurie pulled out the folders on the three cases she'd posted on Thursday: Stuart Morgan, Randall Thatcher, and Valerie Abrams. Using a scratch pad, she jotted down each of the three's address.

In another minute, Laurie was out the door. She caught a cab and visited each of the three scenes. At each residence, Laurie talked with the doorman. After explaining who she was, she obtained the names and telephone numbers of the doormen who had been on duty Wednesday evening.

Back at the office, Laurie began her calls. The first she put through was to Julio Chavez. "Did you know Valerie Abrams?" Laurie asked after explaining who she was.

"Yes, of course," Julio said.

"Did you see her Wednesday night?" Laurie asked.

"No, I didn't," Julio said. "At least I don't remember."

Lou was probably right, Laurie told herself after she'd thanked the man and hung up. She was probably wasting her time. Still, she couldn't resist dialing the next name on the list: Angel Mendez, the evening doorman at Stuart Morgan's apartment.

Laurie introduced herself as she had before, then asked Angel if he knew Stuart Morgan, and the answer was the same: "Of course!"

"Did you see Mr. Morgan Wednesday night?" Laurie asked.

"Of course," Angel said. "I saw Mr. Morgan every night I worked. He jogged after work every day."

"Did he jog on Wednesday night?" Laurie asked.

"Just like every other night," Angel told her.

Again Laurie wondered about the inconsistency of a guy who thought enough of himself to run every night taking drugs. It didn't make a lot of sense.

"Did he seem normal?" Laurie asked. "Did he seem depressed?"

"He seemed fine when he went out," Angel said. "But he didn't jog as far as usual. At least he came back very soon. He wasn't even sweaty. I remember because I told him he'd not worked up a sweat."

"What did he say in return?" Laurie asked.

"Nothing," Angel said.

"Was it usual for him not to say anything?" Laurie asked.

"Only when he was with other people," Angel said.

"Was Mr. Morgan with other people when he came back from jogging?" she asked.

"Yes," Angel said. "He was with two strangers."

Laurie sat up. "Can you describe these strangers?" she asked.

Angel laughed. "No, I don't think so," he said. "I see so many people in a day. I just remembered he was with strangers because he didn't say hello."

Laurie thanked the man and hung up. Now this was something. She could still hear Lou's admonition warning her not to play detective, but this striking similarity to the Myerholtz case could be the beginning of a big break.

Finally, Laurie called the last name on her list: David Wong. Unfortunately David couldn't remember seeing Randall Thatcher on Wednesday night. Laurie thanked him and hung up.

Laurie decided to turn her attention to one more case before returning to her paperwork. She went to Histology and asked for the slides of Mary O'Connor. Back in her office, she scanned the heart slides under her microscope to study the extent of atherosclerosis. It was moderate on microscopic just as Paul had said it had been on gross. She also didn't notice any cardiac myopathy.

With that out of the way, Laurie couldn't think of another reason to avoid her work. Pushing her microscope to the side, she pulled out her uncompleted cases and forced herself to begin.

"So this is it?" Lou asked. He waved a typed sheet of paper in the air.

"That's what we've been able to come up with," Norman told him.

"This is a bunch of doctor gobbledygook. What the hell is 'keratoconus'? Or here's a gem: 'pseudophakic bullous keratopathy.' What is this crap? Will you please tell me?"

"You wanted the diagnoses of the victims who were seeing Dr. Jordan Scheffield," Norman said. "That's what the teams came up with."

Lou read the page again. Martha Goldburg, pseudophakic bullous keratopathy; Steven Vivonetto, interstitial keratitis; Janice Singleton, herpes zoster; Henriette Kaufman, Fuchs endothelial dystrophy; Dwight Sorenson, keratoconus.

"I was hoping they would all have the same condition," muttered Lou. "I'd hoped to catch twinkle-toes Scheffield in a lie."

Norman shrugged. "Sorry," he said. "I can get someone to translate those terms to regular English—if there's any English to cover it."

Lou settled back in his chair. "So what do you think?" he asked.

"I don't have any bright ideas," Norman said. "When I first saw the doctor's name pop out of the data, I thought maybe we had something. But now it doesn't look that way."

"Any of the patients unhappy with their care?" Lou asked.

"Only positive in that arena is the Goldburgs," Norman said. "Harry Goldburg had initiated a malpractice suit against Dr. Scheffield after the doctor took out his wife's cataract. Apparently there was some complication and she wasn't seeing much through that eye."

"What's all this other stuff?" Lou asked, grasping at a fat file folder filled with typed pages.

"That's the rest of the material that has been gathered by the investigative teams," Norman said.

"Jesus Christ," Lou said. "There must be five hundred pages in here."

"More like four hundred," Norman said. "Nothing's jumped out at me yet, but I thought you'd better go through it, too. And you might as well get started: there'll be more coming as we interview more people."

"What about Ballistics?" Lou asked.

"They haven't gotten to us yet," Norman said. "They're still on last month's homicides. But preliminary opinion is that there were only two guns involved: a twenty-two and a twenty-five caliber."

"What about the housekeeper?" Lou asked.

"She's still alive but has yet to regain consciousness," Norman said. "She was shot in the head and she's in a coma."

"Do you have her protected?" Lou asked.

"Absolutely," Norman said. "Around the clock."

Having finally made some progress on her paperwork, Laurie made a neat stack of her completed cases. With them out of the way, she pulled out the records of the overdose cases. Sorting through, she set aside the three she wanted: Duncan Andrews, Robert Evans, and Marion Overstreet. These were the cases she had autopsied on

Tuesday and Wednesday. She copied the addresses and packed up.

Laurie made the same kind of tour she'd made that morning. Only this time she found that the doormen she wanted to question were on duty again.

She was disappointed with the results at the Evans and Overstreet residences. Neither doorman could tell her very much about the evenings in question. But it was a different story at Duncan Andrews'.

When the cab pulled up to the building, Laurie recognized the blue, scalloped canvas awning and the wrought-iron door from her previous visit. As she got out of the cab, she even recognized the doorman. He'd been the same one on duty on her last ill-fated visit. But recognizing the doorman did not deter her. Although she thought there was an outside chance that her visit might get back to Bingham, she was willing to risk it.

"Can I help you?" the doorman asked.

Laurie looked for signs of recognition on the doorman's part. She didn't see any.

"I'm from the medical examiner's office," Laurie said. "My name is Dr. Montgomery. Do you remember my coming here Tuesday?"

"I believe I do," the doorman said. "My name is Oliver. Is there something I can do for you? Are you here to go back up to the Andrews apartment?"

"No, I don't want to disturb anyone," Laurie said. "I just want to speak with you. Were you working Sunday night?"

"Yes I was," Oliver said. "My days off are Monday and Thursday."

"Do you remember seeing Mr. Andrews the night he died?"

"I think I do," he said after thinking about it. "I used to see him most every night."

"Do you remember if he was alone?" Laurie asked.

"That I can't tell you," Oliver said. "With as many people who go in and out of here, I wouldn't be likely to remember a thing like that, especially almost a week later. Maybe if it was the same day or if something happened out of the ordinary. Wait a minute!" he suddenly cried. "Maybe I do remember. There was one night that Mr. Andrews came in with some people. I remember now because he called me by the wrong name. He used the superintendent's name."

"Did he know your name?" Laurie asked.

"For sure," Oliver said. "I've been working here since before he moved in. That was five years ago."

"How many men were with him?" Laurie asked.

"Two, I think. Maybe three."

"But you're not positive which night?" Laurie asked.

"I can't be sure," Oliver agreed. "But I remember he called me Juan and it confused me. I mean, he knew my name was Oliver."

Laurie thanked Oliver and headed home. What to make of this odd streak of similarities? Who were these two men, and were they the same pair in each case? And what did it mean that a young, intelligent, dynamic man would mix up the names of his doorman and his superintendent? Probably nothing. After all, Duncan could have been thinking about calling Juan for a problem in his apartment just as he was arriving home.

Entering her own tenement, Laurie cast an appraising glance around the interior as she walked to the elevator. She noted the cracked and chipped tiles on the floor and the peeling paint on the walls. Comparing it to the residences she'd been visiting, it was a slum. The depressing thing was that all the overdose victims had been about Laurie's age or younger, and obviously had been doing a lot better than she was financially. Laurie was already paying more rent than she thought she could afford on her salary, and she was living in a comparative dump. It was depressing.

Tom lightened Laurie's mood the moment she entered

her apartment. Having been sleeping all day as well as through the previous night, the cat-kitten was a ball of energy. With truly awesome leaping ability he caromed off walls and furniture in a fantastic display of exuberance that made Laurie laugh to the point of tears.

Unaccustomed to the luxury of free time to splurge on herself, Laurie took full advantage of the next several hours by taking a nap as well as a bath. Since there had been no message from Jordan to the contrary, she assumed their dinner plans had not changed from the prearranged nine P.M.

After taking a half hour to decide what to wear, which encompassed trying on three different outfits, Laurie was ready by five of nine. Contrary to the previous two outings, Jordan himself showed up on time at nine sharp.

"You're really going to get my neighbors talking now," Laurie told him. "I'm sure they're thinking I've been seeing Thomas."

Jordan had made reservations for them at the Four Seasons. As with the other restaurants he favored, Laurie had never dined there. Although the food was excellent, the service impeccable, and the wine delightful, Laurie couldn't help but compare it unfavorably to the nameless restaurant Lou had taken her to the night before. There was something so winning about that chaotic, bustling little place. The Four Seasons, on the other hand, was so quiet it was distracting. With the only sounds being the tinkle of ice against the waterglasses or the clink of the sans-serif flatware against the china, she felt she had to whisper. And the décor was so purposefully daunting with its stark geometry, she felt intimidated. Laurie choked on her water when a pesky thought occurred to her: What if it wasn't the restaurant she preferred so much as the company?

Jordan was relaxed and expansive, going on about his office. "Things couldn't be better," he said. "I got a replacement for Marsha who is ten times better than Marsha ever was. I don't know why I was so worried about replacing her. And my surgery is going fine. I've never done so much surgery in such a short period of time. I just hope it keeps up. My accountant called me yesterday and told me this is going to be a record month."

"I'm glad for you," Laurie said. She was tempted to mention her day's revelations but Jordan didn't give her a chance.

"I'm toying with the idea of adding an additional exam room," he said. "Maybe even taking in a junior partner who would see all the junk patients."

"What are junk patients?" Laurie asked.

"Nonsurgical ones," Jordan said. He spotted a waiter and called him over to order a second bottle of wine.

"I looked at Mary O'Connor's slides today," Laurie said.

"I'd prefer to keep the conversation on happier subjects," Jordan said.

"You don't want to know what I found?" Laurie asked.

"Not particularly," Jordan said. "Unless it was something astonishing. I can't dwell on her. I have to move on. After all, her general medical condition was not my responsibility but rather her internist's. It's not as if she died during surgery."

"What about your other patients who were killed?" Laurie asked. "Would you like to talk about them?"

"Not really," Jordan said. "I mean, what's the point? It's not as if we can do anything for them."

"I just thought you'd have a need to discuss it," Laurie said. "If I were in your shoes, I'm sure I would."

"It depresses me," Jordan admitted. "But it doesn't help to talk about it. I'd rather concentrate on the positive things in my life."

Laurie studied Jordan's face. Lou had said he'd seemed nervous when questioned about his patients' deaths. Laurie didn't see any nervousness now. All she saw was a deliberate denial: he'd just rather not think about any unpleasantness.

"Positive things like the fact that you operated on Paul Cerino yesterday?" Laurie asked.

If Jordan caught the facetiousness in her tone, he didn't let on. "That's the ticket," he said, responding eagerly to a change in the subject. "I can't wait to do the second eye and see the last of him."

"When will that be?" Laurie asked.

"Within a week or so," Jordan said. "I just want to make sure his first eye goes well. I shudder every time I think about the possibility of complications. Not that I expect any. His case went perfectly well. But he refused to stay in the hospital overnight so I can't be a hundred percent sure he's getting the medication he needs."

"Well, if he didn't, it wouldn't be your fault," Laurie said.

"I'm not sure Cerino would see it that way," Jordan said.

After dessert and coffee, Laurie agreed to go back to see Jordan's apartment in the Trump Tower. She was impressed the moment she went through the door. Directly in front of her, almost at the same height as Jordan's apartment, was the illuminated top of the Crown Building. Walking into the living room, Laurie could see south down Fifth Avenue to the Empire State Building and to the World Trade Center beyond. Looking north she could see a wedge of Central Park with its serpentine pathways fully illuminated.

"It's gorgeous," Laurie said. She was transfixed by the view of the New York skyline. As her eyes swept the horizon, she realized that Jordan was standing directly behind her.

"Laurie," he said softly.

Turning around, Laurie found herself enveloped by Jordan's muscular arms. His angular face was illuminated by reflected light streaming in through the windows from the golden apex of the Crown Building. With his lips slightly parted, he leaned forward intending to kiss her.

"Hey," she said, disengaging herself. "How about an after-dinner drink?"

"Your wish is my command," Jordan said with a rueful smile.

Laurie was a little surprised at herself. Surely she was not so naive to believe Jordan's gesture wasn't expected. After all, she'd gone out with the man nearly three nights in a row, and she did find him attractive. Yet for some reason she was beginning to have serious second thoughts.

"Well?" Tony mumbled as Angelo came back to the table from the phone outside the men's room. Tony's mouth was full. He'd just finished shoveling in a huge bite of tortellini con panna. Lifting up his napkin, he wiped off the ring of cream and cheese from his lips.

Angelo and Tony were in a small all-night restaurant–sub shop in Astoria. It was Tony's idea to stop, but Angelo didn't mind since he had to call Cerino anyway.

"Well?" Tony repeated after he'd swallowed the tortellini in his mouth. He washed it down with mineral water.

"I wish you wouldn't talk with food in your mouth," Angelo said as he sat down. "It makes me sick."

"I'm sorry," Tony said. He was already busy stabbing tortellini with his fork in preparation for the next bite.

"He wants us to go out again tonight," Angel said.

Tony shoveled the forkful of tortellini into his mouth, then said, "Great!" It sounded more like "rate."

Having had yet another disgusting look at the mash of pasta in Tony's mouth, Angelo reached over and picked Tony's bowl from the table and crammed it upside down on Tony's place mat.

Tony flinched at the sudden movement and stared at his upturned bowl with shocked surprise. "Why did you do that?" he whined.

"I told you not to eat with your mouth open," Angelo snapped. "I'm trying to talk with you and you keep eating."

"I'm sorry, all right?"

"Besides it pisses me off about Cerino sending us out," Angelo said. "I thought we were finally finished with all this crap."

"At least the money is good," Tony said. "What are we supposed to do?"

"We're supposed to stick to the supply side," Angelo said. "We might be finished with the demand side, which is fine by me. That's where we got into trouble."

"When?" Tony asked.

"As soon as you get your ass out into the car," Angelo said.

Fifteen minutes later, as they were approaching the Queensboro Bridge, Angelo spoke up: "There's another thing that bothers me about this. I don't like the timing. Late Saturday night is not a good time. We may have to change things around and be creative."

"Why don't we just use the phone?" Tony said. "We can make sure things are copacetic before we do anything else."

Angelo shot a glance in Tony's direction. Sometimes the kid surprised him. He wasn't dumb all the time.

13

□

Bending over and trying to point the umbrella into the wind, Laurie slowly made her way up First Avenue. It was hard for her to believe that the weather could change as much as it had in a single day. Not only was it windy and rainy, but the temperature had plummeted during the night to just a tad above freezing. Laurie had taken her winter coat out of its mothballed storage container for the occasion.

Standing on the corner, Laurie vainly waved at the few cabs that streaked past, but all were occupied. Just when she had resigned herself to walking to the office, a vacant taxi pulled up to the curb. She had to leap away to keep from being splashed.

Having finally made significant progress on her paperwork the day before, Laurie was not planning on working

313

that Sunday, yet she felt compelled to go to the office because of a superstitious feeling. It was her idea that if she'd
made the effort to go, there wouldn't be any additional
cases in her series.

Stomping off the moisture in the reception area, Laurie
unbuttoned her coat and walked through to the ID office.
No one was there, and nor was there a schedule for the
day's cases. But the coffee machine was on and someone
had made coffee. Laurie helped herself to a cup.

Leaving her coat and umbrella, Laurie descended a floor
to the morgue and walked back to the main autopsy room.
The lights were on, so she could tell it was in use.

The door creaked open to her touch. Only two of the
eight tables were occupied. Laurie tried to recognize who
was working. With the goggles, face masks, and hoods, it
was difficult. Just when she was about to go into the locker
room to change, someone noticed her and, leaving the autopsy table, came over to speak with her. It was Sal D'Am-
brosio, one of the techs.

"What the hell are you doing here?" Sal asked.

"I live here," Laurie said with a laugh. "Which doctor is
on today?"

"Plodgett," Sal said. "What's the problem?"

"No problem," Laurie said. "Who's at the other table?"

"Dr. Besserman," Sal said. "Paul called him; we got a lot
of cases today. More than usual."

Laurie nodded to Sal, then called over to Paul. "Hey,
Paul. Anything interesting?"

"I'd say so," he replied. "I was going to call you later. We
got two more overdoses that can go into your series."

Laurie felt her heart sink. So much for superstition. "I'll
be right in," she said.

Once she had changed into her full protective gear, Laurie went to Paul's table. He was working on the remains of
a very young woman.

"How old?" Laurie asked.

"Twenty," Paul said. "College student at Columbia."

"How awful!" Laurie said. This would be by far the youngest in her series.

"That's not the worst of it," Paul said.

"How so?" Laurie asked.

"Dr. Besserman is doing the boyfriend," Paul said. "He's a thirty-one-year-old banker. That's why I thought you'd be interested. Apparently they injected themselves simultaneously."

"Oh no!" Laurie felt almost dizzy: as a double tragedy the incident was doubly poignant. She moved over to Dr. Besserman's table. He was just lifting the internal organs out of the body. Laurie looked at the dead man's face. There was a large discolored bruise on his forehead.

"He convulsed," Dr. Besserman said, noticing Laurie's curiosity. "Must have hit his face on the floor. Or it could have happened in the refrigerator."

Laurie switched her attention to Dr. Besserman. "This man was found in a refrigerator?" she asked.

"That's what the tour doctor told us," Dr. Besserman said.

"That's the third one, then," Laurie said. "Where was the girlfriend?"

"She was in the bedroom on the floor," Dr. Besserman said.

"Find anything special on the post so far?" Laurie asked.

"Pretty routine for an overdose," Dr. Besserman said.

Laurie stepped back to Paul's table and watched him slice off several samples of liver.

"What kinds of specimens have you been sending up to Toxicology on these cases?" he asked when he noticed Laurie by his side.

"Liver, kidney, and brain," Laurie said. "In addition to the usual fluid samples."

315

"That's what I thought," Paul said.

"Have you found anything remarkable on this case?" Laurie asked.

"Not so far. Certainly consistent with a cocaine overdose. No surprises. But we have the head to go."

"I hear you have a lot of cases today. Since I'm already here would you like me to help?"

"It's not necessary," Paul said. "Especially since Dr. Besserman's come in."

"Are you sure?" Laurie asked.

"Thanks for the offer, but I'm sure."

Going through all the paperwork on the cases, Laurie got the names of the victims as well as the male's address. It had been at the male's apartment that the bodies had been found. Then she went back to the locker room and changed. She was extremely disheartened. There was something particularly tragic about two young lovers losing their lives so senselessly. She began to regret anew Bingham's decision not to inform the public about the potentially tainted drug. If he had, those two people might be alive today.

With sudden resolve, Laurie decided to call Bingham. If this Romeo and Juliet–style tragedy didn't wake him up to the fact that they were potentially facing a major public-health crisis, nothing would.

Upstairs in her office she found Bingham's home number in the directory. Taking a deep breath, she placed the call.

Bingham himself answered. "This is Sunday morning," he said crisply when he understood who was on the other end of the line.

Laurie immediately told him about the two new overdose cases. Once she had finished, she was met with silence. Then Bingham said sharply, "I fail to see why you felt compelled to call me about this on a Sunday."

"If we had made a statement, this couple might be alive today," Laurie said. "Obviously we can't help them, but perhaps we can help others. With these cases I now have sixteen in my series."

"Look, Montgomery, I'm not even convinced you have a bona fide series, so stop throwing the term around as if it's an a priori assumption. Maybe you have a series, maybe you don't. I appreciate your good intentions, but have you come up with any proof? Has the lab come up with a contaminant?"

"Not yet," Laurie admitted.

"Then as far as I'm concerned, this conversation is just a rehash of the one we had the other day."

"But I'm convinced we can save lives—"

"I know you are," Bingham said. "But I'm also convinced it is not in the best interests of the department and for the city as a whole. The media will want names, and we are not prepared to give names, not with the pressure we're under. And it's more than Duncan Andrews' family who'd like to keep these cases out of the headlines. But I am meeting with the commissioner of health this week. In all fairness to you I will present the issue to him and he can decide."

"But, Dr. Bingham—" Laurie protested.

"That's enough, Laurie. Goodbye!"

Laurie looked at the phone with frustration. Bingham had hung up on her. She slammed the phone down in anger. The idea that he would take the problem to the commissioner was not a consolation to her. As far as she was concerned, it was merely shuffling the problem from one political hack to another. She also felt Bingham had been closest to the real reason for keeping a lid on the series when he mentioned Duncan Andrews. Bingham was still worried about the political ramifications of going public with a connected name.

Laurie decided to give Jordan a call. Since he didn't work for the city and was beholden to no special group or interest, maybe he could speak out. Laurie wasn't sure he'd be inclined to get involved, but she decided to chance it. Jordan picked up on the second ring but sounded out of breath when he answered.

"I'm on my exercise bike," he explained when Laurie asked. "Good to hear from you so soon. I hope you had a nice evening. I know I did."

"It was lovely," she said. "Thank you again." It had been a nice evening and Laurie had been relieved when Jordan didn't pressure her after that brief, aborted kiss.

Laurie filled Jordan in on the latest additions to her overdose series. To her relief he sounded genuinely upset.

"Now I have a question for you," Laurie said. "And a favor to ask. The medical examiner is not willing to make a public statement about my series. I want it made because I'm convinced it will save lives. Do you know any other way to get this information to the public and might you be willing to put the word out?"

"Wait a second," Jordan said. "I'm an ophthalmologist. This isn't exactly my area of expertise. You want me to make some kind of statement about a series of drug deaths? No way, it's inappropriate."

Laurie sighed. "Would you think about it?"

"I don't need to think about it," Jordan said. "This is the type of thing I have to stay clear of, pure and simple. Remember, you and I are coming at medicine from the opposite ends of the spectrum. I'm in the clinical end. I've got a very high profile clientele. I'm sure they wouldn't want to hear I'm mixed up in any drug affair no matter which side of the law I'm on. They'd start to wonder about me, and before I knew what was happening, they'd be going to someone else. Ophthalmology is extremely competitive these days."

Laurie didn't even try to argue. She understood more clearly than ever: Jordan Scheffield was not about to help her. She merely thanked him for his time and hung up.

There was only one other person to whom Laurie could turn. Although she was far from optimistic about the reception she'd meet there, she swallowed her pride and called Lou. Since she didn't have his home number, she called police headquarters to leave word for him. To her surprise, he returned her call almost immediately.

"Hey, how are you?" He sounded pleased to have heard from her. "I knew I should have given you my home number. Here, let me give it to you now." Laurie got a pen and paper and jotted the number down.

"I'm glad you called," Lou continued. "I got my kids here. You want to come down to SoHo for some brunch?"

"Another time," Laurie said. "I've got a problem."

"Uh-oh," Lou said. "What is it?"

Laurie told him about the double overdose and her conversations with Bingham and Jordan.

"Nice to know I'm at the bottom of your list," Lou commented.

"Please, Lou," Laurie said. "Don't play wounded. I'm desperate."

"Laurie, why are you doing this to me?" Lou complained. "I'd love to help you, but this is not a police matter. I told you that the last time you brought it up. I can understand your problem, but I don't have any suggestions. And if you want my opinion, it's not really your problem. You've done what you could and you've informed your superiors. That's all you can expect from yourself."

"My conscience won't let me leave it at that," Laurie said. "Not while people are dying."

"What did big bucks Jordan say?" Lou asked.

"He was afraid his patients wouldn't understand," Laurie said. "He said he couldn't help me."

"That's a pretty flimsy excuse," Lou said. "I'm surprised he's not falling all over himself trying to prove what a man he is by helping his damsel in distress."

"I'm not his damsel," Laurie said. Even as the words

came out of her mouth, she knew she shouldn't be rising to his bait.

"Not always charming, that prince of yours, eh?"

Laurie hung up on Lou. The man could be so infuriatingly rude. She got her things together, including the address of the double-overdose scene, and was ready to go when the phone started to ring. Figuring it was Lou, she avoided answering. The phone rang about twenty times before it stopped just as she reached the elevator.

Laurie hailed a cab and headed for the address on Sutton Place South. When she arrived, she flashed her medical examiner's badge at the doorman on duty and asked to see the superintendent. The doorman readily obliged her. "Carl will be down in a minute. He lives right here in the building so he's almost always available."

A diminutive man with dark hair and a thin black moustache soon appeared and introduced himself as Carl Bethany. "I guess you're here about George VanDeusen?" Carl asked.

Laurie nodded. "If it wouldn't be too much trouble, I'd like to view the scene where the bodies were found. Is the apartment empty?"

"Oh, yeah," Carl said. "They took the bodies out last night."

"That's not what I meant," Laurie said. "I want to be sure there aren't any family members up there. I don't want to disturb anyone."

Carl said he'd have to check. He conferred with the doorman, then returned to assure Laurie that the VanDeusen apartment was vacant. Then he took her up to the tenth floor and unlocked the door for her. Stepping aside, he let Laurie go in first.

"Nobody's cleaned in here yet," Carl said as he followed Laurie through the door. Laurie noticed a musty, almost fishy smell as she entered the apartment.

Laurie surveyed the living room. An antique butler's-style coffee table with only three legs lay at an odd angle. The fourth leg was on the floor just by it. Magazines and books were haphazardly scattered across the carpet; it looked as if they had been spilled when the leg was broken. A crystal lamp lay smashed between an end table and the couch. A large, old-master oil painting hung askew on the wall.

"A lot of damage," Laurie said. In her mind's eye she tried to imagine the kind of seizure that could have resulted in such breakage.

"That's just the way it looked when I came in here last night," Carl said.

Laurie started toward the kitchen. "Who found the bodies?" she said.

"I did," Carl said.

Laurie was surprised. "What brought you in?"

"The night doorman called me," Carl said.

Laurie was going to ask about him next. She hoped to speak to him, too, and said so. "Why did he call you?" she asked.

"He said another tenant had called him to report strange noises coming from 10F. The caller was worried that someone was hurt."

"What did you do?" Laurie asked.

"I came up here and rang the bell," Carl said. "I rang it several times. Then I used my passkey. That's when I found the bodies."

Laurie blinked. Her mind was mulling over this scenario, and something wasn't making sense. She could remember reading an hour earlier in the investigator's report that both bodies had significant rigor mortis, even the woman in the bedroom. That meant that they had to have been dead at least several hours.

"You said the tenant called down to the doorman because sounds were coming out of the apartment at that time? I mean at the same time he was calling."

"I think so," Carl said.

Laurie began to wonder how the other victims in her series had been found. Duncan Andrews and Julia Myerholtz had been found by their lovers. But what about the others? Laurie had never considered the question before now. Now that she thought about it, she did recognize one strange thing: all the victims had been found relatively quickly. Their bodies were discovered in a matter of hours whereas in many cases single people who unexpectedly died in their apartments weren't found for days, sometimes only after the smell of decay had alerted neighbors.

The scene in the kitchen was all too familiar. The contents of the refrigerator had been strewn helter-skelter across the floor. The refrigerator door was still ajar. Laurie noticed that the smell of spoiled milk and rotting vegetables permeated the air.

"Someone is going to have to clean this up," Carl said.

Laurie nodded. Leaving the kitchen, she looked into the bedroom. Again she started to feel incredibly sad. Seeing the apartment where these people had lived made them all the more real. It was easier to remain dispassionate down at the medical examiner's office than it was in the deceased's home. Laurie felt her eyes well with tears.

"Is there anything else I can do to help?" Carl asked.

"I'd like to speak to that night doorman," she said, pulling herself together.

"That's easily arranged," Carl said. "Anything else?"

"Yes," Laurie said, gazing around the apartment. "Maybe you shouldn't let anyone clean this place up just yet. Let me talk to the police."

"They were here last night too," Carl said.

"I know," Laurie said. "But I'm thinking of someone a little higher on the ladder in the homicide department."

Downstairs Carl got the night doorman's phone number

for Laurie. The man's name was Scott Maybrie. He even offered to allow Laurie the use of his phone if she wanted to call immediately.

"Wouldn't he be asleep at this time?" Laurie asked.

"It won't hurt him," Carl insisted.

Carl's tiny apartment was on the first floor and faced the street, in contrast to VanDeusen's, which had faced out over the East River. Carl allowed Laurie to sit at his cluttered desk amid notes to plumbers and electricians. Being particularly helpful, Carl even dialed Scott's number and handed Laurie the phone. As she'd feared, the man's voice was hoarse with sleep when he answered.

Laurie identified herself and explained that Carl had suggested she call. "I wanted to ask you a few questions about the VanDeusen case," she continued. "Did you see Mr. VanDeusen or his girlfriend last night?"

"No, I didn't," Scott said.

"Carl told me that one of the other tenants called you about noises coming from the VanDeusen apartment. What time was that?"

"Around two-thirty, three o'clock," Scott said.

"Which tenant called?" Laurie asked.

"I don't know," Scott admitted. "He didn't say."

"Was it one of the immediate neighbors?" Laurie suggested.

"I really don't know. I didn't recognize the voice, but that's not unusual."

"What did he say exactly?" Laurie asked.

"He said there were strange noises coming from 10F," Scott said. "He was concerned someone might be hurt."

"Did he say they were occurring at the moment he was calling?" Laurie asked. "Or did he say they had happened sometime in the past."

"I think he said they were happening right then," Scott said.

"Did you notice two men leaving the building during the

night?" Laurie asked. "Two men you'd never seen before?"

"That I couldn't say," Scott said. "People come and go all night. To be honest, I don't pay much attention to people leaving. It's the ones who are arriving I'm most concerned about."

Laurie thanked Scott and apologized for disturbing him. Then, turning to Carl, she asked if she could speak to the doorman who'd been on duty earlier in the evening.

"Absolutely," Carl said. "That would have been Clark Davenport." Again Carl dialed the number, then handed Laurie the phone.

Laurie went through the same explanation when Clark picked up.

"Did you see Mr. George VanDeusen come into his apartment last night?" Laurie asked after the introductions.

"Yes," Clark said. "He came in around ten with his girlfriend."

"Was he behaving normally?" Laurie asked.

"Normal for a Saturday night," Clark said. "He was a little tipsy. His girlfriend had to give him a little support. But they seemed to be having a good time, if that's what you mean."

"Were they alone?" Laurie asked.

"Yup," Clark said. "Their guests didn't come in for about half an hour."

"They had a party?" Laurie asked with surprise.

"I wouldn't call it a party," Clark said. "Just two men. A tall guy and a shorter one."

"Can you remember what these men looked like?" Laurie asked.

Clark had to think about it. "The tall one had bad skin, like he'd had acne as a kid."

"Did they give their names?" Laurie asked. She could feel her pulse quicken.

"Yeah, of course they gave their names," Clark said.

"How else was I to call up and ask Mr. VanDeusen if they were expected? Otherwise I wouldn't have let them in."

"What were the names?" Laurie asked. She'd taken out a pen and a piece of paper.

"I don't remember," Clark said. "On a Saturday night I have a hundred people coming in."

Laurie was disappointed to be so tantalizingly close to a real breakthrough. Although she wasn't able to get the names, this was progress. Yet again two men were spotted at the scene of the OD shortly before the deaths occurred.

"Did you see these men come out again?" Laurie asked.

"Nope," Clark said. "Of course, I went off duty not too long after they arrived."

Laurie thanked Clark before hanging up. She also thanked Carl profusely for all his help before she left the building.

Even though it was ugly and quite cold, Laurie decided to huddle under her umbrella and walk for a bit before catching a cab home. She wanted to mill over what she had learned and what it might mean for the case as a whole.

By far the most significant discovery was the surfacing of these two mystery men. Laurie wondered if the pair was involved in the drug trade. She wondered if this revelation would be enough to get the police narcotics squad interested. She began to hope Lou might feel differently now that more similarities between the cases were falling into place.

Laurie wished she could speak to the tenant who complained of noise. What did he hear and when did he hear it? When it began to rain in earnest, Laurie hailed a cab and headed for home. Over a salad and some hot tea, she got out all the material she had concerning her series and made a new sheet listing the cases in order. She started two columns beside the column of names: "Found by"; "Two Men at Scene?"

She filled in what answers she had. The rest of the afternoon she devoted to filling in the blanks. It meant a lot of
legwork, but Laurie knew she had to be thorough if she was
ever going to get anyone to believe in her theory.

By late afternoon, Laurie was convinced her efforts had
been worthwhile. In each of the scenes the bodies had been
discovered by a doorman or superintendent investigating
after a neighboring tenant's complaint of strange noises
coming from the deceased's apartment. With the information on her sheet nearly complete, Laurie headed home
convinced more than ever that there was something sinister
afoot. There were too many coincidences. Now if only she
could persuade someone in a position to do something
about it.

By the time she got home, it was dark. She wasn't sure
what her next move should be. Out of curiosity, Laurie
opened the Sunday *Times* to see if the media had picked up
the story of the banker and the Columbia coed who'd
OD'd. She found a brief mention of the deaths in the depths
of the second section. The article made the deaths sound
like just another couple of overdoses and made no mention
of other demographically similar occurrences in the recent
past. Another day, another opportunity to alert the public
lost.

Laurie decided to try Lou's home number. She wasn't
sure she had enough to convince him of anything, but she
was eager to give him an update. She got Lou's answering
machine but decided against leaving a message.

Hanging up the phone, Laurie pondered the thought of
calling Bingham. Believing it would be an exercise in futility
at best, and might get her fired at worst, she gave up the
idea. He clearly stated that he intended to do nothing, at
least not until he spoke with the commissioner of health.

Laurie's eyes moved from the phone to the open newspaper. Slowly the idea of leaking the story herself began to

occur to her. She'd had a bad experience with giving her opinion to Bob Talbot the last time, but in all fairness to him, she'd not specifically said her remarks were confidential.

With that thought in mind, she got out her address book to see if she had his number. She did, and she gave him a call.

"Well, well," he said when he heard it was Laurie. "I was afraid I was never going to hear from you again. I didn't know what else to do beyond apologizing."

"I overreacted," Laurie admitted. "I'm sorry I never got back to you. It was just that I got an awful chewing out by the chief over your story."

"I apologize again," Bob said. "What's up?"

"This might surprise you," Laurie said, "but I may have a story for you, a big story."

"I'm all ears," Bob said.

"I don't want to talk on the phone," Laurie said.

"Fine by me," Bob said. "How about I buy you dinner?"

"You're on," Laurie said.

They met at P. J. Clark's on the corner of Fifty-fifth and Third. They were lucky to get a table on a rainy Sunday evening, especially one by the far wall where they could talk above the usual hubbub. After a clear-eyed Irish waiter took their order and slid two brimming draughts in front of them, Laurie began.

"First, I'm not sure I'm doing the right thing talking to you. But I'm desperate. I feel I have to do something."

Bob nodded.

"I want you to promise me you will not use my name."

"Scout's honor," Bob said, holding up two fingers. Then he took out a note pad and a pencil.

"I don't know where to begin," Laurie said. She was hesitant at first, but once she began explaining recent events, she warmed up a bit. She began with Duncan Andrews and her first suspicions and took him through to the double death of George VanDeusen and Carol Palmer. She emphasized that all the victims were single, educated, successful people with no hint of drug use or illegal activity in their pasts. She also mentioned the pressure brought to bear on the medical examiner to keep a lid on the Duncan Andrews case in particular.

"In a way it's too bad he was the first. I think part of the reason Bingham keeps rejecting my series theory is because the series began with him."

"This is unbelievable," Bob said when Laurie had to pause with the arrival of their food. "I haven't seen anything about this in the media at all. Nothing. Zip."

"There was a mention of the double death in this morning's *Times,*" Laurie said. "But it was in the second section. It got barely a squib. But you're right, there's been no mention of the other cases."

"What a scoop," Bob marveled. He glanced at his watch. "I'll have to move on it if I'm going to make tomorrow morning's paper."

"But there's more," Laurie said. She went on to tell him that the cocaine involved was coming from one source, was probably contaminated with a trace of a very lethal compound on top of being extremely potent, and was probably being distributed by a single pusher who somehow came in contact with upscale young people.

"Well, that's not exactly true," Laurie corrected herself. "It might be two people. On most of the cases that I've investigated, two men have been seen going into the victim's apartment."

"I wonder why two?" Bob asked.

"I haven't the slightest idea," Laurie admitted. "There are a lot of mysteries about this whole affair."

"Is that it?" Bob questioned. He was eager to leave. He hadn't even touched his food.

"No, that's not all," Laurie said. "I've begun to get the

feeling that these deaths are not accidental, that they are deliberate. In other words they are homicides."

"This keeps getting better and better," Bob said.

"All of the bodies were found shortly after death," Laurie said. "That in itself is unusual. Single people who die alone are usually not found for days. In all the cases I've investigated, a phone call led to the discovery of the body. In two cases the victims called their significant other beforehand. In all the others, an anonymous tenant in the victim's building called the doorman to complain about strange sounds emanating from the victim's apartment. But here's the catch: based on medical evidence, these complaints about noise came several hours after the time of death."

"My God!" Bob said. He looked up at Laurie. "What about the police?" he asked. "Why haven't they gotten involved in all this?"

"Nobody buys my series theory. The police aren't the least suspicious. They consider these cases to be simple drug overdoses."

"And what about Dr. Harold Bingham? What has he done?"

"Nothing so far," Laurie said. "My guess is he wants to steer clear of such a potential hot potato. Duncan Andrews' father's running for office; his people have really been leaning on the mayor, who's been leaning on Bingham. He did say he'd talk to the commissioner of health about it."

"If these are homicides, then we're talking about some new kind of serial killer," Bob said. "This is hot stuff!"

"I think it's important for the public to be warned. If this can save one life, it's worth it. That's why I called you. We've got to put the word out about the contaminant in this drug."

"Is that it then?" Bob asked.

"I think so," Laurie said. "If I think of anything I forgot to mention, I'll call you."

"Great!" Bob said, getting to his feet. "Sorry to run, but

if I'm going to get this into tomorrow morning's paper, I've got to go directly to my editor."

Laurie watched Bob weave through the crowd of people waiting for tables. Looking down at her veal swimming in a pool of oil, she decided she wasn't hungry herself.

She was about to get up when their Irish waiter reappeared with the bill.

Laurie looked after Bob, but he was long gone. So much for his offer to pick up the tab.

"What time is it?" Angelo asked.

"Seven-thirty," Tony said, checking the Rolex he'd picked up at the Goldburg place.

They were parked on Fifth Avenue just north of the Seventy-second Street entrance to Central Park's East Drive. They were on the park side of the avenue but had a good view of the entrance to the apartment house they were interested in.

"Must take this Kendall Fletcher a long time to put on his jogging shorts," Angelo said.

"He told me he was going jogging," Tony said defensively. "You should have called him yourself if you weren't going to believe me."

"Here comes somebody," Angelo said. "What do you think? Could that be Kendall Fletcher, banker?"

"He doesn't look like a banker in that getup," Tony said. "I don't understand this jogging stuff. Who'd want to dress up in Peter Pan tights and run around the park at night? It's like asking to be mugged."

"I think it's him," Angelo said. "Looks like the right age. How old did you say Kendall was?"

Tony took a typed sheet of paper out of the glove compartment. Using the map light, he searched for the Kendall Fletcher entry, then read: "Kendall Fletcher, age thirty-four, Vice President Citicorp."

330

"That must be him," Angelo said. He started the car. Tony put the list back in the glove compartment.

Kendall Fletcher had come out of his apartment building dressed to run. He crossed Fifth Avenue at Seventy-second Street and began jogging as soon as he reached the park.

Angelo headed for the East Drive. He and Tony kept their eyes glued to Kendall as he made his way down the Seventy-second Street transverse to the drive, where he turned north into the jogging lane.

Angelo motored about a hundred yards past the man, then pulled over to the side of the road. With the blinkers on, he and Tony got out.

Kendall wasn't the only runner out on the drive. As Angelo and Tony watched him approach, a half dozen other runners passed by.

"I just don't get these people," Tony said with wonderment.

Just before Kendall reached them, Angelo and Tony stepped into the jogging lane.

"Kendall Fletcher?" Angelo asked.

Kendall came to a stop. "Yes?" he said.

"Police," Angelo said. He flashed his Ozone Park police badge. Tony flashed his. "Hate to bother you while you're running," Angelo continued, "but we want to talk to you downtown. We're involved with a Citicorp investigation."

"This is not a good time," Kendall said. His voice was firm but his eyes gave him away. He was definitely nervous.

"I don't think you want to make a scene," Angelo said. "We won't take much of your time. We wanted to talk with the vice presidents before we convened a grand jury."

"I'm in my jogging shorts," Kendall said.

"No problem," Angelo said. "We'll be happy to give you a lift home and let you change. You can be out jogging in another hour if you cooperate."

Kendall appeared wary but finally agreed. He climbed

331

into Angelo's car and they drove back to his building on Fifth Avenue.

Leaving a card on the dash, Angelo and Tony got out of the car with Kendall and followed him into the building. Tony was carrying the old black leather doctor's bag. They walked as a group past the doorman, who ignored them, got on the elevator, and went up to the twenty-fifth floor.

No one spoke as Kendall opened his apartment door, went in, and held the door for Angelo and Tony.

Tony nodded several times as he viewed the apartment. "Nice layout," he said. He put down his doctor's bag on the coffee table.

"Can I get you men anything while I change?" Kendall asked. He motioned toward the bar.

"Nah," Tony said. "You understand, we're on duty. We don't drink while we work."

Angelo checked out the apartment quickly while Tony watched Kendall. Kendall in turn watched Angelo with confused curiosity.

"What are you looking for?" Kendall called after Angelo.

"Make sure there aren't any other people up here," Angelo said as he returned from glancing into the kitchen. He then disappeared back toward the master suite.

"Hey!" Kendall called. "You can't search my apartment!" He turned to Tony. "You have to have a warrant for this."

"A warrant?" Tony questioned. "Oh, yeah, the warrant. We always forget the warrant."

Angelo returned.

"I'd like to see your identification again," Kendall said. "This is an outrage."

Angelo reached into his Brioni jacket and withdrew his Walther pistol. "Here's mine," he said. He motioned for

Kendall to sit down. Tony snapped open the latches on his doctor's bag.

"What is this, a robbery?" Kendall asked, staring at the gun. He sat down. "Help yourself! Take what you want."

"I'm the candy man," Tony said. He lifted a long, clear plastic bag and a small cylinder out of the bag.

Angelo moved behind Kendall, gun in hand. Kendall watched nervously as Tony used the cylinder to inflate the plastic bag with a gas that was obviously lighter than air. Once the bag was completely full, he occluded the end and put the cylinder back in the doctor's bag. With the plastic bag in hand, he approached Kendall.

"What's going on?" Kendall demanded.

"We're here to offer you a wild trip," Tony said with a smile.

"I'm not interested in any trip," Kendall said. "Take what you want and get out of here."

Tony opened the base of the plastic bag so that it looked more like a miniature transparent hot air balloon. Then, holding two sides of the base, he crammed it down over the top of Kendall's head.

The unexpectedness of the move caught Kendall by surprise. He reached up and grabbed Tony's forearms and halted the bag at his shoulders. As he tried to stand up, Angelo threw the arm with the gun around his neck. Angelo's other hand grabbed Kendall's right wrist in an attempt to free its grip on Tony's forearm.

For a second the three people struggled against one another. Kendall, terrified at this point, opened his mouth and bit Angelo's forearm through the plastic bag.

"Ahhhh!" Angelo cried, feeling Kendall's incisors break his skin. Angelo let go of Kendall's arm and was about to punch Kendall in the face inside the plastic bag when he saw it wasn't necessary.

After having taken only a few breaths in the plastic bag,

Kendall's eyelids sagged and his whole body, including his jaws, went limp. While Tony followed Kendall to the floor, maintaining the plastic bag in position, Angelo got his arm back.

Quickly Angelo undid his cuff link and pulled up his sleeve. On the inside of his forearm, about three inches from his elbow, was an elliptical ring of puncture wounds corresponding to Kendall's dentition. A few of them were bleeding.

"The bastard bit me!" Angelo said indignantly. He put his gun into its shoulder holster. "In this line of work you never know what the hell is going to happen."

Tony stood up and went back to the doctor's bag. "Every time we use that gas, I'm amazed," he said. "Old Doc Travino sure knows his stuff." He got out a syringe and a piece of rubber tubing. Returning to Kendall, he used the rubber tubing as a tourniquet. "Look at these veins, will you!" he said. "God, they look like cigars. No way we can miss these. You want to do it or should I?"

"You do it," Angelo said. "But you better get that bag off his head. We don't want another Robert Evans–type screw-up."

"Right," Tony said. He worked the plastic bag free, then shook it out. "Ugh," he said. "I hate that sweet smell."

"Give him the coke, will you?" Angelo said. "He'll wake up before you're finished."

Tony took the needle and pushed it into one of Kendall's prominent veins. "There, what did I tell you?" he said, pleased to have scored on his first try. He pulled off the tourniquet, then pushed in the plunger, emptying the syringe into Kendall's arm.

Tony left the used syringe on the coffee table and put the rest of his paraphernalia back into the doctor's bag. At the same time he took out a small glassine envelope. Going back to Kendall, he poured a small amount of the white powder into Kendall's nostrils. Then he dabbed a little onto his thumb and snorted it. "I love leftovers," he said with glee.

"Stay away from that stuff!" Angelo commanded.

"Couldn't resist," Tony said. He put the glassine envelope next to the used syringe. "What do you think, into the fridge with him?"

"Let's skip it," Angelo said. "I was talking with Doc about it. He says that as long as the body's not out longer than twelve hours we're okay. And the way we've been working this, everybody's been found way before twelve hours."

Tony looked around. "Did I get everything?"

"Looks good," Angelo said. "Let's sit down and see how Kendall likes his trip."

Tony sat on the couch while Angelo sat in the armchair that Kendall had been occupying.

"Nice apartment," Tony said. "What do you say we glance around a little to see if there's anything we might want to pick up?"

"How many times do I have to tell you: we don't take anything when we do these drug trips."

"Such a waste," Tony said wistfully as he surveyed the room.

A few minutes later, Kendall stirred and smacked his lips. Moaning, he rolled over on his stomach.

"Hey, Kendall, baby," Tony called. "How you feel? Talk to me!"

Kendall pushed himself up to a sitting position. He had a blank expression on his pale face.

"How is it?" Tony asked. "With as much snow as you got coursing through those veins, you must be in heaven."

Without any warning, Kendall vomited onto the rug.

"Oh, God!" Tony cried as he scrambled out of the way. "This is disgusting."

Kendall coughed violently, then looked up at Tony and Angelo. His eyes were glazed. He looked confused.

"How do you feel?" Angelo asked.

Kendall's mouth tried to form words, but the man seemed utterly incapable of them. Suddenly his eyes rolled back so that only the whites were showing and he began to convulse.

"That's our cue," Angelo said. "Let's get out of here."

Tony picked up the doctor's bag and followed Angelo to the door. Angelo peered through the peephole. With no one in sight, he opened the door and stuck his head out.

"Hallway's clear," he said. "Come on!"

They exited the apartment quickly and ran to the stairwell. Descending a single floor, they relaxed and waited for the elevator.

"Are you hungry?" Tony asked.

"A little," Angelo said.

To avoid being seen by the doorman, they got off the elevator on the first floor and returned to the stairwell. They exited the building via the service entrance.

Arriving at the car, Angelo stopped. He was astonished. "Look at this!" he said. "I can't believe it. We got a ticket. Some nerve. I hope the cop who gave us this never tries to bring his car out to Ozone Park."

"So what's next?" Tony asked as soon as they were seated in the car. "Another job or dinner?"

"I don't know what you like more," said Angelo, shaking his head, "whacking or eating."

Tony smiled. "Depends on my mood."

"I think we should do the other hit," Angelo said. "Then when we stop to eat it will be just about the right time to call back here to tell the doorman about noises coming from 25G."

"Let's do it," Tony said. He sat back. With his snort of cocaine, he felt great. In fact, he felt like he could do anything in the world.

As Angelo pulled away from the curb, Franco Ponti put his own car in gear. He allowed several cars to pass before pulling out into Fifth Avenue traffic. He'd watched while Angelo and Tony picked the jogger up in the park and escorted him back to his apartment. Although he hadn't been privy to what had transpired in the apartment, he thought he could guess. But the real question wasn't what had happened, but why?

14

□

6:45 A.M., MONDAY
MANHATTAN

The alarm went off and Laurie went through her usual
routine of rapidly fumbling with it to get it turned off. As
she set the clock on her windowsill, she realized that for the
first time in many days she'd not awakened with the anxiety
of having had her recurrent nightmare. Apparently her conscience had been temporarily appeased by her visit with
Bob Talbot.

But as Laurie slipped into her sheepskin slippers and
turned on the bedroom TV to the local news, she began to
feel progressively nervous about what the day would bring
vis-à-vis Dr. Bingham. She was particularly anxious to get
a copy of the paper to see Bob Talbot's piece and how
prominently it would be featured. It was quite apparent
Bingham would suspect her as the source. What would she
say if he asked her directly? She doubted she would be able
to lie to the chief.

Pausing in the kitchen on her way to the bathroom, Laurie hazarded a glance out at the tiny wedge of sky she could see from her window. The dark swirling clouds suggested that the weather had not improved since yesterday.

Later, after her shower and with a second cup of coffee balanced on the edge of the sink, Laurie started applying her makeup, all the time going over various scenarios of what she might say to Dr. Bingham. In the background she heard the familiar theme music to *Good Morning America* as the show came on the air. A little later she heard the equally familiar happy voices of the hosts.

As Laurie was about to apply her lipstick she heard Mike Schneider come on and talk about more weapons of mass destruction that a UN team had found in Iraq. Laurie had her upper lip done and was about to do the lower when she flinched. She'd heard Mike Schneider say a surprising name. It was her name!

Laurie dashed into the bedroom and turned up the volume. Her expression changed from disbelief to horror as Schneider gave an overview of her overdose series starting with Duncan Andrews, son of senatorial hopeful Clayton Andrews. He went on to cite three cases unfamiliar to Laurie: Kendall Fletcher, Stephanie Haberlin, and Yvonne Andre. He mentioned the double overdose at George VanDeusen's. Most disturbing of all, he repeated Laurie's name, saying that according to Dr. Laurie Montgomery, there was reason to believe these deaths were deliberate homicides, not accidental overdoses, and that the whole affair potentially represented an extraordinary cover-up on the part of the New York City police and the medical examiner's office.

As soon as Mike Schneider moved on to other news, Laurie dashed into her living room and literally threw papers aside searching for her address book. Finding Bob Talbot's number, she punched it into the telephone.

"What did you do to me?" she screamed as soon as he picked up the phone.

"Laurie, I'm sorry," Bob said. "You must believe me. It wasn't my fault. To get the story into the morning paper my editor had me write up a memo to him. I wrote that your name was not to be included, but he stole the story from me. It was totally unethical in every regard."

Laurie hung up the phone in disgust. Her heart was pounding. This was a disaster, a catastrophe. She'd surely be out of a job. There was no question of Bingham's response now; he'd be furious. And after this, where would she ever find a job in forensics?

Laurie walked over to the window and gazed out at the sad, refuse-strewn warren of neglected backyards. She was so distressed she felt numb. She couldn't even cry. But as she stood there looking at the depressing vista, her emotions began to change. After all, her actions had come from a need to follow her conscience. And Bingham had admitted, during her call to him yesterday, that he knew her intentions were good.

Laurie's initial fear of total calamity mellowed. All at once she didn't think she would be terminated. Reprimanded, yes; suspended, possibly; but fired, no. Turning from the window, she went back into the bathroom to finish her makeup. The more she thought about the situation, the calmer she became. She could see herself explaining that she had been true to her sense of responsibility as a person as well as a medical examiner.

Returning to the bedroom for the last time, Laurie completed her dressing. Then, gathering her things, she left her apartment.

As she was standing at the elevator awaiting its arrival, she noticed a newspaper in front of a neighbor's door. Stepping over to it, she slipped it from its plastic cover. There on the front page as a second headline was the story of her overdose series. There was even an old picture of her taken in medical school. Laurie wondered where the picture had come from.

Opening the paper to the proper page, Laurie read the first few paragraphs, which were a repeat of Mike Schneider's summary. But, true to tabloid-style journalism, there was much more lurid detail, including reference to a number of victims having been stuffed into refrigerators. Laurie wondered where that distortion had come from. She certainly hadn't mentioned anything like that to Bob Talbot. There was also more emphasis on the alleged cover-up, making it sound far more sinister than Mike Schneider had.

Hearing the elevator arrive behind her, Laurie dropped the newspaper in front of the proper door and hurried back before the elevator left. When she was halfway into the car, she heard Debra Engler's hoarse voice.

"You shouldn't read other people's papers," the woman said.

For a moment Laurie stood holding the insistent elevator door from closing. She wanted to turn around and bash her umbrella against Debra's door to frighten the woman. But she controlled herself, and finally boarded.

As she descended, Laurie's calmness crumbled and was replaced by apprehension of meeting with Bingham. Laurie dreaded confrontations. She had never been good at them.

Paul Cerino was hunched over his favorite meal of the day: breakfast. He was enjoying a hearty feast of eggs over easy, pork sausage, and biscuits. He was still wearing the same metal patch over his eye, but he was feeling terrific.

Gregory and Steven were momentarily quiet, eating their own choice of sugar-coated breakfast cereal which they had selected from a bewildering choice of single serving boxes. Each had his own empty box in front of him which he was studying intently. Gloria had just sat down after having retrieved the newspaper from the front stoop.

"Read me about yesterday's Giants and Steelers game," Paul mumbled with his mouth full.

"Oh my!" Gloria said, staring at the front page.

"What's the matter?" Paul asked.

"There's a story about a bunch of drug deaths of wealthy and educated young people," Gloria said. "Says here they think they were murders."

Paul choked violently, spraying most of the food that he'd had in his mouth out over the table.

"Daaad!" Gregory whined. A layer of partially chewed egg and sausage had settled on the surface of his Sugar Pops.

"Paul, are you all right?" Gloria questioned with alarm.

Paul held up a hand to indicate he was fine. His face had become as red as the heeling patches of skin on his cheeks. With his other hand he picked up his orange juice and took a drink.

"I can't eat this," Gregory said looking at his cereal. "It's going to make me puke."

"I can't either," Steven said, who tended to do just about everything Gregory did.

"Get yourselves clean bowls," Gloria directed. "Then pick another cereal."

"Better read me that article about the drug deaths," Paul said with a hoarse voice.

Gloria read the whole article straight through. When she was finished, Paul headed for his den.

"Aren't you going to finish your breakfast?" Gloria called after him.

"In a minute," Paul said. He closed the door of the den behind him and pressed the button on his automatic dialer that would connect him to Angelo.

"Who the hell is this?" Angelo muttered sleepily.

"Did you read this morning's paper?"

"How am I going to read this morning's paper? I've been sleeping. I was out doing you know what until all hours."

"I want you, Tony, and that harebrained pill-pusher Travino over here this morning," Paul said. "And read the paper on the way. We got a problem."

"Franco!" Marie Dominick said with surprise. "Isn't this a little early for you?"

"I have to talk with Vinnie," Franco said.

"Vinnie's still sleeping," Marie said.

"I figured he was, but if you could please wake him up—"

"Are you sure?"

"I'm sure," Franco said.

"Well, come on in then," Marie said as she opened the door wide.

Franco stepped inside. "Go on into the kitchen," Marie said. "There's coffee already made."

Marie disappeared up a short flight of steps while Franco wandered into the kitchen. Vinnie's little boy, Vinnie Junior, was seated at the table. The six-year-old was busy slapping a short stack of pancakes with the back side of a spoon. His older sister, Roslyn, age eleven, was at the stove poised to turn over the next batch of flapjacks.

Franco poured himself a cup of coffee. Then he wandered into the living room and sat on a white leather sofa and gazed at the new peppermint-colored shag carpet. He was amazed. He didn't think you could buy shag carpet anymore.

"This better be good!" Vinnie thundered as he came into the room. He was dressed in a silky, paisley print robe. His hair, which was normally immaculately slicked back, was virtually standing on end.

Instead of explaining, Franco handed Vinnie the paper. Vinnie grabbed it and sat down. "So what am I supposed to be looking at?" he growled.

"Read the article about drug deaths," Franco said.

Vinnie's forehead wrinkled as he read. He was silent for about five minutes. Franco sipped his coffee.

"So what the hell?" Vinnie said, looking up. He slapped the paper with the back of his hand. "What the hell are you doing waking me up for this?"

"See those names at the end of the list? Fletcher and the other ones? I followed Angelo and Tony last night. They whacked those people. My guess is that they've whacked the whole bunch."

"But why?" Vinnie demanded. "Why with cocaine? They giving the stuff away?"

"I still don't know why," Franco admitted. "I don't even know if Angelo and Tony are on their own or taking orders from Cerino."

"They're taking orders," Vinnie said. "They're too stupid to do anything on their own. God! This is a disaster. The whole city is going to be crawling with feds and narcs on top of normal, everyday cops. What the hell is Cerino doing? Has he gone crazy? I don't understand."

"I don't either," Franco said. "But I just established a connection that goes through a couple of people who know Tony. Someone will get in touch with you."

"We got to do something," Vinnie said, shaking his head. "We can't let this go on."

"It's hard to know what to do until we know what Cerino's up to," Franco said. "Give me one more day."

"Only one," Vinnie said. "After that we move."

Laurie was filled with dread as she faced her office building. What a difference a day made! Yesterday and the day before she had breezed in and out like she owned the place. Now she was afraid to cross the threshold. But she knew it was what she had to do. The calmness she'd felt in her apartment had vanished.

As she drew closer, she saw that a swarm of restless reporters had already descended on the place to get the story—her story. Her thoughts had been so focused on Bingham, she hadn't been thinking of them. There were at least as many there now as there had been for the preppy murder II case. Maybe more.

Might as well get it over with, she decided. Entering the reception area, she was instantly recognized. Microphones were pushed in her face along with a cacophony of questions and the pop of camera flashes. Laurie pushed her way through to the inner door without a word. A uniformed security man checked her photo identification before admitting her. The reporters were unable to pursue her beyond that door.

Trying to maintain her composure, Laurie went directly to the ID office. Vinnie was there reading his paper. Calvin was there too.

Laurie gazed into the black man's face. He stared back at her, hiding his feelings. His eyes were like black marbles, perfectly framed by his wire-rimmed glasses.

"Dr. Bingham wants to see you," Calvin said flatly. "Unfortunately he can't see you until he finishes dealing with these reporters. He'll call you in your office."

Laurie would have liked to try to explain, but there wasn't much she could say. And Calvin didn't seem interested. He returned to whatever work he was doing when Laurie had entered. Laurie decided to check the autopsy schedule before going to her office. Her name was not on the list. She noticed the three names she'd read in the newspaper: Kendall Fletcher, Stephanie Haberlin, and Yvonne Andre. Apparently they were new cases that fit her series.

Laurie approached Calvin. "I guess you know I'd like to do the posts on these overdoses," she said.

Calvin looked up from his work. "Personally I don't care what your preferences are," he said. "The fact of the matter is that you are to go to your office and wait for Dr. Bingham's call."

Embarrassed at this obvious snub, Laurie glanced at Vin-

nie, but he seemed riveted to the sports page as usual. If
he'd heard the exchange, he wasn't about to show it.

Feeling like a child banished to her room, Laurie went up
to her office. Deciding she might as well try to get some
work done, she sat at her desk and pulled out some folders.
She was just about to start when she sensed someone's
presence. She looked to the open doorway and saw a rumpled Lou Soldano. He didn't look happy.

"I personally want to thank you for making my life miserable," Lou said. "Not that I wasn't under enough stress
from the commissioner before your little revelation to the
press, but this just puts the icing on the cake."

"They distorted what I said," Laurie said.

"Oh, sure!" Lou said with sarcasm.

"I never said anything about a cover-up," Laurie said.
"All I said was the police didn't believe the affair involved
them. That's essentially what you told me."

"My own little mischief-maker. It's like your call to Internal Affairs wasn't enough. You had to be sure to really get
me."

"That call was deserved," Laurie snapped. "And talk
about calls, you couldn't have been much ruder when I
called you yesterday. I've had quite enough of your glib
sarcasm."

Laurie and Lou glared at each other until Lou broke off
and averted his gaze. He stepped into the room and sat
down in his usual chair.

"The comment on the phone was juvenile," he admitted.
"I knew it the second it came out of my mouth. I'm sorry.
The problem is that I'm jealous of the guy. There, I said it.
Whatever is left of my ego, you can kick around as much as
you like."

Laurie's anger subsided. She let her head fall into her
hands, her elbows on the desk. "And I'm sorry if I caused
you any trouble at work," she said, rubbing her eyes. "I

certainly didn't mean to. But you know how desperate I'd become. I had to do something in order to live with myself. I couldn't see any more of these people die without trying something."

"Did you have any idea of the upheaval you'd be causing?" Lou asked. "And the effects?"

"I still don't know completely," Laurie said. "I knew there would be some fallout from the story, otherwise I wouldn't have given it. But I didn't know the extent. And I didn't know they'd distort the facts. On top of that they reneged on my condition of remaining anonymous. I haven't seen my chief yet, but from the way the deputy chief spoke with me, it's not going to be a pleasant talk. I could even be fired."

"He'll be mad," Lou said. "But he won't fire you. He's got to respect your aims if not your methods. But he's going to take a lot of heat for this. He won't be a happy man."

Laurie nodded. She appreciated the reassurance she'd not be terminated.

"Well, I'd love to stick around to see how this all turns out, but I've got to go. My office is in an uproar, too. I just had to come down here and get it off my chest. I'm glad I did. Good luck with your boss."

"Thanks," Laurie said. "And I'm glad you came too."

After Lou left, Laurie put in a call to Jordan. She could have used some moral support, but he was in surgery and wasn't expected back in the office until much later.

Laurie was just settling down to work again when there was a knock on her door. She looked up to see Peter Letterman standing before her.

"Dr. Montgomery?" Peter said tentatively.

Laurie welcomed him in and offered him a seat.

"Thank you," Peter said. He sat and gazed around the office. "Nice place."

"You think so?" Laurie questioned.

348

"Better than my broom closet," Peter said. "Anyway, I won't take too much of your time. I just wanted to let you know that I've finally picked up a trace contaminant or at least a foreign compound in the sample you sent up from Randall Thatcher."

"Really!" Laurie said with interest. "What did you find?"

"Ethylene," Peter said. "It was only a trace since the gas is so volatile, and I haven't been able to isolate it from two other cases that I tested."

"Ethylene?" Laurie questioned. "That's odd. I don't know what to make of that. I've heard of using ether in free basing, but not ethylene."

"Free basing is associated with smoking cocaine," Peter said, "not taking the drug IV the way the folks in your series did. Besides, even in smoking, ether is only used as a solvent for extraction. So I don't know why ethylene turned up. It could even be a laboratory error for all I know. But since you've been so interested in the possibility of a contaminant, I wanted to let you know right away."

"If ethylene is so volatile," Laurie said, "why don't you look for it in the samples from Robert Evans? Since you determined he'd died so quickly, maybe there would be more of a chance to find it if it had been involved."

"That's a good idea," Peter said. "I'll give it a whirl."

Laurie kept her eyes on the empty doorway for a moment after Peter had left. Ethylene was hardly the kind of contaminant she'd expected. She thought that they might find some exotic central-nervous-system stimulant like strychnine or nicotine. Laurie wasn't familiar with ethylene. She'd have to do a little research.

Glancing through the pharmacology book she and Riva kept in the office, Laurie didn't find much on the gas. She decided to check the office library upstairs. There she found a long article on ethylene in an old pharmacology book. Ethylene was featured more prominently in the older book

349

because it had been used as an anesthetic agent a number of years ago. It had ultimately been abandoned because it was lighter than air and flammable. Those two qualities made the gas too dangerous for use in operating rooms.

In another book Laurie found that ethylene had been noted around the turn of the century to prevent carnations in Chicago greenhouses from opening. The ethylene had been in the greenhouse illuminating gas. On a more positive note she read that the gas was used to hasten the ripening of fruit and in the manufacture of certain plastics like polyethylene and Styrofoam.

Although this background information was interesting, Laurie still didn't see why ethylene would turn up in cocaine overdose/toxicity cases. Feeling discouraged, she replaced the books on their respective shelves and returned to her office, hoping she hadn't missed Bingham's call. Maybe Peter was right: his finding of ethylene had resulted from a laboratory error.

When Lou got back to police headquarters, he was handed a stack of urgent messages from his captain, the area commander, and the police commissioner. Clearly all of officialdom was in an uproar.

Going into his office, he was surprised to find a newly appointed detective sitting patiently by his desk. His suit was new, suggesting he'd only recently become a plainclothesman.

"Who are you?" Lou asked.

"Officer O'Brian," the policeman said.

"You have a first name?"

"Yes, sir! It's Patrick."

"Nice Italian name," Lou said.

Patrick laughed.

"What can I do for you?" Lou asked, trying to decide on the order in which to return his messages.

"Sergeant Norman Carver asked me to come by to try to collate the medical information you have relating to those gangland killings. You know, all those people who were also patients of Dr. Jordan Scheffield. He thought I might be good at it because I'd been premed for a while in college and had worked in a hospital summers before switching to law enforcement."

"Sounds reasonable," Lou said.

"I came up with something that might be important," Patrick said.

"Uh huh," Lou said. He stared at the messages to call the police commissioner. That was the one that was the most disturbing. He'd never gotten a message to call the police commissioner. It was like a parish priest getting a call from the pope.

"All the patients had different diagnoses," Patrick continued, "but they did have one feature in common."

Lou looked up. "Oh?"

Patrick nodded. "They were all scheduled to have surgery. They were all going to have operations on their corneas."

"No kidding?" Lou said.

"No kidding," Patrick said.

After Patrick had left, Lou tried to make sense of it. He'd been disappointed when he'd failed to find a common link between the murder victims besides the fact they'd been patients of Jordan Scheffield. But now there might be something after all. It couldn't be simple coincidence.

Looking at his stack of phone messages, Lou decided to postpone returning the calls. He'd be better off following up on this new information. After all, he already knew what his higher-ups were calling him about. They wanted to complain about his lack of progress in the gangland murders and probably give him an earful about Laurie's overdose series to boot. If there was a chance he could start to break the case with this cornea stuff, he'd be better off pursuing it now before he spoke to them.

Lou decided to start with the doctor himself. He figured he'd get the usual runaround, but he was determined to speak with the man, patients or no.

But when Lou asked for Jordan, Scheffield's receptionist told him that Jordan was in surgery over at Manhattan General and that he had many cases scheduled. He wouldn't be back in the office until late in the day.

Lou pondered his options. Returning his urgent messages still wasn't his next choice. He decided persistence was the virtue of the day; he'd pay the eye doc another visit even if it meant barging in the operating room. He'd witnessed about a dozen autopsies that week; could surgery be much worse?

"What the hell happened?" Paul bellowed. Angelo, Tony, and Dr. Louis Travino had been hauled on the carpet. They stood like errant pupils before the school principal. Paul Cerino was seated behind his massive partners desk. He was not happy.

Dr. Travino wiped his forehead nervously with a handkerchief. He was a balding, overweight man with a vague resemblance to Cerino.

"Isn't somebody going to answer me? What's the matter with you people? I asked a simple question. How'd this story get into the papers?" He swatted the newspaper on his desk in front of him. "All right," Paul said when it was clear no one was about to volunteer anything. "Let's start from the beginning. Louie, you told me this 'fruit gas' would not be detectable."

"That's right," Louie said. "It's not. It's too volatile. Nothing was said about the gas in the papers."

"True," Paul said. "But then why are they describing these overdoses as murders?"

"I don't know," Louie replied. "But it wasn't because they detected the gas."

"You'd better be right," Paul said. "I don't think I have to remind you I've been covering your sizable gambling debts. The Vaccarro family would be very unhappy with you if I suddenly wasn't good for the money."

"It wasn't the gas," Louie reiterated.

"So what was it? I'm telling you, this article has given me a very bad feeling. If someone's screwed up, heads are going to roll."

"This is the first suggestion of trouble," Louie said. "Otherwise everything has been doing fine. And look at you, you're doing great."

"Then how did this female doc come up with the real story?" Paul asked. "This Laurie Montgomery is the same broad who blabbed to Lou Soldano about the acid being tossed in my face. Who is this chick?"

"She's one of the medical examiners in the Manhattan office," Louie said.

"You mean like that character Quincy that used to be on TV?" Paul asked.

"Well, it's a little different in real life," Louie said. "But basically the same."

"So how did she suspect something?" Paul asked. "I thought you said there'd be no figuring this. How did this Laurie Montgomery guess what was going on?"

"I don't know," Louie said. "Maybe this is something we should ask Dr. Montgomery."

Cerino considered the suggestion for a moment. "To tell you the truth," he said, "I'd been thinking the same thing. Besides, this Laurie Montgomery could become a big pain in the ass if she keeps up the detective work. Angelo, you think you might arrange a little, er, interview with the little lady?"

"No problem," Angelo said. "You want her, I'll get her."

"It's the only thing I can think to do," Paul said. "And after we've had a little chat, I think the best thing this lady doc could do is disappear. I mean completely. I'm talking no body, nothing."

"Isn't the *Montego Bay* going to be leaving soon?" Angelo asked.

"Yeah," Paul said. "She's about to pull anchor and head for Jamaica. Good idea. Okay, bring her to the pier. I want Dr. Louie to question her."

"I don't like being directly involved in something like this," Louie said.

"I'm going to pretend I didn't hear you say that," Paul said. "You're involved in this operation up to your eyeballs, so don't give me any crap."

"When do you want us to move?" Angelo asked.

"This afternoon or tonight," Paul said. "We can't wait around for things to get worse. Doesn't that Amendola kid work over there at the morgue? What's his name? The family's from Bayside?"

"Vinnie," Tony said. "Vinnie Amendola."

"Yeah," Cerino said. "Vinnie Amendola. He works at the morgue. Talk to him, maybe he'll help. Remind him what I did for his old man when he had trouble with the union. And take this." He pointed to the newspaper. "I understand the lady doc's picture's in the paper. Use that to make sure you get the right person."

After his guests had departed, Cerino used his automatic dialer to call Jordan's office. When the receptionist explained that the doctor was in surgery, Cerino told her he wanted his call returned within the hour. Jordan got back to him in fifteen minutes.

"I don't like what's going on," Jordan said before Paul could say a word. "When we talked about some sort of business association, you told me there would be no problems. That was two days ago and already there's a major scandal brewing. I don't like it."

"Calm down, Doc," Cerino said. "All businesses have some start-up pains. Stay cool. I just wanted to be sure you didn't do anything foolish. Something you'd regret."

"You got me involved in this by threatening me. Is this the same kind of scare tactic?"

"I guess that's what you could call it," Paul said. "Depends on your point of view. Me, I thought we were talking one businessman to another. I just wanted to remind you you're dealing with professionals like yourself."

The call, when it came, was from Bingham's secretary. She asked Laurie if she would come to Dr. Bingham's office. Laurie had said of course.

Bingham's expression was solemn when Laurie stepped into his office. Laurie could tell he was trying to maintain his composure much as she was trying to retain her nerve.

"I truly don't understand you, Doctor," Bingham said finally. His face was hard, his voice firm. "You have deliberately countermanded my directive. I specifically warned you about going to the media with your own opinions, yet you willfully disobeyed me. Given such willful disregard for my authority, you leave me no choice but to terminate your employment at this office."

"But Dr. Bingham—" Laurie began.

"I don't want any excuses or explanations," Bingham interrupted. "According to regulations I have the right to terminate you at my discretion since you are still within the probational first year of your employment. However, if you demand in writing a hearing on this issue, I will not block it. Beyond that, I have nothing more to say to you, Dr. Montgomery. That will be all."

"But Dr. Bingham—" Laurie started again.

"That will be all!" Dr. Bingham shouted. The tiny capillaries that wrapped around his nostrils dilated, turning his whole nose a bright red.

Hastily Laurie scrambled from her chair and fled out of

Bingham's office. She consciously avoided the stares of the administrative secretaries who'd undoubtedly heard Bingham's outburst. Without stopping, she went up to her office and closed the door. Sitting at her desk, she looked at its cluttered surface. She was in shock. She'd talked herself out of the possibility of being fired, yet that was exactly what had happened. Once again she found herself fighting tears and wishing that she had more control over her emotions.

With trembling fingers she opened her briefcase and emptied out all the files she had in it. Then she packed it with her personal belongings. Books and that sort of thing she'd have to come back for at a later date. She did take out the summary sheet of the overdose series from the central desk drawer and put it into her briefcase. With her coat on, her umbrella under her arm, and her briefcase in her hand, she closed and locked her door.

She didn't leave the building immediately. Instead she went down to the toxicology lab to find Peter Letterman. She told him that she'd been let go but that she was still interested in the results of his tests with respect to her series. She asked if he'd mind if she checked in. Peter said that he wouldn't mind at all. Laurie knew he was eager to ask about what had happened with Bingham, but he didn't.

Laurie was about to head out when she remembered the test she'd requested from the DNA lab one floor below. She was interested to know about the sample she'd taken from Julia Myerholtz's fingernail. What she was hoping for was something positive even though she did not expect it. To her astonishment her wish came true.

"The final result won't be ready for a long time," the technician explained when Laurie inquired about the status of the specimen. "But I'm ninety-nine-percent sure that the two samples came from two different people."

Laurie was stunned. Here was another baffling piece to the puzzle. What could it mean? Was it another clue that pointed to homicide? She didn't know. The only thing she could think to do was call Lou. She went back to her office and tried to reach him but was told that he was out. The police operator didn't know when he'd be back and had no way to reach him unless it was an emergency. Laurie was disappointed. She realized she would also like to tell Lou about getting fired, yet she could hardly justify saying it was an emergency. She thanked the operator and didn't leave a message. She relocked her door.

Laurie thought it best to leave via the morgue. That way she'd stand less of a chance of running into either Bingham or Calvin. She'd also have a chance to avoid the press. However, when she reached the morgue level, she thought of one more thing she wanted to do: get the addresses and the details of the three cases that had come in overnight. Her only chance at possibly getting her job back lay in proving her allegations. If she could do that, then she thought she'd request that hearing Bingham had mentioned.

Laurie quickly changed into scrub clothes and entered the autopsy room.

As usual on a Monday morning, all tables were in use. Laurie went to the master schedule and saw that the three cases she was interested in had been given to George Fontworth. She joined him at his table. He and Vinnie had already gotten a start.

"I can't talk to you," George said. "I know it sounds crazy, but Bingham came down here to tell me you'd been fired and that I absolutely was not to speak to you. If you want you can call me tonight at home."

"Just answer me this," Laurie said. "Are these cases like the others?"

"I guess," George said. "This is the first one, so I don't know for sure about the others, but from glancing through the folders, I'd say so."

"For now all I want are the addresses," Laurie said. "Let me take the investigator's reports for a minute, then I'll bring them right back."

"I don't know what I've done to deserve this," George said, rolling his eyes. "Just make it quick. If anybody asks, I'm going to say you came in here and took them when I wasn't looking."

Laurie got the papers she wanted from George's folders and went back to the locker room. She copied down the three addresses and put them in her briefcase. Back in the autopsy room, she slipped the reports into their respective folders.

"Thanks, George," Laurie said.

"I never saw you," George answered.

Returning to the locker room, Laurie slowly put on her street clothes. Then, with her things in hand, she walked the length of the morgue, past the mortuary office, and past the security office. At the morgue loading dock were several mortuary vans with HEALTH AND HOSPITAL CORP. stenciled on the sides.

Walking between the vans, Laurie emerged on Thirtieth Street. It was a gray, rainy, clammy day. Opening her umbrella, Laurie began to trudge up toward First Avenue. As far as she was concerned, it was the nadir of her life.

Tony got out of Angelo's car. He was just slamming the door when he noticed that Angelo hadn't moved. He was still sitting behind the wheel.

"What's the matter?" Tony asked. "I thought we were going inside."

"I don't like the idea of going into the morgue," Angelo admitted.

"You want me to go in there by myself?" Tony asked.

"No," Angelo said. "I like that idea even less." Angelo reluctantly opened his door and stepped out. He pulled an umbrella from the floor of the backseat and snapped it open. Then he locked the car.

At the security office Angelo asked for Vinnie Amendola.

"Go on into the mortuary office," the guard said. "It's just ahead, on your left."

Angelo didn't like the city morgue any better than he'd thought he would. It looked bad and smelled bad. They hadn't been there three minutes and already he couldn't wait to get out.

At the mortuary office he again asked for Vinnie. He explained that it was something about Vinnie's father. The man asked Angelo and Tony to wait there; he'd be right back with Vinnie.

Five minutes later Vinnie came into the mortuary office in his green scrub clothes. He looked upset. "What about my father?" he asked.

Angelo put an arm around Vinnie's shoulder. "Could we speak in private?" he asked. Vinnie let himself be led into the hall.

Vinnie looked him straight in the eye. "My father has been dead for two years," he said. "What's this about?"

"We're friends of Paul Cerino," Angelo said. "We were supposed to remind you that Mr. Cerino helped your father once with the unions. Mr. Cerino would appreciate having his favor returned. There's a doctor here by the name of Laurie Montgomery—"

"She's not here anymore," Vinnie interrupted.

"What do you mean?" Angelo asked.

"She was fired this morning," Vinnie said.

"Then we need her address," Angelo said. "Could you get that for us? And remember, this is just between us. I'm sure I don't have to spell it out for you."

"I understand," Vinnie said. "Hang on, I'll be right back."

Angelo sat back down, but he didn't have to wait for

long. Vinnie came back with Laurie's address and even her phone number as speedily as promised. He explained he got the information from the on-call schedule.

Relieved to be leaving the morgue, Angelo nearly jogged back to his car.

"What's the plan?" Tony asked once Angelo had started the engine.

"No time like the present. Let's go to the broad's apartment now. We're even in the neighborhood."

Fifteen minutes later they had parked on Nineteenth Street and were walking toward Laurie's apartment building.

"How are we going to handle this?" Tony asked.

"We'll try the usual way," Angelo said. "Use our police badges. As soon as we get her in the car, we're golden."

In the foyer of Laurie's building they got her apartment number from her mailbox. The inner door was not much of a barrier to the likes of Angelo. Two minutes later they were in the elevator heading for the fifth floor.

They went directly to Laurie's door and pressed her buzzer. When there was no response, Angelo hit it again.

"She must be out looking for another job," Tony said.

"Looks like quite a set of locks," Angelo said, studying the door.

Tony's eyes left the door and roamed around the tiny hall. His eyes instantly locked onto Debra Engler's. Tony tapped Angelo on the shoulder and whispered, "We got one of the neighbors looking at us."

Angelo turned in time to see Debra's probing eye through her narrowly opened door. As soon as his eye caught hers, she slammed the door shut. Angelo could hear her locks clicking in place.

"Damn!" Angelo whispered.

"What should we do?" Tony asked.

"Let's go back to the car," Angelo said.

A few minutes later they were seated in Angelo's car in full view of the entrance to Laurie's building. Tony yawned. In spite of himself, Angelo did the same.

"I'm exhausted," Tony complained.

"Me too," Angelo said. "I'd expected to sleep all day today."

"Think we should break into the apartment?" Tony asked.

"I'm thinking about it," Angelo admitted. "With all those locks it might take a few minutes. And I don't know what to do about that witch in the other apartment. Did you catch her face? How would you like to wake up with that in bed with you."

"This chick's not bad looking," Tony said, gazing at the picture of Laurie in the paper. "I could go for something like that."

Lou helped himself to another cup of coffee. He was waiting in Manhattan General Hospital's surgical lounge, where he'd surprised Jordan on their last encounter. But that time Lou had had to wait for only twenty minutes. Already he'd been there well over an hour. He was beginning to doubt the wisdom of putting this hoped-for interview with Jordan ahead of returning his superior's calls.

Just when Lou was thinking about leaving, Jordan entered the room. He went directly to a small refrigerator and pulled out a carton of orange juice.

Lou watched Jordan take a long drink. He waited until Jordan came over to the couch to look through the newspaper lying there. Then Lou spoke up.

"Jordan, old boy," Lou said. "Imagine running into you here, of all places."

Jordan frowned when he recognized Lou. "Not you again."

"I'm touched you're so friendly," Lou said. "It must be

all the surgery you've been doing that's got you in such an affable mood. You know what they say, make hay while the sun shines."

"Nice seeing you again, Lieutenant." Jordan finished the juice and tossed the carton into the wastebasket.

"Just a second," Lou said. He got up and blocked Jordan's exit. Lou had the definite impression Jordan was being even less cooperative than he'd been during their previous meeting. He was also more upset. Beneath the brusque façade the man was definitely nervous.

"I have more surgery to perform," Jordan said.

"I'm sure you do," Lou said. "Which makes me feel a little better. I mean, it's nice to know that not all your patients scheduled for surgery meet violent deaths at the hands of professional hit men."

"What are you talking about?" Jordan demanded.

"Oh, Jordan, indignation becomes you. But I'd appreciate it if you'd cut the crap and come clean. You know full well what I'm talking about. Last time I was here I asked you if there was anything these murdered patients of yours had in common. Like maybe they were suffering from the same ailment or something. You were happy to tell me I was wrong. What you failed to tell me was that they were all scheduled to undergo surgery by your capable hands."

"It hadn't occurred to me at the time," Jordan said.

"Sure!" Lou said sarcastically. He was certain Jordan was lying, yet at the same time Lou was not sure of his objectivity in judging Jordan. As Lou had recently admitted to Laurie, he was jealous of Jordan. He was jealous of the man's tall good looks, of his Ivy League education, his silver-spooned past, his money, and his relationship with Laurie.

"It didn't occur to me until I got back to the office," Jordan said. "After I looked at their charts."

"But even once you did realize this connecting factor,

you failed to let me know. We'll let that go for the moment. My question now is: How do you explain it?"

"I can't," Jordan said. "As far as I can tell, it's extraordinary coincidence. Nothing more, nothing less."

"You don't have the slightest idea why these murders were committed?"

"None," Jordan said. "And I certainly hope and pray there are no more. The last thing I want to happen is see my surgical population decreasing in any form or fashion, particularly in such a savage way."

Lou nodded. Knowing what he did about Jordan, he believed this part.

"What about Cerino?" Lou asked after a pause.

"What about him?"

"He's still waiting for another operation," Lou said. "Is there any way this murder streak could be related to Cerino? Do you think that he's at risk?"

"I suppose anything is possible," Jordan said. "But I've been treating Paul Cerino for months and nothing has happened to him. I can't imagine he's involved or specifically at risk."

"If you have any ideas, get back to me," Lou said.

"Absolutely, Lieutenant," Jordan said.

Lou stepped out of the way and Jordan pushed through the swinging doors and disappeared from view.

Laurie decided that even if nothing panned out, if she failed to turn up any useful information, at least she was keeping busy. And keeping busy meant she couldn't dwell on her situation: she was unemployed in a city that was hardly cheap to live in and she might even be out of forensics. She could hardly expect a recommendation from Bingham. But she wouldn't think about that just then. Instead she decided to follow through and get more information for her series. There were three more overdoses to be investigated. How were the bodies discovered and were the deceased seen going into their apartments that fateful evening in the company of two men?

Inside an hour, Laurie hit pay dirt at Kendall Fletcher's apartment building, and it all sounded familiar. Fletcher had gone out to jog but had returned very soon after—with two men. The doorman never saw the two men leave the apartment. Several hours after Fletcher had returned, an unnamed tenant called to complain about noise in 25G. The tenant feared that someone inside 25G might be hurt. The superintendent responded to the call; that's when Fletcher's body was discovered.

Laurie had less luck at Stephanie Haberlin's. The woman lived in a converted brownstone with no doorman. Laurie decided to leave that case for the time being and head on to the third and final location.

Yvonne Andre lived in a building similar to Kendall Fletcher's. Laurie made use of her medical examiner's badge just as she had at Fletcher's. The doorman, who introduced himself as Timothy, was more than happy to help. Just as with Kendall Fletcher, Ms. Andre had entered her building along with two men. Timothy couldn't describe the men, but he distinctly remembered their coming.

When Laurie asked who'd found the body, Timothy replied that Jose, the super, had. Laurie asked if she could speak with him. Timothy said of course. He called out to a lean man in a tan uniform who was at that moment repairing a piece of furniture in the foyer. Jose immediately joined them and introductions were made.

"So how was it that you found the body?" Laurie asked.

"The night doorman called me asking me to check the Andre apartment."

"Let me guess," Laurie said. "The night doorman had been called by a tenant complaining that strange noises were coming from the Andre apartment."

Jose and Timothy gazed at Laurie with surprise and respect.

"Ah," Jose said with a smile. "You've been talking with
the police."

"Where in the apartment did you find the body?" Laurie
asked.

"In the living room," Jose said.

"What did the apartment look like?" Laurie asked.
"Was anything broken? Did it look as if there'd been a
struggle?"

"I didn't really look around," Jose said. "Not after I
spotted Ms. Andre. The police were here, of course, but no
one has touched anything. You want to see it?"

"I'd love to," Laurie answered.

They went directly to Yvonne's apartment on the fourth
floor. Jose opened the door with his passkey and stepped
aside.

Laurie went in first. She hadn't taken more than five steps
in the door when she nearly collided with an elegantly
dressed, middle-aged woman who had responded to the
sound of the key in the lock. The woman was quite stunning
although she looked as if she'd been crying. She clutched a
tissue in her hand.

"Excuse me," Laurie said with embarrassment. She was
appalled that the apartment was occupied.

The woman started to say something when she recognized Jose.

"I'm sorry, Mrs. Andre," Jose said. "I didn't know anyone was here. This is Dr. Montgomery from the medical
examiner's office."

"Who is it, dear?" A tall, gray-haired man appeared in
the doorway to the kitchen.

"It's the superintendent," Mrs. Andre managed. "And
this is Dr. Montgomery from the medical examiner's office."

"From the medical examiner's office here in Manhattan?" Mr. Andre questioned.

"That's right," Laurie said. "I'm terribly sorry for this intrusion. Jose suggested I come up here. I had no idea you'd be here."

"Nor did I," Jose added quickly.

"It's all right," Mrs. Andre said. She raised the tissue to dab at the corners of her eyes as she wistfully looked around the living room. "We were just going through some of Yvonne's things."

"If you'll excuse me," Mr. Andre said. He abruptly turned and disappeared back toward the kitchen.

"I can return at a later time," Laurie said, taking a step back toward the door. "I'm terribly sorry about your loss."

"Oh, don't go," Mrs. Andre said, holding out a hand toward Laurie. "Please. Come in. Sit down. It's better for me to talk about it."

Laurie glanced at Jose. She wasn't sure what she should do.

"I'll leave you people," Jose said. "If you need anything, please call."

Laurie wanted to leave. The last thing she should be doing was consoling the loved ones of the deceased. Look where it had gotten her when she'd tried to comfort Sara Wetherbee, Duncan Andrews' girlfriend. But Laurie didn't feel she could simply walk out on the obviously bereaved mother now that she'd burst in on her. With some misgivings Laurie allowed herself to be guided toward the sitting area. Mrs. Andre sat on a love seat. Laurie took a side chair.

"You can't imagine what a shock this has been to us," Mrs. Andre said. "Yvonne was such a good, generous daughter, selfless to a fault. She was always devoting herself to one charitable cause or another."

Laurie nodded sympathetically.

"Greenpeace, Amnesty International, NARAL. You

name a good liberal cause, chances were she was active in it."

Laurie knew she didn't need to say much. It was enough just to listen.

"She had two new ones," Mrs. Andre said with an aggrieved laugh. "At least they were new to us: animal rights and organ donation. It's such an irony that she died of a heart attack. I think she'd really hoped some of her organs would be used to a good purpose someday. Oh, not anytime soon, mind you, but she very much did not want to be buried. She was quite adamant about it; she thought it was a terrible waste of resources and space."

"I wish more people felt as your daughter did," Laurie said. "If they did, doctors could really begin to save more lives." She wanted to be very careful not to contradict the poor woman's notion that her daughter had died of a heart attack, not because of cocaine.

"Maybe you'd like to have some of Yvonne's books," Mrs. Andre said. "I don't know what we are going to do with them all." Clearly the woman was desperate to talk to someone.

Before Laurie could respond to her generous offer, Mr. Andre stormed back into the room. His face was flushed.

"What's the matter, Walter?" Mrs. Andre asked. Her husband was clearly upset.

"Dr. Montgomery!" Mr. Andre sputtered, ignoring his wife. "I happen to be on the Board of Trustees of Manhattan General Hospital. I also happen to know Dr. Harold Bingham personally. Having spoken with him earlier about my daughter, I was rather surprised when you showed up. So I called him back. He is on the phone now and would like a word with you."

Laurie swallowed with some difficulty. She got up and walked past Mr. Andre into the kitchen. Hesitantly, she picked up the phone.

"Montgomery!" Bingham thundered after Laurie answered. She had to move the receiver a few inches from her ear. "What in God's name are you doing at Yvonne Andre's apartment? You've been fired! Do you hear me? I'll have you arrested for impersonating a city official if you keep this up! Do you understand me?"

Laurie was about to reply when she caught sight of a business card tacked to a bulletin board on the wall behind the phone. It was a business card for a Mr. Jerome Hoskins at the Manhattan Organ Repository.

"Montgomery!" Bingham shouted again. "Answer me. What the hell do you think you're up to?"

Laurie hung up without saying a word to Bingham. With trembling hand, she took the card off the board. Suddenly the pieces fit together, and what a terrible, hideous picture they formed. Laurie almost couldn't believe it, yet from the moment everything clicked, she knew the awful, inexorable truth could not be refuted. The thing to do, of course, was to call Lou. But before she did that, there was one other place she wanted to visit.

15

□

Lou Soldano was back in the surgical lounge at Manhattan General for the second time that day. But on this visit he wouldn't have long to wait. This time he'd called the operating room supervisor and asked when Dr. Scheffield would be through with his surgery. Lou had timed his arrival so that he'd catch Jordan just as he was coming out.

After waiting for less than five minutes, Lou was pleased to see the good doctor as he strode confidently through the lounge and into the locker room. Lou followed, hat in hand and trench coat over his arm. He kept his distance until Jordan had tossed his soiled scrub shirt and pants into the laundry bin. It had been Lou's plan to catch the man in his skivvies, when he was psychologically vulnerable. It was Lou's belief that interrogation worked better when the subject was off balance.

369

"Hey, Doc," he called softly. Jordan spun around. The man was obviously tense.

"Excuse me," Lou said, scratching his head. "I hate to be a bother, but I thought of something else."

"Who the hell do you think you are?" Jordan snapped. "Colombo?"

"Very good," Lou said. "I didn't think you'd get it. But now that I have your attention, there is something I wanted to ask you."

"Make it fast, Lieutenant," Jordan said. "I've been stuck over here all day and I got an office full of unhappy patients." He went to the sink and turned on the water.

"When I was here earlier, I mentioned that the patients who'd been killed were all waiting for surgery. But I failed to ask what kind of operations they were scheduled to have. I mean, I was told they were going to be corneal operations of some sort. Doc, fill me in. Just what was it you were going to do for these people?"

Jordan stood up from having been bent over the sink. Water dripped from his face. He nudged Lou to the side to get at the towels. He took one and vigorously dried his skin, making it glow.

"They were going to have corneal transplants," Jordan said finally, eyeing himself in the mirror.

"That's interesting," Lou said. "They all had different diagnoses but they were all going to get the same treatment."

"That's right, Lieutenant," Jordan said. He walked away from the sink to his locker. He spun the wheel on the combination lock.

Lou followed him like a dog. "I would have thought different diagnoses required different treatments."

"It's true these people all had different diagnoses," Jordan explained. He began dressing. "But the physiological infirmity was the same. Their corneas weren't clear."

"But isn't that treating the symptom and not the disease?" Lou asked.

Jordan stopped buttoning his shirt to stare at Lou. "I think I have underestimated you," he said. "You are actually quite right. But often where the eye is concerned, we do precisely that. Of course, before you perform a transplant you have to treat the cause of the opacity. You do that so you can be reasonably sure the problem will not recur in the transplanted tissue, and with the proper treatment, it generally doesn't."

"Gee," Lou said, "maybe I could have been a doctor if I'd had the chance to go to an Ivy League school like you."

Jordan went back to his buttoning of his shirt. "That comment was much more in character," he said.

"One way or the other," Lou said, "isn't it surprising that all your murdered patients were scheduled for the same operation?"

"Not at all," Jordan said as he continued to dress. "I'm a superspecialist. Cornea is my area of expertise. I've just done four today."

"Most of your operations are corneal transplants?" Lou asked.

"Maybe ninety percent. Even more, lately."

"What about Cerino?" Lou asked.

"Same thing," Jordan said. "But with Cerino I'll be doing two procedures, since both eyes were affected equally."

"Oh," Lou said. Once again he was running out of questions.

"Don't get me wrong, Lieutenant. I'm still shocked and distressed to know that these patients of mine were murdered. But knowing that these patients were killed, I'm not at all surprised to know they were all slated for corneal transplants. As my patients, almost by definition that would have to be expected. Now, is there anything else, Lieutenant?" He pulled on his jacket.

"Was there anything about the corneal transplants these people were waiting for that set them apart from other recipients?"

"Nope," Jordan said.

"What about Marsha Schulman? Could she have been associated with these patients' deaths?"

"She wasn't waiting for an operation."

"But she'd met the people," Lou said.

"She was my main secretary. She met practically everyone who came into the office."

Lou nodded.

"Now if you'll excuse me, Lieutenant, I really must go to the recovery room to check on my last case. Good seeing you again." With that, he was gone.

Discouraged again, Lou returned to his car. He'd been so sure that he'd hit on the crucial fact when Patrick O'Brian had come into his office to tell him that the dead patients were all to have the same operation. Now Lou thought it was just another dead end.

Lou pulled out into the street and instantly got bogged down in traffic. Rush hour was always murder in New York, and on rainy days it was even worse. When Lou glanced over at the sidewalk, he realized the pedestrians were moving faster than he was.

With time to think, Lou tried to review the facts of the case. He had a hard time getting past Dr. Jordan Scheffield's personality. God, how he hated the guy. And it wasn't just because of Laurie, although there was that. The guy was so smug and condescending. He was surprised Laurie didn't see it.

Suddenly the car behind Lou's rammed into his. His head snapped back, then forward. In a fit of anger, Lou jammed on the emergency brake and leaped out. The guy behind him had gotten out, too. Lou was chagrined to see that the man was at least two hundred and fifty pounds of solid muscle.

"Watch where you're going," Lou said, shaking his finger. He walked around to check the back of his Caprice. There was a bit of paint from the guy's car on his bumper. He could have played tough cop but he chose not to. He rarely did; it took too much effort.

"Sorry, man," the other driver said.

"No harm done," Lou said. He got back into the car. Inching forward in the traffic, he turned his head to the left and right. He hoped he wouldn't suffer any whiplash.

Suddenly the glimmer of an idea started to take shape in Lou's head. Getting hit had worked some sense into him. How could he not have seen? For a moment he stared into space, mesmerized by the solution that had crystallized so suddenly in his brain. He was so deep in thought, the big guy behind him had to beep to get him to move ahead.

"Holy crap," Lou said aloud. He wondered why it had not occurred to him before. As hideously outlandish as it was, all the facts seemed to fit.

Snapping up his cellular phone, he tried Laurie at the medical examiner's office. The operator told him she'd been terminated.

"What?" Lou demanded.

"She's been fired," the operator said and hung up.

Lou quickly dialed Laurie's home number. He kicked himself for not having tried to call her earlier to find out what had happened when she saw her chief. Obviously the meeting had not gone well.

Lou was disappointed to get Laurie's answering machine. He left a message for her to call him ASAP at the office and if not there, at home.

Lou hung up the phone. He felt badly for Laurie. Losing her job had to have been an enormous blow for her. She was one of those rare people who liked her job as much as Lou liked his.

"There she is!" Tony cried. He gave Angelo a shove to wake him up.

Angelo shook his head, then squinted through the windshield. It had gotten dark during the short time he'd been asleep. His mind felt fuzzy. But he could see the woman Tony was pointing at. She was only ten feet from her building and heading for the door.

"Let's go," Angelo said. He piled out of the car, then almost fell on his face. His left leg had gone to sleep in the weird position he'd assumed when he'd closed his eyes.

Tony was significantly ahead as Angelo tried to run on a leg that felt more like wood than bones and muscle. By the time he got to the door, the leg was feeling like pins and needles from the crotch down. He pulled open the door to see Tony already conversing with the woman.

"We want to talk with you down at the station," Tony was saying, trying to imitate Angelo.

Angelo could see that he was holding his badge too high so that Laurie Montgomery could read what it said if she so chose.

Angelo pulled Tony's arm down and smiled. He noticed that Laurie was as good-looking a woman as Tony had guessed from the photo.

"We'd like to talk to you just for a few moments," Angelo said. "Purely routine. We'll have you back here in less than an hour. It has to do with the medical examiner's office."

"I don't have to go anyplace with you."

"I don't think you want to create a scene," Angelo said.

"I don't even have to talk with you."

Angelo could tell Laurie was not going to be an easy broad. "I'm afraid we have to insist," he said calmly.

"I don't even recognize you men. What precinct are you from?"

Angelo cast a quick glance over his shoulder. No one was coming into the building. This pickup was going to take force. Angelo glanced at Tony and gave a tiny nod.

Getting the message, Tony reached into his jacket and pulled out his Beretta Bantam. He pointed it at Laurie.

Angelo winced as Laurie let out an ear-piercing scream that could have awakened the dead as far away as Saint John's Cemetery in Rego Park.

With his free hand, Tony reached out and grabbed Laurie by the neck, intending to force her to the car. Instead, he got a briefcase in the groin. He doubled over in pain. As soon as he straightened back up, Tony pointed his gun at the woman's chest and fired two quick shots. Laurie went down instantly.

The shots were deafening; Tony hadn't put his silencer on, not thinking he'd have to resort to force. The smell of cordite hung in the air.

"What the hell did you shoot her for?" Angelo demanded. "We were supposed to bring her in alive."

"I lost my head," Tony said. "She hit me in the nuts with her goddamn briefcase."

"Let's get her the hell out of here," Angelo ordered.

Together they each grabbed one of Laurie's arms. Angelo bent down and grabbed her briefcase. Then the two men half-dragged, half-carried Laurie's lifeless body to their car. Dead or alive, they could still get her to the *Montego Bay*.

As quickly as possible they shoved her into the backseat of the car. A few pedestrians eyed them suspiciously, but no one said anything. Tony climbed in beside her while Angelo jumped into the front seat and started the car. As soon as the engine responded, he pulled out into Nineteenth Street.

"She better not be bleeding on that upholstery," Angelo

said, glancing in the rearview mirror. He could see Tony struggling with the body. "What the hell are you doing?"

"Trying to get her purse out from under her," Tony said. He grunted. "It's like she's got a death grip on it, as if it matters at this point."

"She dead?" Angelo asked. He was still furious.

"She hasn't moved," Tony said. "Ah, got it!" He held up the purse as if it were a trophy.

"If Cerino asks me what happened," Angelo snapped, "I'm going to have to tell him."

"I'm sorry," Tony said. "I told you. I lost my head. Hey, look at this! This broad is loaded." He waved a handful of twenties that he pulled from a wallet.

"Just keep her out of view," said Angelo.

"Oh, no!" Tony cried.

"What's the matter now?" Angelo demanded.

"This chick isn't Laurie Montgomery," Tony said, looking up from a piece of identification. "It's a Maureen Wharton, an Assistant D.A. But she looks just like that photo." Tony leaned forward and picked up the newspaper with Laurie's photo. Brushing Maureen's hair to the side, he compared her face to the one in the photo. "Well, it's pretty close," he said.

Angelo gripped the steering wheel so hard that the blood drained from his hand. He was going to have to tell Cerino about Tony whether he asked or not. Because of Tony they had whacked the wrong woman, an Assistant D.A., no less. This kid was driving him berserk.

"It's me—Ponti," Franco said. He'd put a call through to Vinnie Dominick. "I'm in the car heading for the tunnel. I just wanted you to know that I just watched the two guys we've discussed hit another young woman in broad daylight. It's crazy. It makes no sense."

"I'm glad you called," Vinnie said. "I've been trying to

get ahold of you. That snitch you set me up with, that friend of a friend of Tony Ruggerio's girlfriend, just clued me in. He knows what they're doing. It's unbelievable. You'd never have figured it out."

"Want me to come back?" Franco asked.

"No, stay on those two," Vinnie said. "I'm heading out now to talk directly with some Lucia people. We'll figure out what to do. We got to stop Cerino but in a way to take advantage of the situation. *Capisce?*"

Franco hung up the phone. Angelo's car was about five carlengths ahead. Now that Vinnie knew what was going on, Franco was dying to know as well.

Cupping her hands around her face, Laurie pressed them against the locked glass doors of the converted brownstone on East Fifty-fifth Street. She could make out a set of marble steps that rose up to another closed door.

Laurie stepped back to view the front of the building. It was five stories tall with a bow front. The second floor had tall windows from which light poured. The third floor had lights as well. Above that the windows were dark.

To the right of the door was a brass plate that said MANHATTAN ORGAN REPOSITORY: HOURS NINE TO FIVE. Since it was after five, Laurie understood why the front doors were locked. But the lights on the second and third floors suggested that the building was still occupied, and Laurie was determined to talk with someone.

Going back to the door, Laurie knocked again just as loudly as she had when she'd first arrived. Still no one responded.

Looking to the left, Laurie noticed a service entrance. Walking over to this door, she tried to peer inside but saw nothing. It was totally black. Returning to the main door, Laurie was about to knock again when she noticed something she'd not seen. Below the brass plate and partially hidden from view by the ivy that snaked up the building's façade was a small brass bell. Laurie pushed it and waited.

A few minutes later the foyer beyond the glass doors illuminated. Then the inner door opened and a woman in a long, tight, unadorned wool dress came down the few marble steps. She had to walk sideways because of the snugness of the dress about her legs. She appeared to be in her mid-fifties. Her humorless face was stern and her hair was pulled back in a tight bun.

Coming to the door, she pantomimed that they were closed. To emphasize her point, she repeatedly pointed at her watch.

Laurie mimed in return, indicating that she wanted to talk with someone by making her hand move as if she were operating a hand puppet. When that didn't work, Laurie took out her medical examiner's badge and flashed it despite Bingham's dire warnings that he'd have her arrested. When that didn't work its usual wonders, Laurie took out the business card she'd taken from Yvonne Andre's apartment and pressed it against the glass. Finally the woman relented and unlatched the door.

"I'm sorry, but we're closed for the day," the woman said.

"I gathered that," Laurie said, putting a hand on the door, "but I must speak with you. I only need a few minutes of your time. I'm with the medical examiner's office. My name is Dr. Laurie Montgomery."

"What is it you wish to discuss?" the woman asked.

"Can I come in?" Laurie suggested.

"I suppose," the woman said with a sigh. She opened the door wide and let Laurie in. Then she locked the door behind them.

"This is quite lovely," Laurie said. Most of the building's nineteenth-century detailing had been preserved when it had been converted from a private residence to office space.

"We're lucky to have the building," the woman said. "By the way, my name is Gertrude Robeson."

They shook hands.

"Would you care to come up to my office?"

Laurie said that she would, and Gertrude led her up an elegant Georgian staircase that curved up to the floor above.

"I appreciate your time," Laurie said. "It is rather important."

"I'm the only one here," Gertrude said. "Trying to finish up some work."

Gertrude's office was in the front, and it accounted for the light streaming out of the windows from the second floor. It was a large office with a crystal chandelier. Vaguely Laurie wondered how it was that so many nonprofit organizations had such sumptuous surroundings.

Once they were seated, Laurie got to the point. She again took out the business card she'd picked up at Yvonne's and passed it to Gertrude. "Is this individual a member of the staff here?" Laurie questioned.

"Yes, he is," Gertrude said. She gave the card back. "Jerome Hoskins is in charge of our recruiting efforts."

"What exactly is the Manhattan Organ Repository?" Laurie asked.

"I'd be happy to give you our literature," Gertrude said, "but essentially we're a nonprofit organization devoted to the donation and reallocation of human organs for transplantation."

"What do you mean by your 'recruiting efforts'?" Laurie asked.

"We try to get people to register as potential donors," Gertrude said. "The simplest commitment is just to agree that in the event of an accident that renders one brain dead, one would be willing to have the appropriate organs given to a needy recipient."

"If that's the simplest commitment," Laurie said, "what's a more complicated one?"

"Complicated is not the right word," Gertrude said. "It is all simple. But the next step is to get the potential donor to be blood and tissue typed. That is particularly helpful in replenishable organs like bone marrow."

"How does your organization do its recruiting?" Laurie asked.

"The usual methods," Gertrude said. "We have charitable fund-raisers, telethons, active college groups, that sort of thing. It's really a matter of getting the word out. That's why it's so helpful when a recipient can command media attention, like a child needing a heart or liver."

"Do you have a large staff?" Laurie questioned.

"It's rather small, actually," Gertrude said. "We use a lot of volunteers."

"Who responds to your appeals?" Laurie asked.

"Mostly college-educated people," Gertrude said, "particularly those who are civic-minded. People who are interested in social issues and are willing to give something back to society."

"Have you ever heard the name Yvonne Andre?" Laurie asked.

"No, I don't believe so," Gertrude said. "Is this someone I should meet?"

"I don't think so," Laurie said. "She's dead."

"Oh, dear," Gertrude said. "Why did you ask if I knew her?"

"Just curious," Laurie said. "Could you tell me if Yvonne Andre was someone Mr. Hoskins recruited?"

"I'm sorry," Gertrude said. "That's confidential information. I cannot give it out."

"I am a medical examiner," Laurie said. "My interest in this is not casual. I was speaking with Yvonne Andre's mother today, and she told me her daughter was committed to your cause before her untimely death. Mr. Hoskins' card was in her apartment. I don't want to know any details, but I would appreciate knowing if she'd signed up with your organization."

"Did Ms. Yvonne Andre's death occur under questionable circumstances?" Gertrude asked.

"It will be signed out as accidental," Laurie said. "But there are some aspects to her death that bother me."

"You know, generally speaking, that for organs to be transplanted the donor must be in a vegetative state. In other words, everything but the brain must still be physiologically alive."

"Of course," Laurie said. "I'm well aware of that caveat. Yvonne Andre was not in a vegetative state before her death. Nevertheless, her status in your organization is something I need to know."

"Just a moment," Gertrude said. She walked over to her desk and punched some information into her computer terminal. "Yes," she said. "Yvonne was registered. But that is all I can say."

"I appreciate what you have told me," Laurie said. "I have one more question. Have there been any break-ins here at your offices in the last year?"

Gertrude rolled her eyes. "I really don't know if I'm at liberty to divulge this kind of information, but I guess it's a matter of public record. You could always check with the police. Yes, we were broken into a couple of months ago. Luckily not too much was taken and there was no vandalism."

Laurie rose from her chair. "Thank you very much. You've been generous with your time. I really appreciate it."

"Would you like to take some of our literature?" Gertrude asked.

"I would," Laurie said. Gertrude opened a cabinet and

pulled out a number of brochures which she handed to Laurie. Laurie put them in her briefcase. Then Gertrude saw her to the door.

Emerging onto Fifty-fifth Street, Laurie walked over to Lexington Avenue to catch a cab downtown. She directed the taxi driver to take her to the medical examiner's office. With her suspicions strengthening and her confidence renewed, she wanted to talk with George Fontworth. There was something about that day's overdose cases that she wanted to ask about. Even though it was after six o'clock, she thought that he might still be at work. He usually worked late.

But as Laurie approached the office, she began to worry about Bingham still being there. She knew that on a number of evenings he also stayed late. Consequently Laurie instructed the cab driver to turn from First Avenue onto Thirtieth Street. When they came abreast of the morgue loading dock, she had him turn in. It was good that she had. There was Bingham's official city car, one of the perks of being the chief medical examiner.

"I've changed my mind," Laurie called to the driver through the Plexiglas screen. She gave him her home address. With some cursing in a language Laurie had never heard, he pulled out of the morgue driveway and returned to First Avenue. Fifteen minutes later she was in front of her tenement building.

It was still raining, so Laurie bolted for the door. She was surprised to find that the lock to the inner door was broken. She'd have to call the super about it in case no one else had reported it yet.

Laurie headed straight for the elevator. She didn't bother collecting her mail. Just then she had one thing in mind: calling Lou.

As the elevator doors began to slide shut, Laurie saw a hand come around its edge to try to stop the doors from closing. Laurie tried to hit the open button but hit the close instead. The hand pulled back, the doors closed, and the elevator ascended.

Laurie was just unlocking her locks when she heard Debra Engler's door open behind her.

"There were two men at your door," Debra said. "I've never seen them before. They rang your bell twice."

Although Laurie didn't like having Debra meddle in her affairs, she wondered who the two men were and what they could have wanted. It was difficult not to think of "two men" in anything but the context relating to the overdose cases, and the thought sent a chill down her spine. She wondered how they'd gotten as far as her door, since she hadn't been there to buzz them in. Then she remembered the broken lock in the second door. She asked Debra what they looked like.

"Didn't get a good look at their faces," Debra said. "But they seemed no good to me. And as I said, they rang your bell twice."

Laurie turned back to her door and unlocked the last lock. It occurred to her that if the two men had malicious intentions, they could have gone up the service stairs and broken in through her rear door in the kitchen.

Laurie pushed open her door. It creaked on its hinges, which had been coated with a hundred layers of paint. From her vantage point in the hall, her apartment appeared as she had left it. She didn't hear anything abnormal or see anything suspicious. Cautiously she stepped over the threshold, ready to flee at the slightest unexpected sound.

Out of the corner of her eye, Laurie saw something coming at her. Letting out a small involuntary cry that was more of a gasp than a scream, Laurie let go of her briefcase and raised her arms to defend herself. At the moment the briefcase hit the floor, the cat was on her, but only for a second. In the next instant it had leaped to the foyer table, and with its ears held flat against its skull, it scampered into the living room.

For a second Laurie stood in her doorway, clutching her chest. Her heart was beating as fast as it did after several games of racquetball. Only after she'd caught her breath did she turn back to her door, close it, and secure the multitude of locks.

Picking up her briefcase, Laurie went into the living room. The manic cat rushed from his hiding place and leaped to the top of the bookcase and from there to the top of the valance over the windows. From that vantage point it glared down at Laurie with playful anger.

Laurie went directly to her phone. Her answering machine light was blinking, but she didn't listen to her messages. Instead she dialed Lou's work number. Unfortunately, he didn't pick up. Laurie hung up and started to dial his home number. But before she could finish dialing, her doorbell rang. Startled, she hung up.

At first she was afraid to go to the door, even to look out the peephole. The doorbell sounded a second time. She knew she had to act. She would see who it was, she told herself. She didn't have to open up.

Laurie tiptoed to the door and peered out into the hall. Two men she didn't recognize were standing there, their faces distorted by the wide-angle lens into exaggerated corpulence.

"Who is it?" Laurie asked.

"Police," a voice called.

A feeling of relief spread over her as she began to unlock her locks. Could Bingham have made good on his threat to have her picked up? But he hadn't said he'd do it, he'd only said he might.

After undoing the chain lock, Laurie paused. She again put her eye to the peephole. "Do you have identification?" she asked. She knew enough not to let anyone in on their word alone as to who they were.

The two men quickly flashed police badges in front of the peephole. "We only want to talk with you for a moment," the same voice explained.

Laurie backed away from the door. Although she'd initially been relieved to learn that her visitors were police, now she was beginning to wonder. What if they were here to arrest her? That would mean they'd have to take her to the police station to be booked. She'd be questioned, held, maybe arraigned. Who knew how long that would take? She had to talk to Lou about much more important matters. Besides, he'd undoubtedly be able to help her if she were to be arrested.

"Just a moment," Laurie called to them. "I have to put on some clothes."

Laurie headed straight for her kitchen and the back door.

Tony exchanged looks with Angelo. "Should we tell her not to bother dressing?" he asked.

"Shut up!" Angelo whispered.

The click of old hardware sounded behind them. Tony turned around to see Debra Engler's door opening a crack. Tony lunged toward the door and clapped his hands loudly to give Debra a scare. The tactic worked. Debra's door slammed shut. About a dozen locks were audibly being secured.

"For Chrissake!" Angelo whispered. "What's the matter with you? This is no time for screwing around."

"I don't like that witch looking at us."

"Get over here!" Angelo ordered. He looked away from Tony, shaking his head. That's when he caught a fleeting glimpse of a woman's silhouette dashing by the wire-embedded, smoked glass of a door to the fire stairs.

It took Angelo a second to appreciate what was happening. "Come on," he said as soon as it hit him. "She's going down the back stairs!"

Angelo ran over to the stairwell door and yanked it open.

Tony sprinted through. They both halted momentarily at the banister and peered down a dirty stairwell that dropped in a series of short flights to the ground floor five stories below. They could see Laurie several floors lower and hear the echo of her heels on the bare concrete treads.

"Get her before she reaches the street," Angelo snarled.

Tony took off like a rabbit, taking the stairs four at a time. He gained steadily on Laurie, but wasn't able to catch her before she went through a door on the ground floor leading to the backyard.

Tony reached the door before it had a chance to swing shut. He pushed through to the outside and found himself in a rubble-strewn backyard overgrown with weeds. He could hear Laurie's running footsteps echo as she sprinted down a narrow passageway leading to the street. Leaping over a short handrail, Tony ran after her. Laurie was only twenty feet away. He'd have her in a moment.

Laurie had known that she'd not slipped out unnoticed and that the police were behind her. She'd heard them coming down the stairwell. As she fled, she'd questioned the advisability of having done so. But, having started, she couldn't stop. Now that she'd run, she was even more deter-mined not to be caught. She knew that resisting arrest was a crime in and of itself. On top of that, the thought of whether they were bona fide police crossed her mind.

As she mounted the final steps to the street, Laurie knew that one of her pursuers was almost on her. At the lip of the steps, pushed against the wall of the building, was a collec-tion of old, dented, metal garbage cans. In a fit of despera-tion Laurie grabbed the top edge of one and pulled it behind her, sending it clattering down the steps to the floor of the pass-through to the backyard.

Seeing her pursuer stumble on the can and fall, Laurie quickly rolled the rest of the cans to the lip of the stairs and sent them crashing down. A few pedestrians passing on the street slowed their pace at this spectacle, but none stopped and no one said anything.

Hoping that her pursuer was momentarily occupied, Laurie ran down to First Avenue. She praised her luck as the first cab she saw came over to her and stopped. Completely out of breath, Laurie jumped in and yelled that she wanted to go to Thirtieth Street.

As the taxi accelerated into the traffic, Laurie was afraid to look back. She was also trembling, wondering what she had done now. As she thought about the consequences of resisting arrest, she changed her mind about her destination. She leaned forward and told the driver that she wanted to go to police headquarters instead of Thirtieth Street.

The driver didn't say anything as he turned left to head over to Second Avenue. Laurie sat back and tried to relax. Her chest was still heaving.

As they worked their way south on Second Avenue, Laurie had a change of heart again. Worrying that Lou might not be at police headquarters, Laurie decided her first destination was better. Scooting forward again, she told the driver. This time he cursed but turned left to go back to First Avenue.

As she'd done with the previous cab, Laurie had this driver turn on Thirtieth and pull into the morgue loading area. She was relieved to see that Bingham's car had left. After paying the fare, she ran into the morgue.

Tony paid the driver and got out of the cab. Angelo's car was where they'd left it, with Angelo behind the wheel. Tony climbed in.

"Well?" Angelo asked.

"I missed her," Tony said.

"That much is clear," Angelo said. "Where is she?"

"She tried to lose me," Tony said. "She had her driver

make a loop. But I stayed with her. She went back to the medical examiner's office."

Angelo leaned forward and started his car. "Cerino doesn't know how right he was when he said that this girl could be trouble. We'll have to nab her from the medical examiner's office."

"Maybe it will be easier there," Tony suggested. "Shouldn't be many people there at this hour."

"It better go more smoothly than it did here," Angelo said as he looked back before pulling out into the street.

They rode up First Avenue in silence. Angelo had to hand one thing to Tony: at least he was fast on his feet.

Angelo turned onto Thirtieth Street and killed the engine. He wasn't happy to be back at the medical examiner's office again. But what choice did they have? There could be no more screw-ups.

"What's the plan?" Tony asked eagerly.

"I'm thinking," Angelo said. "Obviously she wasn't so impressed with our police badges."

Laurie felt relatively safe in the dark, deserted medical examiner's building. She got into her office and locked the door behind her. The first thing she did was dial Lou's home number. She was pleased when he picked up on the first ring.

"Am I glad to hear from you," Lou said the moment Laurie identified herself.

"Not as glad as I am to get you."

"Where are you?" Lou asked. "I've been calling your apartment every five minutes. If I hear your answering machine message one more time, I'll scream."

"I'm at my office," Laurie said. "There's been some trouble."

"I heard," Lou said. "I'm sorry about your being fired. Is it final or will you get a hearing?"

"It's final at the moment. But that's not why I called. Two men came to my apartment door a few minutes ago. They were policemen. I got scared and ran. I think I'm in big trouble."

"Uniformed policemen?" Lou asked.

"No," Laurie said. "They were in street clothes. Suits."

"That's strange," Lou said. "I can't imagine any of my boys going to your apartment. What were their names?"

"I haven't the slightest idea," Laurie said.

"Don't tell me you didn't ask them their names," Lou said. "That's ridiculous. You should have gotten their names and badge numbers and called the police to check on them. I mean, how do you know they were really police?"

"I didn't think of getting their names," Laurie said. "I asked to see their badges."

"Come on, Laurie," Lou complained. "You've lived in New York too long to act like that. You should know better."

"All right!" Laurie snapped. She was still overwrought. The last thing she needed from Lou was a lecture. "What should I do now?"

"Nothing," Lou said. "I'll check into it. Meanwhile, if anybody else shows up, get their names and badge numbers. Do you think you can remember that?"

Laurie wondered if Lou was deliberately trying to provoke her. She tried to remain calm. This was no time to let him get to her. "Let's change the subject," she said. "There's something even more important we have to talk about. I think I've come up with an explanation about my cocaine overdose/toxicity cases, and it involves someone you know. I finally even have some evidence that I think you'll find convincing. Maybe you should come over here now. I want to show you some preliminary DNA matches. Obviously I can't meet you here in the daytime."

"What a coincidence," Lou said. "Sounds like we've

both made some progress. I think I've solved my gangland murder cases. I wanted to run it by you."

"How did you manage to solve them?"

"I went by to see your boyfriend, Jordan," Lou said. "In fact I saw him a couple of times today. I think he's getting tired of me."

"Lou, are you deliberately trying to irritate me?" Laurie questioned. "If so, you are doing a wonderful job. For the tenth time, Jordan is not my boyfriend!"

"Put it this way," Lou said. "I'm trying to get your attention. You see, the more time I spend with that guy, the more I think he's a creep and a sleazeball, and this is going beyond that jealousy crap I admitted to in a moment of weakness. I can't imagine what you see in him."

"I didn't call you to get a lecture," Laurie said wearily.

"I can't help it," Lou said. "You need some advice from someone who cares. I don't think you should see that guy anymore."

"OK, Dad, I'll keep it in mind." With that, she hung up the phone. She was tired of Lou's condescending paternalism, and for the moment she couldn't talk with him. She had to give herself some time to calm down. The man could be so infuriating, especially when she needed support, not criticism.

Laurie's phone started ringing almost as soon as she'd hung up, but she ignored it. She'd let Lou stew for a little while. She unlocked her office door and walked down the silent hallway and took the elevator to the morgue. At that hour the morgue was desolate, with most of the skeleton evening staff on dinner break. Bruce Pomowski, however, was in the mortuary office. She hoped he hadn't heard about her being fired.

"Excuse me!" Laurie called from the doorway.

Bruce looked up from his newspaper.

"Is the Fletcher body still here?" she asked.

Bruce consulted the log book. "Nope," he said. "Went out this afternoon."

"How about Andre or Haberlin?" Laurie asked.

Bruce referred to the book again. "Andre went out this afternoon, but Haberlin is still here. The body is going out to Long Island someplace any minute. It's in the walk-in."

"Thanks," Laurie said. She turned to leave. Obviously Bruce hadn't heard she'd been taken off the payroll.

"Dr. Montgomery," Bruce called. "Peter Letterman was looking for you earlier and I'm supposed to tell you to be sure to go up and see him if I run into you. He said it was important and that he was going to be around for a while tonight."

Laurie felt torn. She wanted to view the Haberlin body, thinking that a brief examination could very well substantiate her suspicions. At the same time she didn't want to miss Peter if he had something to tell her.

"Listen," Laurie said to Bruce. "I'm going to run up and see if Peter is still here. Don't let that Haberlin body go until I see it."

"You got it," Bruce said with a wave.

Laurie went to the fourth floor and the toxicology lab. When she saw a light coming from Peter's door, she breathed a sigh of relief: Peter was still there.

"Knock, knock," Laurie called out, pausing at the door. She didn't want to give Peter a scare.

Peter looked up from a long computer printout he was studying. "Laurie! Am I glad to see you! I have something I want to show you."

Laurie followed Peter to the gas chromatograph/mass spectrometry unit. Peter picked up another computer printout and handed it to Laurie. She studied it with little comprehension.

"It's from Robert Evans," Peter said proudly. "Just as you suggested."

391

"What am I looking at?" Laurie asked.

Peter pointed with his pencil. "There," he said. "That's a positive for ethylene, and it's a lot more evident than it had been in Randall Thatcher's case. It is no laboratory error or false positive. It's real."

"That's weird," Laurie said. She'd really come to think the ethylene reading in the Thatcher case had been an error.

"It might be weird," Peter said, "but it's real. No doubt about it."

"I need another favor," Laurie said. "Can you open the DNA lab for me?"

"Sure," Peter said. "You want me to open it now?"

"If you don't mind."

Peter got his keys and led Laurie down a flight of stairs to the lab on the third floor.

As they went in, Laurie explained what she was up to. "I was shown a Polaroid of a match but it was just a preliminary. It concerns the Julia Myerholtz case. You probably recognize the name."

"Certainly," Peter said. "I've run lots of samples on her."

"I want to find that Polaroid," Laurie said. "I need a copy of it. I don't need a duplicate photograph; a copy from the copy machine will be fine."

"No problem," Peter said. He knew exactly where to look. Once he had the Polaroid in hand, he went to the copy machine. Laurie followed.

While the copy machine warmed up, Peter looked at the photo. "It's pretty obvious they don't match," he said. "Is that what you expected?"

"No," Laurie said. "It was a shot in the dark."

"Interesting," Peter said. "Do you think it is significant?"

"Absolutely," Laurie said. "I think it means Julia was fighting for her life."

"You think she's still in there?" Tony asked. He was more antsy than usual. "She could have left while I was going back to get you. And if she's not in there, then we're wasting our time sitting here like a couple of chumps."

"You've got a good point," Angelo said. "But before we move in I wish we could make sure she didn't call the cops. I still don't understand why she split unless she didn't think we were real cops. I mean, isn't she the solid-citizen type? What does she have to hide from cops? It doesn't make sense, and when something doesn't make sense, it means I'm missing something. And when I'm missing something, it scares me."

"God, you're always worrying," Tony said. "Let's just go in there, get her, and be done with it."

"All right," Angelo said. "But take it easy. And bring the bag. We're going to have to play this one by ear."

"I'm with you all the way," Tony said eagerly. Due to the unconsummated chase after Laurie, Tony's appetite for action had been honed to a razor's edge. He was a bundle of nervous energy.

"I think we'd better put the silencers on our guns," Angelo said. "No telling what we're going to meet. And we're going to have to work fast."

"Great!" Tony exclaimed. With obvious excitement he pulled out his Bantam and attached the silencer. It took him a moment because his hand trembled with pleasurable anticipation.

Angelo gave him a hard look, then shook his head in exasperation. "Try to stay calm. Let's go!"

They got out of the car and ran across the street and between the two mortuary vans. They ran hunched over, trying to avoid the drizzle as much as possible. They entered the same way they had that afternoon, through the morgue loading dock. Angelo was in the lead. Tony followed with the black doctor's bag in one hand and his gun in the other. In an attempt to conceal the gun, he had it partially under his jacket.

Angelo was almost past the open door to the security

office when someone inside yelled, "Hey! You can't go in there."

Tony collided with Angelo when his partner stopped abruptly. A guard in a blue uniform was sitting at his desk. In front of him was a game of solitaire.

"Where you guys think you're going?" he asked.

Before Angelo could respond, Tony raised his Bantam and aimed it at the surprised guard's forehead. He pulled the trigger without a moment's hesitation. The slug hit the guard in his head, just above his left eye, so that he fell over onto his desk, his head landing with a solid thump on his card game. Except for the pool of blood forming on the desk top, a passerby might have thought the man was simply asleep on the job.

"What the hell did you shoot him for?" Angelo snarled. "You could have given me a chance to talk with him."

"He was going to give us trouble," Tony said. "You said we had to be fast."

"What if he has a partner?" Angelo said. "What if the partner comes back? Where will we be then?"

Tony frowned.

"Come on!" Angelo said.

They peered into the mortuary office. There was cigarette smoke in the air and a live butt in an ashtray by the desk, but no one was in sight. Leaving the office and advancing cautiously into the morgue proper, Angelo glanced into the small auxiliary autopsy room used for decomposed bodies. The dissecting table was barely visible in the half-light.

"This place gives me the creeps," he admitted.

"Me too," Tony said. "It's nothing like the funeral home I worked at. Look at the floor. This place is disgusting."

"Why are so many lights off?" Angelo asked.

"Saving money?" Tony suggested.

They came to the huge U-shaped mass of refrigerator compartments stacked four-high, each with its own heavily hinged door. "You think all the bodies are in here?" Angelo asked, pointing toward the bank of cooler doors.

"I guess so," Tony said. "This is just like in those old movies when they have to identify somebody."

"It doesn't smell like this in the movies," Angelo said. "What the hell are all those simple coffins for? They expecting the bubonic plague?"

"Beats me," Tony said.

They wandered past the large walk-in cooler, heading for the light that was coming through the windows of the double doors that led into the main autopsy room. Just before they got there, the doors burst open and out walked Bruce Pomowski.

Everyone recoiled in surprise. Tony hid his gun behind his back.

"You guys scared me," Bruce admitted with a nervous laugh.

"The feeling's mutual," Angelo said.

"You must be here for the Haberlin body," Bruce said. "Well, I got good news and bad news. The good news is that it's ready. The bad news is you have to wait until one of the doctors examines it."

"That's too bad," Angelo said. "But as long as we're waiting around, have you seen Dr. Laurie Montgomery?"

"Yeah," Bruce said. "I just saw her a few minutes ago."

"Can you tell us where she went?" Angelo asked.

"She went up to Toxicology," Bruce said. He was becoming curious and even a little suspicious about these two men.

"And where might Toxicology be?" Angelo asked.

"Fourth floor." Bruce tried to remember if he'd ever seen these two on a body pickup before.

"Thanks," Angelo said. He turned, motioning for Tony to follow him.

"Hey, you can't go up there," said Bruce. "And what funeral home are you from?"

395

"Spoletto," Angelo said.

"That's not the one I've been expecting," Bruce said. "I think I'd better make a call. What are your names?"

"We're not looking for any trouble," Angelo said. "We'd just like to talk with Laurie Montgomery."

Bruce took a step backward and eyed Angelo and Tony. "I think I'll give Security a call."

Tony's gun appeared and pointed at the mortuary tech. Bruce froze in place, looking cross-eyed at the barrel. Tony pulled the trigger before Angelo could say anything. Similar to the security man, the slug hit Bruce in the forehead, and he swayed for a second, then crumbled to the floor.

"Damn!" Angelo said. "You can't shoot everybody."

"Hell!" Tony said. "He was about to call Security."

"A lot of good that would have done him," Angelo said. "You already took care of Security. You have to learn to restrain yourself."

"So I overreacted," Tony said. "At least we know the chick's still here. We even know where to find her."

"But first we have to hide this body," Angelo said. "What if somebody comes along." Angelo glanced around. His eyes settled on the cooler compartments. "Let's stick him in one of the refrigerators," Angelo said.

Quickly Angelo and Tony began checking compartments, searching for an empty one. In every one the first thing they spotted was a pair of bare feet with a manila tag around the big toe.

"This is disgusting," Angelo said.

"Here's an empty one," Tony said. He pulled out the drawer.

They went back to Bruce's limp body. Tony discovered the man was still alive and making weird noises when he breathed. "Should I give him another slug?" he asked.

"No!" Angelo snapped. He didn't want any more shooting. "It's not necessary. He won't be making much noise in the refrigerator."

Together they dragged the body to the open refrigerator compartment and managed to lift him onto the drawer.

"Sleep tight," Tony said as he slid the drawer into the wall and closed the door.

"Now put your goddamned gun away," Angelo commanded.

"All right," Tony said. He stuck his Bantam into his shoulder holster. With the silencer in place, the butt of the gun showed at Tony's lapel.

"Let's get up to the fourth floor," Angelo said nervously. "This isn't going very well. We have to get the woman and get out of here. All hell is going to break loose if someone comes across this trail of corpses you've been leaving."

Tony picked up his doctor's bag and hurried after Angelo, who'd already headed for the stairs. Angelo did not want to chance running into anyone in the elevator.

Emerging on the fourth floor, they saw only one room was lit. Assuming that had to be the toxicology lab, they headed straight for it. They entered cautiously, only to find Peter cleaning some equipment.

"Excuse me," Angelo said, "we're looking for Dr. Laurie Montgomery."

Peter turned around. "You just missed her," he said. "She went down to the morgue to look at a body in the walk-in cooler."

"Thanks," Angelo said.

"Not at all," Peter said.

Angelo took Tony by the arm and quickly led him out into the hall. "Nice of you not to shoot him," Angelo said sarcastically.

The two retraced their steps, heading back downstairs to the morgue.

After looking in the mortuary office and the main autopsy room, Laurie gave up on finding Bruce. He'd probably gone on break. She had it in her mind to ask him for help, but she decided to check the walk-in for the Haberlin body herself.

Laurie put on rubber gloves before entering the large refrigerator. Straining against the door's weight, she pulled it open, reached in, and switched on the light.

The walk-in looked much as it had when she'd gone in in search of Julia Myerholtz. Most of the bodies on the wooden shelves had not been disturbed since her last visit. Those on gurneys represented a new batch. Unfortunately, there were more bodies than there had been before. In an attempt to be methodical, she began by checking the bodies closest to the door. As usual, all the bodies had been tagged for identification. Laurie had to lift the sheets shrouding the feet to check the names. After checking each gurney, she moved it aside to allow her to work deeper into the cooler.

Finally, near the back of the walk-in, and after checking a dozen bodies, she found the tag with Stephanie Haberlin written on it. It was none too soon; Laurie was shivering. Covering the feet back up, Laurie jockeyed the gurney around to get to its head. Then she pulled back the sheet.

Laurie winced at the sight. Seeing a young person's pale corpse was never a pleasant sight. No matter how long she stuck with forensics, Laurie didn't think she'd ever get used to this part of the job. With uncharacteristic reluctance, Laurie reached over and placed her thumb and index finger on Stephanie's upper eyelids.

For a moment Laurie hesitated, wondering what she wished for more: to be wrong or right. Taking a deep breath, she lifted the lids.

Laurie winced for the second time. She even felt her legs go weak. In a split second her suspicions had been validated. She'd been correct. It could no longer be considered a coincidence. The dead woman's eyes were gone!

"You awful, awful man," Laurie said aloud through chattering teeth. How could any human being perpetrate such a heinous crime? This scheme was truly diabolical.

The resonant click of the cooler's latch shocked Laurie from her musing. Anticipating Bruce, she was surprised to see two strangers enter, one carrying an old-fashioned doctor's bag.

"Dr. Montgomery?" the tall one called out.

"Yes," Laurie answered. She was afraid she recognized these two as the same men who'd come to her door.

"We want to talk with you downtown," Angelo said. "Would you mind coming with us?"

"Who are you?" she demanded. She began to tremble.

"I don't think that really matters," the shorter one said as he started pushing gurneys to the side with his free hand. He was cutting a path to Laurie. Angelo started to move toward her, too.

"What do you want with me?" Laurie asked, her terror mounting.

"We just want to talk," Tony said.

Laurie was trapped. She had no place to run. She was snared in a virtual sea of corpse-laden gurneys. Tony was already pushing aside the last two of the remaining gurneys that lay between them.

With no other recourse, Laurie stripped her shoulder purse from her arm and let it drop to the floor. She then stepped to the head of Stephanie Haberlin's gurney and grasped the sides.

Screaming to bolster her courage, Laurie started wheeling Stephanie's gurney, desperately trying to build up speed in the confined space. She aimed the gurney directly at the surprised Tony. At first Tony suggested he would stand his ground. But as Laurie's efforts accelerated, he tried to get out of the way.

Laurie crashed the gurney into Tony with enough force to knock him off balance as well as to cause Stephanie's corpse to topple off. Haphazardly a stiff dead arm draped itself around Tony's neck as he fought to regain his footing.

Not allowing the man to recover, Laurie grabbed another

gurney and ran it into Stephanie's. Grabbing still another, she ran it at Angelo, who slipped on the tile floor trying to avoid being struck, and totally disappeared from view.

Tony struggled from Stephanie's embrace, pushing the corpse away from him. He was wedged between the gurneys, which he attempted to push away as he pulled out his gun. He tried to take aim, but Laurie crashed another gurney into the others, throwing him off balance once again. Angelo struggled to his feet and tried to make a space for himself to stand upright, pushing more gurneys in Tony's direction.

Tony fired as Laurie crashed one last gurney. The sound, even with the silencer, was deafening within the insulated cooler. The bullet passed over Laurie's shoulder as she scrambled for the door. She was out of the cooler in an instant, slamming the heavy door behind her. Frantically she searched for a lock to secure the walk-in refrigerator, but there wasn't one. She had no other choice but to make a run for it. She hadn't gotten far when she heard the cooler door open behind her.

Running as fast as she could, she rounded the corner of the mortuary office. Seeing no one, she continued on to the security office. Dashing inside she called out to the sleeping guard.

"Help me!" she cried. "You've got to help me. There are two men—"

When the guard did not move, Laurie desperately reached out and roughly grabbed the man's shoulder, yanking him to an upright sitting position. But to Laurie's shock, the man's head flopped back like a rag doll, dragging playing cards with it. With horror she saw the bullet hole in his forehead, his unseeing eyes, and bloody froth oozing from his mouth. Where his head had been on the desk was a pool of partially dried blood.

Laurie screamed and let go of the guard. He collapsed backward in the chair, his head hyperextending, and his arms limply dangling with his fingers just brushing the floor. Laurie wheeled around to flee, but it was too late. The shorter of the two men came flying through the door, his gun held out in front of him, a demonic smile spread like a gaping wound across his face. He pointed the gun directly at Laurie. At such close range she could even see a short distance up the barrel of the silencer.

The man advanced toward her as if in slow motion until the tip of the gun was a mere inch from Laurie's nose. She didn't move. She was paralyzed with dread.

"Don't shoot her!" cried the other, taller man, who suddenly appeared over Tony's shoulder. "Please don't shoot her!"

"It would be so rewarding," Tony said.

"Come on," Angelo urged. "Gas her!" Angelo put the black doctor's bag on the corner of the desk. With his foot, he gave the desk chair a shove to get it out of the way. The dead guard rolled out of the chair and fell to the floor. Then Angelo stepped into the corridor to look in both directions. He'd heard voices.

Tony lowered his gun. It had been all he could do to keep from firing it. Placing it in his jacket pocket, he opened the black bag and took out the gas cylinder and the plastic bag. After inflating the bag, he stepped over to Laurie, who'd backed up against a table.

"This will be a nice rest," Tony said.

Wide-eyed with terror, Laurie was shocked when Tony crammed the bag over her head. The force bent her back over the table. Both hands splayed out to support herself. As they did, her right hand hit up against a glass paperweight. Clutching it, Laurie swung it underhand, hitting Tony in the groin.

Tony's grip on the plastic bag released as he reflexively grabbed his genitals. After their recent run-in with the briefcase, they were particularly sensitive.

Laurie took advantage of his pain to tear the plastic bag

from her head. The smell inside it had been sickeningly sweet. Pushing off the table, Laurie dashed by Tony, who was still doubled over, and then Angelo, who'd been standing guard outside.

"Goddamn it!" Angelo shouted. He started after Laurie. Tony, partially recovered, limped after Angelo, carrying the black bag, the plastic bag, and the gas cylinder.

Laurie ran out the way she'd come, passing the stack of Potter's Field coffins and the walk-in refrigerator. She was hoping to run into some of the custodial staff—anyone who might be able to help her.

When she saw the light in the main autopsy room, she was encouraged. She went through the swinging doors at a full run. Inside, Laurie was thrilled to find a man mopping the floor. "You've got to help me!" she gasped.

The janitor was shocked by her sudden appearance.

"There are two men chasing me," Laurie cried. She dashed to the sink and snatched up one of the large autopsy knives. She knew it wouldn't be much help against a gun, but it was the only defense she could think of.

The confused janitor looked at her as if she were crazy, and before she could say anything else, the door burst open a second time. Angelo entered at a run with his gun drawn.

"It's over!" Angelo snarled between harsh, winded breaths. Behind him the door opened again. Tony came charging inside, clutching the black bag and the gas paraphernalia in one hand, his gun in the other.

"What's happening?" the janitor demanded. His shock had changed to fear with the sight of the guns. He gripped his mop in both hands as if he were prepared to use it as a weapon.

With no further provocation, Tony raised his gun and shot the man in the head. The janitor staggered and collapsed. Tony stepped over to shoot the man a second time.

"It's the girl we want," Angelo yelled. "Forget the janitor! Gas her!"

As he'd done in the security office, Tony inflated the plastic bag and approached Laurie.

Paralyzed with shock from having seen the janitor killed in front of her, Laurie was temporarily incapable of resisting. The autopsy knife slipped from her hand and clattered to the floor.

Tony went behind her and pulled the bag over her head. After taking a few breaths of the sweet gas inside the bag, Laurie reached up as if to pull the plastic off her. But her efforts came too late. Her knees gave way and she sank to the floor, unconscious.

"Run out and get one of those pine coffins," Angelo said. "Make it quick!"

A few minutes later Tony returned with a coffin, nails, and a hammer. He put the coffin down next to Laurie. With Angelo at her head and Tony at her feet, they lifted her into the box, then pulled off the plastic bag. Tony put on the lid and was about to nail it shut when Angelo suggested putting more of the gas inside.

Tony held the cylinder under the lid and tried to fill the coffin. Quickly he smelled the gas. Pulling his hand out, he closed the lid.

"That's about all I can get in," Tony said.

"Let's hope it holds her," Angelo said. "Get one of those wagons over here." He pointed to a gurney pushed against the far wall.

Tony wheeled the gurney over, while Angelo nailed down the coffin's lid. Then they both lifted the coffin onto it. Tony threw the plastic bag and gas cylinder into the doctor's bag and set the bag on top of the coffin. Together he and Angelo wheeled the gurney out the door. They headed for the loading dock. Moving at a run, they passed the mortuary office, then turned and passed the security office.

While Tony waited on the lip of the loading dock and made sure the gurney didn't roll away, Angelo went to check inside the mortuary vans. In the first one he found the keys in the ignition. Running back to Tony, he told him they'd use the truck. As quickly as possible, and using the keys to unlock the rear doors, they loaded the coffin containing Laurie into the back of the van. Angelo dropped the keys into Tony's hand.

"You drive her," Angelo said. "Go directly to the pier. I'll see you there."

Tony climbed into the front of the van and started the engine.

"Move it out," Angelo yelled. Frantically waving, he guided Tony as Tony backed up into Thirtieth Street. Again Angelo could hear voices within the morgue.

"Get moving," Angelo said as he slapped the side of the mortuary van. He watched until Tony had turned onto First Avenue, then he sprinted over to his own car, started it, and followed.

As soon as Angelo caught up to the van, he gave Cerino a call from his cellular phone. "We got the merchandise," he said.

"Beautiful," Cerino said. "Bring her to the pier. I'll call Doc Travino. We'll meet you there."

"This wasn't a clean operation," Angelo said. "But we seem to be clear. No one is following us."

"As long as you got her, it's OK," Cerino said. "And your timing is perfect. The *Montego Bay* departs tomorrow morning. Our little lady doc is due for a cruise."

16

□

Lou pulled into the morgue loading dock and parked his car to the side. There was only one van in the drive instead of the usual two, so he could have pulled right up to the entrance, but figuring the other van would be back soon, he didn't want to be in the way.

He put his police identification card on the dash and got out. Lou could have kicked himself for pushing Laurie as he had on the phone. When was he going to learn to back off? Criticizing Jordan was sure only to make her more defensive about the man. He must have really set her off this time. He could understand why she hadn't picked up the phone when he'd called back, but even if she was mad he would have thought she'd have called him back. When she hadn't gotten back to him after half an hour, Lou decided to head over to the medical examiner's office to talk to her in person. He hoped she hadn't left.

Lou passed the security office and glanced in through the window. He was a little surprised to see that no one was there, but he assumed that the security guard was making his rounds. Farther down the hall, Lou checked the mortuary office, but it was empty as well.

Lou scratched his head. The place seemed deserted. It was dead quiet, he thought with a laugh. He checked his watch. It wasn't that late, and wasn't this place supposed to be open around the clock? After all, people died twenty-four hours a day. With a shrug of his shoulders, Lou walked to the elevators and rode up to Laurie's floor.

As soon as he stepped off the elevator he could tell that she wasn't there. Her door was closed and the room was dark. But he wasn't about to give up. Not yet. He remembered her having said something about some laboratory results. Lou decided to see if he could find the right lab and maybe then Laurie. He took the elevator down one floor, unsure of where to find the appropriate lab. At the end of the fourth-floor hall he saw a light. Lou walked the length of the hall and peered in the open door.

"Excuse me," he said to the youthful man in a white lab coat stooped over one of the room's major pieces of heavy equipment.

Peter looked up.

"I'm looking for Laurie Montgomery," Lou said.

"You and everyone else," Peter said. "I don't know where she is now, but half an hour ago she went down to the morgue to look at a body in the walk-in cooler."

"Someone else been looking for her?" Lou asked.

"Yeah," Peter said. "Two men I'd never seen before."

"Thanks," Lou said. He turned back toward the elevator and hustled down the hall. He didn't like the sound of two strangers looking for Laurie, not after what she'd said about two alleged plainclothes policemen coming to her apartment.

Lou went straight to the morgue level. Exiting the elevator, he was surprised he still hadn't seen a soul besides the guy in the lab. With growing concern, he hurried down the long hall to the walk-in cooler. Finding its door partially ajar only added to his unease.

With mounting dread he pulled the door the rest of the way open. What he saw was far worse than he could have imagined. Inside the cooler, bodies were strewn helter-skelter. Two gurneys were tipped on their sides. Several of the sheets covering the bodies had been pulled aside. Even after a few days' experience in the autopsy room, he still didn't have the stomach for this. And whatever had happened to Laurie, this body-strewn battleground was hardly an auspicious sign.

Lou spotted a purse among the wreckage. Pushing gurneys aside, he picked it up to check for ID. He snapped open the wallet. The first thing he saw was Laurie's photo on her driver's license.

As he rushed from the cooler, Lou's concern turned to fear, especially if his current theory about all the gangland-style murders was correct. Frantically he looked for someone, anyone. There was always someone available at the morgue. Seeing the light in the main autopsy room, he ran down to it and pushed open the doors, but no one was there either.

Turning around, Lou dashed back to the security office to use the phone. Entering the room, he immediately saw the guard's body on the floor. He knelt down and rolled the man over. The man's unseeing eyes stared up at him. There was a bullet hole in his forehead. Lou checked for a pulse, but there wasn't any. The man was dead.

Standing up, Lou snatched up the phone and dialed 911. As soon as an operator answered he identified himself as Lieutenant Lou Soldano and requested a homicide unit for the city morgue. He added that the victim was in the security office but that he would not be able to wait for the unit to arrive.

Slamming the phone down, Lou raced to the morgue loading dock and jumped into his car. Starting the engine, he backed up with a screech of his tires, leaving two lines of rubber on the morgue's driveway. He had no other choice than to head directly for Paul Cerino's. It was cards-on-the-table time. He slapped his emergency light on the car's roof and arrived at Cerino's Queens address after twenty-three minutes of hair-raising driving.

Racing up the front steps of the Cerino home, he reached into his shoulder holster and unsnapped the leather band securing his .38 Smith and Wesson Detective Special. He rang the bell impatiently. Judging by all the lights blazing, someone had to be home.

Lou knew that he was operating on a hunch that depended on his theory about the gangland slayings being correct. But at the moment it was all he had, and his intuition told him that time was of the utmost importance.

An overhead light came on above Lou's head. Then he had the feeling that someone was looking at him through the peephole. Finally the door opened. Gloria was standing there dressed in one of her plain housedresses.

"Lou!" Gloria said pleasantly. "What brings you here?"

Lou shoved past her and into the house. "Where's Paul?" he demanded. He looked into the living room, where Gregory and Steven were watching TV.

"What's the matter?" Gloria asked.

"I have to talk with Paul. Where is he?"

"He's not here," Gloria said. "Is there something wrong?"

"Something's very wrong," Lou said. "Do you know where Paul is?"

"I'm not positive," Gloria said. "But I heard him on the phone with Dr. Travino. I think he said something about going down to the company."

"You mean at the pier?" Lou asked.

Gloria nodded. "Is he in danger?" Gloria asked. Lou's distress was infectious.

Lou was already half out the door. Calling over his shoulder, he said, "I'll take care of it."

Back in his car, Lou started the engine and made a sweeping U-turn in the middle of the street. As he accelerated he caught sight of Gloria standing on her stoop, anxiously clutching her hands to her chest.

Laurie's first sensation was nausea, but she didn't vomit, although she retched. She woke up in stages, becoming progressively aware of movement and uncomfortable bumps and jostling. She also became aware of dizziness, as if she were spinning, and a terrible sense of air hunger, as if she were smothering.

Laurie tried to open her eyes, only to realize with a terrible shock that they were already open. Wherever she was, it was pitch black.

When she was more awake, Laurie tried to move, but when she did, her legs and arms immediately hit up against a wooden surface. Exploring with her hands, she quickly determined that she was in a box! A wave of frightful claustrophobia passed through her like a cold wind as she realized she'd been sealed into a Potter's Field coffin! At the same time the memory of what happened at the medical examiner's office flooded back with searing clarity: the chase; those two horrible men; the dead guard, the poor janitor murdered in cold blood. And then another horrid thought occurred to her: what if they were planning to bury her alive!

Gripped with terror, Laurie tried to draw up her knees, straining against the top of the coffin. Then she tried to kick, but it was all to no avail. Either something extremely heavy was on the lid or it had been nailed firmly down.

"Ahhhh," Laurie cried as the coffin jarred severely. It was then that she realized she was in some sort of vehicle.

Laurie tried screaming but only succeeded in hurting her own ears. Next she tried pounding the underside of the lid with her fists, but it was difficult in the confined space.

Abruptly the jarring stopped. The vibration of the engine also stopped. Then there was the distant sound as if the doors of the vehicle had opened. Laurie felt the coffin move.

"Help!" Laurie cried. "I can't breathe!"

She heard voices, but they weren't speaking with her. In a wave of desperate panic, Laurie again tried to pound the underside of the lid as tears came. She couldn't help herself. She'd never been so terrified in her life.

Laurie knew she was being carried for a time. She hated to think where they were taking her. Would they really bury her? Would she hear the dirt raining down on the lid?

With a final thump the coffin was put down. It hadn't hit ground. It sounded like wood.

Laurie gasped for air between sobs as a cold sweat appeared on her forehead.

Lou wasn't exactly sure where the American Fresh Fruit Company was, but he knew it was in the Green Point pier area. He'd been there once years before and was hoping it would come back to him.

When he got to the waterfront district, he took his emergency light down and turned it off. He continued on Greenpoint Avenue until he could go no further, then turned north on West Street, the whole time scanning the abandoned warehouses for some sign of life.

He was beginning to feel discouraged and progressively desperate until he saw a road marked Java Street. The name rang a bell. Lou turned left onto it, heading ever closer to the river. A block down stood a high chain-link fence. Over the open gate was a sign bearing the name of Cerino's company. Several cars were parked on the inside of the gate. Lou recognized one as Cerino's Lincoln Continental. Beyond the cars was a huge warehouse that extended out over the pier. Above and behind the warehouse Lou could see the very top of the superstructure of a ship.

Lou drove through the gate and parked next to Cerino's car. A wide overhead door to the warehouse was open. Lou could just make out the rear of a van parked in the darkness within. He shut off his engine and got out. All he could hear was the distant screech of some sea gulls.

Lou checked his gun but left it in his holster. He tiptoed over to the open door and peered in for a better look at the van. When he saw HEALTH AND HOSPITAL CORP. on its side, he was encouraged. Glancing around in the darkness of the warehouse, Lou saw nothing but the vague outlines of stacks of bananas. No one was in sight, but toward the end of the pier, in the direction of the river, perhaps a hundred yards away, he could see a glow of light.

Lou debated calling for backup. Proper police procedure required such a move, but he feared there wasn't time. He had to be certain Laurie wasn't in immediate danger. Once he did that, he could take the time to call for help.

Avoiding the central corridor through the bananas, Lou worked his way laterally until he found another corridor that led out the pier. Groping ahead, he moved in the general direction of the light.

It took him about five minutes to get abreast of the light. Carefully he again moved laterally until he could see that the light was coming from a windowed office. Inside were people. Lou recognized Cerino immediately.

Inching even closer, Lou got a better view of the interior. Most important, he saw Laurie. She was sitting in a straight-back chair. Lou could even see that her forehead gleamed with perspiration.

Sensing that Laurie was all right momentarily, Lou

began to carefully retrace his steps. Now he wanted to use his radio in his car to call in some backup. With as many people as there were in the office, he wasn't about to play hero and go barging in.

Back at his car, Lou climbed in and picked up his police radio. He was about to speak when he felt the press of cold metal against the back of his neck.

"Get out of the car," a voice commanded.

Lou turned slowly and looked up into Angelo's gaunt face.

"Out of the car."

Lou carefully replaced the microphone and got out onto the asphalt.

"Face the car," Angelo ordered.

Angelo quickly frisked Lou, removing his gun when he found it.

"OK," Angelo said. "Let's go down to the office. Maybe you'd like to go on a little cruise, too."

"I don't know what you're talking about," Laurie said. She was trembling. The coffin she'd been in was off to the side. She was terrified that they were going to force her back into it.

"Please, Doctor," Travino said. "I'm a doctor myself. We speak the same language. All we want to know is how you figured it out. How did you guess that these cases were not the garden-variety overdoses you people see day in, day out?"

"You must be thinking of someone else," Laurie said. She tried to think, but it was difficult with her terror. Yet she had the idea that the reason she was still alive was because they were desperate to know how she'd solved the case. Consequently she didn't want to tell them anything.

"Let me at her," Tony pleaded.

"If you don't talk with the doctor," Paul said, "I'll have to let Tony have his way."

At that moment the door to the warehouse proper opened and Lou Soldano was propelled inside the office. Angelo followed, his gun held at his side. "Company!" he said.

"Who is it, Angelo?" Paul demanded. His patch was still in place over his operated eye.

"It's Lou Soldano," Angelo said. "He was about to use his radio."

"Lou?" Cerino echoed. "What are you doing here?"

"Keeping an eye on you," Lou said. Looking at Laurie, he asked, "Are you all right?"

Laurie shook her head. "As well as can be expected," she said through tears.

Angelo grabbed a chair and set it next to Laurie's. "Sit down!" he barked.

Lou sat down, his eyes glued to Laurie. "Are you hurt?" he asked.

"Travino," Paul said angrily, "this whole affair is getting too complicated. You and your big ideas." Then to Angelo he said: "Get someone outside to make sure Soldano was alone. And get rid of his car. To be on the safe side let's assume he had a chance to call in before we got him."

Angelo snapped his fingers at several of the low-level hoodlums who'd accompanied Paul. The men immediately left the office.

"Want me to take care of the detective?" Tony asked.

Paul waved him away. "The fact that he is here means he knows more than he ought to know," he said. "He's going on the cruise, too. We'll have to talk with him just like we have to talk with the girl. But for the moment let's get them on the *Montego Bay* quickly. I'd prefer if the crew saw as little as possible. What do you suggest?"

"Gas!" Angelo said.

"Good idea," Paul said. "Tony, you're on."

Tony leaped at the opportunity to prove himself in Paul's presence. He got out a couple of plastic bags and the gas cylinder. As soon as he had the first bag inflated, he tied it off and started on the second while the first slowly floated toward the ceiling.

One of the hoodlums came back and reported that no one else was around and that Soldano's car had been taken care of.

A sudden vibrating blast from the *Montego Bay*'s ship's horn made everybody jump. The ship was just on the other side of the uninsulated wall of the office. Paul cursed. Tony had let go of the second bag and some of the gas escaped into the room.

"Is that stuff bad for us?" Cerino questioned, smelling the gas.

"No," Dr. Travino said.

In the confusion, Laurie turned to Lou. "Do you have your cigarettes with you?" she asked.

Lou looked at her as if he'd not heard correctly. "What are you talking about?"

"Your cigarettes," she repeated. "Give them to me."

Lou reached into his jacket pocket. As he was about to pull out his hand, another hand grabbed his wrist. It was the hoodlum who'd reported on his car.

The thug glared at Lou and pulled Lou's hand from his jacket. When he saw that Lou was only holding a pack of cigarettes with matches under the cellophane, he let go of Lou's arm and stepped back.

Still baffled, Lou handed the cigarettes to Laurie.

"Are you alone?" Laurie asked in a whisper.

"Unfortunately," Lou whispered back. He tried to smile at the thug who'd grabbed his wrist. The man was still glaring at him.

"I want you to have a cigarette," Laurie said.

"I'm sorry," Lou said. "I'm not interested in smoking at the moment."

"Take it!" Laurie snapped.

Lou looked at her in bewilderment. "All right!" he said. "Whatever you say."

Laurie took one of the cigarettes out of the pack and stuck it into Lou's mouth. Then she slipped out the matches. Tearing out a match, she glanced up at the hoodlum who was watching them so intently. His expression hadn't changed.

Laurie shielded the match and struck it. Lou leaned toward her with the cigarette between his lips. But Laurie didn't light it. Instead she used the match to fire the entire pack of matches. Once the pack started to flare, she tossed it toward Tony and his plastic bags. In the same motion she fell sideways off her chair, tackling a surprised Lou in the process. Together they fell to the floor.

The resulting explosion was severe, especially around Tony and upwards toward the ceiling, where the escaped ethylene had layered and the second bag had positioned itself. The concussion of the blast blew out all the office windows as well as the door and all the overhead lights, sparing only a lamp on the desk. Tony was consumed by the fireball. Angelo was thrown against the wall, where he sagged to a sitting position, his eardrums blown out. His hair was singed to his scalp, and he suffered some internal damage to his lungs. All the others were knocked momentarily senseless to the floor and superficially burned. A few managed to push themselves up on all fours, groaning and totally befuddled.

On the floor, Laurie and Lou were relatively spared, having been below any of the layered ethylene, although both had suffered some minor burns and mild ear damage from the severe deflagration. Laurie opened her eyes and released her grip around Lou's middle.

"Are you all right?" she questioned. Her ears were ringing.

"What the hell happened?" Lou said.

Laurie scrambled to her feet. She pulled Lou's arm to get him to his feet. "Let's get out of here!" she said. "I'll explain it later."

Together they stepped around and over moaning people strewn about the floor. They coughed in the acrid smoke.

Beyond the blown-out door of the office, their feet crunched over shattered glass. Down the corridor of bananas, they saw a flashlight bobbing in the dark. Someone was running toward them.

Lou yanked Laurie laterally away from the office in the direction from which he'd originally come. As they huddled behind a stack of bananas, the running footfalls drew closer. Soon another one of Cerino's thugs stood gasping at the threshold of the office. For a moment he stood there with his mouth open in amazement. Then he went to his boss's aid. Paul was sitting on the floor in front of the desk, holding his head.

"This is our chance," Lou whispered. He held on to Laurie as they worked their way back toward the entrance of the warehouse. The going was slow because of the dark and the fact that they wanted to stay away from the main corridor in case there were other Cerino people in the area.

It took them almost ten minutes before they could see the vague outline of the opening of the overhead door. In front of it was the black silhouette of the morgue van. It was still parked where it had been when Lou had entered.

"My car is probably gone," Lou whispered. "Let's see if the keys are in the van."

They approached the van cautiously. Opening the driver's side door, Lou felt along the steering column. His fingers hit the keys, still dangling from the ignition.

"Thank God," he said. "They're here. Get in!"

Laurie climbed in the passenger side. Lou was already behind the wheel.

"As soon as I start this thing," Lou whispered urgently,

"we're out of here fast. But we might not be in the clear. There might be some shooting, so how about you going in the back and lying down."

"Just start the van!" Laurie said.

"Come on," Lou said. "Don't argue."

"You're the one who's arguing," Laurie snapped. "Let's go!"

"Nobody's going nowhere!" a voice said to Lou's left.

With a sinking feeling, Laurie and Lou looked out the window on Lou's side. A number of faceless men in hats were standing in the dark. A flashlight snapped on and played over Lou's face, then over Laurie's. They each blinked in its glare.

"Out of the truck," the same voice ordered. "Both of you."

With hopes dashed, Laurie and Lou climbed back out of the van. They could not see the men for the bright light shining at them, but there seemed to be three.

"Back to the office," the same voice commanded.

Discouraged, Laurie and Lou led the way back. Neither of them said a word. Neither wanted to think about Cerino's fury.

The scene at the office was still chaotic. Smoke still hung heavily in the air. One of Cerino's goons had helped his boss into the desk chair. Angelo was still sitting on the floor with his back against the wall. He looked confused, and a trickle of blood was dripping down his chin from the corner of his mouth.

An additional light had been turned on, and the extent of the damage was more apparent. Laurie was surprised by the amount of charring. That old pharmacology text hadn't been kidding: when it said ethylene was flammable it meant flammable. She and Lou were lucky not to have been injured more severely.

Laurie and Lou were given the same seats they'd occupied only minutes before. Sitting down, Laurie got a glimpse of Tony's burned remains. She grimaced and looked away.

"My eye hurts," Paul wailed.

Laurie closed her eyes, not wanting to think what the consequences were to be of her having ignited the ethylene.

"Someone help me," Cerino cried.

Laurie's eyes opened again. Something was wrong. No one was moving. The three men who'd accompanied them back to the office were ignoring Cerino. In fact they were ignoring everyone.

"What's happening?" Laurie whispered to Lou.

"I don't know," he said. "Something weird is going on."

Laurie looked up at the three men. They appeared nonchalant, picking at their nails, adjusting their ties. They hadn't lifted a finger to help anyone. Looking in the other direction, Laurie saw the man who'd run back into the office just after she and Lou had gone out. He was sitting in a chair with his head in his hands, looking at the floor.

Laurie heard the sound of footsteps approaching. It sounded as if whoever was coming had metal taps on his heels. Out the blasted doorway, Laurie saw beams from several flashlights bobbing toward them.

Presently a rather dapper, darkly handsome man came to the blown-out door. He stopped to survey the scene. He was dressed in a dark cashmere coat over a pin-striped suit. His hair was slicked back from his forehead.

"My God, Cerino," he said with derision. "What a mess you have made!"

Laurie looked at Cerino. Cerino didn't answer; he didn't even move.

"I don't believe it," Lou said.

Laurie's head spun around. She looked at Lou and saw the shock registered on his face. "What's happening?" she asked.

"I knew something weird was going on," Lou said.

"What?" Laurie demanded.

"It's Vinnie Dominick," Lou said.

"Who's Vinnie Dominick?" Laurie asked.

Vinnie shook his head, surveying what was left of Tony, then walked over to Lou. "Detective Soldano," Vinnie said. "How convenient that you're here." He pulled a cellular phone from his coat pocket and handed it to the detective. "I imagine you'd like to contact your colleagues to see if they'd be so good as to come over here. I'm sure the D.A. would like to have a long talk with Paul Cerino."

In the background Laurie was aware of the three men who had been lounging around before Vinnie Dominick arrived. They were now going around the room collecting guns. One of them brought Lou's over to Vinnie, having retrieved it from Angelo. Vinnie proceeded to give it back to Lou.

In disbelief Lou looked down at the phone in one hand and his gun in the other.

"Come on, Lou," Vinnie said. "Make your call. Unfortunately I've got another appointment, so I can't be around when the men in blue arrive. Besides I'm kind of a shy sort of guy and I wouldn't feel comfortable with all the acclaim the city would want to throw my way for saving the day. Obviously you know what Mr. Cerino has been up to, so you don't need my help there. But if you don't, don't hesitate to give me a call. You know how to get ahold of me, I'm sure."

Vinnie started for the door, motioning for his men to follow him. As he passed Angelo he turned back to Lou. "You'd better call an ambulance for Angelo here," he said. "He doesn't look so good." Then, looking down at Tony, he added: "The mortuary van out there will be fine for this dog turd." With that, he left.

Lou handed Laurie his gun while he used the cellular

phone to call 911. He identified himself to the 911 operator and gave the address. When he was finished, he took back his gun.

"Who is this Vinnie character?" Laurie asked.

"He's Cerino's main rival," Lou said. "He must have found out what Cerino was up to and this is his way of turning him in. Very effective, I'd say, with us here as witnesses. It's also a clever way to get rid of his competition."

"You mean Vinnie knew Cerino was behind all these overdoses?" Laurie asked. She was stunned.

"What are you talking about? Vinnie must have figured out that Cerino was killing off patients ahead of him on Jordan Scheffield's corneal-transplant waiting list."

"Oh, my God!" Laurie exclaimed.

"What now?" Lou asked. After the night he'd been having, he wasn't ready for much more.

"It's twice as bad as I thought it was," Laurie said. "The drug overdoses were really homicides to get eyes. Cerino was having people killed who'd signed up with the Manhattan Organ Repository for organ donation."

Lou glanced at Cerino. "He's more of a sociopath than I could ever have imagined. My God, he was working both sides of the problem: supply and demand."

Cerino lifted his head from his hands. "What was I supposed to do? Wait like everybody else? I couldn't afford to wait. In my business, every day I couldn't see, I risked death. Is it my fault the hospitals don't have enough corneas?"

Laurie tapped Lou on the shoulder. He turned to face her.

"There's a strange irony to this whole affair," Laurie said, shaking her head. "We argued with one another about whose series was more socially relevant and therefore more important, your gangland-style murders or my upscale overdoses, only to learn that they were intimately connected. They were just two sides of the same horrid affair."

"You can't prove a thing," Cerino growled.

"Oh, really?" Laurie said.

Epilogue

□

Lou Soldano stamped the wet snow off his feet and walked into the morgue. He smiled at the man in the security office, who didn't challenge him, and went directly to the locker room. Quickly he changed into green scrubs.

Pausing outside the main autopsy room doors, he donned a mask, then pushed through. His eyes traveled from one end to the other, inspecting the people at each table. Finally his eyes spotted a familiar figure that even the bulky gown, apron, and hood could not hide.

Walking over to the table, he looked down. Laurie was up to her elbows in a huge corpse. For the moment, she was by herself.

"I didn't know you did whales here," Lou said.

Laurie looked up. "Hi, Lou," she said cheerfully. "Would you mind scratching my nose?" She twisted away

423

from the table and closed her eyes as Lou complied. "A little lower," she said. "Ahhh. That's it." She opened her eyes. "Thanks." She went back to her work.

"Interesting case?" Lou asked.

"Very interesting," Laurie said. "It was supposed to be a suicide, but I'm beginning to think it belongs in your department."

Lou watched for a few minutes and shuddered. "I don't think I'll ever get accustomed to your work."

"At least I'm working," Laurie said.

"That's true," Lou said. "Yet you shouldn't have been fired in the first place. Luckily things have a way of working out for the best."

Laurie glanced up. "I don't think the families of the victims feel that way."

"That's true," Lou admitted. "I just meant in relation to your job."

"Bingham ultimately was gracious about it," Laurie said. "Not only did he give me my job back, he also admitted I had been right. Well, partly right. I was wrong about the idea of a contaminant."

"Well, you were right about the important part," Lou said. "They weren't accidental, they were homicidal. And your contribution didn't end there. In fact that's why I stopped by. We just got an airtight indictment against Cerino."

Laurie straightened up. "Congratulations!" she said.

"Hey, it wasn't my doing," Lou said. "You get the credit. First you were able to match that skin sample under Julia Myerholtz's fingernail with Tony Ruggerio's remains. That was critical. Next you exhumed a number of bodies until you made a match with Kendall Fletcher's teeth on Angelo Facciolo's forearm."

"Any forensic pathologist could have done it," Laurie said.

"I'm not so sure," Lou said. "Anyway, faced with such incontrovertible evidence, Angelo plea-bargained and implicated Cerino. That was what we needed. It's downhill from here."

"You did pretty well yourself," Laurie said. "You got the Kaufmans' maid to pick Angelo out of a lineup and Tony out of mug shots."

"That wouldn't have been strong enough for an indictment," Lou said. "Or, even if I'd gotten an indictment, I wouldn't have gotten a conviction. Certainly not of Cerino. But anyway it's over."

"I shudder to think that there are people like Cerino out there," Laurie said. "It's the combination of intelligence and sociopathy that is so frightening. As heinous as the whole Cerino affair was, it had some ingenious aspects. Imagine having his thugs put people into refrigerators to preserve the corneal tissue longer! They knew that we'd erroneously ascribe that to the hyperpyrexia that cocaine toxicity causes."

"The point is," Lou said, "the vast majority of people who play by the rules and abide by the laws don't realize that there is a large number of people who do the opposite. One bad side to Cerino's indictment is that Vinnie Dominick is unopposed. He and Cerino used to keep each other in check, but no longer. Organized-crime activity has gone up in Queens with Cerino's departure from the scene, not down."

"Now that it is all over," Laurie said, "I wonder why it took us so long to figure out what was happening. I mean, as a doctor I knew that New York is behind the times with its medical-examiner laws and that there is a waiting list for corneas. So why didn't I see it earlier?"

"I bet the reason you didn't see it was because it was too diabolical," Lou said. "It's hard for the normal mind to even think of such a possibility."

"I wish I could make myself believe that," Laurie said.

"I'm sure that it's true," Lou said.

"Perhaps," Laurie said.

"Well, I just wanted to let you know about Cerino," Lou said. He shifted his weight clumsily.

"I'm glad you did," Laurie said. She studied him. He avoided her eyes.

"Guess I'd better get back to my office," Lou said. He nervously glanced around, making sure no one was paying them any attention.

"Is there something you'd like to say?" Laurie asked. "You're acting suspiciously familiar."

"Yeah," Lou said, finally making eye contact. "Would you like to go out to dinner tonight, purely social, no business?"

Laurie smiled at this replay of Lou's painful social awkwardness. It was particularly unexpected now that they had worked together on the Cerino case and knew each other better. In all other respects Lou was decisive and confident.

"We could go back to Little Italy," Lou said in response to Laurie's hesitation.

"You never give a girl much warning," Laurie said.

Lou shrugged. "It gives me an excuse to myself if you refuse."

"Unfortunately I have plans," Laurie said.

"Of course," Lou said hastily. "Silly of me to ask. Well, take care." Lou abruptly turned. "Say hello to Jordan for me," he called over his shoulder.

Laurie felt a surge of old irritation as she watched Lou stride toward the double doors. She fought against the urge to snap back at him. He had not lost his penchant to be infuriating.

The doors to the autopsy room shut behind Lou, and Laurie turned back to her job at hand. But she hesitated.

Then, stripping off her rubber gloves, her apron and

gown, Laurie strode from the autopsy room. The hall was clear. Lou had already disappeared. Guessing he was in the locker room, Laurie pushed directly into the men's side.

Laurie caught Lou with his scrub shirt half off, exposing his muscled and hairy chest. Self-consciously he lowered the garment.

"I resent your implication that I'd be seeing Jordan Scheffield," Laurie said, her arms akimbo. "You know full well he was implicated in this whole affair."

"I know he was implicated," Lou said. "But I also know the grand jury did not indict him. I also made it a point to learn that the Board of Medicine didn't even discipline him even though there was a strong suspicion that he knew what was going on. In fact, some people believe that Jordan discussed the affair with Cerino but did nothing because he liked the increase in surgery it provided. So Jordan's out there pulling in the big bucks like nothing happened."

"And you think I'd still be seeing him under these conditions?" Laurie asked incredulously. "That's an insult."

"I didn't know," Lou said sheepishly. "You never mentioned him."

"I thought it was clear," Laurie said. "Besides, with as close as we have been working together, you could have asked."

"I'm sorry," Lou said. "Maybe it's more that I was afraid you were still seeing him. You remember that I admitted I've always been a bit jealous of him."

"He is the last person you should feel jealous of," Laurie said. "Jordan would be lucky to have an ounce of your honesty and integrity."

"I'd like an ounce of his schooling," Lou said. "Or his sophistication. He always made me feel like a second-class citizen."

"His urbanity is superficial," Laurie said. "The only thing he is truly interested in is money. The embarrassment

for me is that I was as blind to Jordan as I was to what
Cerino was doing. I was bowled over by the rush he gave me
and his apparent self-confidence. You saw through his façade, but I couldn't, even when you told me directly."

"That's not your fault," Lou said. "You think better of
people than I. You're not the cynical bastard I am. Besides,
you're not laboring under a hangup about your background like I am."

"You should be proud of your background," Laurie said.
"It's the source of your honesty."

"Yeah," Lou said. "But I'd still rather have gone to
Harvard."

"When I told you I had plans tonight, I was hoping you
might have suggested we get together tomorrow night or
next week. As prosaic as it sounds, I'm going to my parents'
tonight. What about you coming with me?"

"You're kidding," Lou said. "Me?"

"Yes," Laurie said, warming to the idea. "One of the
positive spinoffs of this whole affair with Cerino is my
relationship with my parents has improved dramatically.
For once my father even recognized that I'd done something he could relate to in a positive way, and I think I've
grown up a tad myself. I've even stopped rebelling. I think
dealing with this affair has finally allowed me to come more
or less to terms with my old guilt in relation to my brother's
death."

"This is starting to sound a bit out of my league," Lou
said.

"I suppose it seems sophomoric and overly analytical,"
Laurie agreed. "But the bottom line is that visiting my
parents can be fun. Lately I've been seeing them about once
a week. And I'd love for you to come along. I'd like them
to meet someone whom I really respect."

"Are you pulling my leg?" Lou asked.

"Absolutely not," Laurie said. "In fact, the more I think

about it the more I hope you'll come. And if you enjoy yourself, maybe you'll still be willing to take me out to Little Italy tomorrow night."

"Lady," Lou said, "you got yourself a deal."